The new Zebra Regency Romance logo that you see on the cover is a photograph of an actual regency "tuzzy-muzzy." The fashionable regency lady often wore a tuzzy-muzzy tied with a satin or velvet riband around her wrist to carry a fragrant nosegay. Usually made of gold or silver, tuzzy-muzzies varied in design from the elegantly simple to the exquisitely ornate. The Zebra Regency Romance tuzzy-muzzy is made of alabaster with a silver filigree edging.

D1551741

A TASTE OF PASSION

King's voice was low and intense as he spoke. "What harm is there in a kiss?" he asked.

"There is every harm," Henrietta answered, meeting his gaze boldly. "There are days past to regret. There are future nights to pine for, knowing they will never exist. There are other kisses to regard forever with disfavor."

He leaned toward her, slipping an arm about her waist, his lips hovering over hers. She thought he would now take his kiss. Instead, he drew back slightly.

"At least take your kiss from me and be done with it!" she cried. "You are driving me to the point of madness!"

He teased her mercilessly as he again drifted his lips over her own, not quite kissing her. He pulled her more closely still. In a slow easy movement, Henrietta put her arm around his neck, leaning into him.

THE BEST OF REGENCY ROMANCES

AN IMPROPER COMPANION   (2691, $3.95)
by Karla Hocker

At the closing of Miss Venable's Seminary for Young
Ladies school, mistress Kate Elliott welcomed the invitation to be Liza Ashcroft's chaperone for the Season at
Bath. Little did she know that Miss Ashcroft's father, the
handsome widower Damien Ashcroft would also enter her
life. And not as a passive bystander or dutiful dad.

WAGER ON LOVE   (2693, $2.95)
by Prudence Martin

Only a rogue like Nicholas Ruxart would choose a bride on
the basis of a careless wager. And only a rakehell like Nicholas would then fall in love with his betrothed's grey-eyed
sister! The cynical viscount had always thought one blushing miss would suit as well as another, but the unattainable
Jane Sommers soon proved him wrong.

LOVE AND FOLLY   (2715, $3.95)
by Sheila Simonson

To the dismay of her more sensible twin Margaret, Lady
Jean proceeded to fall hopelessly in love with the silver-
tongued, seditious poet, Owen Davies — and catapult her
entire family into social ruin . . . Margaret was used to
gentlemen falling in love with vivacious Jean rather than
with her — even the handsome Johnny Dyott whom she se-
cretly adored. And when Jean's foolishness led her into the
arms of the notorious Owen Davies, Margaret knew she
could count on Dyott to avert scandal. What she didn't
know, however was that her sweet sensibility was exerting a
charm all its own.

THE Willful Widow

VALERIE KING

ZEBRA BOOKS
KENSINGTON PUBLISHING CORP.

*To my parents, Dick and Myrna Humphreys,
with love and gratitude.*

ZEBRA BOOKS

are published by

Kensington Publishing Corp.
475 Park Avenue South
New York, NY 10016

First printing: February, 1991

Printed in the United States of America

And, to begin, wench,—so God help me, la!—
My love to thee is sound, sans crack or flaw.
                                   —William Shakespeare

Chapter One

We are all flawed, Henrietta thought as she glanced about the small parlor of Fair Oaks Manor. She was seated at a writing desk, her quilled pen in hand, reviewing the menus Cook had prepared for the forthcoming week, but she was of the moment completely distracted by the complacency of her family. Her gaze lit upon her four sisters and her widowed mother, each in turn. By midsummer, Mr. Huntspill, a cousin of the late Mr. Leighton and a stranger to the inmates of Fair Oaks, would eject them from the manor and take possession of his inheritance. The ladies would then be left to fend for themselves in a world known to be hostile to females of gentle birth and penurious circumstances.

Henrietta gave her brown curls a disbelieving shake as she watched her docile family pursuing their homey tasks. There were no frowns marring a single visage present, no exclamations of dismay to disrupt the air of tranquility in the wood-panelled chamber, and no grasping of distressed bosoms where the difficulties of living could often wreak havoc. Indeed, Charlotte sat on a footstool at her mother's feet, a skein of amber yarn wrapped about one elbow as she crunched happily upon an apple. Mrs. Leighton regaled both Charlotte and Arabella about the size and cost of an exquisite diamond tiara she had recently discovered in *La Belle Assemblee,*

Angel gently plucked a Bach prelude upon the strings of her harp, and young Betsy held a glass jar toward the window, smiling with pleasure at the several inhabitants living within the small, glass house.

A stranger might have wondered at so much disinterest in the face of disaster, but Henrietta knew the truth and tapped a finger nervously against her lips. As she turned back to her own housewifely task of examining and approving each of Cook's menus, she again thought, *We are all flawed, for none of us will admit that our fate hangs by a mere thread.*

Mr. Huntspill was that thread. He had inherited Fair Oaks upon the death of Mr. Leighton because the property had been entailed solely to heirs male. Henrietta's papa had been both an indifferent husband and an improvident father. Not only had he failed to provide in his will for his wife and daughters, but he had permitted his wife, during the course of their marriage, the purchase of each and every frippery that took her fancy regardless of her obvious need to practice economy.

Mrs. Leighton in particular seemed unaware that unless fortune smiled suddenly upon them all, they were soon to be cast upon the world without a feather to fly with.

Of course Mrs. Leighton firmly believed that Huntspill would provide for them all, but Henrietta was not in the least convinced that this would indeed happen. In the little correspondence he had graciously deigned to bestow upon the widow, he gave no indication that he meant to lift a finger for Mrs. Leighton and her daughters. The former's belief in his goodness was based more upon her own hopes for the future than upon any solid evidence that Mr. Huntspill possessed either an honorable character or a generous disposition. And from Henrietta's knowledge of the world, as well as from Mr. Huntspill's brief, pompous letters, she was fully inclined to believe he was more of a clutch-fisted bore than the

6

saint that Mrs. Leighton wished him to be.

Setting her thoughts of Huntspill aside, Henrietta turned back to the menus only to have Betsy, the youngest of the Leighton ladies, interrupt her.

"Henry!" she cried. "I cannot find Vincent anywhere! Have you seen him? Do you know where he is?"

"No," Henrietta responded absently as she dipped her pen into the inkwell and scratched a note on one of the menus before her. "But he's probably off on another adventure of his. He'll undoubtedly return when he cannot keep his ears from dragging on the ground or when his appetite gets the better of him."

Betsy, who was just recently turned twelve years of age, set her jar on the table beside the inkwell. Henrietta glanced at the small glass container and saw Betsy's usual collection of twigs, flowers, leaves and at least three swallowtail caterpillars. Betsy tapped the glass several times and, with a frown between her brows, said, "But I am afraid he may have gotten into Lord Ramsdean's home wood. I heard recently that his bailiff has ordered a number of springtraps set up in hopes of discouraging the poachers. And well, what if Vincent were to get hurt by mistake? Besides, the bailiff told me that if he ever found my dog near Lord Ramsdean's stock again, that he'd shoot him!"

Henrietta said, "I don't think you need to worry just yet."

"But you don't understand. Vincent has been gone since yesterday!"

At that, Henrietta looked up from her small stack of papers and queried, "Are you sure?"

Betsy nodded, her large blue eyes dark with concern. She was a very pretty girl, with thick lashes, the delicate arched brows that characterized all of the Leighton ladies, and a smattering of faint freckles across her nose. She would probably blossom into one of the fairest of the young women, second only to Angel, who was the acknowledged beauty of the family, but of the moment,

7

her concerns were exclusively of a childish nature. She preferred her dogs to painting watercolors, her explorations throughout the South Downs of Hampshire to mastering French knots, and collecting bugs to practicing her scales upon the pianoforte. To all of the ladies, except Arabella—who had an extremely rigid view of how a lady ought to conduct herself—she was a beloved pet and was permitted to indulge her young interests as much as she wished.

Henry leaned her elbow on the table, her chin resting in the palm of her hand, and watched Betsy with a mixture of amusement and envy. Her own girlhood had slipped away so quickly that at three and twenty she could scarcely remember it at all. She was herself a widow, and was known among their neighboring families by her married name, Mrs. Harte. And how long ago even that seemed, for she had been wed at seventeen and widowed the same year when her dear Frederick had scandalized the family, the neighborhood and his vast London acquaintance by shooting himself in the head after losing his entire fortune in a desperate game of hazard. He had been handsome, his smile jaunty and his kisses as reckless and impulsive as his manner of living. But why, Henrietta wondered for the thousandth time, could he not have stayed his final impulse and sought her counsel first? She could have given him hope. She could have persuaded him not to take his life.

Betsy interrupted her thoughts and asked, "Will you not help me look for Vincent? Please?"

Henrietta heard her as through a fog and pressed her fingers to her temples. She rubbed her head in an effort to still the unhappy memories that still haunted her even after six years. Finally, she said, "Of course I'll help you find dear old Vincent. We shall go as soon as I have spoken with Cook."

Betsy's face lit up with a beatific smile as she picked up her jar of caterpillars and removed to the mullioned windows where she began searching for more intriguing insects.

A few minutes later Henrietta returned the menus to Cook and learned that she had hidden Betsy's infamous sling, used to hurl stones at any moving object that happened to catch her practiced eye, in the salt box next to the roasting pit.

"I wrapped it in a length of white linen and hid it before she'd done turned around. She killed another of my layers, she did, with that wicked weapon of hers! And I won't have it! I don't like to spoil Miss Betsy's fun, but I can't have the chickens all stirred up or they'll be off layin' for a fortnight or more. And we need them eggs, as ye well know, what with Mr. Huntspill holding his purse so close as he does!"

Henrietta agreed that it would do no harm for Cook to withhold Betsy's catapult—as it was known among the boys of her acquaintance—and after requesting Cook's singularly delectable raspberry tarts for the tea tray that afternoon, she returned to the entrance hall. There she found not only Betsy preparing for a trek through the country lanes about Fair Oaks, but Charlotte as well. Each had donned a stiff, small poke bonnet and tied it securely beneath her chin against the April wind that was known to bluster across the downs with a vengeance at times. Charlotte held out a thick merino wool pelisse for Betsy to wear. But Betsy took great exception to the cumbersome article, arguing that she would be quite comfortable with her old shawl. Charlotte, however, insisted her younger sister protect herself against the cold weather, particularly since it was just as likely to rain as not. Betsy still refused to cooperate until Charlotte informed her that neither she nor Henrietta would assist her in searching for Vincent unless she did as she was told.

Henrietta immediately joined her sisters, aligning herself firmly with Charlotte. Betsy glared at them both

9

and slipped her arms into the warm pelisse, all the while muttering that it was quite clear she was made of sterner stuff than her paltry siblings!

When Henrietta had also buttoned her pelisse of a royal-blue merino, and tied her poke bonnet over her dark, brown hair, she glanced at herself in the mirror beside the stairwell. Fluffing the curls upon her forehead, she saw reflected in the looking glass a serious young woman with large blue eyes, well-shaped brows, a straight nose and rosy lips. Frederick had once told her she had the sweetest lips he had ever partaken of. She wondered briefly if she would ever be kissed again. What an odd notion to strike her at such a time!

Her reveries were interrupted suddenly by Betsy, who cried, "You are quite presentable, Henry, but I wish you wouldn't dawdle so when poor Vincent may be lying wounded and bleeding in Lord Ramsdean's home wood!"

Chapter Two

King Brandish drained his tankard of ale and eyed the serving girl with appreciation. She was of medium height, had large, dazzling hazel eyes, sported a head of guinea-colored hair, and possessed a figure Venus would have envied. Even her ankles were well-turned, he noted with pleasure as she bent over slightly to wipe a recently vacated table. He was seated in the dining parlor of the Bell and Angel Inn, where he was enjoying a quiet luncheon. He could have dined at Broadhorn Hall, but he was unable to bear the thought of enduring one more forced meal with his father, Lord Ennersley, his jovial uncle, Lord Ramsdean, and his father's sister, Lady Ramsdean. In addition, two more country guests made the enjoyment of his uncle's sideboard an impossibility—Mrs. Kempshott and her daughter (the polished, decorous, and hopelessly virtuous Widow Marshfield) also drank their toasts to all of his father's opinions.

The poor widow had been selected by his elders to serve as a sacrificial lamb to his bachelorhood. That they provided a widow, and not an innocent young lady of tender virtue, spoke volumes regarding their opinion of his character as that of a hopeless libertine. What pure, virginal female would be easily beguiled into a union with the infamous King Brandish? As for the widow, he had no ill feelings toward her to speak of. She was comely, well

11

bred, elegant, and at times, witty. Unfortunately, he valued his independence considerably more than he cherished her company.

The truth was, he had been for years heartily sick of Aunt Margaret's machinations and his father's lectures regarding his duty to his ancestors to take a wife and provide an heir for the distinguished family of Brandish. King, himself, would one day inherit the Ennersley peerage and enjoy all the attending benefits of nobility. But his father would only feel he had fulfilled his duty as the fifth Viscount Ennersley once his son married and produced a male child in line to inherit his exalted title.

All King wanted of the moment, however—as he reveled in the sight of the serving maid bending over yet another table—was a cuddle or two from an affectionate, warm, generous female. In short, a kiss would suffice to satisfy him, at least until the dinner hour. Just one fleeting pressure of his lips upon the mouth of that exquisite creature might recompense him for all his trouble in journeying down to Hampshire. One taste of the maid's full lips, and he was certain his sense of feeling ill-used, harassed and brow-beaten would dissipate like the early morning dew when the sun has risen. Oh, that she would take pity on him!

As these thoughts swirled about in his mind, he contented himself with sipping a second tankard of ale and smiling roguishly now and then upon the flaxen-haired wench. She smiled often in return, giving him great hope that his desires would very soon be fulfilled. All he had to do was wait until the dining parlor had emptied of patrons, and he would be alone with the hazel-eyed beauty.

As the last of the inn's guests quit the parlor, the maid glanced curiously at him, but not unkindly, he thought. His reward, he was certain, would very shortly be forthcoming, and he moved swiftly to close the door lest any priggish matron should discover the wench in his arms and take strong exception to his mode of conduct.

12

"What—what are you doing?" the maid cried, apparently surprised to find herself alone with King as he leaned against the door, barring her way.

She held a dirty plate in one hand and two empty tankards in the other. As comprehension of his intentions dawned on her, she lowered her head, scowled at him and demanded he step aside, for she had no intention of engaging in a hopeless piece of dalliance with him or any other man for that matter.

King, conversant with the habits of recalcitrant maids throughout the quiet and varied villages of England, ignored her feisty speech. Smiling in a devilish manner, he said, "I beg only to know your name. That's all, truly. But tell me your name, oh, fairest of maids, and I shall be satisfied."

"My name is Eleanor, sir, but I beg you—" she began.

He lifted a hand, cutting her off gently as he said, "You may call me by my Christian name, for your beauty has won my heart and my devotion—pray call me King, as my friends do."

She rolled her eyes slightly and laughed outright. "I suppose next, *your majesty*, you will tell me all the ways you now expect me to *serve* you. Have I the right of it?"

He was pleased, infinitely so. She was as clever as she was pretty, and with a contented sigh, he said, "Yes. Oh, yes, indeed. And your wit has further enslaved my heart, oh, beauteous one. Only ease my longings now by placing a kiss upon my lips. I've not been kissed in a sennight, and I'm like a man suffering from a terrible ague who needs only a cool cloth pressed against his brow to ease his distress. Ease my torment, now, my lovely Eleanor, and grant me one, poor kiss."

Her lips parted slightly as she readied an answer, her eyes full of consternation. "I've never heard such talk before," she said at last. "Your speech is all flowers cloaking your thorns, and were I of a mind to, I shouldn't hesitate in giving what you ask. But I cannot give that which does not belong to me."

13

"How's this?" he asked affably. He was certain of success as long as he refused to give up the chase. She was merely offering a perfunctory resistance to his advances, a pattern of steps necessary to the performance of the lively country dance they had enjoined.

Suddenly, however, her rosy, provincial features were overcome by an expression that turned his confidence into the merest shadow of hope. Her face was alive with a love that he could easily observe as she became caught up in a reflection that had absolutely nothing to do with his charm, his wit, or any other enchanting aspect of his person.

"I'm to be married Saturday next to the handsomest smithy in all of Hampshire," she said, her eyes filled with a soft glow.

His spirits fell. He may not have hesitated to seduce a willing serving maid, but the bride-to-be of a hardworking man, especially one whose heart was pure, did not have a place in his exploits.

He sighed heavily. "I am lost," he said. "You were my only hope of salvaging what has been one of the most tiresome sennights of my existence."

He stepped away from the door, opening it for her, and with a broad sweep of his arm, gestured for her to depart in peace.

She giggled and told him he was a good man, for all his roguish flirtations. She still held the plate and the tankards in hand, and as she passed by him, she stopped suddenly, placing a sweet, impulsive peck upon his cheek. Then she was gone.

King paid his shot and left the Bell and Angel feeling more irritable than when he had arrived. Mounting his bay stallion he was soon cantering down the High Street. He passed the blacksmith's shop and with a vague sensation of envy noticed the towering smithy, his arms heavily muscled in evidence of his demanding trade, as he pounded a glowing shoe against an anvil. This was no doubt the very man the serving wench was to marry, and

14

he was struck with how much simpler the life of country folk appeared when compared to his own. They seemed to take pleasure in their toils, married whom they wished regardless of such matters as property and dowry, and bore their children out of desire instead of duty. He longed for his life to have similar, unremarkable boundaries, but the gods had not blessed him so kindly. Instead he was heir to a peerage, and his father's endless scoldings had caused him more than once to despise his birthright.

Once beyond the village, he rode toward the lane that led to an obscure manor house near the southern end of Ramsdean's home wood, then curved about the rolling downs to the gated entrance of Broadhorn Hall, Lord Ramsdean's county seat. The air had grown decidedly cooler, and a brisk wind had begun whipping the tops of the tall elms and pollarded oaks that lined the lane. The starry blue flowers of the periwinkle vine clambered about the bushes of the hedgerow, dancing in the mounting wind as Brandish pressed his hat more firmly about his ears. He wore a blue coat, fitted buckskin breeches, rugged top boots and spurs. In short, he wore the proper attire for a young gentleman visiting his family in the country. He was fagged to death with ruralizing with his relations and determined that very moment that he would quit Hampshire on the morrow.

The decision made, the terrible weight attached to his spirits seemed to disengage, and his heart felt considerably lighter. The breeze on his back was no longer harsh, but invigorating. He needed only one thing now to completely restore his faith in the goodness of life—the kiss sweet Eleanor had been unable to give him.

He began mentally reviewing all of the various maids, undermaids, chambermaids, scullery maids and abigails that traversed the long halls of Broadhorn, speculating upon which female in particular might prove best suited for the purpose. Dalliance, he thought with a smile as he turned down the lane, was his most favorite of all

15

occupations! But what was this?

In the distance he saw three females—what great fortune, three! A trio from which to choose a proper victim. In his renewed interest in life, he quickly spurred his horse on and within a matter of seconds drew abreast of the ladies.

Scrutinizing them carefully, he found that the first young woman was young, indeed. She could not even have left her childhood yet. The second, though walking with a certain grace he found pleasing, wore spectacles and would not even meet his gaze as he tipped his hat to them all. But the third! Faith, he now believed in fortune's favor again, for she was a lovely creature, with eyes as beautiful as the periwinkles adorning the hedges. Her face was a perfect oval in shape, and her brows were delicately arched. Her complexion, while pink from walking in the wind, was creamy and uniform. In short, he had just tumbled violently in love—at least for this one precious moment in time.

But what charmed him most about this Hampshire beauty was how firmly she returned his gaze, neither flinching, nor blushing, nor even smiling in response. She merely looked at him, her periwinkle eyes beckoning him to speak.

Before he could, however, the youngest of the ladies called out to him suddenly, in her little girl's voice. "Sir! Why do you stare at my sister in that odd manner? You are being uncommonly rude!"

He glanced at Betsy and inquired, "Am I? But can a worshipper of beauty be accused of discourteous conduct when he has found a new object to admire? A precious artifact, existing in human form, and worthy of the palaces of Olympus?"

Betsy stopped in her tracks and regarded him directly for a long moment as though assessing his words with every ounce of her blossoming feminine intuition. "What a rapper!" she cried at last. "You are merely trying to get up a flirtation!"

16

"You are too observant," King responded with a smile, his gaze never leaving his quarry's precious face. "And you are exposing me abominably, Miss, er—"

"Leighton, if you please! Betsy Leighton. You have a fine horse there, you know."

King, who had paid a dear price for the spirited bay stallion now sidling across the lane, brought his horse under control with a careful lifting of the reins. "Thank you, Miss Betsy. And if you would permit me to say so, I would hazard a guess that in a few more years, you will be that lady's equal in both face and figure." He gestured to her sister with his riding crop. "And she, I will add, is by far the prettiest female I have ever encountered in my life."

Betsy laughed outright as she approached the stallion and clucked several times to him. "Then you have not seen my sister Angel," she said. "Henrietta cannot hold a farthing-candle to her!" She completed the distance to the restless horse and stroked his nose several times. The stallion quivered once, but permitted her to run a hand down his long neck with only a flicker of his ears to express his discontentment.

King glanced at Henrietta, caught her gaze and whispered her name. "Henrietta." He saw her blush and turn away, as the two ladies then conferred together. Addressing Betsy, he said, "I have a great difficulty believing that Angel could be comelier than your sister here. In fact, if I had not already ascertained that you were frank to a fault, I would have accused you of prevaricating."

Betsy leaned away from the horse's head and lifted her gaze to look at him. Blinking once, she asked, "Are you trying to flatter me, sir?"

He had been watching Henrietta, who was whispering to the other young lady. But at these words, he glanced down at Betsy and responded, "Why, yes, of course. I am hoping you will introduce me to your sister"—here he gestured to Henrietta again—"because I long to make

17

her acquaintance. My heart fails within my breast at the mere sight of her."

"Oh, stuff," Betsy cried with a laugh. "I doubt your heart ever fails you, and as for *failing* you now, I can only say you sound like a regular bleater!"

He laughed and tapped Betsy on the top of her bonnet with his crop. "Well, Miss Mischief, will you make me known to your sister or not?"

She looked up at him speculatively, and asked, "Are you perchance Mr. Brandish? Lady Ramsdean's nephew?"

He seemed surprised, but bowed readily, acknowledging his identity as well as his unfortunate relationship to a woman he felt was a hypocritical, ungenerous, Old Tabby. "But how do you know of me?" he asked. "I am not a frequent guest at Broadhorn."

Betsy nodded in a knowing fashion and whispered, "That is because you are quite often in disgrace with her ladyship. You are a very bad man, a wicked scapegrace, at least that is what my sister Arabella says of you! And she, if you must know, is well informed about everyone and everything in the entire parish!"

He leaned down to Betsy, who had taken a confiding step toward him, and said, "A gabblemonger, eh?"

"Oh, indeed, yes! A tittle-tattle of the highest order, though if she's been particularly fusty and interfering, I'll always put a toad in her bed, or something equally as odious, just to bring her down a peg or two."

He laughed uproariously, throwing his head back, and almost lost his beaver hat in the process. When he patted it back down about his ears, Henrietta cried, "Come, Betsy! We ought not to be detaining this gentleman. It is bad form, you know, to be speaking to him since we have not been privileged with a proper introduction."

"But I like him, Henry, and I think you would, too. He's not at all like his aunt, I assure you!"

"I certainly hope not!" Brandish cried, laughing in response to Betsy's most improper observation. "She's a regular cross-crabs." He smiled down at her, then added, "So, Miss Betsy, I thank you for your kind opinion of my character, and I ask only that as you approach your coming out ball in the not too distant future, you will always retain your candor and dislike of toad-eaters and gossips."

Betsy straightened her shoulders and said, "I won't have a come-out ball, that much I can promise you, for I intend to journey all over the world once I am released from the schoolroom. I mean never to marry, and I shall keep a hundred dogs in my house if I so desire! Oh! Speaking of dogs, we have been out looking for my own dog, Vincent, for quite some time! Have you seen any dogs in the lane this afternoon, Mr. Brandish? He's yellow and big and thinks he's a great hunter, but he's too clumsy by half to do more than alert all the quarry in the district that we are about!"

Brandish shook his head. As he glanced at the ladies' clothing, noticing that they were remarkably dirty and their shoes were cloaked with dust, he lifted his brows in surprise. "Have you been hunting this dog all morning and past nuncheon?"

"Oh, no!" Betsy cried. "Only for about three hours now, but we can't find him. We intend to turn west at the next sheep-track and search the southern edge of your uncle's home wood. I have been worried terribly that he might have been killed by one of Lord Ramsdean's spring-traps."

"I certainly hope that is not the case, and if it pleases you—and your sister—I should be happy to return to Broadhorn at once and see if Vincent wandered onto my uncle's property. Besides, I can tell by the reproachful look in *Henry's* eye that I will not be making her acquaintance today."

Betsy said, "You ought to call upon us at Fair Oaks, Mr. Brandish. Of course, we'll only be residing there for another three months, after which, Charlotte—my other sister—" she nodded toward the young lady standing beside Henrietta—"says we shall most likely go directly to the poorhouse."

"*Betsy!*" her sisters cried in unison, both stepping forward to take charge of the unhappily verbose young lady.

King wondered what this cryptic statement could possibly mean. He would have asked, but Betsy's older and wiser sisters had already whirled the young hoyden about, planting her solidly between them so that she could no longer chat with him.

Henrietta then dismissed him with a curt nod of her head, and the trio set off down the lane at a brisk pace.

The wind whipped at their pelisses, and King had a sudden impression of a closeness between the ladies that he had never known in his own family life. He had but one sister, who was five years his senior and who was now positively buried in a northern county with a husband and a large brood of eight hopeful children. He rarely saw any of them. He knew another fleeting sensation of envy, and he was struck by the very odd thought that his own existence had been devoid of many fine, yet mundane, advantages. The smithy came to mind as well, along with Eleanor and her simple devotion to her future husband. Would he ever know such ordinary pleasures as this? he wondered. Somehow, it did not seem at all likely.

He soon lost sight of the ladies as he cantered up the lane heading for Broadhorn. After a few minutes, he reached the gates of the expansive country house, and instead of riding straight up the long drive, he guided his horse toward the kennels. He knew his uncle's bailiff by reputation and did not doubt for a second that the man would either shoot Vincent on sight or have him locked up in the kennels until it pleased him to release the poor dog.

It was not long, as he marched about the ancient, stone buildings, before he spied a muddy, yellow dog. The poor beast looked quite lonely and dejected as he lay on the ground, his head resting sadly upon his paws.

"Vincent!" he called sharply. "Come here, boy!"

When the big dog pricked up his ears, rose briskly to his feet and trotted over to the gate, Brandish was left in little doubt that he had found Betsy's beloved pet. After a brief, albeit harsh, exchange with the kennelmaster, King secured Vincent's release. For his efforts, he received a wet lick on his face. King realized, as he scratched the dog's neck, that fate had given him a wonderful gift in Vincent, for what woman, possessing even the hardest of hearts, would not be moved by the reunion of a younger sister and her adored pet.

"Vincent, dear doggy," he said, addressing the yellow retriever and smiling into his furry face. "You may be the very means by which I am at last able to secure the kiss I have been seeking all day. What do you say to that, old fellow?"

Since Vincent, excited by Brandish's kind words, placed a series of hearty licks on his savior's chin and face, King could only assume that the beast wished to assist him in any way he could.

Brandish stepped away from the hound, eyed him warily for a moment, then said, "But do you suppose she would value you sufficiently to offer a kiss as a reward for your safe return?"

The dog whined and grovelled before him which caused King to click his tongue reproachfully. "Decidedly not, you wretched toad-eater."

21

Chapter Three

Henrietta knew of one other place poor, old Vincent might be found. Perhaps it was because she thought it would be more efficient to form two separate parties to search for the dog that she suggested the scheme to her sisters, but in her heart, she knew what she really wanted was a respite.

A desperate confusion had taken possession of her mind the moment King Brandish had captured her attention and held her gaze so steadfastly. She had wanted fiercely to simply turn away from him, to look anywhere but into his sharp, blue eyes. Instead, she had regarded him mutely, obeying the silent command of his reckless spirit. Did he know the effect he had had upon her? She prayed he did not, else he would pursue her mightily until he held dominion over her soul.

Henrietta pressed a hand to her heart as she stumbled slightly across the field leading to the wooded dell. She had striven for the past six years to master this wretched flaw that held sway over her mind. It was as though at birth a gypsy had cursed her with an unaccountable passion for gentlemen of a wild and haunted nature.

Brandish was just such a man.

For the past sennight, the ladies of Fair Oaks had known that King Brandish and his father, Lord Ennersley, were visiting the inmates of Broadhorn Hall.

But there had been for so long no contact between Lady Ramsdean and Mrs. Leighton that none of the ladies would have expected to have been introduced to either the viscount or to his notorious son.

Henrietta, therefore, had been completely unprepared to meet Mr. Brandish. Had she had occasion to encounter him over teacakes or in a crowded ballroom, she would have long since steeled herself against the man before ever he could look at her. As it was, he had unwittingly taken her by surprise and caught a glimpse of her own wayward soul before she had been able to adequately protect herself.

I am horridly flawed, she thought yet again.

Moving swiftly in the opposite direction of Betsy and Charlotte, she crossed two lanes and another field which was bordered at the far end by what appeared to be a thick coppice. A passerby would presume that another field lay immediately beyond the thicket. Instead, the shrubby, wooded growth led to a small ravine blanketed with moss and dotted with lilac flowers as well as an occasional wild hyacinth. Alder, birch and willow adorned the sides of the elegant cleft in the earth where a centuries-old rivulet of water had rent the land in two. At one end of the cleft, the ravine opened up into a soft meadow where lambs and ewes frolicked or rested according to their need, and in this place, Henrietta felt her heart grow calm again.

In the far distance she could hear Betsy cry out, "Vincent!" But the farther away her sisters moved, the fainter the calls sounded until they disappeared entirely. The wind blew steadily, sweeping the tops of the trees, but in the ravine all was peaceful.

Henrietta's reflections drifted to the first love of her life, Frederick Harte. Their courtship had been madcap and exciting, full of fun and gig and every merriment he could concoct to please her.

She had loved him immensely.

Her mind grew very still at this thought. Had she truly

loved him? Was it love that had enslaved her heart? Or was it some strange moon-madness that had invaded her intellect and turned her reasoning powers to dust? After so long a time, she wasn't certain.

Their honeymoon had been brief, and Henrietta had very soon been brought up short by the knowledge that for all his dash and boldness, Frederick was dangerously heedless with money. He gambled recklessly, leaving her alone at night as he went from one gaming hell to the next. Creditors soon pelted their small establishment on Mount Street with bill after endless bill. But of all his habits of conduct, none affected her more wretchedly than his former associations with a variety of mistresses. On at least a dozen separate occasions, she was ogled by elegant Cyprians at Hyde Park, at the Royal Italian Opera House, and at Drury Lane.

Henrietta wished the memories would not haunt her so, but they persisted still. Seating herself upon a ledge of rock that was surrounded by tufts of oxlips and cowslips, she placed her hands over her face, trying to force the painful recollections from her mind. Six years! And she could still hear the sound of Frederick's pistol reverberating through the halls of his father's ancient hunting box in Somerset.

Brandish had culled forth these harsh memories, not because he physically resembled Frederick, but because his reputation was as hapless as her husband's had been. In addition, both men shared a certain haunted expression of both *ennui* and daring. Over the years, when the ladies of Fair Oaks would dance at local balls or at the assembly rooms in Bath, Henrietta had learned to recognize such men at a mere glance and to avoid them whenever possible. She knew who they were, for they always walked with a certain swaggering challenge to the *beau monde*, they wore their hats at a devilish angle, and always their smiles. . . .

"Do we intrude?"

Henrietta removed her hands quickly from her face as

24

a bolt of fear struck cleanly through her heart. Somehow, Brandish had found her. Oh, lord, it was not possible!

She watched his descent into the ravine and realized that Vincent was close upon his heels, whining the moment he caught scent of her.

"Vincent!" she cried, rising to her feet. She was grateful for the distraction the retriever presented. "How overjoyed Betsy will be to see that you are alive and well!" She bent over slightly to pet the unfortunate dog and to rub his ears. "Where have you been? We have been searching for you for hours!"

Vincent nuzzled her hands, jumped wildly about her feet and barked at her several times as though trying to recount his adventures. Henrietta grasped his lower jaw playfully and told him he was a very naughty dog to have disappeared as he did and to have caused Betsy so much heartfelt worry. He growled and sneezed as if in apology.

She released him with a friendly shove against his strong neck, and he bounded clumsily away. Soon afterward, he caught a whiff of rabbit, lowered his muzzle to the ground and began a familiar sweeping pattern across the short turf of the ravine in search of his prey.

Henrietta lifted her gaze to regard Brandish and immediately felt a smattering of gooseflesh prickle her neck as she looked into his eyes. They were cool, fiery eyes, full of blue heat. He smiled at her, lowering his head slightly, his expression replete with invitation. She knew he had come for a purpose. Every movement of his entire person indicated an improper design.

She chose to ignore the meaning evident in the enticing language of his face and asked politely, "Where did you find him, Mr. Brandish?"

He took a step toward her, not a large step, but a familiar one, a maneuver intended to invoke confidence. "I am loath to say that Vincent had been detained overnight by Lord Ramsdean's bailiff in the kennels at Broadhorn. I found him there shortly after I spoke with the delightful Betsy. Naturally, I felt it incumbent upon me to return him to Fair Oaks at once. But when I saw you marching across the fields in the direction of this enchanting, *secluded* dell, I decided to bring him to you directly."

Henrietta took a marked step away from him, lifting her chin slightly and turning her gaze toward Vincent. The retriever was now some twenty yards away digging furiously into the soft bank of the ravine. "It was very kind of you, I'm sure, to bring Vincent to me, but you must have seen Betsy. And if you did not see her, you certainly knew where she was headed, for she told you her intentions earlier. You would have done much better to have taken Vincent to her, rather than to me."

He closed another few inches of the distance between them by stepping toward her in a purposeful manner, his hands clasped behind his back. "You are right, of course," he responded. "But I had no desire to demand a reward from either of those fine ladies, for you must know I am asking a kiss for Vincent's safe return in payment for my excessive labors in rescuing the ill-fated brute. And as for having chosen you to discharge this exhilarating office, I am sorry to say it was a logical process of elimination. Your sister Charlotte, for instance, would no doubt have blushed to the roots of her lovely hair at such a demand, and I cannot bear the blushes of flustered females. As for Betsy, she would surely have kicked me hard in the shins at such a request."

"I shall do so as well if you don't take care!" Henrietta cried. "And I must say that you are by far the most arrogant, dishonorable man I have ever met. Where is your chivalry?"

"Alas," he said sadly. "I left it all at the Bell and Angel. I begged a kiss of a serving maid there only to discover that she is engaged to be married. You would have been amazed at my conduct—I left her unscathed." He sighed deeply, a mischievous twinkle lurking in his eye.

His falsely aggrieved expression performed a serious

injury upon Henrietta's intention to ward off this hopeless rake. She found a bubble of charmed laughter ready to burst inside her. She liked his flirtatious manner of speech excessively, and with every word he spoke, she found her resolution slipping. She knew she ought to turn heel and run at a mad pace from the dell, yet she remained.

"I am only amazed," Henrietta responded in kind, "that you showed such supreme self-control! And I don't know that I have a single reason to believe a word you are saying anyway, for you are clearly a disreputable fellow, even if you did return Vincent to me."

He took another step toward her and, with a devilish smile, said, "I am a rogue, a wastrel, a scoundrel, anything you like, *Henry*. But one thing I promise you—I am not a liar."

Henrietta scarcely noticed the use of her nickname as she fell victim again to Brandish's soporific gaze. His eyes ought not to be so blue, she thought, else she could easily resist his advances. And it wasn't only his gaze that drew her to him but his strong, manly presence as well. He was a tall man, powerfully built, clearly a Corinthian in his habits of exercise. His hair was black, cut somewhat longer than the usual mode, and not a little wild in appearance. His tight, buckskin breeches revealed muscular thighs, and his blue riding coat fit his broad shoulders and chest to perfection. He was a Man about Town, a Corinthian, a rogue.

Henrietta felt her heart betray her. He stood but two feet from her now, his eyes regarding each of her features in turn—first her brow, then her eyes and nose, her chin and lastly her lips. He lingered there longest, finally returning to her eyes. His expression had altered subtly, Henrietta noted, as he moved closer still. He searched her face as though trying to remember something long since forgotten.

"Have I met you before," he queried suddenly. "For a moment you looked familiar to me."

"I do not recall having made your acquaintance previously," Henrietta said quietly, a blush rising to her cheeks. "It is possible I met you some years ago, for I was used to reside in London, though for only a few short months."

He frowned slightly, still scrutinizing her features.

She felt sick at heart, her spirits failing her. Perhaps he was remembering the scandal that shocked so many members of the *ton*. He would have been acquainted with Frederick then; their worlds were so similar. He would have known that Freddy Harte had married a chit scarcely out of the schoolroom and then taken his life not two months after the wedding vows had been spoken.

She swallowed hard as she watched his thoughts float in waves across his face. She waited uneasily for him to associate her with Frederick. She wanted to end the anxiety of the moment and simply blurt out her identity as Mrs. Frederick Harte, a woman who would live in disgrace forever. But she could not.

When he finally gave voice to his speculations, his words surprised her. "You are beautiful, you know. I may have spoken in an affected manner when I first saw you in the lane with your sisters, but I truly meant what I said. You could grace the palaces of Olympus."

Henrietta felt her breath desert her. Even Frederick had never addressed her so prettily. "I must go," she whispered at last, a sudden desperation to escape him overtaking her. "I do thank you for returning Vincent to us, but I must go! I must!"

She found enough strength to turn away from him, but he caught her arm and held her fast. "Don't leave just yet, Henry, please."

She glanced back at him, straining against his hand as he prevented her from leaving. She wanted to go, but she longed to stay. Never before had she known such dissension in her heart. He drew close to her, maintaining all the while a firm grip on her arm. When he spoke, she could feel his sweet breath on her cheek.

28

"I can't let you go," he whispered. "I must hold you once in my arms before I can permit you to leave. I must have my reward. I must. I will!"

He was standing very close to her now, and she was surprised at how much his hand, which still gripped her arm, eased her heart in a way she could not explain.

"You do not know, Mr. Brandish, the harm you're inflicting upon me. Please don't do this. Please go away and leave me in peace, I beg of you."

He moved to stand in front of her and placed his other hand on her opposite arm. His voice was low and intense as he spoke. "What harm is there in a kiss? How can one salute upon your fair lips possibly bring you anything but pleasure?"

When she would not meet his gaze, he caught her chin in his hand and forced her to look at him. "I ask you again, Henry, what harm is there in a kiss? One kiss?"

"There is every harm," she answered, meeting his gaze boldly. Her words measured and low, she continued, "There are days past to regret. There are future nights to pine for and yet to know will never exist. There are other kisses to regard forever with disfavor."

He leaned toward her, slipping an arm about her waist, his lips hovering over hers. "I only want a kiss for this moment, nothing more. You must learn to think as I think—to live only for this present hour. The future orders itself however it will, regardless of our efforts to mold it to our liking."

"I promise you, King," she responded in a murmur. "If you do this thing, I shall haunt your future, I shall trample your midnight dreams, and every woman's lips you violate from this day forth will be as a shadow to mine." She did not know why she was speaking these words to him. Perhaps she wanted to punish him, to place a curse on his roguish ways.

"You have charmed me, indeed, Henry," he said, brushing his lips against hers. She thought he would now take his kiss. Instead, he drew back slightly and pulled

29

hard on the ribbons of her bonnet.

"No!" she cried. "At least take your kiss from me and be done with it! You are driving me to the point of madness. Why must you now do this?"

He pulled the ribbons apart and pushed the bonnet away from her dusky curls until it fell to the ground. "Because I mean to live in your dreams, as well," he responded.

Her curls had also been held captive by a ribbon, and he pulled the bow until her hair cascaded to her shoulders in a tangle of ringlets. Gently, he began entwining his fingers among her brown locks as he drew her against him and held her very close, his cheek pressed against her own.

Henrietta felt tears sting her eyes as she leaned into him, taking forbidden solace in the nearness of his body. A loneliness rose from deep within her, passing in an empty wave over her soul.

"You don't know what you are doing, Mr. Brandish," she said at last. "You don't know how you are hurting me."

"Your hair smells very sweet" was his only response as he began gently brushing his lips against her cheek. "Your skin is as soft as I knew it would be." Revelling in the silken texture of her complexion, his mouth sought the gentle curves of her face. Henrietta could scarcely breathe, his touch was so wondrously delicate as his lips moved from her brow to her cheek to the warm, tender place beside her mouth.

He teased her mercilessly as he again drifted his lips over her own, not quite kissing her. He pulled her more closely still. In a slow easy movement, Henrietta slipped an arm about his neck, leaning into him.

He still would not kiss her. "Brandish," she whispered, as his mouth played havoc upon her own. "Kiss me, I beg of you!"

He waited for no further invitation as he pressed his lips hard upon hers, full upon the mouth. He crushed her

30

to him until she felt as though she had blended into his soul and become one with him. Years of heartache burned within her, rising from the despair Frederick's death had brought to her. But King's mouth was a cool drink, easing the burn, a balm upon her lonely heart. She did not want the moment to end. She wanted to disappear into the long hallways of time, caught up in his arms forever.

He seemed to sense the need within her and held her fast, kissing her wildly, his lips bruising hers again and again. His hand found her face as he touched her lightly upon her brow, her cheek, then drove his fingers into her curls. He seemed mad with pleasure, tasting her lips with the tip of his tongue, then kissing her hard again.

The wind pressed against them as a sudden gust blew down into the ravine, swirled about them, then disappeared across the meadow. The cold air washed over them, breaking the spell that had taken them from the present, transporting them to a netherworld where time stopped.

Vincent had returned and had begun whining at Henrietta and sniffing at Brandish's boots. The smell of rain on the wind greeted Henrietta's senses as she pulled away from King at last, her gaze lowered to the moss at her feet. She pulled at the curls now hanging about her shoulders and turned around to search for her bonnet.

"I must go," she said quietly. "Betsy and Charlotte will be wondering what has become of me." Her voice sounded as though it had travelled a very long distance. Her heart felt weighted with pain. Brandish's kisses had opened a wound she had believed long since healed. His embraces showed her how wretchedly fragile her defenses really were.

A tear trickled down her cheek, and she wiped her eyes with the sleeve of her pelisse. She searched unseeingly for her bonnet and stumbled through her tears. Brandish was beside her instantly, supporting her arm and retrieving her bonnet at the same time.

31

"What is it?" he cried. "What is the matter? Are you ill? Have I hurt you, Henry? I didn't mean to hurt you?"

She looked at him, feeling frenzied inside, hating that she had yielded to that part of her that would always long for something destined to hurt her.

"Go away," she breathed.

"I won't," he countered quickly. "Not when you are so deeply distressed. I am not a completely heartless libertine, even though you may think so. Only answer me truthfully, you are not a maiden, are you?"

She looked at him intently, searching his eyes. "No," she responded quietly. "No, I am not a maiden. I am a widow of some six years standing. I was married to a man very much like you. Don't you know who I am, Brandish? I thought for a moment, before you kissed me, that you had recognized me from my few weeks in London. Cannot you guess who I am?"

He shook his head, appearing bewildered.

She took the bonnet from his hands and placed it over her curls, not caring that her hair hung loose, trailing down her back.

Tying the ribbons beneath her chin, she said, "Well, I shall tell you, then. And afterward, you may run to your aunt and ask her for all the particulars, because from the very day I was widowed, Lady Ramsdean refused to even speak with my mother. Do you need another hint?"

"You are not making a great deal of sense," he said, scowling at her. "I wish you would not speak in circles."

Henrietta looked away from him, at the sheep grazing in the meadow, and said simply, "Harte."

"Your *heart?*" he queried.

She glanced back at him, laughing slightly at his error. "No," she responded, placing a hand against her bosom. "Not *heart*. But Harte. Mrs. Frederick Harte."

Comprehension broke over him as a distant clap of thunder rent the air. "You are Freddy Harte's widow! Good God! I saw you once at Drury Lane, and I remember thinking at the time you were the most ravishing

32

creature—" he broke off suddenly, then continued, "He shot himself, didn't he?"

"Yes, King, he did." She watched him steadily for a moment as the horror of the suicide broke over him. His expression grew distant, and a great sadness welled up within her. She again turned to watch the lambs leap about in the meadow, her heart empty once more. She had learned from many years' experience that few persons believed her innocent of the affair, that she had somehow caused her husband to take so final and desperate a step. How could she explain that she had never really known Frederick, that when she had awakened upon the morning following her wedding night, she had beheld a stranger in her bed.

Brandish's voice shattered her unhappy thoughts. "Are you telling me, then," he asked sharply, "that you believe I am as—as flawed as Freddy?"

Henrietta looked at him, her brows lifted in faint surprise. "Aren't you?" she queried softly.

A martial light entered his eyes as he held her gaze steadfastly. Henrietta knew a faint quavering of her heart as she saw a compressed anger harden the handsome lines of his face. Still, she remained standing before him, returning stare for stare.

"Were you a man," he said at last, his deep-timbred voice closing the distance between them, "I should make you account for that. With all respect to the fact that Mr. Harte had shown at least some sense in having wed you, he was a rapacious fool, quick-tempered, a consorter with every Captain Sharp in London, a seducer of innocent maids."

Henrietta lifted her chin slightly. She disliked having the few fond memories she possessed of Frederick treated so cruelly. In response, she cried, "And what object, pray tell, Mr. Brandish, have you been trying to accomplish in this dell with me? Your motives have not been entirely pure and proper. We did not exactly play at Ducks and Drakes, now did we?"

33

Narrowing his eyes, he bowed to her ever so slightly and said, "I was enjoying a kiss with a beautiful woman, that's all."

With that, he turned briskly away from her and retraced his steps to the top of the ravine.

Henrietta watched him go, a rumble of thunder echoing across the meadow and funneling deep into the ravine. She shivered, for the air grew steadily colder as the spring storm rolled inexorably across the downs.

For the barest moment, she wanted to stop him, to apologize for her harsh words and accusations. She didn't know Brandish's character at all; it was wrong of her to have judged him as severely as she had.

Lifting her hand toward him, as though to call him back, she stayed the impulse and let her arm drop back to her side. She watched him disappear through the break in the thick coppice. King Brandish may not have been of a completely similar stamp as Frederick, but he was still, with respect to her vulnerable heart and sensibilities, a dangerous man. Better to let him go, for in all likelihood she would never see him again, and her life could then return to its former state of repose.

Chapter Four

Henrietta rejoined Charlotte and Betsy a few minutes later with Vincent in tow, his tongue lolling from his mouth in a contented manner. The reunion between Betsy and her dog was filled with woofs and squeals primarily emanating from the former, while the latter, exhausted from his search for rabbits among the ravine as well as his overnight vigil in Ramsdean's kennels, trotted wearily beside her.

When Betsy learned that she had King Brandish and his kindness to thank for the safe return of her beloved retriever, she begged to be permitted to hurry after him so that she might be able to thank him properly for his magnanimous efforts on Vincent's behalf. But Henrietta persuaded her to confine her boisterous gratitude to the contents of a well-composed letter and attend, instead, to Vincent's neglected grooming and appetite.

Betsy agreed readily, and with Vincent bounding along the lane next to her, the happy pair bolted in the direction of Fair Oaks, far outstripping Henrietta and Charlotte within a scant few seconds of their departure.

A droplet of rain struck Henrietta's bonnet, and she quickened her steps as did Charlotte. As soon as Betsy was out of earshot, Charlotte spoke in a concerned voice. "I know how worried you have been regarding our future, Henry," she said, blinking rapidly as was her manner. "And that you believe none of us have been giving the matter the least consideration. But I wish to assure you that a day does not pass when I do not give our desperate circumstances some thought, some careful attention. For all my efforts, however, I have as yet to compose one reasonable course of action that would keep all of us together as a family once we quit Fair Oaks. And I despise the thought of being separated from any of you."

Henrietta slipped her arm about Charlotte's waist, giving her sister a hug. "I'm certain we shall contrive somehow, though I daresay not in a fashion to which our mother is accustomed." Another drop of rain tapped upon the brim of her poke bonnet.

Charlotte clicked her tongue. "I deeply fear that Mama hasn't the least notion of precisely how hopeless our straits are. Why, only this morning she was speaking of purchasing a diamond tiara! And though I don't approve of Arabella having laughed at her, she was not too far off the mark when she asked, 'But where, Mama, would you wear it when we are very soon to be turned out of our home?' So, you see, all of our thoughts are never far from the encroaching summer months when our fate shall be altered forever!"

She then smiled at Henrietta, and noticing that her curls had escaped the confines of her bonnet, she cried, "Whatever happened to your hair?"

Henrietta blushed slightly and said that her bonnet had become caught in a thicket while she was searching for Vincent. She had only with great difficulty been able to extricate it from the tangled shoots of a clinging woodbine shrub.

Charlotte paused in her steps, laying a hand upon her sister's arm. Gazing hard into Henrietta's eyes, she said, "You are telling me a whisker, dear Henry! I can always tell. Your cheeks betray you even now, though if they didn't, you have an odd inflection to your speech when you tell a rapper that warns me everytime. Come now!" she cried. "What happened? You appeared very con-

36

scious when you found us a few minutes ago. Was it Mr. Brandish? Did he—?"

Henrietta took her sister's arm and wrapped it about her own. "You won't like it one whit! Indeed, I fear you will lecture me once I have told you the truth."

Charlotte sighed in a long-suffering manner. "I knew this would happen," she said, her musings leaping far ahead of Henrietta's confession. "I knew the moment Brandish looked at you that you would be lost to his flirtations. And the worst of it is, even I was not unmoved by his charming discourse with Betsy earlier today. Oh, my dear Henry, do take great care that you do not lose your heart to this one!"

"This one!" Henrietta exclaimed. "Why, you make it sound as though I have had a full regiment of rakish beaux, when Frederick was the only one I had ever met before, or so much as encouraged an acquaintance with since."

"Yes, but you married Freddy," Charlotte pointed out with devastating wisdom. "You must admit you have a remarkable susceptibility to the sort of man more interested in stealing kisses from young ladies than from finding any useful employ in the daily activities of his life. I have watched you at the various balls and assemblies we have attended. You always seem to search out the most incorrigible of men, watching them with a longing in your eyes."

Henrietta admitted it was true. But after she pointed out that she carefully avoided the society of such men and that they were unlikely to ever lay eyes on Brandish again—particularly if they were to adjourn to the poorhouse as Betsy had suggested—she felt she stood in little danger of falling victim to her unfortunate flaw.

Charlotte agreed reluctantly that Henrietta's point was well taken.

A gust of wind swept down upon them, the air heavy with rain. The newly leaved elm trees, compressed into the hedgerows, sang with the wind, a shimmering sound that reminded the young ladies that a lusty spring squall would soon be upon them, and they picked up their steps.

Of all her sisters, Henrietta found the greatest cama-raderie in Charlotte, who was next to her in age. And, of all the ladies of Fair Oaks, Charlotte was by far the most deserving of a fine, noble future. She habitually placed the interests of others before her own, and had she been just a trifle prettier, she would now at one and twenty be happily married; Henrietta was certain of that. In addition, the lack of a dowry for any female—and especially one not endowed with beauty—was a hard obstacle to overcome. It was not that Charlotte was plain or ill-favored, but rather that her nature was such that she never put herself forward. Her clothes, however, were always chosen and stitched with elegance. Where beauty might be lacking in form, her eye seemed always to find it.

The wind rose dramatically, and Henrietta found it difficult to hear her sister. Leaning close to Charlotte as they moved down the lane at a brisk pace, she addressed their former subject. "I, too, confess to being greatly concerned about our future, and I don't know, either, how we will go on or whether we will be able to remain together. I could certainly find a post as housekeeper somewhere, as I am fully persuaded you could do as well. But what of Betsy and our mother, not to mention Angel. For though she has been graced with exceptional beauty and an extraordinary—and quite inexplicable—talent for musical composition, she is wholly unsuited for teaching young girls the use of the globe or even their letters, I'm afraid."

Charlotte shook her head, a smile hovering at the edges of her lips. "Henry, I don't like to mention it, but I don't think Angel even knows all of her letters."

She looked at Henrietta with a mischievous twinkle in her eye, and both ladies broke into laughter. Charlotte, for all her lackluster qualities, possessed in abundance a penetrating sense of humor. It was well known that Angel was not a scholar. Her intelligence rested at a pole completely opposite her comeliness. She was as stupid as she was beautiful.

"I have often thought nature seeks a balance in everything," Henrietta said. "The gods endowed Angel with the face of a goddess but left great gaps in her reasoning prowess. They must have been supping in Jupiter's palace at the very moment they should have been attending to the perfecting of her intellect. Poor, dear, Angel. I do not possess even a fraction of her proficiency upon the pianoforte, but what will her end be, for the world is uncommonly cruel to gentle but witless young ladies."

Charlotte queried, "Do you remember her first presentation at the Lower Assembly rooms in Bath last summer? I am still astonished when I recall how much her beauty collected the gentlemen about her—like bees to honey. Really, it was remarkable to watch. Not that her dull wit did not frighten some of her beaux away, but there were enough who remained either to dance with her or to stand against the walls ogling her, to cause a great deal of comment amongst the ranks of ladies bereft of partners because of it. And do you remember, Henry, that she also received two proposals of marriage that very evening? Papa was shocked but not a little pleased as well."

Henrietta felt a prickling of gooseflesh spread over her entire body at her sister's words. "Oh, my dear!" she cried. "You have just given me the most amazing notion, only it would be such a gambit—and could it possibly succeed? We should be required to invest heavily in so daring a scheme in order to attract the proper suitor. What do you think, Charlotte? Do you think it would work?"

"I cannot answer you," her sister responded dryly, "unless of course you wish to inform me of the particulars."

Henrietta realized she had imparted only the smallest portion of her newly conceived stratagem to her sister. She laughed and then gave Charlotte's arm a squeeze.

"The answer is so simple!" she cried. "And so perfect.

39

We must return to Bath this summer. Surely we could scrape together enough funds to do so, to rent a charming town house in Laura Place, or even in the Royal Crescent. Perhaps we could sell some of our jewels or the furniture. We could prepare a very fine array of costumes for Angel. You and I could sew them all if need be. And what with her beauty and elegance, surely we could find a husband for her before the cat could lick her ear!"

Charlotte's blue eyes glittered as she responded fervently, "The simplest trick imaginable! Of course! And Angel could accomplish the task; I know she could. Why, all she would have to do is smile and bow, and surely one eligible gentleman would fall at her feet. He would have to be wealthy, though, or the rest of us would still end up quite in the basket!"

"Yes, as rich as Croesus if we can manage it! You and I shall see to that by discouraging all but the most promising of suitors! Oh, I can see her now, bedecked in the finest silks and satins and silver lace!"

At that moment, the skies parted, sending a furious squall of rain crashing down upon the earth. The ladies had been so caught up in their schemes, they hadn't realized how close the storm had progressed. They now found themselves running the rest of the distance to the manor, laughing all the while. They were still giggling as Henrietta threw open the door to the entrance hall and fairly pushed Charlotte inside.

Just as they were shaking off their wet pelisses, Henrietta noticed that they were not alone. Arabella, the middle sister, stood by the stairs, a hand pressed to her cheek as she perused a letter. She appeared stunned, an unusual expression for the most stoic of the Leighton ladies.

Henrietta watched Arabella for a moment as she removed her wet bonnet. She saw an expression of intense anxiety overtake her sister's face. Startled by Arabella's evident distress, Henrietta cried, "What is it, Bella? You look almost ill."

Chapter Five

Arabella looked up from the missive that had overset her. Blinking once as a blush crept up her cheeks, she cried, "It is nothing, truly! That is, I have had an astonishing letter from a—an acquaintance of mine, and I'm not certain what to think of the news that he, rather that *she*, had to impart to me."

She forced a thin smile and began refolding the letter, her fingers trembling slightly.

Charlotte passed by her sisters, pausing on the first step of the stairs, and glanced over her shoulder. "Henry," she said. "We ought to remove these wet clothes and dry our hair. You know what Cook is like if she should discover us in this state. She would surely force us to drink one of her putrid restorative draughts before we retired for the night." Lowering her voice to a conspiratorial whisper, she added, "And though I cannot speak for you, for myself, I always suffer abominably from the contents of her potions. Do save yourself, and hurry!"

"I'll only be a moment," Henrietta said, smiling up at her sister. "But I have a matter of some import to discuss with Arabella first."

Charlotte shrugged her shoulders and ascended the stairs, adding that she would take great delight in laughing at Henrietta should Cook discover her with damp tresses.

"Yes, do withdraw to your bedchamber, Henry," Arabella said, voicing her agreement with Charlotte. Clearing her throat in a nervous manner, she continued, "I would be most unhappy were you to become afflicted with an inflammation of the lungs."

Henrietta did not know what to say to her sister. Arabella rarely needed the comfort or help of her family in anything. She possessed a fortitude, a strength of will, that kept her to a degree distanced from those who loved her. Of the moment, Henrietta had never seen her so agitated in her entire existence.

When Charlotte had disappeared into the hallway abovestairs, Henrietta said, "Then, at least join me in my bedchamber while I put on a new gown. Besides, I wanted to speak with you anyway about a particular scheme Charlotte and I have in mind for repairing our fortunes."

Arabella opened her mouth as if to speak, then closed it, all the while holding her letter and stroking it lightly. "Of course," she said finally. Henrietta hooked her arm about her sister's elbow and gently drew her toward the stairs.

The ladies mounted the steps in silence as Henrietta glanced at Arabella. Her sister was of a precise nature, her tone and emotions modulated to suit her ordered sense of the world. Even her blond hair was kept pinned into a careful loop of braids at the nape of her neck. Upon her forehead she wore several identical curls, her one concession to the fashion of the day that dictated a profusion of frizzed ringlets about the face. Her features were angular, consisting of wide cheekbones, a pointed chin, a straight nose and clear, direct blue eyes. Of all the sisters, Henrietta thought Arabella was the least engaging and yet could have been a remarkably handsome woman had not her somewhat autocratic personality inhibited the warmth necessary to soften her sharp features. Betsy came closest to the truth when she described Arabella as a cold fish.

When Henrietta closed the door of her bedchamber

behind her, she turned to face her sister, noting the severe distress in her eyes. She felt compelled to offer her support. "If you wish for it," she said kindly, "I would certainly lend you an ear, for you seem uncommonly distrait!"

Arabella again cleared her throat, clasping her hands together before her in a formal manner as she moved to stand by the window overlooking the topiaried gardens behind the manor. "I don't know, Henry. I would like to discuss this letter with you, which is the source of my uneasiness, but I am not certain that anything useful would come of it. Not that I don't value your opinion, it is just that the difficult circumstances described herein are all but settled. You see, my, er, friend is in the worst quandary, not knowing how to tell her family that she has recently become engaged."

Henrietta thought about this for a moment. As she moved to her wardrobe and began hunting about for a suitable gown, she asked, "Has she entered this engagement without her parents' knowledge?"

Arabella spoke in her clipped manner. "Precisely."

"I think your friend would do well to speak frankly with her family. I'm sure they would understand and undoubtedly approve her course, provided the young man is unexceptionable."

"Oh, he is very agreeable!" Arabella responded enthusiastically. "I have been privy to his mode of correspondence, and he speaks like a man of great sense! His intellect is of a high order, and his prospects, though not grand, are certainly comfortable. I think my family, that is, my *friend's* family, would be quite content with the match."

"Then, I perceive no difficulty at all," Henrietta responded, removing a white cambric morning gown from the wardrobe.

Arabella said, "I suppose part of the dilemma resides in the fact that the engagement will come as a complete shock to her family. My friend and her betrothed have only known one another through an exchange of letters. They have never met before. And though the correspondence has been vigorous and stimulating—enough to prompt my friend to accept his proposal of marriage— there is an unhappy flaw in the arrangement."

"I think the flaw," Henrietta said smiling, "is that they have not as yet met *vis-à-vis*. It is the common course of courtship to begin with a physical approval of a prospective mate, then to proceed to the more daring aspects of discovering intellectual compatibility. It has frequently been my observation that if a woman's figure does not please, her mind be hanged!"

"I wish you would not be so flippant, Henry," Arabella responded tartly. "Nor so base in your evaluation of people and life. Besides, your words only serve to increase my belief that this man"—here she tapped the letter three times—"is quite superior to the general realm of mankind!"

Henrietta suppressed a desire to respond equally as brusquely, for she could see she had greatly offended her sister. Moving to stand behind a tall painted screen, she said, "I did not mean to disparage your friend's betrothal, and I apologize if I have done so. But I cannot imagine then, what flaw there could be in such a happy troth, if it is all as you have described it to be! Is there a mother who would not be content to approve such a husband for her daughter?"

"These are my sentiments as well," Arabella responded, her face growing quite animated. Henrietta peered over the top of the screen and was slightly taken aback by the pink glow on her sister's cheeks. She wondered briefly if more resided behind their discussion than Arabella was confiding.

As Henrietta slipped out of her dress and quickly donned the white morning gown, she noticed that Arabella's expression had again grown puckered and anxious.

"It would seem," Arabella said at last, still looking out

the window as rain pelted the soft spring landscape below, "that the gentleman in question, though well-circumstanced as I mentioned before, is unwilling to bestow a significant settlement upon the lady's nearest relations. You see, her family is quite impoverished, not unlike our own."

"But does she love the young man, do you think?"

"Yes, I'm sure she does, at least, as much as one can through only an exchange of letters. They are, in fact, exceedingly well-suited in temperament and general philosophies, so much so that I think she, in particular, would be satisfied throughout her entire life being the wife of such a fine gentleman. The problem lies in the fact that my friend feels a great sense of duty to her family—a loyalty—"

"And this speaks highly of her character. I esteem her immensely for this."

Arabella pressed the letter against her chin, her brow furrowed. "You do not think, then, it is selfish of my friend to wish for the match even if her family will not benefit from it?"

Henrietta slipped her arms through the long sleeves of her gown and begged her sister to fasten the buttons. Considering how best to answer Arabella, her thoughts turned naturally to the possibility that their own family might face a similar quandary. If they actually proceeded with their scheme to bring Angel into fashion, presenting her to the finest of Bath society this summer, the Beauty could just as easily fall in love with an impoverished young man as with a gentleman of fortune. What then would they do? Would Henrietta raise a hue and cry, refusing to let Angel marry where she wished? There could be only one acceptable response—of course not!

Answering Arabella's query, she said, "If the young lady truly loves her betrothed, then she must do as her heart bids her."

"You speak your opinion firmly," Arabella responded as she systematically closed each button, working her way up to the neck of the gown in a measured cadence. "But I am not so easily convinced. What of family duty? Isn't she obligated to help her relations? Is not this the solid foundation upon which our great society is formed? And how can you purport that it is perfectly acceptable for one to make a decision based upon something as unpredictable as the shiftings of the human heart? You of all people, Henry!" Her tone was incredulous and indicated the source of her discord. "Your life has been so wretchedly altered because you followed a course completely dominated by your senses that I wonder you would even offer similar advice to anyone."

"Oh, Bella," Henrietta began wistfully. "You are the only female I know who manages her life with such resolute adherence to her mind. But for most of us, I am afraid that life does not always fall neatly within the parameters of one's ideals and precepts."

"But it ought to," Arabella insisted as she completed her task of buttoning Henrietta's gown. "How else does one find stability and peace in one's life?" Before she permitted her sister to leave the protection of the screen, Arabella smoothed out invisible wrinkles at the shoulders of Henrietta's gown and gave the skirt several jerks. When she was at last satisfied with her sister's appearance, she stepped aside to let Henrietta pass.

Crossing the chamber to her dressing table, Henrietta seated herself, picked up her mother-of-pearl brush and began tugging at her tangled, wet curls. "I have grown weary arguing with you," she said. "And I begin to think your original assessment of my proposed assistance to you an accurate one. I have given you nothing, except a set of opinions with which to quarrel."

She expected her sister to disclaim or at least to apologize, instead, Arabella said, "Yes, my first intuitive appraisal was correct—the point is moot anyway since the decision has already been made."

Henrietta then glanced at her sister in the mirror and said, "So tell me then, Bella, who is this fine gentleman

46

you have decided to wed unbeknownst to your family."

Arabella stared into the mirror, her expression disbelieving as she met Henrietta's gaze steadily. Blinking rapidly, her mouth agape, she cried, "But how did you guess?"

"You slipped too many times in your speeches, for me to not have noticed. But I do wish you joy! Indeed, I do, and as for the settlements, I know we all would want your happiness to preclude our own security. Only tell me who this man is? I am all agog to know. Do we know him or even of him?" She laughed slightly and cried, "I only wish it were Mr. Huntspill, for at least then we would be guaranteed of a home."

Arabella turned away abruptly, tears starting to her eyes. Henrietta was on her feet immediately and placed an arm about her sister's shoulders. "Don't cry, dearest! You are feeling guilty and you shouldn't. It isn't your fault your betrothed feels unable to help your family. I'm sure his reasons are sound."

"It is ungenerous of him," Arabella said quietly. "I had hoped that he would do more for my family, but he feels a duty to our own progeny. I'm so sorry, Henrietta. Do you know, for a moment, when he first spoke of marriage between us, I was convinced I would be the means by which my family could escape the terrible effects of poverty. I am grievously disappointed."

"Why, Belle," Henrietta cried, tears stinging her own eyes. "I have never known this part of you, that your heart is so noble and magnanimous!"

"I fear what the neighbors will think," Arabella responded with devastating candor. "It cannot look well for me that I am blessed with prosperity while my family must search out their own fortunes however they might."

With that, Henrietta broke into a trill of laughter, releasing her sister. She should have known that Arabella's thoughts or motives would not have wandered very far from her own self-interest.

Ignoring her sister's indignant request to inform her precisely what she had found so amusing, Henrietta begged again to be told who Arabella's beloved was.

"I shan't tell you—I've already made up my mind to that—nor will I say more at this present time. He will be arriving at the Bell and Angel on Wednesday about midday at which hour he will send me word of his arrival. You shall all meet him shortly thereafter."

With this matter settled, Henrietta broached the subject of her scheme to take Angel to Bath for the summer and attempt to find a suitable husband for her.

"It is a wise course," Arabella said, nodding firmly. "She is hardly suited to be any man's wife, in my opinion. But she is even less fitted to be cast upon the world to earn her own fodder."

However coldly expressed the opinion, or however inelegant the description of future need, Henrietta could not help but agree with Arabella. Angel's only hope was to find a man of substance who would not mind gazing, night after night, over his turbot, peas, puddings and claret, into exquisitely beautiful, yet hopelessly doltish blue eyes.

Chapter Six

A few minutes later, Henrietta stood at the entrance to the parlor and gazed down at Angel Leighton. Much to her consternation, her sister was actually lying on her stomach, on the floor alongside Betsy. The two youngest ladies were alone in the room, which accounted for their singularly hoydenish behavior. Had any of the older sisters or Mrs. Leighton been present, this most improper conduct would have been halted immediately.

Angel's laughter floated about the room suddenly, a melodic warbling as delicious to hear as it was infectious. Betsy soon joined her, and even Henrietta could not resist smiling in spite of her disapproval of the ladies' reprehensible posture. "And what," she demanded to know at last, "are the pair of you doing on the floor? What would Mama say?"

"Oh," Angel cried, squirming up to a sitting position as she leaned upon her heels. Turning around to look at Henrietta, she continued, "I did not know you were there. And as for Mama, she is not here; she went to the village hours ago, to see her favorite seamstress. And she couldn't have the least notion of what we are doing, could she? Besides, only look, Henry, Betsy found some caterpillars. Do but look! Aren't they adorable?" She gestured elegantly toward the carpeted floor with an exquisitely molded hand. "It is so exciting! They are racing toward my lavender glove."

Henrietta advanced into the room to inspect the object of Angel's enthusiasm. On the thick Aubusson carpet of pink and gold, crept two caterpillars.

"My man is on the left," Betsy cried. "Do you care to lay a wager with me? I have bet Angel that my caterpillar will beat hers before the clock strikes the hour."

Henrietta noticed that the afternoon was far advanced and that it would very soon be five o'clock. Rain still beat upon the windows as the spring shower continued to pummel the earth, the sky growing steadily dark as night began infringing upon day.

Henrietta glanced toward Angel and then Betsy and realized there was nothing for it but to wait out the race. Just as the hour presented itself in the chimes of the clock, Betsy's caterpillar reached Angel's glove. Angel squealed and praised the delicate, green-striped creature for being so very intelligent. When Betsy pointed out, however, that not only was she complimenting the wrong caterpillar, but that she had lost the wager, Angel opened her eyes wide, exclaiming, "I did?"

Even Betsy groaned.

At that point, Henrietta wasted no time marshaling Angel off to the library where Charlotte awaited them both.

"But I don't want to be married," Angel said at last, tears rising to her lovely, large eyes and sitting on her lashes. One tear shaped itself into a pretty, sparkling drop, bounced off her cheek, then splashed upon her hand. She brushed her face with the sleeve of her pink muslin gown, sniffing delicately.

Henrietta leaned forward in her chair and regarded Angel intently. How was it possible for any female to cry and not show a single, red blotch. When Henrietta cried, her nose invariably turned a brilliant, shiny vermillion, and her eyes became pink and swollen. But there it was—

Angel could shed tears and still her skin appeared as unmarred as a baby's soft complexion.

When another tear rolled down Angel's cheek, Henrietta exchanged a concerned glanced with Charlotte. Perhaps their scheme overlooked the most important factor of all—Angel's desire to take part in it.

Charlotte rose to her feet and moved to a desk of Macassar ebony. There she began struggling with a tinder box preparing to light a branch of candles. "Angel, dearest," she began, her voice low and kind. "We have not suggested this scheme to upset you. Indeed, if you don't wish for it, of course we would never force you to comply. We only ask that you give it some serious consideration."

Angel turned to look at Charlotte with a wounded expression, then back to Henrietta, who sat across from her. She swallowed visibly and said, "But Mama said that when Mr. Huntspill arrived, we should all be taken care of. And yet you are telling me that we are to go to the poorhouse unless I marry someone very quickly. I don't understand. I don't understand at all."

Henrietta, who sat very close to her, took her hand and pressed it gently. She wanted to explain her own perception of the situation carefully, but she didn't think her sister would be able to comprehend any of it. Instead, she smiled and said, "Mr. Huntspill cannot care for all of us. It is impossible."

"But Mama says—"

"I know, dearest, but do you think if Mr. Huntspill took a wife, he would permit us to stay here as well?"

"Whyever not?" she asked ingenuously. "I'm certain once he got to know all of us he would think it a wonderful thing. If I were him, I should enjoy being part of a large family. Why, it always pained me to think that he had only one brother who had got himself killed at Waterloo."

Henrietta stopped breathing. When she and Charlotte had discussed the notion of removing to Bath and

51

parading Angel before every eligible young gentleman they could possibly find, nothing seemed simpler. But now, when Angel was proving not only recalcitrant, but particularly obtuse as well, Henrietta knew a fierce doubt that her plans could ever succeed.

Taking a deep breath, she began again. "Regardless of how much Mr. Huntspill might, or might not, enjoy our continued presence here at Fair Oaks, neither myself nor Charlotte, nor our mother wish to remain. Surely you have heard Mama say that her desire is for Mr. Huntspill to provide her with an annuity?"

Angel nodded. "Yes, that is true," she said. "I have heard her say so often and often. 'Ten thousand pounds or even five would be delightful.'" She smiled suddenly and clapped her hands. "Well, then, it is all settled. We have only to persuade Mr. Huntspill to give us a lot of money."

Charlotte, who had succeeded in lighting the candles, bit her lip and turned away from Angel, clearing her throat several times. Henrietta caught her eye and regarded her severely.

Returning her attention to Angel, she continued, "Dearest, Mr. Huntspill will not give us the money Mama hopes for. He will in all likelihood provide us with something, but not enough to secure all our futures." In the same vein, she continued to press upon Angel the dire nature of their circumstances, especially Mrs. Leighton's need to be going about in society and to not be trapped in a small cottage somewhere, unable to afford even a single day's holiday to any of the seaside resorts where she had for years been a faithful patron. Next, she spoke long and eloquently about Angel's own future, that her alternatives would very soon align themselves into two reprehensible parts were she not to very soon find a husband—she could become a governess or a companion to an elderly invalid—and which did Angel think she would prefer?

"Oh, lord, Henry!" she cried, her eyes full of fear. "I

52

could not teach a child anything. I could give little girls as much love as my heart can hold, and I could play happily with them; but I always get my finger stuck in the bar that holds the globe of the world. I should end up crying! And as for being a companion, I know I would be expected to read." Her blue eyes appeared enormous at this frightening thought. She shook her head slowly, the candlelight playing upon her guinea-curls in a madcap fashion quite at odds with the solemnity of her appalled expression.

"Do you begin to see, then, my dear, all the difficulties before us?" Henrietta asked. "And were you to become the wife of a man of excellent prospects, then in all likelihood, you could help both our mother and Betsy. For myself, I intend to pursue an occupation as a housekeeper—"

"Yes," Angel said, cutting her off. "That is because you are a disgraceful person."

Charlotte's laughter caught in her throat. "Not a *disgraceful* person, Angel," she interjected. "Henry is living *in disgrace*. Quite a different matter altogether, I assure you."

"Oh," Angel said, looking at Henry with renewed respect. "I could never understand why you were a *disgraceful* person. You have always seemed to me to be very nice—considerate, kind, and you are quite intelligent, too. Now I understand." Her brow puckered slightly. "At least I think I do. I know it's all because of Freddy—and I liked him! He made me laugh!"

Henrietta felt both exasperated and charmed by her dear sister. Having her husband presented in this innocent fashion reminded her suddenly of all the many good qualities he had possessed. "He made me laugh, too," she said quietly.

Angel was silent apace, appearing to digest all that had been thrust upon her over the past hour. Finally, she said, "I would be willing to go to Bath and to wear the pretty clothes you have described. I want Mama to be

53

able to go sea-bathing when she wishes to, and though I know you say you will enjoy being a housekeeper for some deserving family, I don't want you to, Henry. You are the one who should be married, not me. I know you wish for a passel of children of your own, though you never mention it. I have seen it in your eyes a dozen times whenever we leave church on Sunday and all the children are running about the yard. At any rate, I will try, if you wish it. Only—" she broke off, chewing her lip. When Henrietta encouraged her to give voice to her thoughts, she continued, "I won't marry a fat man, for they always wheeze, and I can't abide that particular noise. I don't have to marry a man high in the flesh, do I?"

Henrietta looked at Charlotte, whose face was quite pinched from restraining her mirth. But this last remark was too much for Henrietta, who gave vent to a peal of laughter. Charlotte joined her, and after a moment their amusement settled into a gentle sense of relief that at least for the time being they had a course charted for the future. Henrietta assured Angel that only if she felt she could love the man who offered for her, would she be expected to marry him. "And even then, my dear, if at the last moment you truly don't wish for it, no one would press you to marry where you did not want to."

Angel seemed to relax at these last words, and the ladies then set about discussing the various gowns, ball dresses, walking dresses, sandals, half-boots, muffs, capes, and any number of miscellaneous furbelows Angel would need in order to cut a dash in Bath society.

Charlotte seated herself at the desk and, pulling a sheet of white paper forward, began composing a list of the items the ladies had agreed would be necessary for their purposes. Once having acquiesced to the project, Angel was now fully prepared to enter enthusiastically into the plans for their siege of Bath. They were laughing together when a knock sounded on the door.

One of the maids entered the library, her face flushed

and her manner seriously discomposed. She addressed Henrietta, "I am sorry, Mrs. Harte, but I didn't know how to answer him. He asked to see Miss Betsy, you see, and it seemed very odd somehow. He is waiting now in the entrance hall, but I am reluctant to call Miss Betsy unless you say it is all right."

"Who is here to see her," Henrietta queried, a fluttering sensation beginning to tickle the edges of her heart.

"He says his name is Brandish. Mr. Brandish. He said he was acquainted with you, and, oh, la, madame, he is the handsomest creature I've ever seen in me life!"

Chapter Seven

Henrietta closed the doors of the library behind her, closeting both Charlotte and Angel within. She could not imagine what had brought King Brandish to Fair Oaks; moreover she was shocked that he had come since Lady Ramsdean surely would have expressed her displeasure at his intention of doing so. What could he mean by it?

In the hall, she paused before a looking glass and fluffed the curls upon her forehead. After having been caught in the rain, she had knotted her dark hair at the crown of her head since the long tresses which had hung down her back after Brandish kissed her had since lost their curl. She was presentable, she thought, as she regarded her reflection, but hardly coiffed or dressed in as elegant a manner as no doubt the ladies of Broadhorn were.

The hall intersected with the entranceway, and in a few seconds she stood on the threshold regarding the man she had thought she would never see again. He was squatting in front of Vincent, rubbing the retriever's ears. Vincent leaned into Brandish's magical hands, a contented rumble issuing from his throat.

"Mr. Brandish," she said. "I must confess I did not expect to see you here at the manor."

He rose to his full height upon hearing her voice and turned to face her. He seemed to fill the small vestibule with his very presence, and her knees felt suddenly weak and fragile. He was dressed in fine evening clothes, sporting a black coat molded to his broad shoulders, an intricately tied neckcloth, a white waistcoat and black pantaloons. Against the night air, he had donned gleaming, tasseled Hessians and had slung a single-caped greatcoat over his shoulders.

His appearance was strictly in the Brummell mode lacking ostentation of any kind. Only a solitary seal hung from his waistcoat. Frederick had tended to dandify his clothes with wide lapels, the use of buckram wadding to pad his coats, and an assortment of fobs and seals. He had jingled when he walked. At the time, she had thought him all the crack. But looking now at Brandish, she realized, yet again, how mistaken she had been in her husband— how foolishly naive and romantic had been her convictions about love and life.

He held his hat and his gloves in hand and bowed to her as she approached him across the tiled floor.

"I realize the hour is undoubtedly inconvenient, but I wished to call upon Betsy since she asked me to. I shall be leaving Broadhorn tomorrow and would not have had the opportunity at that time of paying her a morning call. May I see her please? I shan't detain her long." His manner was stiff as he regarded her unwaveringly. In the candlelit entrance hall, his blue eyes appeared softer than she remembered.

"I'm not certain where she is of the moment," Henrietta responded politely, her heart beating unsteadily. She could not help but recall their turbulent encounter in the mossy ravine. Finding herself quite nervous in his presence, she excused herself to discover her sister's whereabouts. Just as she reached the hall leading to the kitchens, she turned about, and with a brief smile, said, "Betsy will be immensely pleased that you took her invitation seriously." But before he could respond, she whirled away, walking briskly down the hall.

From Cook, she learned that Betsy had taken a lantern to the barn since the stableboy had arrived earlier to inform her that a colt had been born to one of the mares.

When she brought this news to Brandish, she expected him to politely make his excuses and leave. Instead, his response surprised her.

"If you'll direct me to the stable, I should like to attend my young friend there. I have the tilbury with me, and I can just as easily bid her farewell in the barn as in the drawing room."

Henrietta tilted her head slightly, looking at him as if for the first time. "The barn is a drafty, dirty place. Are you sure you wish for it? I daresay your valet would object strenuously were he to comprehend your intentions!"

Slapping his hat against his muscular leg, he narrowed his eyes at her, his expression measuring. "I have not been acquainted with you for very long, but I have the strongest impression I have just been issued a challenge. I shall counter therefore with this. Will you not accompany me to the stables, or are you a missish, *hen*hearted female, my dear *Hen*rietta?"

She liked him. This afternoon in the dell, he had brought hurtful feelings surfacing to her heart, and he had angered her. But in this moment, heaven help her, she liked him very much. And if he weren't positively leaving Hampshire on the morrow, she would have simply pointed in the direction of the barn and left him to his own devices. Instead, she responded, "I have a burning desire to see the colt myself, suddenly. I should be happy to join you."

"What a lovely manner you have of expressing yourself. I wish you would join me."

Henrietta felt a blush creep up her cheeks. He was thoroughly a rogue, and the worst, most delicious weakening sensation assailed her stomach. *Join him*, indeed! Thank heaven he would be gone by tomorrow! She ignored the wastrel's smile on his face and quickly donned her pelisse.

Once outside, he helped her climb aboard the light, two-wheeled gig. A single brown horse pulled the carriage along, and she noticed with a slight grimace that he did nothing more than encourage the horse to walk—very slowly.

In an effort to keep the conversation from more dangerous turf, she said, "You became an instant favorite with Betsy, you know. She rarely warms to people so quickly. You should feel honored."

"I do," he said with a smile. "Your sister has great charm, almost as much as you."

Henrietta looked at him, surprised. "Oh, indeed!" she cried facetiously. "I am replete with charm. In fact, I must certainly be the most charming woman of your acquaintance, now that I think on it. What other female, I ask, who had scarcely exchanged a dozen words with you and who had no real knowledge of your attributes or your flaws, would condemn your character as roundly as I did?" When he chuckled, she continued, "I don't like to mention it, Brandish, but if that is your notion of charm, I begin to question your reasoning prowess."

He laughed outright this time, then gave the reins the gentlest of slaps, for the horse had almost drawn to a complete halt.

The rain had stopped momentarily, but a thick layer of clouds still hovered in the sky, chilling the air and silencing the land. A single carriage lamp lit the gravelled drive leading to the barn. Henrietta crossed her arms, hugging herself against a cold wind that occasionally gusted across the downs, her breath shaping into little puffs of mist each time she spoke.

The peaceful night held them both captive for a long moment. Henrietta glanced at Brandish's profile. His brow was furrowed slightly, his thoughts cloaked from her because she did not know him very well. She wondered if a small part of him was still angry with her for the cruelty of her accusation that he was just like

59

Frederick. She decided to beg forgiveness for her harsh, undeserved judgements.

"I'm sorry if I offended you this afternoon, Brandish. I was overcome by our unfortunate meeting, and if I said anything hateful, I do apologize. But I hope you will understand that I was very young when I knew and married Frederick. I had not been a bride longer than two months when he died. My life has been so completely altered by his death that I found myself entirely overset by your embraces. That was still no excuse for my unkindness toward you, and I do apologize."

Brandish did not answer her right away. When he did, his voice was low. "My conduct was so thoroughly unsatisfactory that I believe you have no need whatso-ever to extend an apology. It is I who ought to perform that office. I am sorry, Henrietta, for condemning your husband as I did. I don't know what possessed me to criticize him so brutally. My life is not an innocent one! Good God, in reflection I felt like the worst sort of hypocrite. When I considered my words later, I will confess I was horrified, because I realized I had begun to sound just like my aunt Margaret. And I detest her sanctimoniousness.

"I will admit also that when I set out for Fair Oaks this evening, I was hoping for a moment's conversation with you. I did not want to leave the district without making amends for my bitter words. When I returned to Broadhorn Hall earlier today, I had occasion to learn of how scurrilous my aunt's treatment of your mother has been. I may not have approved of Frederick entirely, nor appreciated being likened to him, but I certainly do not blame you for his death or for his excessive habits which were the true cause of all his misfortune. And I must say that it seems the greatest injustice in our society that a woman such as you, as well as your family, must forever bear his guilt. I am here, therefore, as much to apologize for my aunt's conduct as for my own."

Henrietta listened to him, her eyes fixed carefully on

the tips of her half-boots. She had not expected so much understanding from a man she believed wholly consumed with his pursuit of pleasure. She found herself astonished and not a little pleased.

She directed Brandish to follow the drive to west of the manor. The barn and home farm were situated a considerable distance from the main house, but a light from the stable could be seen some two hundred yards away.

Henrietta appreciated Brandish's apology very much and told him so. As they neared the stables, he pressed her arm with his hand. "There is only one thing," he said, smiling faintly, "for which I have no regrets whatsoever with regard to this afternoon's adventure and subsequent quarrel." The carriage lamp cast a dull glow on his face, and though his features were dimly illuminated, she could see that his expression was warm and teasing.

Henrietta felt a familiar tug of longing as she looked up at him. The wind pulled at the ends of his unruly black hair, whipping them against his cheeks and the edge of his neckcloth.

"I command you not to give voice to the words readied on your tongue," she cried. "The dell must be forgotten."

"Never," he responded quickly. "And don't you remember, you promised me that the kiss we shared would haunt my dreams?"

"I was speaking foolishly."

"No, I don't think so. I believe you spoke prophetically."

"Brandish," Henrietta cried out of a mounting sense of frustration. "You are the most hopeless, incorrigible rascal I've ever encountered. You are leaving on the morrow. Why not let us part friends."

He drew the gig to a halt several yards away from the barn and slipped an arm about her waist. "Friendship is not at all what I desire of you."

He leaned close to her, and she could smell the sweet redolence of sherry on his breath. His mouth was inviting, she thought, as her gaze drifted to his parted lips. To her horror, she realized she wanted nothing more than to enjoy his kisses again. She should not have come with him to the stable; she should have simply instructed him as to the route to the barn, then let him find his own way. Instead, she was seated beside him, her heart beating a sudden and furious cadence in her breast, her breathing light and uneven. She felt dizzy as his lips touched her cheek.

"Mr. Brandish!" Betsy cried, the tone of her voice indignant as she called out to him. "Whatever are you doing with my sister? Stop, I say! And Henrietta, I don't like to mention it, but he was about to kiss you!"

Henrietta was grateful for the dark cover of night, since her face felt warm with acute embarrassment. Brandish, however, seemed oblivious at having been discovered in a shocking embrace, for though he immediately released her, he called out a friendly greeting to Betsy and then jumped easily down from the gig as though nothing untoward had happened.

He then moved behind the tilbury to help Henrietta alight, holding his hand outstretched to her.

"You ought not to be quite so observant, Miss Betsy," he cried, smiling at her over his shoulder. Betsy stood near the stable doors shaking her head in disapproval.

As Henrietta placed her hand somewhat reluctantly in his, he clasped her hand firmly and with a quick jerk succeeded in setting her entirely off balance so that she landed squarely in his arms.

"Oh!" she cried, startled. Realizing he had orchestrated this little piece of tomfoolery, she rebuked him. "How could you! And would you please set me down. You are scandalizing my young sister!"

"But you would have fallen had I not caught you as I did," he exclaimed, feigning great innocence as he relaxed his hold on her. She pushed away from him and

62

began shaking out the skirt of her pelisse as he turned toward Betsy.

"You pulled her down," Betsy cried, astonished. "I saw you do it! You forced her to tumble into your arms. But why?"

"I know it was wrong of me to have done so," he answered with a wink. "But Henry blushes so prettily when I tease her in this manner that there is no help for it. I felt compelled to torment her."

"Oh, I see. You are *flirting* with her. Well, if that is all it is, then I don't give a fig for it, though I suggest you avoid letting Mama see you hugging her. But do come into the barn. That is why you've come, isn't it? But however did you learn a colt had been born?"

"I didn't know a thing about it until I arrived at the manor just a few minutes ago. I came here, you see, at your invitation, but only to say good-bye. I shall be leaving on the morrow for London, and I knew I wouldn't be able to pay you a morning call; so I came this evening, without warning. I hope you don't mind this rather informal visit of mine."

"Of course not," Betsy responded magnanimously. "Besides, now you will get to see the colt which I think you will find a great deal more amusing than doing the pretty with me and my sisters." He agreed readily. "And only think, Mr. Brandish, the colt was born today. Isn't that famous! And you will be but the second person of consequence to see him."

"Who was the first?" Brandish asked, like a lamb to the slaughter.

"Why, the stableboy of course!"

To this, Brandish laughed heartily, refusing to answer Betsy's query as to what he found so amusing.

Henrietta heard Betsy's last remark and could not help but smile at her sister's youthful disregard for Brandish's elevated station in life. She wondered if he was the least bit offended that Betsy had spoken of him with the same regard she held for the man who mucked their stables.

She was struck with the knowledge that though Brandish might be many things, he was not so vain that he could lose the meaning of Betsy's innocent compliment. Another man, considerably higher in the instep than King, would undoubtedly have been indignant. But not Brandish. Not when he had laughed with such enjoyment.

Henrietta stood by the gig for a full minute, collecting her thoughts. She could admire Brandish for his lack of pretension, but in all other respects she found herself greatly disturbed. For one thing, he had not shown the least amount of confusion when he had been caught embracing her, and this seemed very odd. She realized that though she had been married—and to all intents and purposes must be considered a woman with some experience of life—she felt but a babe when it came to King Brandish. He seemed to have little conscience where matters of the heart were concerned. He could kiss her one moment, then unabashedly proclaim he only meant to tease her. An unwelcome thought intruded: What precisely did she expect him to think or feel? She knew what he was, and he had made no false profession of love for her, as well as having admitted freely that he was a man who simply enjoyed kissing.

With no small degree of irritation, she moved toward the stable realizing that she could not fault him. If she must blame someone, then she had to blame herself. Refusing to give the matter one more thought, she picked up her skirts to enter the stable. Just as she did, however, Vincent came running up behind her, knocking her in the back of the legs and barking. The horses in the stable immediately grew restive, snorting and stamping their hooves.

"It be that curst mongrel again!" the stableboy cried. "Out with you now, Vincent. You'll do more harm than good in here."

Henrietta called sharply to the retriever and brought him to heel. She bade him wait at the entrance of the stable as she crossed the hay-strewn floor to where Betsy leaned on the wood gate of the mare's stall, peering through the slats.

"Do but look, Henry," she cried. "Isn't he beautiful?" She glanced up at her sister, her eyes shining with wonderment. "I think I'll call him Thunder because he was born during a storm. I shall train him, too, and I shall be the first to ride—him—" she broke off suddenly, backing slowly away from the gate. Henrietta was instantly alerted that something serious had gone awry.

Betsy's face had grown pale, her brow wrinkled, as though a thought, never before having intruded into her little girl's mind, had burst over her in a wave of grievous disappointment. She looked up at Henrietta, tears brimming in her eyes. "I just remembered," she said quietly, the tears spilling down her cheeks. "Thunder doesn't even belong to me, nor his mother. He doesn't belong to any of us. He is Huntspill's property now. Oh, Henry, I don't want to leave Fair Oaks. This is my home!" She ran to Henrietta, threw her arms about her waist, and held her tightly. She drew in several deep breaths to keep from sobbing but with little success.

Henrietta enfolded her in her arms and returned her unhappy embrace. "My dear Betsy, I'm so sorry. But we'll find a good home very soon, and then maybe we can persuade Mr. Huntspill to give us Thunder, if you still wish for him by then." She petted Betsy's head and kissed her gently on her forehead.

When Betsy had grown calm, Henrietta instructed her quietly, "But now, my dear, you must remember that you have a guest who has come to bid you farewell." She glanced up at Brandish, hoping he would understand what had happened. But the expression on his face stunned her, for he was looking at her fiercely, his eyes penetrating and bold. She did not know what to make of it.

Betsy swallowed hard and drew herself up straight as she pulled herself away from Henrietta. She then addressed Brandish politely, explaining that they were to quit Fair Oaks by mid-summer and that none of them were certain where they were next to go. She then shook hands with him, thanking him for coming to see her, and as though unable to bear more, she curtsied and said good-bye. She walked over to where Vincent waited, fidgeting on all fours at Betsy's approach. "Oh, Vincent," she wailed. "At least you are mine!" She then threw her arms about the dog's neck and, after giving him a quick hug, ran back to the manor.

Henrietta could not prevent tears from rushing to her eyes as she watched Betsy leave the stables. She turned back to gaze at the beautiful black colt which had so quickly stolen her sister's heart, then broken it in the same moment. The colt was fast asleep on a bed of hay, and Henrietta, too, felt a sudden sense of painful separation from so many precious objects and memories that she had known and loved since she was a child. All of Mrs. Leighton's daughters had been born at Fair Oaks, and summer suddenly seemed a mere breath away.

Henrietta walked with Brandish back to the gig. She realized he had fallen silent, and she thought perhaps he was feeling uncomfortable. "Please forgive us, King," she began. "This is a most difficult time for my family."

He took her hand in his and kneaded it gently. She was standing by the tilbury and felt suddenly weary. King did not try to engage her in conversation, but merely looked kindly at her. She felt full of pain all over again and did not want to be feeling so much, particularly when Brandish was waiting to leave. She didn't want him to go, however. She felt somehow that he understood her unhappiness.

After a few minutes, she felt a little better. Returning the pressure of his hand, she said, "I must go."

"Not yet," he whispered. "Will you be all right?"

She nodded. "Of course."

He took her chin in his hand and lifted it to better see her eyes. He wore the same expression she had seen earlier, and she asked, "What is it? What's wrong?"

"You have a generous heart, Henry," he said. And without waiting for her to protest, he placed a full kiss upon her lips.

Henrietta felt again the sweet pressure of his mouth as his lips brushed hers tenderly. His lips were parted and warm, and as before, were a comfort to her. She responded by kissing him in return, leaning into him slightly.

He withdrew from her, though remaining very close, his breath on her cheek. "I meant only to express my admiration for you," he said, "and to offer what little succor I could in your misfortune. I promise you, I have not kissed you out of sole self-gratification."

He still held her hand and was gripping it tightly. He continued, "But it very likely will become a great deal more if you do not walk away from me now. For a reason I cannot fully comprehend, I am fraught with desire for you."

Henrietta heard his words and felt his lips on her cheek. She knew she should part from him, just as he said, but she could not. She felt bound to him in this moment, her soul clinging to him. Instead of leaving him, she turned her head slowly, seeking his mouth with her own, until she felt the sweetness of his lips upon hers. "King—" she breathed.

She got no farther, for he suddenly drew her to him in a crushing embrace, releasing her hand to enfold her in his arms. He kissed her hard upon the mouth, bruising her lips again as he had done in the ravine, holding her fiercely, until she could scarcely breathe. The damp, night air cooled her burning cheeks and forehead as King ravished her mouth, kissing her again and again. She wanted to beg him to stay with her, to take her to bed, then chided herself for such an unchaste thought. His mouth was unearthly sweet as his tongue touched her lips. She had never known such desire as this, a yearning to belong to this man, to be possessed by him.

After a long moment, when she had grown breathless, King drew back from her, pressing his forehead against her own. He took her hands and clasped them tightly, holding them against her bosom. In a low voice, he spoke intensely. "It is a good thing that I leave tomorrow, Henry. I do not desire to marry anyone at this time, and if I stayed, I swear I would make you my mistress. Do you understand?"

Henry nodded, tears burning her eyes. "I want you to go as well, King," she replied. "Even if you were to ask me to be your wife, I don't know that I could accept you."

He looked at her, stunned beyond belief. "Do you deem me unworthy?" he cried, disbelieving.

"No," she said, shaking her head. "No, do not misunderstand me. But what is this mystery that exists between us? I have never before permitted any man to kiss me in this manner. Why do I allow you such liberties? And yet I am unwilling to call this sensation, *love*. I am not certain I even know what love is. Do you? And should I ever marry again, it will be for no other reason than for a love I am certain will be strong enough to bear all the trials and adversities of life. I have suffered too much to make a second disastrous mistake."

He looked at her very hard. "Why do you do this, Henry? Why do you constrain me by your forthrightness to examine my motives and the paths I choose for my day-to-day existence?"

He tried to disengage her hands, but she held his fast, forcing him to look at her. "You are right in one thing, King, this I want you to know: If you remained, I should become your mistress." She kissed him once again upon his lips, then released him entirely.

He did not look at her further, but climbed immediately into the tilbury and within seconds was gone.

Betsy watched Brandish give the reins a sharp jolt, the

horse moving quickly into a trot as the entire equipage began bowling back up the drive. She then turned to look at her sister, wondering what she was thinking at this moment. She knew Henrietta could not see her, for she had remained hidden in the shadows of the hedge near the back entrance to the manor's formal gardens, but still she feared discovery. She did not want Henry to know that she had been witness to her quite improper tryst with Mr. Brandish.

She had at first been greatly shocked by the sight of Henrietta engulfed in Brandish's arms. But very soon she realized, even with her child's view of the world, that something quite powerful and rare was happening. That they spoke to each other so intently for a long moment after he had stopped kissing her, struck Betsy as significant. She wondered if they had tumbled in love with one another, though she found it hard to believe it only took a day. She had observed that with Angel, for instance, the business of love usually took a full month or more! Angel was unaccountably fussy where her heart was concerned.

When Henrietta wiped a tear from her cheek and made as if to head up the path toward her, Betsy stole quickly through the stone-arched opening in the garden and ran the rest of the distance to the house.

Her mother and her sisters might speak of Huntspill or journeying to Bath for the summer as the answer to their family's wretched dilemma, but Betsy knew of a better one—King Brandish. Once inside the house, she went immediately to the hallway outside the kitchen where she spied on Cook. When she could see her disappear into the buttery, she stole into the kitchen and retrieved her sling from the salt box.

She then hastened to her bedchamber to change her gown for dinner. When she was fully dressed, she picked up the sling, made up of a short strap with strings fastened to its ends, and began whirling it about in a practiced movement. The stableboy had taught her two years ago how to use a catapult and had even made one for her. No one supposed when she developed a fascination for the toy that her proficiency would improve to such an extent that she could actually hunt small game with it if she wished to. Of course, she had not meant to kill the chicken. That was a most unfortunate accident. She had intended merely to whip off a few of its tail feathers, but had not counted on the bird moving as it had.

The sling made a whirring noise as it cut through the air, and Betsy hoped her aim would be true enough tomorrow to prevent Brandish from leaving Hampshire. She also knew a fleeting concern that if something untoward happened she could possibly do him an injury. This she dismissed as negligible. The stableboy had taught her well, and she was confident of her ability.

Chapter Eight

Henrietta stood upon the threshold of the entrance-way, faintly aware of the bustling of her mother amidst a dozen or more packages and bandboxes. She remained fixed in one spot, a hand pressed to her cheek as she remembered her parting words to Brandish, that if he remained in Hampshire, she would indeed become his mistress. Even now, her heart fluttered at the thought, yearning for what she knew must never be.

As through a tunnel of time, she heard her mother's voice: "Henry! Whatever is the matter with you?" she cried. "Your cheeks are flushed and your eyes wild-looking. Are you well or are you suffering from the ague?"

Henrietta glanced toward her mother, her vision clouded slightly. In slow stages she released the memories that dogged her heels, preventing her from embracing the present. When her mother came fully into focus, she looked her up and down and drew in a horrified breath. "Mama," she cried. "What have you done?"

Mrs. Leighton swelled her bosom with great indignation. "I can't imagine what you mean, Henrietta," she cried, her creamy cheeks turning a rosy hue with embarrassment. "And why do you speak to me in that disrespectful tone of voice?" She wore a new bonnet trimmed with a pink ostrich feather, bright yellow gloves adorned her fingers and on her feet gleamed a smart pair of half-boots.

She began stripping off her gloves in a quick succession of jerks, as she continued, "I cannot possibly have my child, my own daughter, speaking to me as though I were a miscreant! Besides, I have done nothing wrong. I have only purchased a few necessary accoutrements to enhance the quite dilapidated collection of gowns now stuffed into my wardrobe."

When she had removed her gloves, she set them on a cherrywood table by the stairway and called loudly for one of the maids to assist her in carting her purchases up to her bedchamber.

Henrietta moved forward toward the mound of booty her mother had scattered haphazardly upon the black and white tiled floor and picked up two of the bandboxes. "Mama," she said, her expression concerned. "You cannot be unaware that we totter on the precipice of disaster. In less than three months we shall be turned out of Fair Oaks with scarcely a guinea to spare."

"Oh, pooh!" Mrs. Leighton cried. "For all your intelligence, Henry, you can be the most annoying creature. Have you forgotten that when Mr. Huntspill arrives in July, he will settle a handsome annuity upon me? I am certain of it! I have little doubt he means to provide me with no less than ten thousand pounds since he is a man of comfortable fortune. He knows I will have the support of my five daughters and has given every indication he means to be generous beyond even my expectations. And I have no cause to doubt his good intentions."

"But, Mama, has it not occurred to you that Mr. Huntspill may have a very different notion of generosity than you do?"

"Nonsense. I am certain I am being quite conservative in my estimation, but it is not a matter over which you are to fret, Henry. The future of this family is my concern, not yours. Oh, there you are, Susan. Be so good

72

as to take these trifles to my chamber."

The stocky maid glanced at the largess strewn about the vestibule and opened her eyes wide with amazement. Blinking several times, she cried, "*Trifles!* More like plunder. La, Mrs. Leighton, but I'll wager ye've made one or two shopkeeper's wives happy today!"

When Mrs. Leighton glared at her, the maid begged pardon for having spoken so boldly and set about burdening her person with as many of the packages as she could manage on her first trip to her mistress's bedchamber.

Mrs. Leighton began mounting the stairs after the maid, bidding Henrietta to follow behind her. She noticed that her eldest daughter was wearing a pelisse. "Where have you been, my dear?" she asked. "Have you been out for a stroll in the gardens? Well, then it is no wonder you are as cross as crabs, for it is far too cold and windy to be marching about in the damp air. Oh, and that puts me in mind of something! Who was the man in the gig who drove past my coach as though the devil was on his coattails. Why, it nearly scared poor Timothy coachman to death, I can tell you!"

"You refer to Mr. Brandish."

They were halfway up the stairs when Mrs. Leighton, upon this pronouncement, turned sharply around to stare at Henrietta. She did not speak for a long moment as her mouth fell agape, and her large blue eyes took on the startled appearance of a hare caught in the vegetable plot. "Brandish, you say? Not *King* Brandish, surely? But what am I saying, of course it must be King Brandish, for he is *that woman's* nephew. What on earth was he doing here, at Fair Oaks?" She pressed a hand to her bosom, and then her other hand to Henrietta's shoulder. Gasping loudly, she exclaimed, "He saw Angel! He saw my beautiful daughter, then he insisted upon learning her name. And when he discovered she resided here—he came as swiftly as he could! Oh, my dear Henry, we are made! We are made! He will fall in love with Angel and

73

marry her! But what wondrous good fortune!"

Henrietta remained stunned by her mother's sudden exuberance and by how swiftly her mind leaped ahead in the fabrication of an entire story to explain Brandish's inexplicable appearance.

Henrietta smiled faintly and shook her head. "You are sadly mistaken, I fear. The truth is, he came to see Betsy. You see, we met him in the lane earlier this afternoon— Charlotte, Betsy and myself—and he was so taken with your *youngest* daughter, who is most unfortunately *not* of marriageable age, that he decided to call upon her."

"But this is excellent!" she cried, not in the least disappointed that her original suppositions had proved false. "We shall have Betsy send him an invitation to dine with us; then he can meet Angel, and the rest shall follow!"

"I don't like to blast your happy schemes, Mama, but Mr. Brandish came to say good-bye. He is returning to London on the morrow, and we shan't see him again."

Mrs. Leighton exhaled all of her disappointment in one great breath and leaned dejectedly toward Henrietta. "How is it," she cried, "that with so much beauty and wit spread out amongst my daughters, none of you can find a husband." She turned to begin trudging up the stairs, all her momentary excitement completely gone.

Henrietta could not force her feet to move as she watched her mother ascend the stairs. She gripped her hands tightly together in front of her in an effort to restrain an enormous sensation of guilt that threatened to flood her soul. Her mother had not meant to be cruel, but there was a hidden truth to her words that laid open a wound in Henrietta's heart. *I should be married,* she thought bitterly. *Then I could share some of this burden that my mother, however ineptly, shoulders day and night.*

Remembering her own scheme to recoup the family's losses, she cried, "Mama, wait. There is something I wish to tell you."

Once in Mrs. Leighton's bedchamber, Henrietta

74

briefly presented her plan, accentuating the fact that Angel had already agreed to it.

Mrs. Leighton was frowning by the end of the recital and said, finally, "I approve of your scheme entirely, Henry. I had a similar notion in mind. But why do you think we must sell our jewels and live in relative poverty? When Huntspill arrives—"

"Never mind that," Henrietta said quickly. "I was only suggesting so desperate a course should Mr. Huntspill prove ungenerous."

When Mrs. Leighton appeared ready to defend him again, Henrietta lifted a hand, laughing. "I should never have spoken so ill of the man!" she cried. "From this moment on, he is all that is openhanded and noble."

"That is much better, my dear. You must not lose faith in the goodness of mankind."

After dinner, when the ladies were again clustered within the cosy parlor and a fire blazed upon the hearth, Henrietta watched a solemn-eyed Arabella approach her mother. Mrs. Leighton was struggling to shape yet another ball of amber yarn from the loop held upon Charlotte's arms, just as she had done only this morning. Betsy sat next to Henrietta, leaning upon her shoulder. They had been reading Milton's *L'Allegro,* when Arabella's procession made her pause.

"Why did you stop?" Betsy cried.

Henrietta told her to hush, for she could see that Arabella was uncommonly upset, almost to the point of tears.

"Mama," Arabella began, the strain in her voice causing even Angel to cease her music. "This letter arrived today for you. I fear it does not bear good tidings. It is from Mr. Huntspill, who had sent me a letter as well, explaining his decision in detail."

Mrs. Leighton appeared astonished, as did all the ladies. Betsy sat up straight, Charlotte pushed her spectacles back up to the bridge of her nose and Angel set her harp back on its supports. Henrietta felt a chill surround her heart.

Mrs. Leighton took the letter and quickly broke the seal. Her frown deepened between her brows as she read the missive. "It can't be!" she cried. "He—he wishes us to quit Fair Oaks by the end of the month! That is only three weeks away!"

Chapter Nine

Later that evening, at Broadhorn Hall, Brandish sat in an elegant, gold silk chair, one knee crossed negligently over the other as he watched Fanny Marshfield sing a delightful air. She stood poised and stately before his aunt's pianoforte of rosewood, gesturing delicately with each flowery climb of the song and in a gracious manner directed portions of the melody to her various listeners. She was charming, dressed in the height of fashion, wearing a soft, white muslin gown gathered at the high waist and flowing to the floor in a demi-train. She wore long white gloves that nearly touched the puffed sleeves of the bodice, and pearls graced her elegantly sloping neck. She looked to be of an age with Henrietta and shared one thing in common with her: Fanny Marshfield, too, was a widow.

Brandish watched her intently, trying to determine why it was he found himself so utterly bored with her. She was an acknowledged beauty, with shimmering auburn hair and large doe eyes. Her manners were polished, and her general air of good breeding had brought her a fine reputation as an altogether unexceptionable young lady. Her widowhood rested lightly upon her. Perhaps that was the rub, Brandish thought as he shifted lower into his chair. Her husband had been dead for a mere eighteen months, and she seemed to have been left untouched, unlike another female of his acquaintance. He chided himself for being so critical, and for comparing her to Henrietta.

The mildest thought of the latter brought a mingled sensation of pleasure and regret surging over his heart. It had taken every ounce of his strength to take his leave of her, for his desire to possess her had grown acute. There was a mystery between them, just as she had said. He, too, was unwilling to call it *love*. But if not love, then what? His experience in pursuing her and violating her lips had been like none other. He grew irritable trying to comprehend all that had transpired between them and reverted his attention to Fanny's song.

She was smiling at him now as she sang the next few lines of the verse. He nodded politely in response but found himself grateful when she moved on to direct the next stanza to his father, who was standing beside his own chair.

"Fine girl!" he heard his father murmur as he pressed a hand upon King's shoulder.

"Yes," Brandish responded perfunctorily, if for no other reason than to keep his parent in a contented state until he had an opportunity of informing him he was leaving Broadhorn in the morning. His father clearly wanted him to offer for Mrs. Marshfield, and he would be furious with his son for leaving the cosy country party.

The song drew to a close, Fanny curtsied elegantly and his aunt immediately rose from her seat and approached her protege with a delicate spatter of applause. "My dear, your execution of the trills throughout the piece set my heart to dancing."

"Thank you, ma'am," Fanny responded with a meek lowering of her gaze to this compliment. "But I could not sing half so well without Mama to accompany me." She stepped aside with practiced grace and gestured to her mother.

Mrs. Kempshott fluttered from her seat, disclaiming any such effect upon her dear Fanny's performance. She

78

was an obsequious creature who had long since won Lady Ramsdean's affections by approving all of her ladyship's opinions and strictures. She wore a fine, cashmere shawl over a gown of amber silk and a matching turban sporting three pheasant feathers.

King Brandish watched the feathers droop and bounce as Mrs. Kempshott nodded her agreement to something his aunt was saying. She was smiling, Fanny was listening politely and his dear aunt Margaret was again pontificating. Stifling a yawn, he turned toward his father and said in a low voice, "I had not wanted to mention it earlier, sir, but I have pressing business in London and must return on the morrow. Quite early, in fact."

He expected a strong resistance to his intention of leaving Broadhorn, but he was not prepared for the awful silence that befell the entire drawing room upon his announcement. His aunt, whom he had believed to be deep in conversation with her female guests, turned instantly upon his words and glared at him with a horrific scowl pinching her face. Mrs. Kempshott looked worried, and Fanny's cheeks were covered in a dull blush as she began inspecting the tips of her gloves. Even his uncle, who had been snoring gently throughout Fanny's song, seemed to awaken suddenly. "Eh, what's that?" he cried. "Leaving tomorrow? Can't say as I blame you. This party's been a curst flat affair from the beginning."

Brandish, who saw the blush deepen on Fanny's cheeks, rose suddenly and exclaimed, "I have been quite happily entertained by my aunt, sir! I merely recalled having left several urgent matters unattended to. My memory has been at fault, not the present company." He felt his father's censure as Lord Ennersley held his hands clasped behind his back, rocked on his heels and glowered at him. He knew a severe dressing down would follow the very instant they were alone.

Lord Ramsdean, who sat in a large, blue-striped chair, chuckled softly as he rose to his feet. "You have a *convenient* memory, King. I used to have one myself before I married your aunt. Now, I find it dreadfully *inconvenient* most of the time." He laughed at his joke and smoothed down his white hair which had become disarranged from leaning against the back of the chair. He was a large man, easing into the mellow years of his life with bluffness, good humor, and the single-minded objective of setting up his wife's back as frequently as he was able.

By the appearance of Lady Ramsdean's wooden countenance, he had succeeded in this instance, mightily.

"I will have words with you later, King," Lord Ennersley breathed harshly, his voice a whisper.

King nodded, quite used to his father's diatribes. He watched his aunt speaking in a low voice to Mrs. Kempshott and could not help but notice that Fanny, who heard their discussion, whispered, "No, I beg you will not—"

He wasn't certain why she was momentarily distressed until Mrs. Kempshott, her eyes wide and theatrical in appearance, placed a hand to her brow and spoke in a manner worthy of the great actress, Sarah Siddons. "My dear Lady Ramsdean, I feel quite faint, of a sudden. I must lie down at once. Would you be ever so kind as to escort me to my bedchamber."

"Good heavens," Lady Ramsdean cried, the tone to her voice false and equally as dramatic as her friend's. "Whatever is the matter? Are you suffering a spasm? Horace, do come help me with Georgianna. She is become quite ill. Do look how pale her complexion is!" To Mrs. Kempshott, she said, "I daresay it was the lobster patties. I always suffer from the vapors when Cook serves the lobster. I should have warned you!"

Fanny, to her credit, did not even try to interfere with this piece of histrionic fiddle-faddle. She glanced at Brandish and shrugged, afterward turning back to the pianoforte, where she seated herself in a composed manner and began glancing through the several sheets of music collected there.

Lord Ramsdean cried, "Why do you not simply suggest the young people have a moment alone together and be done with it, rather than affect all this nonsense?"

His wife regarded him with a choleric eye. "You are the only one here who is being nonsensical. Now, do aid me in helping Georgianna to her chamber. Charles!" she added, addressing Lord Ennersley. "I rely upon you to go at once to the kitchens and beg Cook to prepare a posset!"

Lord Ramsdean sighed heavily, holding his hands out in a helpless gesture toward Brandish. "I am sorry, King, but at times it is simply best to give them their heads!"

Lord Ennersley permitted the party to precede him from the chamber. He remained for a moment beside his son, his expression still severe. He seemed to deliberate within himself for a few seconds before grasping King's arm hard and saying, "Just this once, I wish you wouldn't disappoint me!" He then released his son, his nostrils flared as he followed in Ramsdean's wake.

Until this moment, King had borne his father's autocratic insistence upon his attendance at the country party with equanimity. Initially, it had seemed a small thing to oblige him by spending a sennight with his relations whom he rarely saw. But when, a day later, Fanny arrived, he realized at once that he had been drawn to Broadhorn under false colors, and his ire had been steadily rising since. It blossomed now as the full import of his father's words struck him brutally like a flush hit from Jackson at his boxing saloon. Only now did he comprehend he was actually expected to offer for Fanny!

He was beyond reason angry and could not look at the widow for fear the fury in his eyes would turn her to stone. He clenched his fists, pivoted sharply on his heel, and walked away from her, heading toward the long windows of the Elizabethan mansion. There he stood for several minutes, watching the wind twist and whip the tall lime trees in the avenue. It would rain again soon. And he would be leaving in the morning, regardless of either the weather or his father's threats.

He heard Fanny's voice a few feet behind him. "I like the sound of the wind as it buffets the windows," she said, her voice composed.

She did not seem overly disturbed by the actions of her elders, and this irritated him. He began to think she was equally blameworthy. Turning toward her, he cried, "I hope you do not think I shall drop to one knee and espouse my love for you? Surely you are not as blind to my sentiments as my family seems to be!" His anger spilled over, burning her as a wash of color stained her cheeks. The moment the words were spoken, he regretted them.

He started to apologize, but she lifted a gloved hand and responded with cool dignity. "Mr. Brandish, I am neither blind to your sentiments nor would I expect you to offer for me when you are obviously quite indifferent to my charms." She smiled faintly. "Though I confess I find it vastly amusing to think your father and your aunt would expect you to do so even though you fairly yawn in my presence."

"I do nothing of the sort," he responded instantly, disliking her accurate perception of his feelings. When she lifted a reproachful brow indicating she knew he was talking fustian, he smiled ruefully. "I have not meant to be uncivil, and I apologize if I have offended you."

"You have not been discourteous in the least," she responded affably. "You merely presumed I was insensitive. I had hoped when we first arrived you would have understood that only your aunt's—and to some degree my mother's—insistence could possibly have persuaded me to come." She laughed suddenly, then continued, "If only you had had occasion to see the horrified expression on your face when I emerged from your uncle's coach! Mr. Brandish, you were quite thunderstruck. I do not blame you at all for being angry, and truly I hoped we would have a chance to speak that I might make my own opinions known to you. As it happens, I have no desire to

82

wed any gentleman of the moment. Not even *King Brandish*."

"Indeed," he responded, greatly surprised and considerably pleased by her speech. He realized this was the second lady in one day who indicated she would have refused him had he asked for her hand in marriage. He wondered what the odds were on such a phenomenon occurring.

"Yes, indeed," she responded with a coquettish twinkle in her large brown eyes. "There is only one thing, however, I wish to beg of you. A favor as it happens, though not an unhappy one to perform, I hope."

He bowed slightly and responded, "It would seem I am deeply in your debt, for I don't think that I could have borne a fit of hysterics at this moment, a display in which any lesser female would undoubtedly have engaged. You have saved me from infinite discomfort and made my impending quarrel with my father a thing no longer to be feared. Whatever you ask, therefore, I shall do for you if it is within my power."

"Oh, it most certainly is. You see, I made a horridly reckless wager with a friend of mine, Miss Taverner, if you recall her?"

"She is a delightful person with a round face, freckles and a cheerful disposition."

"Too cheerful at times," Fanny cried. "At any rate, I bet her—and I blush to say so—that though I knew you had no interest in courting me, I could steal a kiss from you. She wagered her new pearl-studded fan, and I—it is wretched of me I know—but I set as my stake next quarter's allowance." She held her hands out in a pleading manner. "So you see, I am quite desperate!"

He was stunned, both by the extent to the stakes she had set as well as by the decidedly flirtatious aspect to her temperament. "This, from the lips of demure Mrs. Marshfield?" he cried. "I don't believe it. Have I not known you, Fanny?"

"No, Brandish, you have not! I am a woman, you

83

know, though I daresay you have hardly had the opportunity of discovering this irrefutable fact because I have been literally shoved in your face for the past month. Now, what do you say? Shall I win my wager, or not?"

"Never let it be said," King cried, approaching her with great enthusiasm, "that I should not help a lady when she is in such obvious distress."

She stood before him calmly, her hands resting easily at her sides, her expression open and welcoming. He took her quickly in his arms, placing a full kiss upon her lips. Her mouth was pleasing as she returned his kisses readily, her figure soft and appealing. He felt desire stir within him and held her more closely still, but she gently pushed him away. When he tried to take her back in his arms, she admonished him with a shake of her auburn curls, saying that her wager most unfortunately had included but one kiss.

"You are flirting with me," he cried, astonished, as she moved away from him and began crossing the room toward the doors leading into the hall.

She turned back to him and, with a slight curtsy, said, "Perhaps." Then she closed the doors firmly behind her as she quit the drawing room.

He smiled, realizing that though she had failed to accomplish the task their respective relatives had set her to, she had surprisingly achieved something more—she had intrigued him.

King stared at the doors for a moment, thinking with satisfaction that this was precisely how he preferred to conduct his trysts. He wondered how long it would take to make her his mistress or even whether he could. She may have kissed him, but something in her cool demeanor bespoke a female of considerable resolution.

His thoughts took an abrupt turn as he remembered his final parting with Henrietta, and he felt bowled over suddenly with the memory. She was his for the plucking, and that awareness should have bored him. Instead, a powerful feeling arose in his breast, of longing, of passion, and for the first time in his existence, he was utterly confused.

Perhaps it was just as well that he had decided to leave Broadhorn on the morrow, because he had an uneasy premonition that were he to stay, his life would be thrown into chaos. He knew a profound need to place distance between himself and Mrs. Henrietta Harte.

Once in London, however, he meant to pursue Fanny and to discover whether or not he could seduce her.

Chapter Ten

On the following morning, Henrietta made her way slowly down the stairs, her gaze fixed on nothing in particular, but her mind absorbed completely with a plaguing thought: Of what use would it be for them to journey to Bath in April, when the *beau monde* would still be in London? And yet how could they possibly afford to remove to the Metropolis, where lodgings in Mayfair were dear beyond belief. The difficulty was, they could lease an affordable town house in Hans Town, but they would never be able to establish themselves in *tonnish* circles!

She reached the bottom of the stairs with a sense of despair encroaching upon her heart. All the Leighton ladies, including Betsy, had remained in the parlor long past midnight on the evening before, discussing their dilemma. To the end, Mrs. Leighton had maintained that good Mr. Huntspill had not meant by his letter that they must leave Fair Oaks within three weeks.

Even when Charlotte pointed out that his letter seemed precise on this very point, Mrs. Leighton still refused to doubt his essential goodness.

"But, Mama," Henrietta cried. "Do but listen again to how he phrases his letter: 'I'm certain three weeks' time will be adequate to situate you in new lodgings; a small cottage perhaps near the High Street where the rent is reasonable would suit your family exceedingly well.'"

Henrietta had read the letter aloud several times, and each reading brought another of the sisters to a sharp awareness that Mr. Huntspill—far from being the openhanded, obliging creature Mrs. Leighton insisted he was—gave all the appearance of being a nip-farthing who grudged every groat.

Even Angel at one point had exclaimed, "But however does he suppose all six of us can share two bedchambers, for I know that's the very cottage to which he refers! Perhaps you are right, Henry! Perhaps he means to do nothing for us!"

"Nonsense," Mrs. Leighton cried. "You are all mistaken, and as soon as Huntspill arrives on Wednesday, he will set everything to rights."

Henrietta wished more than anything that her mother's optimism was well founded, but in the bright reckoning of daylight, as she reached the bottom of the stairs, she knew Mr. Huntspill was a false hope to the solution of their hardships. She wished she could keep so many distressing thoughts from rattling about in her brain, but she could not. They were on the brink of poverty, an existence from which, once the world had placed them thus, they would have enormous difficulty extricating themselves. A gentlewoman without a dowry had a future as hopeful as a butterfly without wings.

Another aspect of the business bothered her. How was it Arabella seemed to know the contents of the letter before her mother even opened it. In the dismayed aftermath of reading Huntspill's missive, Henrietta had forgotten all about Arabella's odd role in the matter. Now she intended to discover the source of her prior knowledge of his decision.

She stood on the threshold of the parlor, watching Angel and Charlotte with their heads bent over the writing desk, where they seemed to be compiling an important list. Neither Betsy nor her mother were present, but Arabella sat near the mullioned window,

87

busily employed mending a tear in one of the linens.

Moving to stand near her sister, she gazed out the window which overlooked the front approach to the manor. A hedge lined the western side of the avenue, and in the center of the gravelled drive, an ancient oak curved and knotted its way toward the sky. A well-scythed lawn rested below the tree clinging to thick roots that sprawled along the grass for a time, then dove into the nurturing earth. Henrietta had climbed that oak at least a hundred times throughout her childhood.

After greeting her sister, she made her inquiry, her voice low, her gaze still fixed upon the gnarled oak.

Arabella did not glance up from her needlework as she replied, "I had exchanged some correspondence with Mr. Huntspill. I know it was improper of me, but I had in my own way hoped to encourage him to help us. I am intensely displeased and disappointed that he refused to do so."

"Then, you do not believe as our mother does, that he will prove generous once he arrives?"

Arabella set another stitch, the merest lifting of a brow giving physical expression to her opinion. "He will not," was all she said.

Henrietta remembered her conversation with Arabella of yesterday, and a faint prickle of gooseflesh travelled over her. Was her sister engaged to the new owner of the manor? But that was impossible. What woman, possessing even an exceptional intelligence, could ever find anything to admire in Huntspill? She glanced down at the neat loops of braid pinned at the back of Arabella's head, her precise stitches, her methodical approach to her life. On the other hand, what could be more orderly or sensible than to marry the man who owns the house you live in? But was it truly possible?

She was about to confront her sister when Cook barrelled into the entranceway, her pudgy face red with exertion as she exclaimed, "There you are Mrs. Harte! It's gone! And Miss Betsy left not half an hour since! I've a miserable feeling that something horrifying is about to happen."

"What?" Henrietta cried. "What is gone? What wretched thing is about to transpire?"

"I don't know. But Miss Betsy's catapult is gone! Remember? I told you about it yesterday. I'd hidden it in the salt box, and now it's gone along with Miss Betsy. And I don't mind telling you she's had something of a wild look in her eye all morning—like when she killed that poor chicken!"

Angel cried, "Well, I know where she's gone, and she certainly can't mean to kill another chicken, for they don't go down to the lane. She told me she was going to wave good-bye to her friend, Mr. Brandish." She paused for a moment and said, "She doesn't intend to fling one of her rocks at him, does she? Why, only last night she was telling me how much she liked him! I would be very shocked to learn she wanted to kill Mr. Brandish."

Even Cook stared at Angel with her mouth at half-cock. Arabella sniggered, and Charlotte simply adjured her scatterbrained sister to attend to their task. Angel shrugged slightly, unconcerned that no one paid the least heed to her remarks, and returned her full attention to Charlotte's query regarding Mrs. Leighton's amethyst necklace. Henrietta listened to them for a moment and realized they were compiling a list of all the precious jewels the ladies owned in an effort to formulate an approximate figure of their worth. Should they come to a place of needing to raise the ready in order to complete their mission of seeing Angel well settled, Charlotte, in particular, wished to know precisely how they stood.

Arabella returned to her mending, shaking her head at Angel's maudlin speech, but Henrietta could not dismiss either Cook's distraught expression or Angel's bizarre fancy quite so easily.

She frowned deeply, a recent conversation with Betsy returning vividly to haunt her. Last night, Betsy had walked upstairs with her, hugging her close but wearing a familiar mischievous smile in her large, blue eyes. She had asked, "Henry, why don't you marry Mr. Brandish? He's very rich, isn't he? Then we wouldn't need to worry about anything. Besides, you know Angel won't be able to really help us because she doesn't fall in love very easily like you do. And you love Mr. Brandish, don't you?"

"I don't know what you mean, Betsy. I only met him yesterday."

She lowered her voice and said, "Yes, but you seemed to like kissing him very much."

Henrietta looked down at her, frowning. "Hush, now! Do not tell me you were spying on me."

Betsy smiled. "Only a little, but he seemed so fixed to you, like he was stuck, or something. I could tell he didn't want to let you go. Does he love you as well?"

Henrietta had looked deep inside herself at this question. Did he love her? She shook her head. "I don't know. He seemed attached to me in a way I can't explain, and I to him; but I wouldn't call it love."

"Well, I would!" Betsy retorted fervently. "You both tumbled violently in love; you just seem unwilling to acknowledge it as such!"

"And what do you know of love, Miss Betsy Leighton, my precocious one!"

"Not a great deal, actually, except that Angel is very bad at it and that you won't be happy once Mr. Brandish leaves Hampshire."

These words had pierced Henrietta's heart, revealing a truth she did not want to admit to herself. "Perhaps," she agreed. "But I won't be marrying Mr. Brandish, so you may set aside that notion at once. He is leaving for London tomorrow, and that is the end of it!"

"Not if I can help it," Betsy had responded cryptically. "Besides, I don't think your scheme to marry Angel off has the least chance of success. You seem to have forgotten that she's not only chuckleheaded, but she's whimsical, too. She may have agreed to do all you requested today, but tomorrow, she's likely to forget she

90

promised to do any of it. You must at least concede this much."

Henrietta had refused obstinately to do anything of the kind.

Last night, Henrietta had dismissed Betsy's conversation as merely the hopeful imaginings of a twelve-year-old girl on the brink of womanhood. Betsy wished desperately to join her elders, to contribute her portion to the happy resolution of their problems, but her child's mind was not suited to the creation of a reasonable course of action.

Could this mean, however, that when she spoke of somehow being able to prevent Brandish from leaving the district she had some childish yet hazardous scheme in mind?

Henrietta regarded Cook's concerned expression as that good woman waited patiently on the threshold of the parlor. And Betsy's catapult was gone. A strong sense of foreboding overtook Henrietta. "I shall go in search of her immediately," she announced.

Chapter Eleven

King glared at his father, who stood in front of the massive, oak doors of Broadhorn Hall, refusing to let him leave. They had engaged in a fierce, explosive argument on the night before, following Mrs. Kempshott's fainting episode, that had lasted for over half an hour. It would have continued longer had not Lord Ennersley turned on his heel and stalked from his son's bedchamber too furious to argue further.

King settled his beaver hat hard upon his head. "There is nothing you can say to me at this time, Father, that would persuade me to remain here one more instant. You should never have asked me to join you at Broadhorn without first informing me that not only had Mrs. Marshfield been invited but that I was expected to offer for her as well! Good God, do you not see how harshly she will be treated by many of her London acquaintance once it is learned that I did not ask her to become my wife? The intimate family nature of this gathering cannot help but give rise to just this sort of speculation amongst every gossip in Mayfair."

Lord Ennersley merely folded his arms stubbornly across his chest and returned King's ferocious stare. "You are past thirty years of age now," he cried venomously. "And what I wish to know is when you will leave off your raffish ways and settle down! You need a bride, a wife, a woman to bear your children and lend stability to your unsteady, rakish habits." He was a tall man, equal in height to King. They were in every physical respect, father and son. They shared the same general tough, masculine physique, the same sharp, blue eyes, and though now streaked with gray, the viscount's hair was thick and black like King's.

Brandish could not resist responding in kind. "I shall change the mode of my existence, sir, the day you do! You profess to be grievously concerned for your progeny, why then don't you take a wife and set up a second nursery! You are not so old that it would be impossible."

Ennersley seemed taken aback by this unexpected attack upon his flank and could only scowl at his son in response. For the moment he was bereft of words.

King took advantage of his father's silence and continued, "I know that you are hopelessly disappointed in me, Papa. But you must try to understand that I have no desire to marry anyone at this time. And how much worse a compliment could I pay to a prospective bride, such as Fanny for instance, than to lead her to the altar, with my heart completely unengaged."

Lord Ennersley frowned heavily and responded, "You make excellent speeches. Why could you not put your abilities to better use than dallying among the lightskirts of Hyde Park and haunting the gaming hells of Mayfair? What will your end be, m'boy? Are you run into dun territory yet? I would not be surprised to learn that you were."

"And were I," Brandish asked in a deceptively calm voice, his eyes narrowed, a painful ire crushing his chest, "could I enlist your aid? Or would you cast me off?"

"I knew it!" his father cried, punching the air with a tight fist. "So how much do the cent-percenters have you in for? Ten thousand? Twenty?"

King was furious beyond words. So this was his father's opinion of him—a reckless scapegrace! A common gamester! He pulled on his gloves of York tan with hard jerks, his temper rising hotly. "Oh, I've little doubt it must thirty by now, perhaps even forty!" he responded between clenched teeth.

"What?" his father spit. "Why, you worthless, irresponsible—and to think I spawned you! Why, were I not—" he broke off suddenly, breathing hard. "So, how much do you need, then? I shall return to London, and we'll begin sorting through your affairs. Damn and blast, I knew I should have long since taken charge of you!"

King watched his father coldly, his heart hardening toward him. "Your face grows quite red when you shout at me. But the truth is, I lied to you. I am not in debt at all." He smoothed his tight-fitting gloves over his hands. Against the threatening clouds that loomed on the western horizon, he donned his caped greatcoat, wanting nothing more than to part from his father before he lost his temper completely.

"Not a penny, eh?" his father queried, disbelieving. "Come, come. The truth, boy!"

King refused to answer him except to beg his father to stand aside since his horses were being kept waiting and he could hear the wind blustering through the lime trees in the avenue. "Not unlike you," he ended, regarding his father with intense dislike.

"Now here! I say, King, don't go getting your hackles up! I've got an interest in you, else I wouldn't pay you the least heed. You're my son! Damme, listen to me! I want what is good for you!"

King had pushed past him and was now moving briskly down the brick steps of the mansion. A pair of finely matched grays were harnessed to his gleaming, black curricle, and a groom stood by the lead horse, keeping the team in check.

"King! Dammit, stop I say! I've not finished with you!"

Brandish leaped lightly into the two-wheeled carriage, ignoring his parent. He grasped the reins quickly, and just as he gave his uncle's groom the office to release the

94

horses, his father jumped up into the carriage, dropping into the seat beside him. "I said, stop, you rebellious care-for-nobody! King—" he cried into the growing wind.

Brandish refused to halt the equipage. He was angry beyond words, and he would be damned before he would bow and scrape before his father. He cracked the whip over the leader's ears, calling loudly to the grays to step lively!

Lord Ennersley held on fiercely to the side and front of the curricle as his son drove the horses swiftly into a headlong gallop. "What are you about?" he cried. "Do you wish to see me killed? Is that it?"

Brandish felt every angry fiber of his being thrill to the reckless pace of the curricle as it flew down the gravelled drive and swung into the macadamized lane that led to the village. Tree-studded hedges and climbing bowers stretched along both sides of the drive as the horses pounded into the coarse bed of rock. A white dust rose from the horses' hooves, cloaking the clean, polished curricle in a fine, gritty powder.

"For God's sake, King! You will have us both killed if you do not take care! The lane takes a sharp turn ahead! Slow down, I say!"

Betsy sat very still on the limb of a walnut tree situated near the lane. She could hear the approach of Brandish's carriage and knew from the sound of the charging horses that he was travelling at a fast pace. Her heart beat wildly against her ribs as she balanced herself on the limb and began whirling her catapult in a practiced circle. The curricle drew closer and soon would be in view as the lane opened to a wide arc, bordered on the far side by a ditch. She knew her aim must be true, for she would have only one chance to bring the curricle to a halt before it swirled quickly by. She intended to strike one of the horses just hard enough to cause it to shy and stumble. The carriage would overturn, undoubtedly, because of the angle of the lane. In her mind's eye, she could see Brandish tumble from the carriage, suffering only a mild injury, of course. He would then be brought to Fair Oaks for a protracted recovery under Henrietta's care where their love could blossom into marriage.

Her heart sang with the simplicity and beauty of her scheme which she felt to be infinitely more sensible than trying to rig Angel out and get her married off to some poor cawker in London.

The curricle rounded the bend at an enormously quick pace. Betsy whirled the catapult faster and faster, waiting breathlessly for the horses to draw opposite her. One second more.

Henrietta heard the curricle before she saw it as she walked briskly across the field to the west of the manor. If Brandish were driving the carriage, she knew at once he was travelling far too swiftly to negotiate safely the wicked turn which would soon be upon him. She quickened her steps and had nearly gained the road when a fluttering movement in one of the trees near her caught her eye. Looking up, she saw Betsy whipping her sling about in an ominous manner.

"Betsy!" she shrieked as a gust of wind slammed into her back.

King gloried in the mad, daring pace of the curricle, avenging his lacerated feelings by forcing the horses heedlessly down the lane. His father again begged him to stop, cursing his foolhardiness.

Without giving the matter any thought, Brandish impetuously passed the reins to his father, shoving them into his hands, as he cried, "You seem to know so well how to manage my life, then take the reins and be damned!"

He watched in horror as his father grasped in-effectually for the brown strips of leather, and the reins slipped down in front of the body of the carriage, instantly becoming tangled in the traces and the crashing hooves of the horses. From somewhere to his left he heard a woman shriek, and at the same time one of the grays screamed with fright. In a fraction of a second, the carriage swung into the air, and he had a bizarre glimpse of horses, hedges and road all swirling together. He felt a heavy weight press down on him and then nothing. . . .

Chapter Twelve

The ditch was half-full of water and deeper than the height of a tall man.

Henrietta broke through the hedge by the lane, a clinging bramble vine dragging at her pelisse. She took in the chaos of the disaster before her, trying desperately to bring her inexplicably sluggish mind to bear on the confusion of the wreckage. She needed to find the most effective course to take charge of a situation that clearly demanded the strength of several men to accomplish properly. One of the grays was down, thrashing about, having been caught in a loop of traces that were pulled tight by the overturned vehicle. The other horse stood quivering and wild-eyed, his coat lathered from exertion as the horse beside him kicked at his own legs and whinnied.

Near the ditch, a fine-looking gentleman with graying black hair lay on his side moaning. She went to him first and begged to know if he was all right. She did not know him by sight and was surprised to find that someone other than Brandish had been tooling recklessly down the lane. She had fully expected to find King in the middle of the calamity.

She stooped beside him as he leaned up on his elbow then sat upright holding his left arm. He seemed dazed, and to Henrietta's query as to his condition, he responded foggily, "Where's my son? Where's Brandish? Oh, my God, the horses!"

"Was King with you?" she asked, feeling a panic strike her heart, for he was nowhere to be seen. He nodded, and she looked around quickly only to discover much to her horror that he had been thrown into the ditch and was lying facedown on the muddy bank, the greater part of his body trailing into the water. The ditch was alive with mud and movement from the recent rains as it tugged steadily at Brandish, draining the overflow of the surrounding fields, leading the water southward to the River Meon.

Without hesitation, Henrietta began clambering quickly down the side of the ditch, anxious to reach Brandish. Every year brought news of disastrous drownings, where some poor fellow or child had fallen into one of hundreds of trenches that crossed the countryside. As Henrietta slid her feet into the water, it was not without some fear that she, too, was at risk. Not more so, however, than Brandish, for the mud gave way beneath him, and she watched, appalled, as he slipped farther down the bank, the current of the stream pulling relentlessly at him.

Henrietta plunged the rest of the way into the stream and found herself standing in water up to her thighs. She felt her face grow flushed with agony as she reached down and turned Brandish's head toward her slightly to better see his face. His complexion was chalky white, his eyes closed, and she could not even determine if he was breathing. She leaned very close to him as the muddy water swirled about her legs and feet, soaking the bottom of her pelisse and making movement difficult. She found to her intense relief however, as she bent near his face, that he was breathing.

The rains had softened the walls of the ditch, and King again slid closer toward the water. She quickly slipped a hand under his arm and held him fast to the side of the trench by pinning her hip against him. But his sheer size, as well as the weight of his wet clothing, made even this effort one she knew she would not be able to sustain indefinitely.

"King," she called to him softly, only vaguely aware that tears had begun pouring down her cheeks. "Whatever were you thinking, dearest?"

She looked up and saw that his father was peering at her from the rim of the ditch. His face was also pale, his eyes wide and desperate. "Is he—?"

She shook her head. "No. But we must get help. I can't hold him like this forever."

"I've broken my arm," he responded, his face contorted with pain, "but I think I could manage to slide down the bank." He began shifting his feet toward the edge of the trench, all the while clutching his arm close to his chest.

"No! Do not!" she cried. "Should you falter, I could do nothing for you. Please stay a moment and let me think!"

Betsy appeared suddenly, and Henrietta breathed a quick prayer of thanksgiving. She had forgotten for the moment that her sister was nearby. Betsy's face was pale with fear as she dropped down beside Lord Ennersley. "I didn't mean any harm, Henry!" she cried, bursting into uncontrollable tears. "Only look what I have done! I've killed Mr. Brandish, and I liked him ever so much!"

Henrietta tried to gain her attention several times by calling loudly to her, but her young, overwrought sister could not hear. She was caught in the midst of a fit of hysterics, from which only the sharp words Brandish's father struck her with brought her to heel. "Stubble it!" he cried. "Enough of this blatheration! We need your help, now, not your infantile wailings!"

Betsy looked at him, wide-eyed and frightened, for his voice was commanding and fierce. She wiped her face hastily with both her hands, and though she continued sobbing, she cried, "Yes, sir! Now, tell me what I am to do!"

Henry addressed her. "You must listen carefully if we

100

are to save these gentlemen. Do you understand?" Betsy nodded. "First, you must go to the stables and send three—no four—of our hands back here. Tell them two men are injured and two horses, as well. Next, you must send another hand, on horseback, to fetch the doctor. And finally, Betsy, I want you to return to the house and go directly in search of Cook. When you find her, tell her everything that has happened and that I intend to see that these gentlemen are brought back to Fair Oaks. Our home is much closer than Broadhorn, and I know that Cook will know precisely what must be done!"

Before Betsy left, Henrietta made her repeat everything she had just told her. Betsy caught her breath once or twice during her quick recital; but she had all of the directions intact, and Henrietta immediately sent her on her mission, bidding her run faster than even Thunder would, once he had grown up!

After but a few minutes, Henrietta felt her legs and feet growing numb with cold. Her hip ached from the constant pressure she needed to bring to bear on King's body in order to keep him from submerging into the water. Already his face was inches away from the murky stream, and she found herself muttering feverish prayers that the farmhands would return quickly to help her.

She felt his body give way again, and he slid to the edge of the water, his chin sunk deeply into the mud. She glanced up at Lord Ennersley in desperation. She could not move King one inch, for he was heavier than she could manage.

Lord Ennersley did not wait for an invitation. Some of the color had returned to his cheeks, and with great care, he began his progress down the side of the ditch. Just as he found his footing in the cold waters, he caught his son's body before it slipped into the muddy stream. He winced as he struggled to keep Brandish against the bank of the trench, but this gave Henrietta enough time to reposition herself and lock one of her legs behind King's, again pinning him to the bank.

101

She remained thus, with Lord Ennersley holding his son tightly about the waist, and her own legs frozen with the cold but securing King to the wall of the ditch, for what seemed an eternity. She could not keep from weeping the entire time, as unbidden tears kept pouring down her cheeks. This loss would have been unbearable, she realized. To have found Brandish one day and to have lost him the next would have been more than she could have endured without enormous grief. At the same time she was astonished at the depths of her feelings for a man she had known scarcely the rising and falling of the sun.

Lord Ennersley struggled mightily with the growing pain of his arm. Henrietta watched him as closely as she did King. Finally she thought it might serve them both well to converse, if nothing more than to give time the appearance of being shorter than it really was. "I hope you will forgive my boldness," she began. "But do I presume correctly if I address you as Lord Ennersley?"

He looked at her through pain-bleared eyes and nodded. "You seem to be acquainted with my son?" he queried, his voice hoarse and breathy.

"Yes, I had the opportunity of meeting him yesterday. He brought Vincent back from Lord Ramsdean's kennels, Betsy's dog, you know. My poor sister was sick with worry."

Ennersley shifted his grip on Brandish's waist slightly, hunching over as a spasm of pain gripped him. He spoke haltingly, "Yes, I remember now. King was very angry about the dog and—and other things." He glanced through narrowed eyes at her and asked, "Are you perchance Mrs. Harte?"

Henrietta nodded. "But I think given the circumstances, I would be much more comfortable if you called me Henrietta." She smiled faintly and in response saw a dart of amusement flash in his eyes. For the first time, as she regarded the viscount, she noticed that he was very much Brandish's father. "King resembles you, sir."

"Yes, he does. For many years it was a source of great

102

pride, but of late, because he also possesses my temper, it is a fount of soreness, for we have done little else but argue at every turn. We were in the midst of a ridiculous quarrel when the—the accident occurred. Betsy mustn't think it was her fault, though I can't imagine why she would—"

"She is very proud of her skill with the sling. I was close enough to see that she had hit her mark, and one of the horses, should he survive, will bear a nasty welt upon his shoulder." Above them, in the lane, they could hear the faint sporadic snortings and blows of the grays. They seemed to have accepted their lot, Henrietta thought, just as she and Lord Ennersley were in the process of resigning themselves to theirs.

"It wouldn't have mattered," the viscount responded. "Just as we approached this wicked bend, King thrust the reins at me, and I lost hold of them." He shuddered, trying to forget the last few moments of the mis-adventure. "It was my fault. I was pushing and prodding him, until his temper snapped, just like mine would have in the same circumstance. Yes, indeed, he resembles me to a fault. We share the same flaws, it seems."

Henrietta's legs ached, and she wondered how much longer she would be able to maintain her position. At least Brandish was safe. "I have sometimes thought that one's family often brings as much pain as it provides happiness. We love so much; but the very act of loving brings us too close, and we begin to rub one another insensately."

"You are a philosopher, Henrietta. My wife was such, and when she was alive, I begin to think her greatest service to me was to show me how to love my son. I seem to have failed miserably in the past several years." At that his strength seemed to give way, and he fell forward, leaning against the side of the ditch, letting out a cry of anguish.

"Sir!" she cried, only to feel King again slip away from her. "Oh, dear God, help me!"

103

At that moment, she heard the trampling of several sturdy country boots, and before she had looked up at the rim of the ditch and blinked twice, it seemed that a host of men were swarming over the edge, hands reaching out to grasp her, as well as the injured men.

Before long, she was seated in the back of a cart, wrapped securely in several blankets and pillowing King's head on her lap. He was still unconscious. Lying next to him, Ennersley, though awake, kept his eyes closed as he endured the painful jolting of the journey back to Fair Oaks.

By the merest breath of good fortune, they were all alive.

Chapter Thirteen

Henrietta sat beside King, her hands clasped tightly in her lap as she looked down upon his pale brow and relived for the hundredth time the horror of finding him facedown in the mud. Cook had seen both men bathed, warmed, and as comfortable as possible before the doctor arrived. Henrietta herself had soaked her legs in a warm tub as one of the serving maids continually added hot water until the chill had left her entirely.

During that time, the doctor had presented himself at Fair Oaks, bustling between the two rooms in which father and son were situated. He set Lord Ennersley's broken arm with the aid of two strapping stable hands, and examined King thoroughly. Regarding the latter, he pronounced a severe jar to the head when the curricle overturned. He gave Cook instructions as to the care of both men as he prepared to quit the manor. The baker's wife was beginning her confinement. "Twins, this time," he cried jovially. "Which will increase her brood to twelve, but a better mother you will not find in three counties, not by half!"

As he fitted his weatherworn hat on his head, Henrietta had rushed down the stairs, only just in time before he crossed the threshold, to inquire as to Brandish's condition.

"He's a strong-looking lad," the doctor had responded.

"He'll do, so long as he wakes up soon. Though I will confess I don't like it that he's been unconscious for over two hours. But if he awakens before nightfall and does not develop a brain fever, he should live to see his grandchildren, I shouldn't wonder. Now I must go!"

Another hour passed as Henrietta sat beside Brandish, her eyes scarcely leaving his face. Cook brought in a nuncheon for her since it was now past noon. Twice, King stirred in his bed, moaning slightly and clutching the cherry-red counterpane as if in great distress. Then he would grow still and quiet, seeming to withdraw deep within himself.

Another hour advanced, and Henrietta found herself pacing the room. She wanted to see how Lord Ennersley fared, but nothing could drag her from her bedchamber until King awoke and she could be easy again.

However, as the clock neared three, a commotion in the entranceway, accompanied by a severe exchange of words—the noise of which reached even to the door of her room—caused Henrietta to step into the hall. Belowstairs, she could hear a feminine voice berating Cook and fairly shouting that she wished to speak with Mrs. Leighton at once. *At once!*

For the life of her, Henrietta could not imagine who could be so ill-mannered as to come to their home and yell at one of their servants!

At the far end of the hall, she saw her mother, Angel and one of the maids depart the chamber in which Ennersley was resting. When her mother drew near, she begged Henrietta to accompany her. "It would seem," Mrs. Leighton cried, "that Lady Ramsdean has arrived, with two carriages, to collect the gentlemen—and they are not fit to travel! I sent her word, you see, informing her that her brother and nephew were here, as well as a description of the nature of their injuries. But even the doctor said they should not be moved—not for several days. However, the viscountess, even now, is arguing with our dear Cook."

She pressed a hand suddenly on Henrietta's arm and

106

continued, "You must come with me, Henry! I can't bear to face *that woman* after all these years. But you know my weakness in this regard. I fear she shall overcome my good sense, and I will then permit her to pull the men from their beds!"

Henrietta did not wish to leave King. At the same time, she agreed that where persons of consequence were concerned, her mother had a deeply ingrained respect and obsequiousness far out of proportion to what society demanded as the deference due them. After a moment's consideration, Henrietta agreed to attend her mother and bade Angel sit with Brandish.

"If he should awaken," she instructed her sister, "you must hasten to assure him that he is well and that his father survived the accident."

Angel nodded vigorously and took up her station on the needlepoint chair beside King. She began humming almost immediately, and though Henrietta wanted to tell her to stop, that it might disturb her patient, Mrs. Leighton took her arm and began pulling her toward the stairs.

King heard a roar in his ears, like a mighty rushing wind, yet he didn't feel the wind, only a coolness beneath his cheek. His head felt odd, like it was moving in a slow circle, bringing a pulsing wave of nausea over him with each pass it made. He saw images in his mind, of boots and legs and a woman weeping over him. He remembered lying in a stream and knew he was in the midst of a dream. He couldn't see the woman, but he could hear her speaking, her voice warm and melodic, but what was she saying? *King resembles you, sir.* She was speaking to his father, he realized.

The wind swept over him again, and he couldn't hear the woman's voice anymore. After a moment, he felt a cool dampness on his cheek and forehead, and the wind subsided enough for him to hear music, a delightful humming. He remembered suddenly that he'd been in an accident. The curricle had overturned.

He opened his eyes and beheld a creature more beautiful than any he had ever seen. She had guinea-colored hair, enormous, twinkling blue eyes, and a great light shone all around her. She was singing a familiar tune, a hymn. He had the impression he was dead, for his body felt strangely detached from him and the wind roved ceaselessly through his mind.

"What is your name?" he whispered.

The creature leaned over him and whispered back. "Angel, but I know who you are even though we've not met before."

So this was heaven, King thought. "Of course," he responded. The beautiful angel would have knowledge far beyond his. She would most certainly know his name.

"You are Mr. Brandish whom Betsy tried to kill. It was very wrong of her, I know, but I hope you will not bear a grudge; I hope you will forgive her, for she is very penitent and cannot stop crying."

He closed his eyes, unable to bear the brilliant light surrounding the heavenly cherub. He turned his head away and wondered why he would need to forgive Betsy. He then felt a great deal of surprise that he had been permitted into the kingdom of God so readily, and he asked, "But are all my sins forgiven, then?"

"Why of course, Mr. Brandish. You were driving quite recklessly, or so Henry seemed to think, but 'all's well that ends well,' that's what I say!"

He found it amusing that his death meant all had ended well. He wanted to inquire about his father, but he felt very tired suddenly and drifted back to the place where the wind possessed his mind and the light did not bother his eyes anymore.

At the bottom of the stairs, three ladies were grouped, all sporting large, ribbon and flower bedecked poke bonnets with wide, fashionable brims. One of the ladies was much younger than the other two, Henrietta noticed.

108

She was quite pretty, actually, as she lifted her gaze to regard Henrietta from a pair of soft, dewy, brown eyes. Next to her, a retiring woman, bearing the same eyes, smiled nervously—the younger woman's mother, no doubt.

But in full command of both ladies stood the third, Lady Ramsdean. She stepped forward, slapping her cane once upon the tiled entranceway floor, and commanded Mrs. Leighton. "I insist you send Mrs. Harte away," she cried. "I will not discuss anything in her presence. You know my sentiments." She regarded Henrietta from cold blue eyes, her thin lips pinched tightly together.

Henrietta felt her mother quaver next to her as they arrived upon the bottom step of the stairs. She quickly grasped her arm, holding it firmly while her mama addressed the viscountess. "I have no desire at all to offend you, Lady Ramsdean, but Henry will remain by my side. She is my daughter, and I am very proud of her."

"I do not take exception to her person, merely the extremely distasteful and unacceptable scandal to which her name must forever be attached. One must learn precisely where societal boundaries are to be drawn and forevermore to abide by them. You should have sent her away as I recommended to you years ago. Then you and your daughters could have benefited from my patronage. But all that is past, and now I have come for only one purpose for which Mrs. Harte need not be present. Now, I direct you again to send her away."

Henrietta was shocked at Lady Ramsdean's speech. She looked at her mother in disbelief and also with a renewed love that brought tears to her eyes. "Mama," she said quietly. "You never said a word to me. I should have gone years ago had I known this was how matters stood. I cannot believe that only my being here prevented future association with Lady Ramsdean. I thought it was the scandal itself. You had no right to withhold such information from me."

Mrs. Leighton looked at her daughter, a horrified expression in her eyes. "I should never have sent a child

109

of mine away. How could you think such a thing! And now I recall the very reason I said nothing to you at the time. I knew you well enough to comprehend that you would have disappeared. And however much I value Lady Ramsdean's patronage, I hope you would always think I would love you more."

Henrietta was so overcome, knowing all that her mother had given up in accepting her back into her home after Frederick's death, that she threw her arms about her and gave her a fierce embrace.

"This is all very touching!" Lady Ramsdean snorted. "But hardly useful." She pointed her cane at Henrietta and said, "And now, take your leave of us, immediately."

Henrietta was prepared to do battle. She did not care for the overbearing and frequently malicious viscountess one whit. She opened her mouth to speak but felt her mother's arm slip about her waist.

Mrs. Leighton gave her daughter a quick squeeze and, holding her close, spoke with dignity. "Your ladyship," she began, lifting her chin firmly. "I beg you will not take that high-handed tone in my house. If you cannot speak civilly to my eldest and most beloved daughter, I shall have you ejected bodily from Fair Oaks."

Henrietta could feel that her mother was shaking, but was pleased beyond words that she had stood her ground with the viscountess. They remained thus, on the bottom step of the stairs, united against their common foe.

Lady Ramsdean lifted her brows in shock and indignation. "Why, I have never heard of such a thing! Are you actually threatening me, Lavinia?"

"Yes, Margaret, I am!"

For some reason, Lady Ramsdean did not appear all that affronted, and it occurred to Henrietta that she was the very sort of person who could only esteem those who defied her.

"Well, then," that lady exclaimed. "I suppose it is useless to argue further. I see that your manners have become sadly degenerate. I can only think that perhaps it was a very good thing that you chose to disregard my advice and to cast off my auspices as you did six years ago."

"I am inclined to agree with you on that score!" Mrs. Leighton responded with elegant indifference.

"Hmph!" was the viscountess's only response.

To Henrietta's surprise, the young woman finally spoke. "We were greatly stunned to learn of Lord Ennersley and Mr. Brandish's most horrifying accident. Pray tell me if they are well. I am a particular friend of Mr. Brandish."

These last words were directed toward Henrietta. She regarded the young woman for a long moment, wondering who she was. She was an elegant, well-mannered female, her features pretty, her voice soft and welcoming.

"I am not acquainted with you, am I, my dear?" Mrs. Leighton inquired, afterward directing her gaze toward Lady Ramsdean and awaiting an introduction.

Lady Ramsdean introduced both Mrs. Kempshott and Mrs. Marshfield. Somehow it disturbed Henrietta to learn that the young woman was a widow, like herself. Was Brandish in love with her, she wondered. But thoughts of King returned her to Mrs. Marshfield's question, and she answered her that though Lord Ennersley was resting quietly, Mr. Brandish had not yet gained consciousness.

All three ladies gasped their dismay.

"Then, they ought to be brought home to Broadhorn at once!" Lady Ramsdean cried, clearly overset by Henrietta's report. She pulled a cambric handkerchief from her reticule and quickly began dabbing at her eyes.

Mrs. Leighton, her heart ever distressed by the plight of others, suddenly released Henrietta and quickly took Lady Ramsdean's arm, drawing her gently into the parlor. "Calm yourself, Margaret. Your brother is well, I promise you, and the doctor assures us that Mr. Brandish will undoubtedly survive to see his children's children. You must be patient."

"I want them to come home," she wailed.

Over her shoulder, Mrs. Leighton begged Henrietta to bring some tea to the parlor for the ladies. "And perhaps a little ratafia as well."

"I should prefer sherry," Lady Ramsdean said.

Mrs. Leighton nodded her acquiescence to Henrietta, then settled the viscountess upon a settee near the fire.

Lady Ramsdean sniffed several times into her kerchief, pressing her side in a delicate manner. "Georgianna," she cried. "Come here and sit beside me; I need your support in this desperate hour. Where is your vinaigrette; I find I am feeling quite unwell."

Mrs. Kempshott moved obediently, rustling in the depths of her reticule as she crossed the room to sit beside her dear friend. "You look very pale," she cried. "But who could wonder at it, for any person of perception must comprehend the depths of love and concern you hold for your brother and nephew."

"It is true," Lady Ramsdean agreed mournfully. "They are my closest relations, and I hold their happiness as dear to my heart as my own."

Henrietta had a difficult time stifling a retort that would assuredly have burned her lips had she given vent to her opinion of Lady Ramsdean's solicitude for her nephew. If the viscountess felt anything for Brandish other than a need to orchestrate his entire existence, she would be greatly surprised.

Much to her discomfort, Henrietta sat for an entire hour with the guests of Broadhorn, wishing, as her mother did, that they would take their leave. But every hint that direction brought another turn of the conversation, initiated each time from the rosy lips of Mrs. Marshfield, and the minutes ticked relentlessly forward.

Henrietta finally excused herself, for she was longing to return to her bedchamber, where Brandish was situated, and discover if he had awakened. She also did not place a great deal of confidence in her sister's abilities to render King assistance, should he require it.

When she rose and shook out her skirts, begging leave

of the ladies, explaining that she had pressing household duties to attend to, Mrs. Marshfield hurriedly gained her feet as well. She appeared as though she meant to accompany Henrietta, which would have been quite malapropos, for the ladies scarcely knew one another. But at the last second, she merely bid Henrietta good-day, expressed her hope that in the future they might have occasion to meet under happier circumstances, and inclined her head politely. A slight frown marred her pretty countenance.

As Henrietta slowly mounted the stairs, she had the distinct impression that somehow Brandish's accident had disrupted the widow's schemes. She decided that for all of Mrs. Marshfield's composure and elegance, beneath her calm demeanor was a woman full of machinations. She had been the first to inquire after Brandish; she alone had prolonged their visit and, in the end, seemed reluctant to let Henrietta leave. Of course it was a great intuitive leap on her part, to presume that Mrs. Marshfield had designs upon Brandish, but it did not take extraordinary powers to conclude that a lovely, available young woman, who also happened to have connections with Lady Ramsdean through her mother, might not make an effort to win the hand of so fine a Matrimonial Prize as Lord Ennersley's future heir. To be the next Lady Ennersley would be a fine position of consequence indeed!

It occurred to Henrietta in the most ungracious of thoughts that she did not care for the notion of Mrs. Marshfield becoming Brandish's wife! He must certainly marry one day, but she hoped he would choose a very different sort of female. She then chided herself for engaging in such absurd speculations. It was no business of hers, whatsoever, who King married.

Having drawn that conclusion, she quickly picked up her steps and hastened to her bedchamber.

Chapter Fourteen

Henrietta's bedchamber faced the downs to the west, and the sun shone steadily through the paned windows the entire afternoon long. Two pairs of windows flanked the wall, through which the friendly spring sun flooded the room with golden light. Flounced, white lace curtains hung gracefully to the polished oak floor, a glass bowl of fresh handmade potpourri sat upon a round, inlaid table beween the windows, and the walls were decorated in a paper trailing with wild strawberries and dark green leaves. The fine, cherrywood bedstead gleamed from a liberal use of beeswax and was draped with thick, red velvet hangings. The bed linens were embroidered and edged with bone lace that Henrietta herself had worked. The room was warm, feminine and comfortable, sporting two overstuffed chairs, also covered in velvet and draped with squares of decorative filet lace.

Henrietta found Angel just as she had left her, sitting in one of the comfortable, well-cushioned chairs and still humming.

"Oh, there you are, Henry!" she greeted her sister cheerfully. "You will be pleased to know that shortly after you left, Mr. Brandish awoke, in a foggy sort of way." She arose from her station and moved around the chair to stand at the foot of the bed, where Henrietta herself had stopped to gaze at Brandish.

Henrietta felt her heart constrict with joy and relief at her sister's words. "What did he say?" she cried. "Was he awake for very long?"

"Only a minute, I think. Not much longer than that. He said several curious things, however. He even wished to know if I had forgiven all his sins. Imagine! Of course I didn't want him to be distressed, so I told him, 'of course you are forgiven.' I told him he needed to absolve Betsy though, for she hadn't meant to try to kill him. His brow had become quite puckered, but soon afterward he sort of drifted away. He's been peacefully asleep since."

Henrietta felt tears sting her eyes as she regarded his pale countenance, his black hair tousled upon the pillow, his breathing shallow. He was dressed in one of her father's old nightshirts which was open at the neck and fit him snugly. He was a much larger man than her papa had been, but for all his strength and firmness of muscle, in this moment, he looked quite vulnerable.

Satisfied with Angel's report, Henrietta resumed her watch as she took up her place on the chair by the bed. Frequently, she placed a hand against his cheek to determine whether or not a fever was developing, but his skin remained cool to the touch. Another hour passed, and the shadows lengthened as the sun descended toward the soft, flowing hills of Hampshire.

Henrietta grew weary of sitting in the chair and rose to stand by the window, looking out on the landscape, the warm sun on her face. So much had happened in the past two days that upon reflection, she could not quite credit that not only had a gentleman, known by reputation as a rogue, kissed her twice in the space of a single day, but now lay in her bed suffering the ill effects of an overturned curricle. In the distance, she could hear the lowing of cows needing to be milked and the bleating of sheep requesting their dinner. And tomorrow Huntspill would arrive.

Upon this last thought, however, Henrietta smiled. Had she tried to arrange some sort of punishment for

115

their cousin who insisted upon sending them away from the manor without a proper warning, she could not have concocted a better one than to have brought two strange, wounded gentlemen into his house for an indefinite sojourn.

"What are you smiling at?" Brandish called from the bed.

Henrietta whirled about at the first sound of his deep voice. His blue eyes regarded her steadily, a faint smile on his lips.

"King!" she cried, returning to her chair and leaning toward him. "How do you feel? Are you all right? Tell me at once, for I have been in the worst state of apprehension for most of the day!"

He swallowed with effort, and she realized he must be suffering from thirst. She immediately poured him a glass of water from a pitcher upon the bedstand and helped him drink it.

"I feel like the devil, if the truth be known! I have a roaring wind rushing about in my head." He glanced up at the velvet canopy over the bed. Blinking several times, as though trying to clear his mind, he asked, "My father. Is he—"

"He is perfectly well; you may be easy on that score. He suffered only a broken arm when your curricle overturned. You were both fortunate beyond words." The vision of his form half protruding from the ditch and sliding toward the murky waters overcame her in that moment, and she shuddered.

He looked at her and reached out a hand to touch her arm. "You were there, weren't you? I don't remember much, but for some reason that seems etched in my mind. I can also recall something you said to my father, but how is that possible?"

Henrietta shook her head as she covered his hand with her own.

"But how did you get there?" he inquired, confused. "I mean, it all seems so providential."

116

"Not amazingly so," Henrietta responded. She told him about Betsy and her sling. He listened quietly, his brow furrowed, his gaze intent upon her face.

When she had finished, he shook his head. "I caused the accident; Betsy must not blame herself. Had I not been cramming the horses and travelling at a break-neck speed—besides having foolishly thrust the reins at my father—we would not have come to such grief. I knew the bend well enough to negótiate it properly. I, and I alone, am to blame."

Henrietta pressed his hand hard and responded, "I must agree with you. Wholeheartedly. You gave way to your temper and nearly killed yourself and your father because of it."

He shifted his head on the pillow to better see her, and with a slight, rueful smile, he said, "You needn't be so steadfast in your opinion—you bruise my pride."

"I had rather do harm to your self-consequence than let you continue without a single check or warning to your heedlessness. I beg your pardon if I offend you by saying so. You must at some time, of course, pay your debt to nature, but I had rather it be when you are old and withered and have a dozen children and grandchildren in attendance upon you."

"Am I grown so precious to you, then, Henry?"

She saw the familiar roguish sparkle in his eyes, and she smiled broadly. "I speak only as one fellow creature to another. I would say the same thing to any poor fellow who has just narrowly escaped death."

"Even to my uncle's bailiff who locked up poor old Vincent?"

Henrietta giggled. "Well, perhaps not to *every* gentleman of my acquaintance, but most of them."

He was silent for a moment, then said, "You know, I had the most intriguing experience while I was asleep. You will laugh when I tell you that I thought I had awakened and spoken with an angel—"

Just as he said this, Angel knocked lightly on the door,

then entered the bedchamber. "I heard voices," she cried. When she saw King was at last awake, she clapped her hands joyously and exclaimed, "You are alive, Mr. Brandish. How wonderful. Do you remember me?"

He looked at her, stupefied, then laughed aloud. "Angel!" he cried. "*Angel!* I asked who you were and you said, 'Angel.' I thought you were a celestial cherub, come to greet me on my first day in heaven. I thought I had died. Though I must confess I had every reason to be mistaken, for your name suits you uncommonly well." He glanced back at Henrietta and cried, "A veritable diamond of the first water! I have never seen such beauty in one—" He broke off as Henrietta teased him with a warning look. He continued graciously, "That is, I have never seen *two* such exquisite creatures in my entire existence."

Angel came to settle herself in an unself-conscious manner upon the side of the bed, her feet dangling over the edge. She had an endearing, childlike quality about her as she immediately began to confide in King. "Betsy told me all about you, Mr. Brandish, that you are a decided flirt and that you have fallen in love with our dear Henry here." She gestured to Henrietta with an elegant wave of her hand, her eyes wide and innocent as she spoke.

Henrietta was mortified by her speech and tried to stop her, to catch her eye, but another wondrous thought seemed to strike her. She ignored her sister and continued, "I say, if you could take it upon yourself to marry Henrietta, why, I would be ever so grateful. For you must know that they are forcing me to go to London and marry a duke."

"A duke?" Brandish queried, his expression both confused and not a little irritated. "They are forcing you to marry a duke? But which one?"

Angel shrugged. "I don't know. That is, I suppose it wouldn't have to be a duke, or even a lord for that matter. We just need someone very rich—like you! Henry says

118

that I must find a wealthy husband and then all our futures will be made secure! But if you are already in love with Henry—"

At this point, Henrietta found her face hot with embarrassment as she cried, "Angel! That is enough! You forget yourself and that Mr. Brandish is very ill. Cannot you see that you are disturbing him?"

"She is not disturbing me at all," Brandish cried angrily, interrupting the sisters as he addressed Henrietta. "For I am not so ill that I was unable to comprehend most of what she just said to me. But is this true?" His voice was filled with disgust. "Are you requiring of this poor innocent that she sacrifice herself for your family's interests? Are you taking her to London?"

Henrietta met King's gaze unflinchingly. She knew her cheeks still burned with color as she responded, "Yes, as it happens, we are, as soon as we are able to raise the funds to do so. Mr. Huntspill, you see, is arriving here tomorrow, and we have but three weeks to find new lodgings, or—as is our present intention—to remove to London and hopefully find a husband for Angel, thereby securing a home and prospects for Charlotte, for Arabella, for my mother, and for Betsy."

She spoke each of the names of her family members in a measured way, hoping that by doing so he might begin to comprehend the enormity of the difficulties before her.

He stared hard at her, his face stiff with anger. "You are no different from my own father and aunt. You are as full of intrigues as every other female I've known. And I suppose next you will tell me, as Angel has done, that were I to offer for you it would be a very good thing!"

Henrietta rose to her feet and answered him quietly. "I gave you my answer to that but yesterday. Nothing at all has transpired since then to alter my opinion. I will only say that you sit in harsh judgement on me, Mr. Brandish, without really giving due consideration to our circumstances."

119

"And you, likewise," he responded. "You are so quick to proclaim my flaws, and yet here I learn that you intend to embark on a course repugnant to me in the extreme." He closed his eyes, appearing quite ill suddenly. "And now, if you don't mind, the wind is again tearing about in my head, and I should like to sleep for a time."

Henrietta was hurt deeply by his lack of sympathy or understanding. She was also greatly concerned that this quarrel might hinder his recovery. Assuring him that Cook would bring him some broth shortly, she ushered Angel from the room, shutting the door behind her.

Brandish closed his eyes, trying to quiet the thoughts that rushed in tandem with the wind about in his mind. He knew a disappointment in Henrietta that seemed inordinate. Afterall, what was she to him that he would give a fig for either her opinions or her intentions with regard to Angel? She had been a brief country flirtation—nothing more.

Still, her face lingered in his mind, the hurt in her eyes reaching into his soul. Cook arrived a few moments later and fed him a sustaining broth, and still he could see Henrietta's large blue eyes cloaked with distress.

Finally, he was left alone in the night to stare at a single candle until it guttered in its socket and the chamber fell to darkness. Only then did he admit that he cared for Henrietta, and this was the reason he despised her machinations so intensely.

Chapter Fifteen

"Are you in any pain, Lord Ennersley?" Mrs. Leighton queried, her brow knit with concern as she placed an embroidered pillow beneath his arm.

Lord Ennersley was seated upon the rose damask settee in the parlor and accepted the pillow gratefully. His arm was bound close to his chest, and with the aid of laudanum, he felt very little discomfort except a slight twinge when he moved his arm too quickly.

"Thank you, Mrs. Leighton," he responded. "But I am most comfortable. You have been very kind."

Mrs. Leighton responded brightly, "Nonsense. We have done only what every good Christian would do. I am only sorry that Betsy—"

"No, no!" he cried emphatically. "I won't have your daughter berated for a second. I take complete and utter responsibility for the accident. It was entirely my own fault. I had become the overbearing parent and literally drove my hapless son to distraction."

Mrs. Leighton looked down at him, tilting her head and smiling. "You are a very good man, my lord, and a humble one to admit so much." After fussing over him for a few minutes more, she left him to his own devices and began busying herself with a large basket of amber yarn.

Before him, on a three-legged table, a cup of tea sat

within easy reach. He lifted the cup to his lips and savored the hot, bitter brew as he glanced about the wood-panelled chamber. It was a cosy nest, he realized after a moment's scrutiny. The chairs opposite the settee were covered in a burgundy and green plaid made of finely woven wool. Occasional hardbacked chairs were scattered about the room in addition to several serviceable yet attractive work tables upon which rested a variety of objects: well-used copies of *La Belle Assemblee*, a pillow and bobbins for working lace, a sewing box for repairing any number of household linens, and an intriguing glass jar in which from across the room he could detect movement but could not imagine what manner of creature resided therein.

Next to the settee, the fireplace glowed with a warm log fire, and on either side of the hearth, shelves ranged to the ceiling forming a tidy library which bore a fine sampling of works, from volumes in Greek to recent editions of *Pride and Prejudice* and *Emma*.

He found himself settling down into the settee, feeling remarkably at ease in the parlor even when the ladies began appearing. They were dressed not in the finery of Broadhorn Hall, but in a warm, country elegance that simply pleased him. Betsy, easily his favorite, entered the parlor first, wearing a round gown of brown merino wool. He had long since made peace with her, explaining that her sling could have had but little to do with the accident since its true cause sprang from the quarrel in which he and his son had been mightily engaged.

He flicked her nose, teasing her about her freckles, and received for his efforts a salute upon his cheek. She then left him, explaining she needed to attend to her caterpillars, who, he learned, were the inhabitants of the jar on the table by the mullioned windows.

Next, Angel tripped merrily into the room, kicking out the ruffles of her pink muslin morning gown in a childish manner and rubbing her cheeks with her lace gloves just to feel the softness of the miniscule designs. She immediately went to her mother and placed a kiss on her cheek. After that she approached Ennersley, asking in her bird-witted way whether or not his arm was still broken. She clicked her tongue when she learned it would take several weeks to mend and, afterward, drifted to the harp where she drew off her gloves and plucked out a melody as beautiful as it was soothing.

Lord Ennersley found himself scrunching lower into the settee and sighing with contentment. He felt relaxed in a fashion he had not enjoyed for many long years—not since his wife passed away. He took pleasure in merely watching Angel play as she flittered her fingers over the strings. She was a true enigma, he realized, for she was clearly a talented musician yet incapable of holding a conversation for longer than five minutes.

A quarter hour passed. He sipped his tea, listened to the crackling fire and felt at peace with the world.

But when Arabella walked into the room, wearing a tidy gown of gray stuff, he sensed immediately that her arrival caused a degree of tension which had not been present before. She greeted her mother—without a peck upon her cheek, he noticed—then sat beside him and inquired laboriously as to the condition of his injured arm. He understood instantly why this daughter's appearance wrought uneasiness, for within two minutes of conversing with her, he felt just as he did when speaking with his own sister. And however much he might be in agreement with Lady Ramsdean that King ought to marry soon, in all other respects he found her society almost intolerable.

Arabella quit the parlor after a perfunctory exchange of greetings, and even he breathed a quiet sigh of relief. When she was a fair distance into the hallway, he chanced to catch Mrs. Leighton's eye. They exchanged a silent understanding, which brought a smile to Mrs. Leighton's face, and for the first time he really looked at her and was delighted with what he saw.

She was pretty in a fresh, country manner, her

engaging spirits evident in the contented expression of her face. He noticed that her clothing was of a fine quality. She wore a violet cambric gown trimmed with a delicate black Chantilly lace, and matched pearls about her creamy neck. She equalled the elegance of Broadhorn, but in a subdued manner he found restful and pleasing.

In her features, he saw all of her daughters bundled up in one. She had finely arched brows—as all the girls did—Henrietta's warm smile, Betsy's nose, Angel's large blue eyes and the twinkle he often found lurking in Charlotte's quiet countenance. He frowned, realizing very little of Arabella resided in her. Happening to glance at a portrait of the deceased Mr. Leighton, he saw at once that the middle daughter had favored her father. An austerity marked the face that stared back at him from the wall beyond the harp where the portrait hung. Mr. Leighton seemed to have lacked an essential good humor that his wife possessed in abundance. He looked back at the widow and wondered if she had been happy in her marriage. Somehow, he didn't think so, or at least not entirely.

Charlotte and Henrietta entered the parlor last, their arms linked, their heads bent together. These ladies had dark brown hair like their father, as did Betsy, while Angel and Arabella sported their mother's fair locks.

Both ladies kissed their mother and afterward approached him. Charlotte exchanged a polite, though restrained, greeting which he could tell emanated from a natural shyness on her part rather than a lack of feeling. She withdrew quickly, but Henrietta sat beside him begging to know if he was feeling much better.

He responded politely, all the while regarding her closely. She was dressed in a deep-blue muslin morning gown, ruffled about the neck. She wore a simple silver locket for ornament, and he found that he approved of her quiet dignity. She wore her hair pulled to the crown of her head and cascading in pretty curls down the back.

A froth of ringlets graced her forehead. He could not help but remember that only yesterday they had stood in a ditch together, shivering and fearful that they might not be able to save his son. He could not keep from shuddering slightly.

"You are ill," she exclaimed gently, placing her hand upon his arm. "Is there anything I can get for you, sir? A little more tea perhaps?"

He shook his head, feeling an ache in his heart. "My difficulty has nothing to do with my arm," he responded in a low voice. "You see, when I looked at you just then, I could not help but remember—" He shifted his gaze away from her, recalling even the feel of the cold water as it rushed into his boots. "I almost lost my boy, yesterday. He could so easily have perished except for your clear-sightedness and courage."

He saw the blush on Henrietta's cheeks and patted her hand brusquely. "Well, I suppose this makes you my kinswoman in some ancient manner. I am in your debt, Henrietta."

"I was so very frightened. You've no idea!" she responded, her hands clasped tightly upon her lap. After a moment, she asked if he had as yet spoken with his son.

"Yes. Earlier this morning I shed tears over his nightshirt, and he begged pardon for his temper." He scowled, sighing heavily. "Of course we began squabbling almost immediately as though nothing untoward had happened." He shook his head and took a sip of tea. "I've made a mull of it, I'm afraid. I didn't always pinch at him as I do now. But his rackety ways—" he broke off, realizing it was improper to be discussing his son with Henrietta. "Well, enough of that. I simply wish to express again my deepest gratitude for all that you did yesterday."

He squeezed her hand in a fatherly manner and wondered briefly how such a fine young lady, who did not seem to want for sense, had actually married a flat like Frederick Harte. He was about to hint at the matter and

125

see if he could coax a response from her, but at that moment, Arabella appeared in the entranceway. She was flustered and bore a spot of color on each pale cheek.

She smoothed out the skirts of her gray gown, patted the braids at the back of her head, and cried, "I believe Mr. Huntspill has arrived!"

Just as the words escaped her lips, a coach was heard in the drive, and Lord Ennersley rose to his feet. He knew of the hard circumstances facing the ladies as well as the fact that for some reason Mr. Huntspill was refusing to help them. Of course, this he had from Betsy, and she could very well be mistaken; but whatever the actuality of the situation, this initial meeting would be better conducted without his presence.

Mrs. Leighton, upon learning of his intention, begged him to remain in the parlor, that he was by no means a hindrance to a happy encounter with her husband's cousin. But he refused her kind offer, saying that it would do him no harm whatsoever to lie down for a while. He was, as it happened, feeling greatly fatigued.

Upon these words, Mrs. Leighton quickly took his arm in a solicitous manner and guided him gently to the stairs. "Of course you must rest, and I now see that you were merely being polite." He wished to argue with her, that he was leaving out of respect for the arrival of the new owner of the manor, but he decided against it. The truth was, he found himself enjoying her kindnesses immensely, so much so that he nodded meekly to her suggestions as she prattled on, adjuring him to follow good Doctor Bingham's orders implicitly. "For he is a very fine surgeon, besides knowing a great deal about phlegm and the like. And though I can see that you are a remarkably strong man, I am convinced you will recover more quickly if you restrain your movements, just for a day or so." She smiled up into his face.

Lord Ennersley looked down into Mrs. Leighton's large blue eyes and, for the oddest moment, felt himself tumble into their cerulean depths. He remained there for what seemed a long time, lost in her gaze, and then the moment passed as she again encouraged him to take great care with his arm. He experienced an odd, floating sensation as he began to mount the stairs, as though his heart had become suddenly set free of its usual constraints.

Chapter Sixteen

Henrietta stood between her mother and Charlotte as all the Leighton ladies waited anxiously for Mr. Huntspill to cross the threshold of his new home. Arabella seemed as though her nerves would break, for she stood in the entranceway, her gaze fixed on the door, her hands gripped tightly together, her body leaning forward as if in dreaded anticipation. Henrietta was now convinced that beyond those doors, Arabella's betrothed marched up the path.

A loud banging resounded from the use of the knocker, and a serving maid—brought from the nether regions strictly for this purpose—opened the door. Henrietta watched Arabella's eyes grow wide, a smile slowly suffusing her face, as she dropped into a deep curtsy.

Mrs. Leighton whispered, "Whatever does she mean by this?"

Henrietta restrained her mother from moving forward and, in a low voice, said, "I have reason to believe they are engaged."

Mrs. Leighton looked swiftly at Henrietta, mouthing the word, "What?"

Then Mr. Huntspill stepped into view, and a ripple of surprised murmurs passed down the line of ladies.

Mr. Huntspill was a very handsome gentleman, indeed! He was a proud man, though, who carried himself with stiff dignity. His clothes were of the finest quality, his silk hat gleaming, his cane bearing a gold handle. He had a firm jaw, an aquiline nose, and brown, wavy hair. He took Arabella's hand in his and drew her up from her curtsy. "So, you are *my* Arabella," he said, taking in a deep breath and swelling his chest. "I can see that I have chosen wisely."

"Mr. Huntspill," Arabella said breathlessly. "Welcome to Fair Oaks, and please let me make you known to my family." She took his arm and gestured in a wide sweeping movement toward her mother and sisters.

She proceeded evenly and smoothly with each introduction, though her cheeks were covered with a dull blush as her siblings stared at her in disbelief. Mrs. Leighton, overcome with delight at this unexpected change of fortune, actually embraced her heartily, an action Arabella appeared more to endure than enjoy.

When they were all acquainted at last, Mr. Huntspill took Arabella's arm and addressed Mrs. Leighton. "I see by your expression that you have guessed our little secret. I had always thought it would be a noble gesture to take one of your daughters to wife, and in part I believed it to be my duty to do so. However, I was not convinced that it was entirely possible for many reasons, not least of which are my somewhat exacting standards. However, I soon found cloaked in Arabella's correspondence the very jewel I was seeking to place in my crown, as it were. And though I believe her heart sometimes takes too great a precedence over her common sense, in all other respects I have found much in her to admire. I knew almost at once she was meant to become my wife, and I consider the entire affair to have been ordained by a Hand mightier than my own."

Mrs. Leighton beamed upon them both, drawing Mr. Huntspill to a place of prominence in the parlor, seating him in the very same spot Lord Ennersley had inhabited but moments earlier. She provided for his comforts, ordering a tea tray to be brought in immediately, and kindly taking his hat, gloves and cane from him.

These, Henrietta collected from her mother, wondering when her dear parent would notice the curious manner in which the betrothal had been conducted. She did not have to wait long.

As Mrs. Leighton settled herself upon the settee next to Mr. Huntspill, and the other ladies grouped themselves politely in an array about their cousin, she asked, "But it seems very odd that you mentioned nothing to me of an engagement in your letters, Mr. Huntspill. I hope you did not think I would refuse to honor your request for Arabella's hand."

"Not at all," the gentleman answered, removing a quizzing glass from his pocket and examining each of the ladies in turn. When he came to peer at Angel, he leaned forward slightly, then returned his attention to Mrs. Leighton. "It was merely that I could think of no reason to inform you of my decision until I arrived here."

Mrs. Leighton opened her eyes wide, her brow furrowed ever so slightly. "No reason?" she queried, perplexed.

He swung his quizzing glass easily, looping the ribbon about his finger, then unlooping it. "None at all. I knew I was prepared to do you a great service by relieving you of the burden of one of your daughters. Your gratitude is all that I require in this moment." He then smiled in a benevolent manner upon her.

Mrs. Leighton shifted her gaze to regard Henrietta directly. Her features appeared slightly frozen, as though a blast of cold wind had just blown fiercely through the parlor. There was no hint of consideration whatsoever in Mr. Huntspill's speech, no indication he gave thought to anyone but himself.

She responded coolly, "But I am her parent. And at the very least I would expect to be consulted, or otherwise informed in a more decorous manner. I would expect this from any of my daughters' beaux."

Mr. Huntspill lifted a brow. "Since you are now subject to my patronage, Mrs. Leighton, I am certain you will agree that a few of these formalities may be dispensed with. I have brought a Special License with me, and I intend to marry Arabella on Saturday."

Mrs. Leighton, who now sat bolt upright beside her future son-in-law, glared at him and said, "Do you wish, then, to put us out of our home on Sunday? That would, afterall, be convenient for you, I'm sure!" She was clearly furious, her blue eyes flashing. The ladies fidgeted at these novel warnings, for Mrs. Leighton was known to be very easy-tempered and long-suffering. If Huntspill had angered her, she was angry indeed.

Mr. Huntspill laughed lightly. "Of course not," he cried. "I would not think of discommoding you."

A general sigh of relief went round the ladies upon these words, until he ended with, "A sennight shall suffice, I think. Arabella and I shall have a brief honeymoon at my town house in Brighton, after which I will naturally desire to return to Fair Oaks and begin to make all the changes I have already observed to be imperative." He lifted his quizzing glass to his eye. Regarding the chair upon which Henrietta sat across from her mother, he cried, "Good heavens! Whoever chose the colors for this chamber!" He wrinkled his hooked nose in disgust.

"I did," Mrs. Leighton responded frostily.

He made no further comment, save the silent lifting of a censorious eyebrow as he rose to inspect the bookshelves. Henrietta watched him with a mixture of fury and amusement as he began plucking every novel from among the books residing there. She then glanced at Arabella, wondering how her sister was responding to her betrothed's brash, imperious manners.

Arabella, however, sat composedly observing Mr. Huntspill and appeared not in the least vexed with him. If anything, she wore an approving expression as she watched her beloved sort through the books and create a large stack of, in her expressed opinion, highly disreputable *literature*. Arabella had never approved of the reading of novels—not even Maria Edgeworth's

131

improving tales.

Mrs. Leighton, however, took great exception to Mr. Huntspill's mode of conduct. "I beg you will stop this instant!" she cried, an angry tremor in her voice causing him to turn around and regard her with a surprised expression. "You have made it perfectly clear that we are to be gone by Saturday next. Until such time, I expect this room, indeed this house, to remain just as it is until I decide what must be shifted about or not! I think you forget yourself, Mr. Huntspill. You do not seem to realize that I have lived here as mistress for over twenty years. And however much you dislike my decor or my choice of books, you have no moral right to barge in here and proclaim yourself master before I have even packed a single bandbox! Had I had some warning of your intentions, I might even now be gone. As it is, I find you, just as Henrietta prophesied you were, high-handed and utterly without consideration for the sensibilities of those around you."

He opened his mouth to speak, but she rose to her feet hastily and cried, "Hush! Not another word, for I vow if I must suffer through one more singularly disrespectful remark, I shall fall into a fit of strong hysterics!"

Again, the infamous brow rose to its noble height as he bowed in acquiescence to Mrs. Leighton's command. Still, he remained unruffled and unmoved as he watched her quit the room, a mild curiosity reflected in his face.

All the ladies, save Arabella, followed in Mrs. Leighton's wake like a trail of ducklings swimming behind their mother.

Mrs. Leighton retired to her bedchamber, where all the ladies scattered themselves, sitting upon the bed or in one of the two overstuffed chairs by the window. The room was a creamy blend of yellows and whites, contrasted with a cherrywood bedstead, dressing table and a lowboy by the door. A golden light poured through

132

the east-facing windows as Mrs. Leighton paced the room, wringing her hands, trying to ease the distress and anger of her heart through her abrupt turns and quick, violent steps.

Betsy sat on the bed, kicking her feet as they dangled over the edge. "Mama!" she cried. "I have never seen your face so red before!"

Henrietta watched her mother with a painful constriction of her heart. She knew that her parent must have, in those few minutes of conversation with Huntspill, realized that she had no hope whatsoever of relying upon his generosity to provide for the future of her daughters.

"I am beyond reason angry, I know," she cried, throwing her arms wide in a hopeless manner. "But never have I met such a person in my entire existence! The insolence, the impudence! Oh, I vow I could have strangled him and would have, had not my dear Arabella—"

She broke off as a light rapping sounded upon the door. She brushed an angry tear from her cheek, trying to compose herself. "Come in," she said.

Arabella entered her mother's bedchamber comporting herself with dignity as she carefully closed the door. She glanced about the long chamber, her expression grave. "I have come to say something, to share sentiments of mine which—were the circumstances different—I should prefer remained unsaid." She paused, her head held high, but her gaze cast upon the floor. She seemed to be experiencing a profound degree of emotion, quite at odds with her habitually stoic demeanor. Indeed, in the past two days, Henrietta had observed in her more sensibility than Arabella usually exhibited in the course of an entire year. She could not imagine what her sister meant to impart to them.

"I know that all of you must think quite poorly of me at this time, but when I originally wrote to Huntspill, it truly was for no other reason than to beg for his

133

assistance, to attempt somehow to reason him into settling even a small portion upon Mama. I had seen early on, just as Henrietta did, that this man would fail to provide for us." Much to Henrietta's surprise, her lip began to quiver, and a tear rolled down her cheek.

"I have also known, ever since I was a little girl, that I was different from the rest of you. I was never able to share in your jokes, and you never seemed to find amusing the very things that I thought witty and droll.

"Papa, however, understood me quite well, but since his death—" she broke off, unable for a moment to continue as she hastily pressed a cambric kerchief to her eyes. "Since his death, I have been quite alone, you see, with no one to share my concerns or my joys. It seemed remarkable to me that within a very brief exchange of letters, I discovered a most pleasing fellowship in Huntspill—though I daresay you will find it very hard to comprehend. I will admit that I was grievously disappointed that he refused to settle even a tuppence on you, Mama—" since this was not generally known, a gasp of dismay went up about the room—"but he is to be my husband. I esteem and love him, and I beg you will forgive his lack of sensitivity and munificence for my sake. That is all I wish to say."

Henrietta had never known her sister to share such painful reflections with anyone before, and her heart went out to her. She had also never realized how isolated Arabella's life must have been, especially during the past year and a half since their papa's death.

As one, Arabella's sisters and mother swarmed over her, begging forgiveness for not understanding her, wishing her joy in her marriage to Mr. Huntspill and expressing their love for her. Arabella received their expressions of sisterly and motherly affection with equanimity and even a little embarrassment.

When Arabella had dried her tears, she addressed her mother. "And now, I have an important request to make."

Mrs. Leighton, overcome by the sadness in her

daughter's eyes, quickly embraced Arabella yet again. "You needn't tell me what my duty is now, my dear child. I shall most certainly make peace with your future husband. Had I known the depths of your regard for him and had I been a little better prepared to meet Huntspill, I would never have addressed him as I did, no matter how angry I might have been by his, er, unusual conduct."

Arabella looked a little conscious as she responded, "No, Mama, you misunderstand me. I'm certain you needn't say anything to Huntspill. He knows very well that you are overwrought because you will be leaving Fair Oaks soon. I'm convinced he has already forgiven you."

"Forgiven me?" Mrs. Leighton asked, incredulous. "But what then, did you wish me to do?"

"I was referring to the seating arrangement at dinner. Would you please make certain that Huntspill is given Papa's place? He wishes for it, and heretofore, of course, we have permitted Betsy to occupy it. I, for one, will be grateful to return to the accepted etiquette at table. Well, I must go now. Huntspill asked me not to be far from his side today. As you may imagine, we have many matters to decide." She smiled benevolently upon them all.

"Well, I feel a great deal better," she said cheerfully. Then she was gone.

They were left, all huddled together, staring at the door. Angel was the first to break from the group as she returned to a chair by the window. Plopping down, she expressed an opinion that Henrietta felt certain represented a joint sentiment. "And to think for a moment," she cried, "I actually felt sorry for her."

Upon these words, Henrietta and Charlotte burst out laughing while Betsy grumbled that she wouldn't mind giving up Papa's chair if it were to anyone but Huntspill.

Mrs. Leighton, however, addressed the larger, more urgent, issue. "But however will we get to London, with no money, no settlement of any kind? And how are we to live from day to day?"

135

Chapter Seventeen

Two days later, Henrietta enjoyed the crunch of gravel beneath her half-boots as she progressed along the path around the formal gardens of the manor. She wore a warm pelisse of dark blue merino wool, trimmed about the neck with a soft sable ruff. The wind fluffed the fur against her neck now and again, the air cool upon her face. She was consumed with trying to solve her family's difficulties. And though she could easily secure a post as housekeeper or governess anywhere in England, she knew that her mother, Angel and Betsy were virtually unprotected against poverty. She refused to leave them until their futures were settled. She knew that Charlotte was of a similar mind, as well.

Somehow her rhythmic steps and the whispered rasp of the coarse pebbles under her feet soothed the turmoil in her mind that had plagued her since earlier that week when they had learned Huntspill would not be helping them.

She shook her head in disgust as she recalled how indifferent Huntspill was to her mother's wishes. When the ladies had returned to the parlor, following Arabella's speech in Mrs. Leighton's bedchamber, Huntspill seemed neither to appreciate their labored courtesies toward him, nor to appear in the least reproved by Mrs. Leighton's earlier criticism of his conduct.

Arabella had been accurate in her assessment of her betrothed's sentiments, that he simply did not care what her mother's feelings were. Henrietta's opinion was of a similar nature, though perhaps a trifle harsher. She did not believe Huntspill owned a proper sentiment, save that which emanated from his own self-interest, and she was having great difficulty speaking to him civilly.

She sighed, thinking the past two days had been a trial for several reasons, not the least of which was Brandish's ill-opinion of her intentions to find Angel a husband. They had conversed but superficially since their brief argument on Tuesday. She had made a point of attending him in his sickbed only twice on the day after, once on Thursday, and today, not at all. He had expressed his regret that he had spoken so severely to her, but when he had begun arguing, however gently, that she was wrong to proceed with her appointed schemes, she had politely excused herself.

Brandish's health had improved rapidly every day, just as the doctor had said it would given his exceptional physical condition. During the few times they conversed, Henrietta had learned that he was an accomplished swordsman, enjoyed boxing with Jackson himself, swam in the streams about his father's county seat whenever he could, even during the freezing winter months, and was more comfortable astride a horse than sitting in a drawing room doing the pretty.

As she resisted making a full peace with Brandish, Henrietta discovered a surprising benefit to holding the rake at arm's length: She was safe for a time from his flirtations. Even so, he had but to smile at her in that wicked manner of his while drinking one of Cook's bitter, restorative draughts, and her heart became full of schoolgirl daydreams. She found herself replete with desire for the rogue, longing to be held fast in his arms again. In short, whenever he looked at her with mischief in his blue eyes, she was in danger of walking straight into his arms. And this must never be! But as long as she

137

reminded herself of how greatly he disapproved of her, she felt a certain measure of safety from his raffish ways.

At the same time, she wondered at this flaw that had stricken her so mightily, that she could be swayed from every sensible course merely by a rogue's kiss. And why had Fate so inexorably brought him in her path at every turn! Why could he not have removed safely to London on Tuesday? Even now, had that been the case, she would be at peace. Instead, she found herself dreading the next encounter with him.

At the corner of the garden, near an arched entranceway that led to a path to the stables, Henrietta stopped suddenly. She had heard a strange noise, like the scuffing of boots on the gravel path near her. She whirled about, but saw no one as she scanned the entire width of the garden. More than fifty years earlier, one of her ancestors had become enchanted with topiaries. The larger part of the garden was now dominated by shrubs that had been wired, trained and clipped into the shapes of animals, chessmen and household objects. Of the latter, there was a teapot, a clock with hands set at the hour of seven, and a huge candlestick. Henrietta waited by the clock, her heart beating very hard. She knew someone was there; she could sense it.

"Betsy?" she queried. "Do stop at once! None of your tricks now." She heard the faintest shift of gravel very close to her, just on the other side of the clock.

"Enough of this nonsense," she cried again, taking a step forward. As she rounded the clock, a hand shot out, taking a firm grasp on her arm, and drew her among the figured shrubs.

"You!" she cried, her heart sounding loudly in her ears as she stared into Brandish's piercing blue eyes. "But whatever are you doing, King! Why are you out of bed? Here? Dressed?"

He pulled her roughly into his arms, his expression roguish. "Is that an invitation, my dear?" he queried.

138

"Perhaps I erred in donning my clothes and going in search of you so hastily. I can see now that I should rather have sent for you! How eager you seem!"

She had difficulty breathing evenly, for she was still suffering the effects of fright from having been accosted by him. "You are being quite absurd, you know!" she exclaimed, drawing in a deep breath. "But tell me how you feel! You cannot possibly be well! The doctor recommended you remain in bed for a sennight or more!"

He ignored her, holding her fast. "Are you still angry with me?" he asked. "You have not come to my chamber once since yesterday."

Henrietta felt her cheeks grow warm. She looked at the notched lapel of his rust coat, refusing to meet his gaze as she replied, "I know you do not approve of my designs with regard to my family, and I had no desire to argue with you further on that score."

He looked down at her and shook his head. "I should never have chided you as I did. But I have apologized for that. Will you not forgive me? You see, the truth is, I—" he broke off for a moment as a thought, novel in its formation, struck him. "I have missed you very much."

Henrietta looked up at him, surprised. For the barest moment, she believed him. His expression as he smiled softly upon her was entirely sincere.

"You missed me?" she queried.

He seemed to recollect himself, and his customary teasing expression again stole over his features. "Of course I did. If I am not in the company of a beautiful woman at least twice per day, I grow uncommonly irritable and fly into the boughs at the least provocation. I become a nuisance to my family and all those around me. As it happens, in particular, I missed your tender ministrations. Cook does not stroke my cheek nor my forehead as you were wont to do on Tuesday. I had hoped to beg you to perform these harmless services again today. But alas, you did not attend my sickbed."

Henrietta cried, "You remember that I had touched your face? But how could you, when you were unconscious?"

"I awoke to it, I think, though I had some difficulty opening my eyes. You rose from your chair after that and moved to stand by the window. I can still see you outlined by the warm light of the sun. Your expression was clouded at first, then you smiled! You are quite beautiful when you smile. Extraordinarily so."

Henrietta tried to disengage herself from his arms, but he held her more tightly still. "Sir, would you please stop all of this cozening nonsense! Besides, what if someone were to see us from the windows. How then would you explain your behavior?"

"I don't fear Huntspill, if that is what you mean."

She looked into his eyes and spoke innocently. "Is he not an agreeable man? Did you not think him one of the finest gentlemen you had ever met?" She wondered whether or not he would comprehend the facetious tone to her voice. Oh, why was she even speaking to him in this comfortable manner and thereby encouraging him to take liberties with her. She knew she should insist that he release her, but somehow she was unable to summon the wherewithal to do so.

He nodded, perusing her face in an appreciative manner. A quirky smile played upon his lips as he responded, "A toad-eater, decidedly."

"He did not seem angry at your presence in *his* home?" Henrietta queried. She had not been present when Mrs. Leighton had introduced Huntspill to the gentlemen.

Brandish lifted a brow in the same manner as Mr. Huntspill was in the habit of doing. Speaking through his nose, he mimicked Huntspill's haughty mode of speech. "He happened to meet my father first and, learning he was a peer, could not help but drop to his knees and lick his boots. As Ennersley's son, I enjoyed almost the same obsequious entreaties to make liberal use of his hospitality." He resumed his normal tone and said, "I vow if I had expressed an intention of remaining a year, he would have blessed me."

"I have no very great opinion of my cousin," Henrietta responded as she tried again to wriggle from Brandish's arms.

He merely clasped her more firmly to him and said, "I confess to harboring the same sentiment. But even you must agree that he will therefore get on famously with my aunt. She adores toadies and gathers them to her, as chicks to a hen. And Mr. Huntspill has just the appearance of a chicken when he walks, I think." He then clucked several times which caused Henrietta to laugh.

From the corner of her eye, Henrietta saw movement at one of the windows of the bedchambers that faced the back of the house. She informed Brandish immediately. He glanced about him quickly and spying the archway demanded to know where it led.

"To the stables," she replied.

"A likely place," he commented as he released her to take her arm in his, fairly dragging her with him toward the vine-laden arch.

"I shan't accompany you to the barn, Mr. Brandish. I am not so foolish as that. Now do let me go! You are become quite obnoxious if you must know!"

"Oh, I shan't take you all the way to the stables!" he exclaimed. The moment they passed through the archway, he swung her toward the wall, away from the peering windows that overlooked the gardens. She found herself again clasped tightly in his arms. "I have missed you very much, indeed!" he cried. He wasted no time in kissing her hard upon the mouth.

From the moment he had accosted her by the topiary clock, Henrietta had felt scattered in her thoughts. Brandish seemed always to overset her completely— whether he was expressing his anger toward her schemes, or whether, as in this case, his lips were tearing at her heart. She gave a soft cry as he continued his assault upon her mouth. He was certainly a practiced rogue, for

141

she had never experienced anything so painfully sweet in her life as his kisses. She returned the pressure of his lips, remembering the last time he had kissed her and how she had told him she would become his mistress if he stayed. And here he was, not four days later, still residing in Hampshire, and much too near her for either her comfort or her continued safety from the danger his embraces presented to her virtue.

His mouth was heaven to her as he began hovering his lips just above her own. "You taste of all the delights of love, my dear Henry," he whispered breathlessly.

His words caused her to groan. "King, pray do not . . . I beg you will release me at once!" she whispered in return.

He laughed lightly as he responded, "Only if you will take your arms from about my neck! Do so, and I'll give you your freedom, though I had much rather you stayed. . . ."

He sought her mouth again as Henrietta clung to him. The feel of his tongue touching her lips gave rise to all the forbidden thoughts that had so completely taken hold of her the last time he had kissed her thus. She tasted of his breath as his lips fluttered over hers, touching her, yet not. His lips teased her painfully until she leaned against him fully, imploring him to kiss her properly. "You are being cruel," she whispered. "What a dangerous man you are!"

At that, he crushed her lips beneath his own, taking possession of yet another portion of her heart. She felt utterly powerless as he held her fiercely in his arms. But how many women had Brandish subjugated in just this manner?

The thought struck fear into her heart, and she knew she could not permit this embrace to continue. She must find some manner of severing his hold upon her. And still, she longed to remain locked in his arms. Tears of frustration welled up from deep inside her as she finally pushed him away, though he did not release her entirely as he placed feathery kisses upon her ear.

She quivered, knowing if she did not think of some manner in which to fend off his attack, she would be lost forever. She searched her mind valiantly for something that could break this spell his wicked lips had cast over her. Suddenly, she knew precisely what she should say to him. "Will you help us?" she asked.

His lips brushed her ear over and over. "In what way?" he queried. She did not think he was attending to her entirely.

She felt a ripple of gooseflesh travel all down her neck and arms as she replied, "Why, to establish Angel amongst the *beau monde,* of course. And to find her a husband. Afterall, your acquaintance in London must be prodigiously large! Surely my kisses are worth this much!"

His mouth drifted slowly away from her ear, and in stages, as comprehension of her request dawned on him, he stiffened.

"Help you?" he inquired, drawing back from her slightly, his expression astonished.

Henrietta unwrapped her arms from about his neck, and knowing that he would become angry with her, she pressed him purposefully.

"Yes," she said, looking past him, not wanting to gaze into his eyes, else she was certain she would again find herself lost. "Would you help us, King? I have every confidence that were the task to belong to you, it would be accomplished readily, with great ease. You are a Leader of Fashion, are you not? A Go Amongst the Goers?" Only then did she dare look at him.

His eyes were half-lidded and burned with anger. "You cannot be serious?" he cried, releasing her entirely. He seemed overcome with rage and unable for a moment to speak. "How dare you ask this of me, when you know my sentiments."

"And how dare you kiss me again," she retorted, "when you know my weakness for men of your stamp! Do

143

you intend to seduce me, King? Is that your purpose here? Well, I will confess I have little respect for your designs. At least my stratagems to see my family's prospects renewed have some nobleness of intention."

He breathed hard through his nostrils as he stepped toward her, staring down into her face. "I will never take part in your intrigues. Never."

Henrietta held his gaze steadily and smiled. "Never is a very long time, King." Just as these words were spoken, a brilliant thought streaked through her mind. "I wouldn't be so sure. In fact, now that I think on it, I believe I know precisely how you might be persuaded to help me."

"Pray tell me," he scoffed. "I long to know the designs you would employ to alter my opinions."

"You would wager for it," she said simply.

He appeared as though she had struck him. His expression grew strangely fixed, and a light shone in his eyes that was as familiar to Henrietta as the sun setting each night upon the downs. "You see," she said, lifting a knowing brow, then turned to walk away from him.

Lord Ennersley sat upon a burnished-gold velvet chair in his bedchamber. He slapped the back of one hand against the palm of the other in a quick manner. Ever since he could remember, he had done so whenever something either distressed or excited him. In this case, the latter had taken full possession of his mind. He had seen his son embracing Henrietta Harte behind a topiaried shrub, and the possibilities latent in this improper hug excited him. At first he had been shocked because Henrietta had seemed like a virtuous young woman, one not given to dalliance.

He had turned away from the window immediately and felt aggrieved at the thought of Brandish seducing that poor, young woman. But after a moment, he remembered something that had been buried in his mind.

Even now, as he sat staring at a needlepoint sampler on

the wall, he recalled the accident of Tuesday and how Henrietta, who scarcely knew his son, had wept over him. His hands rapped out a nervous cadence. Could it be possible that she loved him? But it was not Henrietta's feelings that intrigued him of the moment, but rather, King's. Yesterday, he had opened the door of his son's bedchamber gently to see if he was asleep and instead found him deep in conversation with Henrietta. He had even stood for a long time, in full view of either of them, but he might as well have been invisible. Brandish was speaking of nothing more significant than some of his sporting interests, but there seemed to exist between the young people a curious, inexplicable bond. He had departed the chamber, confused by a sudden desire not to disturb their rapport.

But now, in light of having seen Brandish with his arms pinning Henrietta tightly, he applied an entirely different meaning to their relationship. In short, he believed his son had at last fallen in love.

"Only, would the damn fool be wise enough to own up to it!" he cried into the air, giving his hands a final hard rap. He determined in that moment to do all that he could to further King's blossoming interest in Freddy Harte's widow.

Chapter Eighteen

In a procession of two coaches, with only the faint flickering of carriage lamps to guide the equipages under a dark, cloudy sky, the ladies of Fair Oaks and Mr. Huntspill wended their way toward Broadhorn Hall. Only Betsy had remained behind, grumbling loudly that even though she was only twelve she still should have been permitted to attend the fete. An engagement party, as it were, in honor of Arabella.

The ladies were bedecked in their best satin gowns, jewels, capes and feathers. Huntspill, sitting across from Henrietta, confessed to having spent a full hour in tying his neckcloth. "For no attention to matters of deportment, however small, can be considered unjustified when being presented to members of our nobility."

Henrietta ignored her future brother-in-law's deferential orations, attending, instead, to her own thoughts as she gazed out the window. She was still astonished that not an hour after the gentlemen had quit Fair Oaks to return to the Hall, hasty cards of invitation had been returned to the entire family.

Mrs. Leighton had cried, "But whatever could be the meaning of this!"

Mr. Huntspill wasted no time in explaining the matter to her. "Why, to give due notice to my recent arrival here, I'm sure. Afterall, I cannot imagine that Lady

Ramsdean would continue her ostracization of Arabella, when she knows—I do beg your pardon if I give you pain—that Mrs. Harte will shortly leave the grounds forever! She is merely being magnanimously condescending, a generous characteristic that often comprises a true Lady of Quality, such as I believe Lady Ramsdean to be!"

Mrs. Leighton had merely stared very hard at him, shrugged and returned to her bedchamber to dress for the occasion.

From the window of the carriage, Henrietta could see the faint shadows of elms, holly shrubs, blackthorn and trailing clematis that formed parts of the hedges along the lane. The smell of dust and rock drifted into the coach as it rumbled toward the Hall. Arabella and her mother soon fell deep into conversation regarding the wedding due to take place on the following day while Huntspill made a point of ignoring Henrietta. That he believed her to be as great a pollution to Fair Oaks as Lady Ramsdean did, was not lost to her. His expression when it rested upon her was habitually cold.

Henrietta was not in the least offended. Indeed, she was grateful for his disapproval of her, for it meant she would not have to converse with him. And she feared, if she were to address him, she might say something that would put her beyond the pale, and out of reach of Fair Oaks, forever. However much she despised him, she still loved Arabella and could not bear the thought of being separated from her sister, or from the place of her birth, because she was unable to restrain her speech.

Only one difficulty plagued her where Huntspill was concerned: how to persuade him to settle even a few hundred pounds upon her mother! Somehow she would achieve this end before the couple left Fair Oaks to enjoy their honeymoon.

As for the evening before her, the very thought of it sent enchanted ripples of excitement coursing through her. From the moment King had released her just outside the arched wall of the gardens behind the manor, Henrietta had been formulating a daring ploy. She meant to inveigle Brandish into presenting Angel to the *ton*. He might be a rake and a rogue, but she did not for a moment devalue his connections in London. Even six years ago, Freddy had boasted of an acquaintance, however remote, with *King Brandish*. And only yesterday, when she had chanced to converse for a few minutes with Mrs. Marshfield, that lady had confirmed her opinion that Brandish's influence was far-reaching.

Mrs. Marshfield had proved to be a sensible young woman, well-accomplished in her manners and conduct, and had insisted the ladies become friends.

"You must call me Fanny, for it seems unreasonable to remain on such formal terms when we all have shared a terrible fright. Lord Ennersley informed me that you had been exceedingly brave in rescuing Mr. Brandish. Had he perished, I hasten to assure you that a formidable portion of Mayfair's finest families would have been greatly aggrieved. I realize you have not been to London in some time, but even you must know how much the leading hostesses of the *haut ton* demand his presence at their fetes, soirees and balls!"

Lady Ramsdean, Mrs. Kempshott and Fanny had called each day upon the gentlemen. Henrietta was at first surprised when both Lady Ramsdean and Mrs. Kempshott suggested Fanny attend Brandish alone in his chamber, but she quickly realized a scheme of long-standing was in progress. Henrietta remembered King's fierce anger upon learning that she, too, had machinations of her own where matrimony was concerned. He clearly had an abhorrence for matchmaking of any kind, and Lady Ramsdean obviously wished her nephew to marry the beautiful, doe-eyed Fanny.

What King's sentiments were with regard to the young widow, Henrietta could not know, nor did she think she wished to. The only thing she did wonder, however, was whether or not he had been in the habit of kissing Fanny.

The very thought that he probably had saluted her frequently, proved to be a boon to her conviction that she must protect herself from his seductive blue eyes and incorrigibly flirtatious manner.

The carriages drew at last before the front entrance of Broadhorn Hall where flambeaux blazed in their sconces on either side of the door. As Henrietta lifted the skirts of her royal-blue satin gown, trimmed with Brussells lace and billowing slightly behind her in a fashionable demi-train, she descended the coach steps. The doors of the mansion swung open as if by magic, and two liveried servants held them wide as the five Leighton ladies swept up the brick steps and into the magnificent entrance hall of Broadhorn.

Henrietta's gaze was drawn upward by the smooth lines of a curved, majestic staircase supported by marble pillars along its entire length. A chandelier lit with several score of candles illuminated the hall in a brilliant blinding light.

Angel, whose gaze was transfixed by the display, exclaimed, "Mama! We could light our parlor for an entire month with all these candles! Good gracious! What a shocking expense!"

Charlotte nipped her on the arm in warning for her undecorous remark, but she scarcely noticed her solecism. She then turned to gaze at the file of footmen supporting the wall by the stairwell. They were all dressed in satin coats and knee breeches, white stockings and powdered wigs.

"Whatever do all these men do?" Angel erupted again. "Henry, do you suppose they are expected to carry the chamberpots in all this finery?"

As several of the footmen began swallowing their laughter with ill-disguised choking and coughing, and Mr. Huntspill was scowling at Angel, Henrietta immediately stepped forward and took her arm. "Come, dearest," she cried, as the others began following the butler toward the drawing room.

Charlotte drew abreast of the two sisters and whispered, "Henry, I have never seen anything so extraordinary, so beautiful as Broadhorn! It has been so many years since we last visited here—and I was but a schoolgirl at the time—that I have forgotten the elegance and stateliness of architecture. Why, one could accomplish great things in a place as brilliant and fine as this house!"

Henrietta agreed that for all of Lady Ramsdean's irascibility, her taste was impeccable.

Angel's perspective was slightly different as they negotiated several antechambers before finally arriving at a large, impressive receiving room. "I would get lost in such a place living here every day of my life! Lord, but this house frightens me!"

The drawing room was decorated in gold and red, the colors blended and swirling in the rich patterns of the draperies, in the two large Aubusson carpets on the floor, and in the silk chairs and settees scattered comfortably about the room. From the walls, several of the Ramsdean ancestors favored the occupants of the drawing room with mild expressions and easy smiles. Henrietta could see Lord Ramsdean, and his good nature, reflected in the portraits.

Mirrors were framed with intricate gold leaf on molded plaster, an abundance of daffodils and ferns from the viscountess's succession houses were amply displayed in vases throughout the chamber, and everywhere candles danced toward a ceiling of white, carved molding and intricate murals portraying the Greek Gods.

Lord Ramsdean stepped forward in his bluff manner, smiling warmly upon them all as he quickly possessed himself of Mrs. Leighton's arm, leading her toward the ladies. Arabella and Huntspill followed immediately in their wake while Henrietta, Charlotte and Angel hung back slightly, awaiting their turn to greet their hostess, Mrs. Kempshott and Fanny.

Henrietta glanced toward Brandish, who stood slightly

behind his aunt, one black-slippered foot resting upon the hearth as he leaned his arm negligently upon the mantel. He smiled at her in that wicked manner of his which shot an arrow flying straight through her heart. She smiled but faintly in return, then shifted her gaze to a less dangerous object as she inclined her head graciously to Lord Ennersley.

When the formal greetings had been completed, Fanny and Angel soon discovered a similar interest in music. Fanny drew her unhesitatingly to Lady Ramsdean's harp and pianoforte, where they began comparing their preferences in composers and opus numbers.

Lord Ramsdean quickly overcame Charlotte's shyness and drew her into a lively discussion of his house of which he was extremely proud. She professed a profound interest in the great houses of their country, a favorite subject of Ramsdean's, and their friendship was sealed forever.

Brandish approached Henrietta and suggested she regard the view of the gardens from the terrace windows. "Aunt Margaret has had her favorite flowering shrubs and climbing vines lit with lamps. The whole garden looks like it has been filled with the twinkling stars of a clear night sky when the breeze rocks the lanterns. You will like the effect, I think."

Henrietta decided the moment had come to wage her war with the kissing rogue. As they stood admiring the gardens through the glass doors, she spoke in a low voice. "Do you dare to strike a wager with me, Brandish? Have you enough bottom for it?" She glanced at him, holding his gaze evenly.

"Methinks," he cried, "I've had a gauntlet flung at my feet."

"You have, at that!"

He leaned near her slightly. "I know what you would want from me, should I win this wager, but have you the faintest notion what devilment I would require of you?"

She felt her heart jump wildly in her breast. Her

cheeks grew warm as she shifted her gaze to the gardens. The lanterns bobbed about in the wind, winking and sparkling, just as Brandish said they would. "A kiss?" she queried hopefully.

His response was merely to lean even closer and whisper, "Not by half."

"Oh," Henrietta breathed. This much she had feared. "What then? Be very precise."

"I would make you blush were I too precise. And the room is full of ears." He leaned away from her and for a full minute spoke in a normal tone and discoursed on the plants to be found in his aunt's gardens. His voice dropped suddenly, and he continued their negotiations. "A sennight in Paris," he said. "Can you imagine a greater pleasure?"

Unseemly visions battered Henrietta's mind. She caught Brandish's reflection in the glass before her. He was smiling wickedly, regarding her reflection as well. He was particularly handsome tonight, she thought. He was dressed elegantly as he had been on Monday evening, in an array of molded, form-fitting, seductive blacks. His hair brushed the top of his neckcloth; his appearance was wild yet controlled. He was an odd mixture of recklessness and restraint, of rebellion and conformity, of anger and love.

"A sennight?" she queried. She turned toward him slightly to better regard him. She unfurled her lace fan and began wafting it slowly across her features. She took hold of his gaze with her own and commanded his attention. "Only a sennight? Would that suffice?"

He appeared as though she had whirled him around twice. "You would offer more?" he cried, incredulous.

"I don't know that I will offer a minute of what you are suggesting."

"You are teasing me, then. Flirting with me."

She smiled faintly. "It is the least you deserve afterall. And if you remember, I married a man similar in temperament. I comprehend something of your whims."

152

"I would not call a sennight in Paris a whim, precisely."

Henrietta played with her fan, stroking it lightly with one finger. She continued to look at him. In a whisper, she said, "You are quite a handsome man, King. Do we have a wager, then? A sennight in Paris against Angel's success in London? Shall we let the Fates decide?"

"They will decide in my favor," he responded confidently. He then turned back into the chamber and taking her arm asked, "And how shall this wager be played out? Let us not do anything ordinary. I should not like our excursion to Paris to have been founded upon anything as mundane as a roll of the dice or a cut of the cards. What do you say?"

Ennersley, his arm held tightly in a sling, interrupted their progress about the long chamber. "My dear," he cried, addressing Henrietta. "You look radiant this evening."

Henrietta was pleased, for she had taken great care in selecting a gown for the party. Charlotte, whose eye for beauty and elegance was perfection itself, proclaimed the royal-blue gown to be the best of the lot. In addition, her mother's abigail had succeeded in dressing her hair in a delicate sweep of curls from the crown of her head, down her back to the very edge of her bodice. A rope of small seed pearls and a blue ribbon entwined her curls. Upon regarding herself in the mirror, she had beheld a woman from another time, from Greece or Rome perhaps, from an ancient era of long ago.

On an impulse, Henrietta exclaimed, "Lord Ennersley, you might be able to help King and myself. You see, we have engaged in a wager, but we do not know how to proceed. Cards and dice seem dull, billiards I would think absurd—I am at a complete loss!"

"What are the stakes? I am all agog to know."

Henrietta watched King grow discomfited, and she could not keep from smiling broadly. "Should I win," she cried, "your son has promised to bring Angel into fashion once we are all established in London. You did know we were removing to the Metropolis once Arabella is married?"

"Indeed?" Ennersley responded mildly. "I think it an excellent notion. But what of you, Henrietta, what do you lose should King win this wager of yours?"

Brandish interjected hastily. "A kiss!" he cried. "A kiss, only."

Ennersley clasped his hands lightly behind his back and rocked upon his heels. "I don't like to mention it, King, but I believe the lady has already paid her stake. Do you not think as a gentleman of honor, you ought now to recompense her with yours?" He regarded his son steadily, his expression cloaked.

Henrietta drew in her breath sharply. So, Ennersley had been at the window this afternoon. A swift shock passed through her mind as the viscount turned now to look at her, a silent message in his eyes. It was he who had arranged this party and for no other reason than to bring them together. How very curious! And he had seen his son accost her! Whatever was he about?

"You must be mistaken, my lord," Henrietta said softly. "I have paid no stake. I have *given* your son no kisses."

"I do not doubt that in the least," he replied with an understanding nod of his head. "He seems to take what he will."

"Whatever the case, I hope I may win this wager, for my need is very great!"

Ennersley pursed his lips together, his eyes narrowed as if deep in thought. "You have asked my son to aid your family, I take it, and he has refused; and now you will wager him for it? You have great courage, Henrietta, but this I already know. Well! It is left to the young to behave foolishly, even recklessly. And in the end who am I to dampen your amusements or your efforts!"

The viscount glanced about the chamber, looking at each of the Leighton ladies in turn. His gaze rested for a moment upon Mrs. Leighton, and it appeared to Henrietta that his expression grew soft and almost pleased as he regarded her mother. He sighed heavily. "I see the hardship before you. It is a deuced difficult matter for any parent to establish one's daughters creditably. For a sister to attempt to help her siblings, though, I find singularly remarkable." He paused for a moment, frowning slightly. "I have not known you very long, my dear, but I would hazard a guess that you mean to garner none of my son's auspices for yourself. Am I right?"

Henrietta was embarrassed and felt her cheeks grow warm. "Sir," she cried. "I had rather you had left the question unasked. The truth remains, however, that I am Freddy Harte's widow. I would do considerable harm to my sisters' and my mother's prospects by putting myself forward amongst the *ton*. I never for a moment contemplated begging King's help for myself. Only for my mother and sisters."

Lord Ennersley glanced at his son, then looked quickly away. Henrietta, too, directed her gaze toward King and took a miniscule step backward. He was staring at her with a familiar expression, one she had witnessed in the stables on Monday evening. He seemed both disbelieving and dumbstruck. Whatever the source of his sudden fervor as he regarded her, Henrietta felt her discomfiture increase. Between the perspicacity of the father, and the intense allurement of the son, she felt overwhelmed and began fanning herself with a quick, rapid motion.

King took her elbow, an inappropriately familiar gesture for his aunt's drawing room. "You mean to take nothing for yourself?" he cried. "I don't believe it!"

Henrietta felt a sudden ire rise within her. "Whyever not, King? Have you never given something to those you love and who love you without requiring that you receive an equal portion in exchange? Besides, it is my own fault that my family has suffered, though not entirely to my knowledge. I owe them as great a chance at happiness as I

155

took some six years ago when I married Frederick." She pulled her arm away from him and continued, "Besides, I have no desires for myself with regard to London. I will be content if I can see Angel wed to a generous, kindhearted man and Mama and Betsy secure. Charlotte and I both intend to seek employment, though naturally I would wish an excellent husband upon Charlotte, too!" She was overcome by emotion at this point and had to look away from Brandish as tears burnt her eyes.

"Then, I have but one purpose," Ennersley inter-jected, addressing her in a soft voice. He took her arm, wrapping it about his own and patting her hand in a fatherly manner. "I intend to see that you win your wager with my son. Come, let us present your dilemma to the ladies. If nothing else, we will give them a great shock when we tell them you have staked a kiss as your portion of the bet. As it happens, I aspire always to set up Margaret's back whenever I can!"

Ordinarily, Henrietta would have laughed at such a remark, but she was still trembling from her outburst. Only at such moments, did she realize that her sensibilities were in a fairly delicate state and that it took very little to provoke her to tears. The painful prospects of leaving Fair Oaks overwhelmed her daily as did the monumental task of trying to fabricate out of so little, an entire, bountiful future for her beloved family.

But as she approached Lady Ramsdean, her heart began to fail her. The viscountess was magnificently arrayed in white satin, white ostrich feathers and a haphazard assortment of costly jewels draped about her neck and wrists, and dangling from her ears. Her appearance was intimidating in its splendor. But worse, was the critical glare of her small, blue eyes.

"Courage," Ennersley whispered to her. "Margaret has a fierce appearance, but if you stand fast, she frequently gives ground before even the battle is engaged!"

"Lady Ramsdean holds my former marriage in

abhorrence. She has never forgiven me for Freddy's horrid, untimely death."

Lord Ennersley responded, "Then it is high time she did."

Henrietta turned her head to better regard the viscount. His expression was assured as they made their progression toward his sister, but Henrietta could not be as sanguine. If in six years the viscountess had seen no reason to forgive her for the scandal her marriage had brought to Hampshire, then there was truly no reason for her to do so now.

As she shifted her gaze to glance quickly about the drawing room, Henrietta noticed that Fanny, Mrs. Kempshott and the viscountess were all watching her with speculative expressions. Fanny missed two or three notes of the sonata she and Angel were in the midst of playing, and Mrs. Kempshott drew close to her benefactress. She knew the worst fear that she had erred grievously by involving Lord Ennersley in the wager.

Chapter Nineteen

The moment Lord Ennersley announced that King meant to take a kiss from Henrietta should he win a wager they had dared to engage in, the red and gold drawing room became charged with a tension akin to the air before a violent storm. Lady Ramsdean cried, "What!" Mrs. Leighton gasped loudly and covered her mouth with a gloved hand, her blue eyes opened wide with surprise. Mrs. Kempshott half swooned into a chair beside her benefactress, Angel and Fanny stopped in the middle of their sonata, Charlotte held her spectacles pinned to the bridge of her nose as though she feared her startled expression would cause them to pop from her face, Lord Ramsdean smiled broadly, and Mr. Huntspill scowled severely upon Henrietta while Arabella's face grew flushed with indignation.

Only the gentlemen of Broadhorn, Henrietta realized as she glanced from Ennersley to King to Ramsdean, seemed to be enjoying the notorious bet. Lord Ramsdean even went so far as to demand what the particulars of the wager were. When Ennersley informed him, and thereby the rest of his stunned audience, Ramsdean offered anyone who was interested a side bet.

"The only difficulty we have," Lord Ennersley cried, "is what device to use. Henrietta has already expressed a dislike of cards, dice and billiards. Has anyone a suggestion?"

158

His sister responded pointedly, "As it happens, Charles, I do! I suggest you quash this most improper wager at once! A kiss, indeed! And what claim does Mrs. Harte have upon King that she can demand of him to establish her sister in *tonnish* society? No claim whatsoever. This is quite unbecoming conduct for any drawing room, though I must confess I am not especially surprised that Mrs. Harte would show such indelicacy of mind as to have suggested it to your son in the first place! It is all of a piece!"

Mrs. Leighton was on her feet in an instant as these words struck the air. She pulled Henrietta's arm fiercely and drew her daughter several yards away. "What are you about?" she whispered anxiously. "And how could you involve Lord Ennersley in this hapless manner?"

Henrietta tried to demur, to explain Ennersley had taken it upon himself to involve the entire chamber in what was intended to be a private matter between herself and King, but she was given no opportunity of doing so. Before she could even open her mouth to speak, she suddenly found herself, as well as her mother, confronted by Huntspill. "I have never before experienced such intense mortification! I knew it was a mistake to permit you to cross the portals of Broadhorn, Mrs. Harte. And I command you now, as the head of this unfortunate family, to cease this reprehensible wager!"

Since Huntspill was bearing down upon her, Mrs. Leighton slid between them, protecting Henrietta, as it were, from Huntspill's choler. "You forget yourself, Rupert!" she cried, calling her future son-in-law brashly by his Christian name. She had never done so before, and the effect was marvelous. He grew red in the face and backed away, as though she had just boxed his ears like a naughty schoolboy. Mrs. Leighton continued, "You have no call to speak to Henry in that horrid manner. Now, I beg you, return to Arabella, at once!"

He bowed meekly, and Henrietta was more shocked by his obedience then by his earlier attack upon her. Mrs.

Leighton turned back to Henrietta and whispered that she rather thought Huntspill's mother had been something of a dragon and had undoubtedly used his first name in connection with some form of severe discipline.

Ennersley, who had approached mother and daughter the moment Huntspill retreated, heard this last remark and, in a low voice, said, "It is always the case with these obdurate gentlemen. I have noticed it times out of mind. The late Mrs. Huntspill undoubtedly beat her son with a stick, all the while exclaiming, 'naughty Rupert, naughty Rupert!'"

Henrietta covered her mouth and swallowed the laughter that swelled in her breast. She contented herself with clearing her throat several times, though she kept her gaze averted from the viscount's face. She was afraid if she saw his smiling eyes, she would fall into a fit of mirth that would again offend Lady Ramsdean, besides discomfiting her mama further.

Even Mrs. Leighton bit her lip for a long moment before she finally entreated Ennersley in a whisper to put an end to this horrid display of ill-breeding.

He stood very close to the unsettled widow and calmed her by saying that if he thought little harm could come of a kiss, he hoped she would trust him enough to relinquish Henrietta to him.

But Mrs. Leighton looked at Henrietta in an agitated, sorrowful manner, wrung her hands several times, then finally blurted out, albeit in a whisper, "But Ennersley, you don't quite understand. You see Henry"—and here she possessed herself of Henrietta's hand and pressed it firmly—"has the worst—oh, dear me! How shall I say this—she tends to fall madly in love with—with, oh, dear, I am in the worst quandary! I shall offend you, my lord, if I say what I really think."

"She falls madly in love with rogues, eh? Like my son?" he asked, his expression bland, though a hint of amusement gleamed in his sharp blue eyes.

Mrs. Leighton breathed a long, relieved, "yes!"

Lord Ennersley merely promised her that he would let nothing ill befall her daughter and that she would do well to put her confidence in him. "You see," he said kindly, "I am not unaware of the difficulties you face, *Lavinia*. Indeed, if you will permit me to do so, I should like to help if I can."

Henrietta, who stood near them both, felt suddenly awkward as she watched a beatific smile suffuse her mother's face. Mrs. Leighton's entire body relaxed upon his words as she leaned slightly toward him, her face upturned, her expression aglow with thanksgiving. "Why, Enners—that is, *Charles*, how very kind of you!"

Lord Ennersley took a small step toward her, then gave his head a quick shake as though clearing his mind. He blinked twice and after bowing to Mrs. Leighton drew Henrietta forward again.

Lady Ramsdean moved to protest, but Fanny, to everyone's surprise, interrupted her. "I hope I am not putting myself forward in an unbecoming fashion, but I should like to suggest a very simple proposition which I think will answer the case very well, indeed!"

Mrs. Kempshott opened her mouth to remonstrate with her daughter, but Lady Ramsdean laid a firm hand upon her arm and said, "No, Georgianna, let Fanny speak. Since it would seem my brother is intent upon letting the young people have their scurrilous wager, we might as well acquiesce graciously." She nodded to Fanny, giving her permission to speak.

Fanny, who was dressed elegantly in a smoothly flowing white cambric gown embroidered with the Greek key pattern in gold floss about the hem, stepped toward King and smiled mischievously into his face. "Mr. Brandish, if you were to promise, for instance, to salute only her fingers should you win the wager, is there anyone here who could possibly object?"

When a general cry went around the assembled guests expressing a universal opinion of approbation at her suggestion, and even Lady Ramsdean cried, "Well done," the wager was let stand.

It was soon determined that the bet would consist of something very simple—how many lanterns Lady Ramsdean had ordered to be placed among the shrubs, flowers, hedges and walkways of the terrace grounds. The viscountess actually smiled at this unusual choice for the elements of the wager because she was especially proud of her gardens. "Now as to the particulars," she said, her hands folded neatly upon her lap. "I think it would be a very good thing to have both King and Mrs. Harte formulate a guess as to the number of the lamps first. Then I shall summon Banwell, who knows the precise amount of lanterns actually placed in the gardens, and he shall reveal that quantity to us."

She then directed the players to hazard a guess, without benefit of returning to the windows and looking at the grounds again. They were then to whisper their speculations to Lord Ennersley and Mrs. Leighton—son to father, daughter to mother.

It was not until this moment that the full impact of Henrietta's misdeed occurred to her. If she lost this wager, she had promised to accompany Brandish to Paris. Her heart began jolting a fierce rhythm against her ribs which sent a shot of fear spiraling into her brain.

What had she done!

As much as she might enjoy kissing the rogue— heavens!—her conscience would hurt her mightily were she to—

She squeezed her eyes shut for a moment, cutting off her thoughts. She tried to concentrate instead upon the lights she remembered winking at her from the gardens, but wretched visions of Paris with Brandish began swirling in her mind. *Attend to the matter before you*, she commanded herself. She opened her eyes and found her mother begging to know if she was all right.

"Of course," she cried.

Mrs. Leighton whispered, "The butler has arrived, dearest, and Lady Ramsdean wishes to know if you are

162

prepared to hear the answer?''

Henrietta made a wild guess and, in low voice, said, ''One hundred ten.''

Ennersley and King agreed that they, too, were prepared, and the butler responded readily that he had himself seen one hundred and twenty-three lanterns placed among the holly, roses, and yew hedges.

Henrietta held her breath. Mrs. Leighton gave her response, but King shouted his triumph as Ennersley revealed that his son had guessed a mere two above the correct answer.

King immediately possessed himself of Henrietta's hand, holding it lightly within the palm of his own. He gently placed his lips upon her trembling fingers, then looked directly into her eyes. She felt his gaze consume her, and she knew precisely what his thoughts were, that he was thinking of Paris. Her heart fairly stopped within her breast. She was part fear and part desire in that moment, the combination causing her knees to weaken abominably. She knew if he continued to hold her hand, and look at her with his blue eyes full of wicked promises, she would faint.

Fortunately, Lord Ennersley's calming voice broke King's spell. As Brandish released her hand, the viscount said, ''King, since you seem to be in fine mettle just now, for a cut of the cards, I would like to wager you for your assistance, just as Henrietta requested, in helping the Leighton ladies become established in London. I shall set as a stake whatever of mine you might wish for.''

King disclaimed wanting anything of his father's of the moment. He then smiled upon Henrietta, bowed to her and, with a singularly pleased air, turned toward Fanny.

''Nothing?'' Ennersley queried. ''Not even the hunting box?''

Brandish, who had appeared ready to converse with Fanny, turned sharply toward his father. ''You are not serious?'' he cried. ''You would give me your hunting box, to use whenever I wished? Why, I can't believe it!

163

You would do this for her, for her intrigues, when I have all but begged you for it over the past five years—and I am your son!" He seemed both incredulous and angry.

"You needn't be rude," Ennersley responded quietly.

Brandish immediately turned to Henrietta and said, "I do beg your pardon for speaking as though you were not present. It is just that I am shocked—" he broke off, unable to fully comprehend the fact that his father would go to such an extreme for Henrietta's cause. He addressed him, "Do you think me hardhearted then, that I have refused to help Henrietta in her schemes?"

"She has been forthright, her intentions are noble, the circumstances are extremely difficult—" Here he paused and cast a scathing glance toward Huntspill, who merely returned his stare with a wooden expression. "In addition, she has asked nothing for herself, and beyond that, I know that every season hundreds of mothers and guardians formulate similar means by which to establish their daughters. But I don't give a fig whether or not you condone Henrietta's motives, I require only that you want the hunting box badly enough to choose one card from a deck of fifty-two."

King removed his snuffbox from his coat pocket and took a pinch. His gaze seemed fixed, quite soberly, to a pattern of red and gold on the carpet at his feet. The drawing room fell to a tense hush as everyone waited to know his decision.

Henrietta watched his face, noting that his jaw worked strongly as he considered his father's words. After a moment, King glanced at Mrs. Leighton, then at Angel and Charlotte, and finally at Henrietta. A log, crackling in the fireplace, chose this moment to fall asunder, and the noise, loud in the unusually still chamber, startled everyone. Several gasps and giggles resulted, though silence soon reigned again.

When he finally seemed to know his mind, King stood before Henrietta and said, "You understand my deepest sentiments on this score, but it would seem my father's arguments have persuaded me. If you come to London, I will do all I can to help your mother establish her daughters." He smiled faintly and continued, "Afterall, it suddenly seems a very small thing to do for the woman who saved my life."

Henrietta could not credit what he had just told her.

Brandish then turned to his father, who was standing beside Henrietta, and said, "We needn't take part in a wager for this."

He then walked away from them both as though nothing untoward had happened and began conversing with Fanny.

Henrietta felt tears brimming in her eyes. She would never have expected this of Brandish. Never. As she watched him chatting with Fanny, she grew to a startling awareness that she did not know this man at all.

Chapter Twenty

Henrietta paused before the heavy, sliding doors of the library at Fair Oaks. She lifted her hand to knock upon the door, but her heart for a moment failed her as she pressed a trembling hand to her mouth. The task before her suddenly seemed enormous, and she wondered how she would be able to accomplish it. For the past hour, she had been pacing her bedchamber, rehearsing aloud a speech meant for Huntspill. When the words finally rose easily to her lips, and she was no longer stumbling from one thought to the next, she had left her room quickly, meeting no one in the halls, and tripping lightly down the stairs. Her confidence had been quite high initially, until just this second, when she knew she must cross the threshold and confront her impossible cousin.

Taking a deep breath, and shaking out her quaking knees, she rapped loudly upon the thick, wood door. When she heard Huntspill's voice bid her enter, gliding the doors easily apart, Henrietta breezed through.

The chamber was small, yet comfortable, with a desk of swirling burlwood sitting adjacent to the windows. In front of the wall to her right, two winged chairs covered in a cheerful flowered chintz of yellow, burgundy and green, were situated. A table rested between the chairs, bearing a heavy branch of candles, a silver snuffer and a large, jeweled box unfamiliar to Henrietta. Its purpose, however, was evident, for a faint scent of tobacco now hung about the chamber. Her cousin enjoyed his snuff prodigiously, of which he mixed his own proclaiming it was far more economical.

He stood now beside one of the long windows overlooking a tidy flower garden to the east of the manor. The early morning sun fell on his face as he grimaced at the busy scene beyond the window where birds chattered and spring flowers bobbed their heads from a light morning breeze. Without turning to look at her, he spoke in a gruff voice. "Please send the gardener to me at once. I can't possibly have this disorganization staring at me throughout the day. I shall be conducting most of the estate's business from this room, and I can't abide all this haphazard color. We need some hedges here, boxed and clipped."

"Mr. White will not like the idea at all, I'm afraid. He is particularly fond of his bulbs, wild flowers and roses," Henrietta responded with a smile, knowing that her cousin had supposed she was the maid. She had hoped by her easy address that she could lay a few of his feathers which were still ruffled from the evening before. She was however greatly mistaken.

He turned to look at her, his eyebrows shooting up in surprise. "You!" he cried, disgusted. "Whatever do you mean by approaching me in private, nonetheless at this unseasonable hour? If you must know, I thought you were one of the maids bringing my coffee."

He presented an awesome figure, Henrietta realized as she regarded him steadily. He was dressed to perfection, he was handsome and his brows were drawn savagely together in obvious disapproval of everything about her. In all respects he appeared formidable. Had she not been made of stern stuff, she would have turned tail and run from the room. As it was, she had but to remember how quickly he had colored up on the evening before when her mama had addressed him by his Christian name, and her courage swelled within her.

167

"I won't detain you long on your wedding day, cousin," she said, speaking firmly. "But we do have an important matter to negotiate."

"*We* can have nothing whatsoever to *negotiate,* as you say! I will speak only with my wife-to-be or Mrs. Leighton. You have been but a guest in your mother's house for these past six years and more, and you are little to me at all save Arabella's sister. To the latter, I might add, you owe a great deal. I had originally refused to come at all knowing that the infamous Mrs. Harte still resided at Fair Oaks, but Arabella persuaded me otherwise. I now regret it infinitely, for you have caused every manner of uproar and scandal since my arrival here. First, there were strangers ensconced in the bedchambers, and then last night, you inflicted the worst manner of disgrace upon the entire assembled guests at my engagement party with that—that horrid wager! I was never more humiliated in my entire existence!

"But beyond that, the scandal resulting from your indecent marriage to Frederick Harte brought a stench to this house which I'm sure in time will only be aired from every chamber once I have taken charge of the manor fully. And since you have chosen to address me privately this morning," he added, walking toward her and pausing to stand but a few feet from her, "I will inform you now that as master of this house, you will never be permitted to return here. I might have been persuaded otherwise were it not for your flagrantly immoral conduct in Lady Ramsdean's drawing room last night."

Henrietta had never known someone she truly disliked. Even Lady Ramsdean had not seemed so harsh as this man before her. The first words that rose to the tip of her tongue were equally punitive, but she held them back, knowing it would serve her ill to quarrel with him further.

Instead, she clasped her hands before her and said, "I pity you, Rupert, but for my sister's sake, I wish you joy in your marriage."

He nodded coldly, turned his back on her and returned to the desk which was stacked high with books, rolled parchment tied with red silk ribbons and various correspondence. "Thank you," he responded stiffly as he sat down at the chair before the desk. "And now, if you don't mind, I should like to request that you leave me in peace. I have a great deal to attend to before my wedding this afternoon." He took a pen in hand and began scratching upon a sheet of paper before him, his eyes downcast.

"I shan't leave you in peace, at all!" she cried with a laugh as she walked briskly up to his desk. She jerked the pen from his hand and bent over his papers, her face scarcely a few inches from his own. "I insist you compose a draft for three thousand pounds, to my mother, else I will never leave Fair Oaks."

He smirked at her, flaring the nostrils of his aquiline nose. "Empty, useless threats."

"I shall not hesitate to encamp upon the grounds of the manor, as a gypsy might, and proclaim to all who will listen to me of your ungenerosity toward your wife's mother. I will make daily pilgrimages to Broadhorn, where I will pound upon the gates and cry out your hardheartedness in our time of need. I had meant to come to you this morning, to appeal to your nobility of character, but I now realize you possess nothing remotely resembling honor or chivalry. You are a clutch-fisted, nip-farthing, unworthy of your ancestors, and even less worthy of your wife, who at least understood your duty to her family." She suddenly felt overcome by his brutish insensitivity and cried, "Cannot you understand that we depend upon you to provide for my mother? She has nothing upon which to live! She is completely impoverished. What would you have her do? She has no one to turn to. You were her only hope. Does this not move you to some compassion?"

He leaned back in his chair in order to distance himself from her. "I have a duty to my progeny. Your father had a duty to both his wife and to his children. If he failed you all, I don't see why I must suffer as well!''

Henrietta realized arguing was futile and reverted to her original threats. For a long time, he refused, whereupon Henrietta seated herself upon one of the chintz chairs and informed him roundly that she would remain fixed there until he had changed his mind. When he summoned servants to remove her, he was shocked to learn that the entire household was prepared to go to battle for Mrs. Harte. When the hallway outside of the library grew filled with the chatter of several servants, including Cook, he began to grow nervous.

Arabella appeared suddenly, her hair still in curl papers and covered with a mobcap. She had dressed herself hastily to attend to the disaster burgeoning in the library, and at first begged Henrietta to leave the chamber. She glanced fearfully at her betrothed and tugged upon Henrietta's arm.

Henrietta, for her part, informed Arabella calmly of her intentions to remain in the library throughout the day and upon the manor grounds ever afterward until Huntspill acquiesced to her demand. It was an obligation, she insisted, which, by every acknowledged dictum of society, belonged to him as their cousin and only living relation.

Arabella listened to her sister, her own spirits quieting as each dogged word rolled from Henrietta's tongue. At the end of this speech, Arabella, who had been kneeling beside her sister, rose to her full height, her expression grave, her complexion suddenly white and drawn.

She turned to face Huntspill at the same time slipping a band of amethyst stones from her finger. She turned it over in her palm once, her gaze cloaked. Huntspill had given her the ring on the day of his arrival, a token of his esteem for her.

On a measured step, she moved toward the burlwood desk and calmly placed the ring before her betrothed.

''What does this mean?'' he cried, utterly astonished.

170

"I can't bear it, my dear Mr. Huntspill, any longer. It is too much of a humiliation to me to have all my neighbors know that you have refused to settle even the smallest annuity upon my mother. Especially when everyone knows that it was only through my father's negligence in providing adequately in his will for Mama that has led to this disaster in her circumstances. And though I cannot approve of Henrietta's conduct, neither can I condone your obstinance, *Rupert*, in refusing to help my family. I hereby release you from this engagement, and I shall trouble you no further with my presence."

Henrietta noted Arabella's marked use of his Christian name, and she regarded her sister with renewed respect for her abilities. She then watched Huntspill shift uncomfortably in his seat as he busied himself with gathering and stacking several papers and parchments.

When he made no move to stop her from going, she spoke quietly. "Very well, have it as you will! Good-bye, Rupert. I intend to remove with my family to London Saturday next." She turned away from him and, on a stately tread, began crossing the chamber toward the door.

Henrietta counted her sister's steps. Seven in all before Huntspill shot from his chair, tipping it over backward and going in pursuit of his dearest love. There, he promised her anything, only not to leave him, for he had grown to depend upon her excellent character in everything!

Arabella received his penitent speech with a quiet spirit, patting his hands as he held one of hers within a tight grasp.

Henrietta decided she ought to leave her sister alone with her beloved and stole from the chamber to stand in the hallway. There, she dismissed the servants, who were all miserable with curiosity, and waited for Arabella to surface from the library.

She did not have long to wait. In a scant five minutes, Arabella emerged from the chamber, her expression calm. She informed Henrietta that Huntspill was even now affixing his name to a draft in the amount she had requested in their mother's name.

Henrietta regarded her curiously. "You were very brave, Arabella. I have never seen you act so courageously."

Arabella twitched the skirts of her lavender muslin morning gown and headed toward the stairs, begging Henrietta both to accompany her upstairs and to stay as far from Huntspill as she could possibly manage during the remainder of the day.

"I shall be only too happy to oblige you in this, my dear sister," Henrietta cried with a laugh. "He does not seem to like me at all."

Arabella glanced sharply at her, a faint smile flickering at the corners of her lips. Finally, she stopped Henrietta at the foot of the stairs and leaning close to her whispered, "I have you to thank, however. Until this moment, I knew I would live in fear of Huntspill's tyranny, and I did not relish the idea at all. But now, knowing that I have but to stand firm with him in those things I hold dear, I know I shall quail before him no longer."

"But you risked your marriage for your family!" Henrietta cried. "What if he had sent you away, with good riddance!"

Arabella thought about this for a moment and shook her head. "I knew he would not. You see, for all his blustery bravado, he has a great fear of public disgrace. Jilting Huntspill on his wedding day would have cast him in the worst possible light." She paused for a moment, then continued, "I feared his anger more than anything else. But now—" she smiled as she led Henrietta up the stairs—"now I comprehend very well how to manage him. He's really very much like a spoiled child, isn't he?"

"Indeed," Henrietta agreed quietly as she trailed in her sister's wake. "But do you know what I really think, about you, I mean?"

Arabella glanced back at her as they mounted the stairs together, her brows lifted in surprise.

"I think your heart is far larger than you ever choose to admit!" The immediate blush that covered Arabella's cheeks confirmed Henrietta in her opinion. Once they had achieved the first floor, Henrietta made a great fuss of telling all the sisters of Arabella's triumph, and the poor young woman, who wished only to be thought of as cool and sensible, again became the center of affection to her family.

Chapter Twenty-One

"I am beside myself with joy!" Mrs. Leighton exclaimed. She was seated in a yellow damask wing chair beside her bed, holding a bank draft in one hand and a letter in the other. The missive was from Lord Ennersley requesting the pleasure of her company, as well as the attendance of her four unmarried daughters, at his town house in London, where they would reside until the end of the season in June.

"Imagine! Two months in London and three thousand pounds! Oh, my dear girls, we are made! Ennersley says in his letter that his sister, Augusta, whom I have never met, extends the invitation to us, that we are to reside with her, as her guests! But I know this is *his* doing. It is all Charles! He is everything that is kind and good and generous!" She clasped the letter to her bosom and sighed deeply, her large blue eyes aglow.

Mrs. Leighton might believe Ennersley was prompted from motives of sheer goodness, but Henrietta had come to believe he had a scheme of his own in mind. Whatever his intentions, however, she could see by the rapt expression in her mother's eyes that Mrs. Leighton had developed a decided *tendre* for the handsome viscount. What would the end be, she wondered, of this fledgling love?

* * *

174

Arabella marched down the aisle of the parish church that afternoon, with only the immediate family in attendance. The ceremony was brief, and after a general round of embraces and tears, the middle daughter climbed aboard Huntspill's gleaming travelling chariot, her looped braids tucked beneath a modest poke bonnet as she set her face toward the future. The postillion wasted no time in setting the horses off at a smart pace, and before the ladies had dried their eyes and returned their kerchiefs to dangling reticules, Mr. and Mrs. Rupert Huntspill were gone.

Five days later, on Wednesday, the Leighton ladies removed to London, making their acquaintance with Augusta Jane Brandish. She was a tall, thin female of indeterminate age, her complexion smooth, but her hair white. Her blue eyes were quite similar to her sister's, Lady Ramsdean, but Henrietta was quick to note that Miss Brandish's eyes smiled kindly upon everyone she met. Her voice was mellow, her gowns of the finest quality, her conversation intelligent. In short, Henrietta liked her very much indeed.

Her first remarks set everyone at ease. "I have longed for some time to have the house full of guests for the Season," she cried, her expression welcoming as she smiled upon each of them in turn. "And never could I have imagined a more charming family. Charles was very right to have brought you here. And you must be Angel," she cried, directing her gaze toward the Beauty. "You shall set every head to spinning, I'm sure! And I've little doubt that within a few weeks, Grosvenor Square will be crawling with fine beaux—for all of you!" she added generously, encompassing the three eldest daughters.

"Not for me!" Betsy cried. "I hate beaux!"

"As very well you should!" Augusta responded with a quick nod of her head. "I was of a similar mind when I was your age, only I never outgrew it for some reason."

"I shan't either!" Betsy responded joyously. "I intend to travel to the Levant as well as to Greece when I am a little older, and spend my days poking among the ruins!"

"A very noble ambition, my child! I hope you will achieve all your dreams!" Augusta responded adroitly. She then addressed Mrs. Leighton. "I beg you will forgive me, Mrs. Leighton—"

"Oh, pray, call me Lavinia! Charles does, and you've been so very kind to open your home to us. Do let us not stand on ceremony!"

"Lavinia! What a pretty name. At any rate, I hope you will not mind terribly that I have put it about that you were a particular friend of mine some fifteen years ago and through the happiest of circumstances you were at last able to come to London."

"I'm certain it must seem very odd to your acquaintance that we should suddenly swoop down upon you!" Mrs. Leighton cried, a concerned furrow between her brows.

Augusta then took Mrs. Leighton's arm and guided her to the stairs. "Of course it does, which is all the better, for then my friends will have a great deal to discuss over the next few weeks as they meet you and try to determine precisely who you are. We shall have to have a comfortable cose, and you must tell me a great deal about yourself—I shall do likewise—then no one shall be able to guess the truth—that we are utter strangers!" Mrs. Leighton's devotion to Augusta was sealed completely in this moment.

The next day, after the ladies were well settled in their bedchambers and had become somewhat accustomed to the routines of fashionable life such as rising not a second before eleven o'clock in the morning, Henrietta tried in vain to prevent Mrs. Leighton from immediately setting out to do "just a little shopping" in Bond Street. Mrs. Leighton's expression put a great fear into Henrietta's breast. With the exception of apricot tarts of which her mother was prodigiously fond, nothing pleased Mrs. Leighton more than "just a little shopping." Three thousand pounds suddenly seemed to Henrietta to be an entirely inadequate amount. For all her fine and

176

excellent qualities, Lavinia Leighton had never mastered the elements of economics. She was therefore in high gig as she set out with her daughters, first to see that Angel was rigged out in the very height of fashion, and secondly to ensure that the rest of her children—Betsy included!—were dressed equally as fine. She succeeded mightily, surpassing what all of the daughters felt was necessary, including Angel, who cried, "I may not be clever with my sums, Mama, but even I can tell that these gowns are very dear and not made up half so well as the dresses I sew myself. Why, the more I think on it, you ought to ask that lady there"—she nodded toward the glowering proprietress of the most fashionable shop in London—"if you might borrow her pattern cards, and I will make up as many of the gowns as I am able! Even Charlotte says I am an accomplished needlewoman."

Henrietta watched her mother blush faintly as *Madame Louise*, a woman of dubious French birth, lifted an offended brow at Angel and stiffened alarmingly. Madame Louise gave all the appearance of a cat prepared to defend its territory. Mrs. Leighton, however, merely told her daughter to hush, and in a carrying voice that rippled over the patrons currently purchasing gowns from the prestigious shop, she requested that all the gowns be sent as quickly as possible to Grosvenor Square. "Lord Ennersley's address," she added with an innocent smile. "I'm certain it must be numbered in your book. Miss Augusta Brandish recommended your fine establishment to me only this morning. I am a particular friend of hers, of long standing, and will be residing with her—along with my daughters—" she waved a hand over her brood of four—"until the end of the Season."

Madame Louise unbent so swiftly that even Charlotte pressed a hand to her mouth to restrain her laughter. Henrietta saw at once the extent of Miss Brandish's patronage as Madame bowed, scraped and otherwise petted Mrs. Leighton from her shop.

By the time the exhausting expedition drew to a close,

two hackneys were required to haul the mass of the ladies' purchases back to Grosvenor Square.

When they drew up to the door of the town house, Henrietta felt the worst qualm assail her as a procession of footmen hurried forward to take charge of the vast assortment of bandboxes and parcels. The ladies were soon in the entrance hall busily removing bonnets and gloves, laughing and chatting about the day's adventure, but Henrietta could not join with them. She had only to look at the mound of packages to feel unsettled all over again.

Later that afternoon, Henrietta tried to speak with her mother regarding the necessity for guarding her guineas carefully, but Mrs. Leighton would not listen.

"Nonsense!" she cried, as she beheld her reflection in the long looking glass in her bedchamber. "You are in a fret for no reason, my dear! Only consider how just a few days ago it seemed we were in the basket, and now we are actually residing in London for the season. And once Angel's ball is accomplished, I have little doubt that all three of you will soon acquire husbands!"

Henrietta tried again to reason with her mother, that she appeared to be depending a great deal too much on Fate to glow happily upon their enterprise, but Mrs. Leighton was not to be moved. She stood before the looking glass, admiring an exquisite peach cashmere shawl she had purchased for herself. She draped it loosely over her elbows, which was the current mode, and scrutinized her reflection.

Ignoring what she obviously felt to be Henrietta's potherings, she cried, "Do you know that Madame Louise—whom I no more believe to be from Paris, than I do Vincent!—actually told me that this shawl was so fine I could pass it through my emerald ring? Imagine!" She then set about doing just that. When the shawl did indeed flow through the small aperture, Mrs. Leighton clapped her hands gleefully. "Oh, Henry," she exclaimed. "I am so very happy to be in London again! I had forgotten how

178

much I enjoyed society. Your father was never one to—well, never mind that. It is just that I am so content, you've no idea!"

Henrietta left her mother's bedchamber shortly afterward, throwing her arms in the air and determining to let the matter rest. For one thing, she sincerely doubted, no matter how erudite her arguments, her mother would ever be convinced she must keep a careful watch over her purse. And for another, the truth was Henrietta enjoyed tremendously the sight of her beloved parent experiencing so great a degree of happiness. She could not remember a time when she had seen her so content, so at ease!

As she walked down the hall, one of the footmen, bearing a missive on a silver tray, approached her. He bowed politely, saying that the letter had just arrived for her.

She did not recognize the script, yet at the same time she suspected the note was from Brandish. He had years earlier formed a separate establishment from his father in Half Moon Street, a circumstance for which Henrietta was profoundly grateful. As she took the letter from the tray, she returned to her own bedchamber, where she quickly entered the lavender room, shut the door firmly behind her and broke the red wax seal.

Her heart began beating out a familiar cadence within her breast at the mere thought of King. She pressed a hand to her stomach as she read the signature and discovered that her guess was correct, the letter was from him.

My dear Mrs. Harte, the missive began innocently. *I cannot begin to express my pleasure at your presence in London. We seem to enjoy a certain* je ne sais quois *together, don't you agree? I look forward to exploring this intriguing aspect of our good-fellowship, though I suspect we shall not find a full blossoming of this mystery, as you once termed it, until*

179

*we are at last caught together in the bosom and
romance of Paris. I shall see you this evening, since I
promised my father to attend his table. Afterward, I
hope we may have an opportunity for a little*
conversation! *Yours, etc. Brandish.*

The word *conversation,* had been underscored several
times, and Henrietta knew very well he meant nothing of
the kind. She was at the same time miserable and yet
expectant. As she held the letter to her lips, she kissed it,
accepting the most wretched of conditions—that she had
developed the worst, most dangerous *tendre* for Brandish. Her mother had been so very right: Her true flaw was
that King Brandish held her heart captive with little more
than his roguery. She smiled faintly, wondering how it
had come about that Fate had decided to plunge them
together in so hopeless an affair. If only she could find
some means of extricating both herself and her heart
from the pending and quite immoral tryst in Paris! If only
she could stop her unruly heart from responding to even
the barest twinkle in King's eye!

If only she weren't so flawed!

Chapter Twenty-Two

Later that evening, after a boisterous dinner, followed by laughter and music as Angel performed exquisitely upon the pianoforte, Henrietta found herself ensconced at a small table of mahogany in a fierce game of piquet. King sat opposite her, his blue eyes hard with determination to best her, as they slapped their cards, one after the other, upon the table, calling out their points, piques, repiques, and tricks. Henrietta rarely spoke but maintained instead a silent conversation with King, composed of nods, sharp glances, smiles, frowns of dismay or frustration, and an occasional whoop of triumph. He was in high spirits, and not even the fact that he lost his game to Henrietta diminished his good humor, though he did demand that she offer him another game later in the evening. Of course these words were spoken with such mischief in his eyes that Henrietta merely regarded him archly and moved to stand beside a tambour frame where Miss Brandish was working an elegant peacock.

Miss Brandish, pausing to select a new color of floss, looked up at Henrietta. "I did not at first comprehend my brother's intentions in bringing your family to London," she stated softly, her gaze shifting for a moment to rest upon her nephew. Brandish was seated on a royal-blue settee, regaling Betsy about his favorite dog from childhood. Glancing back at Henrietta, the spinster

181

continued, "But now it is all so perfectly clear! He wishes you to marry his son!"

Henrietta agreed with Miss Brandish's opinion, though she was convinced the viscount's wishes would remain unfulfilled. She was startled, however, that Ennersley's schemes were so easily comprehended.

Leaning forward to stroke her fingertips across the embroidered peacock, Henrietta found the long stitches feathery soft to the touch. She did not know Miss Brandish very well and was reluctant to address the subject at hand, to admit she held a similar opinion. Finally, she said, "I only wish Ennersley knew how unfounded his hopes are. Brandish has no desire to marry anyone, nonetheless me."

"I fear you are right, my dear. I trust I do not give you offense when I say that I hope you will continue to be wiser than my brother. You do not depend overly much on King's obvious interest in you?"

Henrietta looked down at Miss Brandish, caught her gaze, held it for a moment, then looked quickly away.

"Oh, dear," Miss Brandish whispered.

"No, no," Henrietta cried in response. "Do not mistake me. It is my heart that has proved unwise, but not my good sense." She turned to glance at Brandish, feeling warm at the mere sight of him and added, "I only wish he were a trifle less handsome. A wart or two would improve my heart's unease immensely."

"Or even a crooked nose!" Miss Brandish cried, as she, too directed her gaze toward King. "I have often wished that Mr. Jackson, who owns that reprehensible boxing saloon, would plant Brandish a well-deserved facer aside his nose, crush it soundly, disfiguring the beast forever. I know many a matron who would rest easier with regard to her daughter's heart should King suffer such a happy misfortune!" The ladies laughed together, and after a moment's silence, Miss Brandish sighed heavily. "Do be wise, if you can, Henrietta. Though I daresay if you are a fair representative of our sex, you will be as heedless as every other hapless female who has loved a rogue."

Henrietta regarded the white head bent over the peacock as Miss Brandish plied the floss easily in and out of the mesh, her hand rocking smoothly. It always intrigued her when she met someone for whom she developed an almost instant rapport. As she turned yet again to regard Brandish, who happened to catch her eye and smile warmly upon her, she thought that to some extent, she felt the same way about him. What was it about the Leightons and the Brandishes that seemed to blend so easily? Even Lord Ennersley and her mother, who were engaged in a heated quarrel about how many persons to invite to Angel's come-out ball, seemed to be able to converse with scant effort.

As the evening progressed past tea, and Betsy was summarily banished to her bedchamber, Angel and Charlotte performed duets upon the pianoforte and harp. Henrietta was not in the least musical; she could neither play her notes with expression—nonetheless accuracy— and as for swelling her song, screeching seemed to be the more apt term for her vocal renditions. Needless to say she had long since relinquished any claim to forming part of the drawing room entertainment.

She took a seat near Miss Brandish, settling her work basket beside her chair. She glanced about the drawing room, her first impression of comfort and elegance confirmed yet again. The style was very much in the lavish mold of the Prince Regent, making liberal use of satin damask to drape the windows in rich panels of royal blue. The same fabric covered the walls, as well as the chairs and settees which were arranged in geometric patterns about the chamber. Embellishments were of gold in the form of the tassels, rosettes and fringe decorating the drapes, in the gold-leaf frames displaying the landscapes and portraits placed unsparingly about the long chamber, and in the gold leaf burnishing the patterned molding on the ceiling. The effect could have been cold, Henrietta realized, but the paintings were all warm and vibrant; even the portraits of the Brandish ancestors reflected a hardihood and good humor she found infinitely soft and appealing. In addition, books, flowers and candles were scattered everywhere, lending a homey ambiance to the otherwise formal chamber.

Taking her own favorite needlework in hand, from a wicker basket lined with green velvet, Henrietta unfolded a delicate piece of white cutwork. Using only a needle and thread, she continued the intricate process of creating a network of lacey patterns to fill in the cloth she had already cut away. King drew a chair forward to sit beside her as the strains of Angel's harp floated throughout the long chamber. Any piece of music Angel found especially pleasing, she easily converted to her harp and was now rippling through a portion of *The Four Seasons*, by Vivaldi. Charlotte, seated before the pianoforte, struggled to match Angel's pace and feeling as she played a complicated accompaniment Angel had composed for the piece. Charlotte's difficulty was enhanced by the fact that by the end of every page, she found it necessary to drop the notes of the right hand in order to push her spectacles back up on the bridge of her nose.

"This is very comfortable," King mused, his brow knit slightly as though trying to comprehend why he was content.

Henrietta glanced up at him from her whitework. "This is not precisely in your usual mode, is it, Brandish?"

"Not by half!" he exclaimed, laughing. He then turned to look at her. Lowering his voice, he said, "Do you realize this is the first I've seen you in an entire sennight? *A mere whisper of time, yet an eternity!*"

Henrietta returned his gaze, smiling. "You have a poetical turn to your speech," she cried. "How many hearts, I wonder, have you invaded with your pretty words?"

"Not as many as I could wish for!" he retorted easily.

Henrietta laughed aloud. "The daring speech of a

184

confirmed rogue!" she cried. "I should have expected you to answer thusly!"

"If you are disappointed, then you should not have asked such a silly question in the first place."

Henrietta smiled, enjoying their discourse a great deal too much for her comfort. She returned therefore to concentrating carefully upon her cutwork.

When the younger ladies had grown fatigued from their energetic performances, they quit their stations, flexing their fingers and discussing the various points at which Charlotte lost her place in trying to keep up with Angel.

The latter eventually sat with Henrietta and soon began to droop, leaning her head against her sister's shoulder. Miss Brandish suggested she retire to bed, and with an apology for being so dull this evening, Angel curtsied to her host and hostess and quit the room. Charlotte joined her soon afterward.

When they were gone, Lord Ennersley offered the ladies some ratafia and for himself and his son, brandy. Mrs. Leighton accepted her glass gratefully but continued her argument with the viscount regarding the size of the ballroom, as well as the attendant receiving rooms, and how many guests she believed they would hold comfortably. To Henrietta, it almost seemed an excuse to continue addressing one another in what was nearly a *tête-à-tête*. After a moment, Ennersley, with pointed looks directed toward both Mrs. Leighton and Miss Brandish, suggested the three of them repair to the ballroom and discuss the matter at length. Once there, they would have the proportions before them. He was convinced only then that they could come to an agreement.

Miss Brandish refused to go, but Ennersley was not to be put off so easily and soon had his sister marching in the direction of the stairs where they would descend to the ground floor where the ballroom was situated at the back of the house. Mrs. Leighton hung back slightly. She seemed unwilling to leave the drawing room as she

185

glanced back at Henrietta, a worried frown between her brows when she glanced from her daughter to Brandish and back again. When she begged Henrietta to join them, Ennersley cried, "I won't have one more female along to bulwark your opinions! No, no, Mrs. Leighton, I insist you permit Henrietta to remain here and see if she can't perhaps reform my son instead!" With that, he ushered the ladies firmly from the chamber.

Henrietta was not in the least concerned that anything untoward would happen. What mischief could King conduct, for instance, in the drawing room where any of the servants were apt to appear at any given moment, or to which the elders would undoubtedly return.

In short, she felt very safe. She was not prepared, however, for King rising to his feet abruptly and exclaiming, "Henry, I have just remembered the most amazing thing! Come! It is an artifact my father has owned for a long time. Have you perchance seen the library? The object of which I speak resides therein!"

Henrietta felt the slightest stir of suspicion as she regarded King's enlivened features. But he seemed so genuinely excited about something he wished to share with her that without giving it a great deal of thought, she wove her needle into the fine, linen fabric, folded her cutwork into a tidy square, returned it to her basket, and rose to go with him.

The entire distance to the library was but a few yards across the hall. The door was open, and a soft, yellow light glowed from within the depths of the chamber. Henrietta had been shown the chamber briefly upon her arrival on Wednesday, but she had not had the opportunity of enjoying the room. So late at night, with only a single branch of candles lighting the chamber, she was struck with the old beauty of the book-lined room. The feel was very masculine with several of the chairs as well as the settee covered in a burgundy damask, which to her touch as she stroked the fabric felt smooth and cool.

At the end of the chamber, above the fireplace, a portrait of father and son rested. King could not have been more than fourteen, but even then, she noted, his smile was replete with mischief.

Henrietta turned back to look at him, her brows lifted inquiringly. "The portrait?" she queried, all innocence and naivete.

He clucked at her. "Are you a simpleton, or are you so in love with me that you actually believed that childish ruse—'let me show you something in the library.'" His gaze was wicked as he shut the door firmly behind him and proceeded with astonishing audacity to lock the door.

"Oh!" Henrietta cried, feeling absurd and hopelessly gullible as she watched him cross the room toward her in three long strides. He gathered her up in his strong arms, holding her tightly to his chest.

He did not kiss her at first, but cried, "I have been longing to kiss you since the moment I entered the drawing room this evening. You are prettier than I remembered you even in a sennight past!" His speeches made, he kissed her hard upon the mouth, his lips tasting of warm brandy.

Henrietta giggled at her stupidity, all the while revelling in the feel of his lips bruising her own. Somewhere in the far reaches of her mind, she wondered if her heart, where Brandish was concerned, did not block her rational processes. She was sure of it as she threw her arms about his neck and returned his kisses fully, the length of her body pressed scandalously against his own. She expected to simply enjoy his embraces and the summery feel of his lips upon her own, just as she had in Hampshire. But this time, something more was at work, and she felt both frightened and consumed by the heady fervor mounting between them. She knew her susceptibility to his lovemaking, but in this moment, an odd, unfamiliar sensation burnt brightly at the very center of her soul, then burst into a pulse of shimmering

187

waves that rolled through her body, overtaking her heart first, causing it to beat rapidly. Then the light swept into her breast, diminishing the air in her lungs and causing her breathing to grow shallow and uneven. Finally, it overpowered her mind so that she grew dizzy as he continued to assault her mouth, his tongue taking possession of her.

She pulled back suddenly, stumbling away from him as she whispered, "King, my darling." He appeared in that fraction of a second when they were apart as though he too were driven by a madness beyond his understanding. His blue eyes glittered strangely, his entire body tense as he recaptured her in his arms and bore down on her with all his might, holding her trapped within his arms.

"My God," he cried. "I have never known—" he broke off, taking her lips hostage again as he forced her down onto the settee, wildly claiming her hair, her face, her arms, her breasts, as his hands roved over her and he stretched out fully upon her.

Henrietta felt herself drowning in his embraces. Her intentions to guard her virtue with care, which she had done since her marriage to Frederick, turned to dust as King's passion engulfed her. His mouth still sought her own in a reckless movement, bruising her lips, his hands wanting to encompass every part of her at once.

She was lost, falling deeply within herself as she surrendered to every advance he made against her virtue, the ferocity of his desire drawing forth her own in painfully exquisite waves. She wanted him to take her fully, and she began begging him to do so. She breathed his name between every kiss.

And then, as though a flood of cold water had washed over him, he stopped suddenly, lifting himself off of her, one hand supporting his weight upon the leather covering of the settee.

"I cannot—!" he cried, as though he was in great pain.

"What is it, King?" Henrietta asked, feeling bemused and dazed. "Why do you stop? I have not refused you."

Even as these words tumbled from her lips, some of the madness of the moment dissipated, and the horror of what had almost been accomplished began to beat upon her heart. "What happened?" she cried. "What have we done?"

He drew back from her, sitting for a time at the end of the settee, his elbow on his knee as he supported his head in his hand. He did not speak to her or even look at her for a long moment.

Henrietta was still in such a bewildered state from the harsh ebb and flow of their passion that she pulled herself upright, but tucked her feet in a most unladylike manner beneath her. She faced King, leaning her head against the back of the settee. She could not see him, however, for her vision was blurred with tears, her mind seething with confusion. What had she done, and why had he ceased his advances so abruptly? She comprehended none of it.

After a few minutes, King looked at her, an anxious frown between his brows as he queried softly, "I did not hurt you, did I?"

Henrietta shook her head. "No, of course not! King, I am so sorry; this should not have happened. I don't know what possessed me, for I have led you to believe—" she then squeezed her eyes shut "—even though I have given my word to attend you in Paris." A sudden, intense fear consumed her as she leaned toward him and cried, "Release me from Paris, I beg of you, King! Release me from this lunacy! With all my heart, I beg you to cease torturing me with your kisses—"

"*I* release *you!*" he cried. Rising to his feet, his face was drawn with anger as he continued, "I will release you from nothing! Paris is a debt of honor you owe me. You enjoined in the wager for your own reasons. I forced you to do nothing!"

He began pacing the library, running a wild hand through his black locks. His speech rambled as he cried, "I shan't release you! I cannot release you. What mysteries? What devilment have you worked?" Finally, he turned toward her and finished with "Well, I won't have it, Henry! You may work all your schemes out upon Angel, but you will not torment me with your charms and machinations. I will not have my world turned upside down because for some reason the sweetness of your lips takes hold of my heart and strangles me. I'll not marry you! Do you understand? I never promised you marriage, and you owe me Paris!"

Then he was gone.

Chapter Twenty-Three

King left his father's town house in a towering passion, a state he could not comprehend at all. He was angry, but at what? At whom? The answers did not come, and he had the worst impression that his fine, simple world had just been cut up into neat little pieces and flung in his face. He felt as though the gods had been creating exotic potions over the past sennight and that they had decided the moment he was alone with Henrietta, they would pour out their libations upon his head for the purpose of tearing up his heart and destroying his peace. Henrietta's kisses had burnt some mysterious place in his soul, like Psyche's hot oil as it splashed onto Eros's unprotected skin.

As he passed through the entrance hall, grabbing his hat, gloves and cane from a startled footman—caught dozing by the front door—he did not stop to bid his parent or his aunt good-bye. He would send a note on the morrow begging forgiveness for his rude conduct, but he supposed that once Henrietta informed her mother of his lascivious advances, he would be forbidden to return to the town house—Angel's coming out ball notwithstanding!

The footman opened the door, hastily adjusting his powdered wig and bowing obsequiously. The cold night air swept over Brandish as he hurried across the threshold, ignoring the servant, and pressing his hat angrily down on his head. He pulled his gloves on with such vehemence that he split the seam of his right thumb and cursed it roundly. Across the square, a fete was in progress, the windows of the town house spilling an ocean of light onto the flagways from all three floors. He could hear the faint sounds of laughter, music and conversation, and he swore a plague down upon the heads of everyone who dared to enjoy the evening when he was in high dudgeon.

A curricle, bearing two bosky souls, bore down upon him as he stepped out into the street. He quickly leapt back as the gentleman drew rein, cursing him soundly until one of them recognized him.

"By all that's wonderful, it's King! Whatever are you doing in London? Thought you was ruralizing."

"The *King?* Must be mistaken!" his friend cried, glancing wildly about, searching for His Majesty, King George III.

"No, you sapskull! Brandish. King Brandish. What ho?" His speech was slurred as he sloppily drew his horses to a halt.

King slapped his cane on the stone flags and scowled at Farley. "What are you doing?" he cried. "Only you, a whipster of the meanest order, would tool his matched bays about London, fit to go! You'll ruin their mouths, you damned brute." He then went to the horses' heads and stroked the leader's forehead and face.

"No need to fly into the boughs!" he retorted, injured at King's fierce blasting of his driving skill. Hugh Farley was a good-natured, large-framed buck with hamlike hands and a friendly smile. "Say, I'm not so foxed that I don't know when you're in a temper. Fanny break your heart and refuse you?" he queried, laughing.

Ordinarily the mere mention of Fanny's name was enough to provoke a sharp retort. The entire *beau monde* was not unaware that his relations and Mrs. Kempshott had been forcing her upon him for the past month. But this time, King felt an odd lifting of his spirits. "Fanny?" he asked. "Is she here?"

The second gentleman, whom King recognized as Lord Wolverton, joined the conversation. "Just danced with her at old Warnborough's ball." He jerked his thumb backward toward the blazing lights of the town house across the square. "In fine mettle, too—"

"Warnborough?" Farley asked his friend, bemused.

"No," Wolverton exclaimed, looking at Hugh as though he were mad. "That old buffleheaded clunch! I am speaking of Fanny! Never seen her so lively." He glanced at Brandish and continued, "Thought you was going to offer for her, but when I asked her if she was to become your wife, she said she had no intention whatsoever of marrying King Brandish! Could only presume she'd refused you, what!"

"I didn't offer for her," Brandish said.

Lord Wolverton appeared astonished. "Why else would you go to a curst dull place like Broadhorn?"

King gave the horse a final pat and responded absently, "Why, indeed."

He remained conversing with his acquaintances for a few minutes and, upon an impulse, bade them good night and walked across the square.

If Lord Warnborough's butler lifted his brow curiously to this late arrival, he gave no other indication that he found it odd that King Brandish—Viscount Ennersley's son and heir to a large fortune!—should appear suddenly, without having been invited to his master's ball. He had not been serving amongst the *ton* for thirty years without knowing when such a breach of etiquette was to be ignored and when it was not. He was quite certain that if he turned the Leader of Fashion away from Lady Warnborough's door, he would be summarily dismissed within the hour—and that without a reference!

King did not give a moment's thought to his conduct. He had but one purpose as he greeted his friends and acquaintances: to find Fanny. As he strolled through receiving rooms, antechambers and hallways, his spirits rose steadily. The moment Farley had mentioned her name, he knew she was precisely what he needed to calm his sorely exacerbated sensibilities. Fanny was coolly elegant and restful. And though he had enjoyed kissing her, *she* certainly did not fill his mind and heart full of *mysteries!* Good God, he wanted nothing to do with Henrietta, except for the pleasures a brief sennight in Paris would bring.

He found Fanny surrounded by beaux. He did not hesitate, even through her sweetly arch protests, to lead her out for a set, a country dance, infuriating all of the men present. She quickly forgave him, however, confessing that she had been unable to decide, at that very moment, which of two gentlemen to bestow her hand upon for the forthcoming dance. One of them was doomed to disappointment, and she could not bear the thought of inflicting such unhappiness upon the poor fellow. King responded in kind saying that it was very fortunate, then, that he arrived to settle the matter for her. She trilled her laughter, a sound that comforted him in his distress.

She blushed prettily as he complimented her half-robe of amethyst-colored cambric and slippers of the same deep shade. When he remarked that the weather was remarkably cool, she agreed, with a smile. He teased her about having so many eligible gentlemen bounding about her heels, and she inclined her head graciously, saying that she was fortunate to have a great many friends in London. She danced precisely and quietly, not missing a single step. Her conversation was agreeable, her countenance poised, and when he teased her about having stolen a kiss from her in Hampshire, she requested he forget entirely about it, while squeezing his hand as they came together during the course of the dance. He smiled, his heart at ease again, his spirits calm.

In short, the dance they went down was as familiar as it was safe.

Chapter Twenty-Four

"Courage, my dear!" Mrs. Leighton whispered to her eldest daughter, holding her arm tightly. "And remember, not only has it been six years since your dear Frederick perished, but everyone will be watching Brandish and Angel—this you must admit is true!"

Henrietta gripped her mother's arm, grateful for her encouragement. The Leighton ladies, Brandish, Lord Ennersley and Miss Brandish formed an awesome procession as they entered the King's Theater in the Haymarket and progressed toward Ennersley's box. The throng of opera and ballet patrons seemed to part like the Red Sea at Moses's command—only this time it was Brandish's quizzing glass that magically performed the feat as he held it to his eye and scanned the various personages present.

When Henrietta had seen Brandish for the first time since he had fled the library on the evening before, she knew at once that something terrible was wrong. He was neither penitent for having deserted her, nor happy to see her again, nor did he appear at all confused or distressed. He was simply cold. And even when she had taken him aside and begged him to speak to her, to forgive her, to rail at her if he wished, but not to be angrily silent with her, he merely stated that he rather thought theirs should be a formal acquaintance only. Henrietta knew this was wise, but her heart rebelled as he strolled easily away from her to chat in a lively manner with Betsy. She longed to call him back to her side and to ask him what fiendish thoughts had hardened his heart to her.

Henrietta watched him now, his black hair just brushing the top of his neckcloth. His head bowed to an acquaintance, and when Henrietta turned to see who it was, she was stunned to find Fanny Marshfield smiling at him with a mischievously adoring expression on her face. Henrietta felt as though someone had just hit her very hard in the stomach. Fanny Marshfield. She knew instinctively that Fate was marching steadily forward, regardless of her wishes. Fanny meant to marry King, and she might just succeed.

As they entered the viscount's box, Henrietta hung well back, as far into the shadows as she possibly could. She and Lord Ennersley had argued bitterly over her attendance at the opera. She had insisted that far from aiding her sisters in her scheme to see them well settled, her own presence would do considerable harm. Ennersley told her she was speaking like a schoolroom miss. "And anyone who would accuse you of wrongdoing in such a case is a simpleton with more hair than wit!" Henrietta longed to point out that his sister, Lady Ramsdean, held such an opinion, but she bit her tongue and instead tried to persuade him to permit her to remain at home where she insisted she would be perfectly content.

Lord Ennersley had finally won the day when he informed her that if she did not attend the season's gaieties, he would permit none of the ladies to enjoy his or his son's auspices.

Therefore, she sat stiffly upon a chair at the back of the box, believing every eye directed toward her was a critical one.

During the first intermission, the box swarmed with people, from Ennersley's acquaintance, to young gentlemen desirous of being introduced to Angel. The acknowledged Beauty of the Leighton clan was dressed entirely in white and silver and appeared as beautiful as her name inferred. She smiled prettily, treating peers and the lowliest country squire's son with equal grace as each fawned over her well-shaped hand which she extended forward to all in warm greeting. She won instant approval from the few ladies and mothers who made her acquaintance, when she ignored their sons' excited interest. It was already understood that Angel Leighton was an impoverished country miss whom Augusta Brandish hoped to marry off to one of the season's wealthy bachelors.

The several acquaintances of Ennersley's to whom Henrietta received an introduction, and who seemed to comprehend that she was Freddy Harte's widow, failed to express the horrendous aversion Henrietta feared they would experience upon learning of her identity. By the second intermission, she had actually relaxed sufficiently to chat easily with Miss Brandish, who had pulled forward a chair to sit beside her.

The spinster, who wore a delicate peach silk turban slanted at a charming angle over her soft white curls, fanned herself gently and in a low voice said, "You look uncommonly pale, Henry!" She had quickly grown accustomed to Henrietta's nickname and made liberal use of it. "I also noticed that my nephew scarcely smiled at you when he arrived this evening. I was struck with how markedly different his conduct toward you was tonight as compared with last night." She turned to gaze at Henrietta and lifted her softly arched brows, hoping for a response. Politeness prevented her from asking a more direct question.

Henrietta breathed deeply, wondering how much she ought to say to the elderly woman. When another young gentleman squeezed by them, bumping Miss Brandish's shoulder in an effort to gain access to Angel, Henry suggested they change seats.

"Nonsense! I am not so old that I cannot tolerate a

little social shoving!" Augusta laughed lightly, then added, "Only do tell me a little of what has happened between you and my nephew, and put me out of at least some of my misery. I am all agog to know what has caused Brandish to poker up so horridly! Why, his expression was so stiff when he greeted you in the drawing room that I thought his face might crack!"

Henrietta sighed. "We quarreled, though I am not certain over what. I daresay, however, that it is for the best!"

Miss Brandish nodded. "Perhaps so. But for a moment last night, even though I still believe I gave you the very best of advice, I thought that I detected in Brandish some little spark of interest in you that I had never seen before—not even in that gypsy-like creature of last season, with lashes as long as one of the feathers on my embroidered peacock. My, my, what an exquisite female she was. She married a duke however, but not before Brandish had grown bored with her and began flirting with that widow—you know, the one he smiled at earlier—the doe-eyed girl with the cold heart."

"Fanny Marshfield," Henrietta responded quietly, almost to herself.

"Yes. Precisely. Now, what is all that racket about?" A humming noise, as of a great number of people whispering excitedly to one another, rose from behind the box, and it was clear that a personage of some distinction was approaching.

"Whoever could it be!" Henrietta exclaimed.

Miss Brandish remained silent until an elegant gentleman with a kind face and a large nose stood at the threshold of the box. He was dressed to perfection in white satin knee breeches, a black coat and a white waistcoat. Henrietta could see an exquisite diamond pin tucked within the folds of his neckcloth. Several fobs and seals dangled from his waist, and he held in his hand a unique cane. Because Henrietta was seated, she could see the cane clearly and noted that the handle had been molded in the shape of a rabbit, a gold rabbit.

Miss Brandish leaned over to her and behind her fan whispered, "It is 'Golden Hare' Phillips! What a triumph! Charles will be infinitely pleased!"

Lord Ennersley rose at once and greeted the most recent arrival to his box. Spectators in the surrounding boxes leaned forward, gasped and buzzed with excitement. Speculation of all manner rose to the lofty ceiling of the horseshoe-shaped theater, and it was wondered by all—would Angel Leighton capture the grandest prize on the Marriage Mart and win Golden Hare Phillips! He was a somewhat reclusive gentleman of immense fortune and was reputed to be the wealthiest man in all of England.

Henrietta was stunned as she watched Golden Hare bow over her sister's hand. Angel nodded politely upon him, greeting him precisely as she had addressed all the others, as though he was of no particular interest to her, much to Ennersley's amusement. Henrietta also found a ripple of laughter tickling her throat, for the truth was, Angel's evenness of spirits in meeting the wealthy man stemmed not from great composure in the face of grandiosity, but rather from her featherheaded intelligence which was simply incapable of discerning a wealthy man from a poor one.

But whatever the source of Angel's display of excellent breeding, Golden Hare was clearly smitten by her loveliness. He remained speaking with her until the orchestra members had again taken their instruments in hand. Only then did he quit the viscount's box, taking a last lingering look at the Beauty before passing into the hallway beyond.

Angel's success, even before her official come-out ball, was now assured.

Angel stared blankly out at the audience. Her gaze drifted aimlessly for a time until it lit upon the dandies parading about in the pit, chatting noisily to one another

199

and seeming to compete with the orchestra. They were curious creatures, who wore lavender satin coats, yellow breeches, enormous quizzing glasses and their hair pomaded and gleaming with a generous quantity of oil. They looked like clowns to Angel, funny little clowns, their waists nipped in tightly, an absurd contrast to their heavily padded shoulders and chests. She watched them wearily, wishing they would be quiet so that she might better enjoy the music. She stifled a great big sigh, her heart feeling weighted clear to the ends of her delicate white slippers which were embroidered with fancy seed pearls. She felt the way these men in the pit looked—ridiculous. She longed for her comfortable muslin gowns and well-worn half-boots. She wanted her supply of heavy parchment paper that she might continue composing music for the pianoforte and harp; she desired intensely to be back at Fair Oaks where everything was familiar and she knew how to find her bedchamber easily. She had gotten lost in Ennersley's town house no fewer than five times since their arrival on Wednesday, and even once walked mistakenly into Miss Brandish's chamber while she was dressing for dinner! She had been mortified beyond words and had not been able to even look at her hostess for the rest of the day.

She felt her lower lip begin to tremble, and she quickly brushed away several tears. Sensing a hand upon her arm, she looked up at Mr. Brandish, who regarded her from concerned blue eyes as he squeezed her arm gently.

"Are you well, Angel?" he asked, leaning close to her.

His obvious sympathy was almost her undoing. She nodded, her throat choked with tears, and smiled bravely. "It is only that I—I am not used to town life, yet," she responded in a whisper. "Everything is so confusing. Do you know how to get back to the town house? I don't even know the direction!"

He assured her that he did, giving her arm a comforting pat, and Angel felt at least some relief. From the moment they had left Ennersley's home heading toward the opera house, she had experienced the worst qualms that they would never be able to find their way back to the enormous square in which the viscount resided. She couldn't even remember the names of the streets!

And she had met so many new faces that she would never be able to remember any of them, except perhaps the last gentleman with the large nose whom she had taken in strong aversion because he jingled when he walked. The seals dangling at his waist clinked together, and she despised the sound. Beyond that, he was a big man, and his sheer size frightened her. She hoped desperately that Henrietta would not make her dance with him should he attend her come-out ball.

Angel glanced back at her sister and wished more than anything that she had not permitted Henry to persuade her to come to London. She was not strong like Henrietta or Arabella or even Charlotte! She tried to tell them it was a mistake, but both Henry and Charlotte had seemed so desperate. She knew she was useless when it came to matters of the heart and that she would never be able to find a husband as they wanted her to. Most men bored her to tears with their idle chatter of horses, soirees and government. But how could she have refused her beloved sisters? The only thing she hoped for was that one of them would find a husband instead. And when that happened, she meant to beg them to return her to Fair Oaks.

As she returned her gaze to the stage, a famous songstress by the name of Catalani again took possession of most of the audience save the clowns in the pit. This was at least one consolation: The evening's music soothed much of the ache in her soul.

But, oh, how she hated London!

Chapter Twenty-Five

Henrietta measured each day by the waning light of the afternoon as it began violating the drawing room windows. She did not know upon which day precisely she had begun this ritual, but she rather thought it had occurred on Sunday, following the opera. As each afternoon advanced, she found herself turning again and again toward the windows, observing the placement of light in order to determine the hour of the day. She knew that had she turned toward the clock as frequently as she glanced at the light now shaping itself on the blue carpet, someone would have surely noticed her odd fixation on time. As it was, she felt safe in her obsessive rite.

By Wednesday, she had discovered that if the sun was not obscured by clouds, she knew the fashionable hour of five o'clock had arrived when the golden beams streamed through the west windows and struck a gold automaton. By Thursday, she comprehended that if clouds overlay the city of London, and the hour had arrived, it was at the precise moment when the long, blue chamber grew just dark enough to obscure the words of a book—if one were trying to read. Not that Henrietta was capable of reading, or doing anything else of a substantial nature at this time of day. Generally, her nerves were so rattled that if she had opened a book to read, she found the sentences jumping about before her eyes until she grew dizzy. She could not concentrate on a book, nor on her whitework, nor even upon a conversation. Miss Brandish had found it necesssary on at least two separate occasions, to ask whether or not Henrietta was feeling well.

Henrietta did not care overly much that when the clocks struck five the *beau monde* would soon join ranks to descend like a grand flurry of snow geese upon Hyde Park. No, she had another reason for finding the hour intolerable, one that increasingly distressed her as the days of the week climbed over one another. And now, on Friday, as she sat in the drawing room threading her needle with fingers that trembled slightly, her gaze moved frequently to the gleaming mahogany table, upon which the gold automaton sat encased in a glass jar. The sunlight was on the table already and shone on the gold rim of the base. In the drawing room, Angel stood by the white lace underdrapes, fingering them absently as she glanced down into the street. She was dressed to perfection in a carriage gown of amber silk. Over her guinea curls, she wore a poke bonnet trimmed with a single white ostrich plume and tied beneath her chin with a pale blue ribbon. Dangling from her gloved hands was a beaded reticule Henrietta recognized as one she had made for Angel last summer.

A carriage was heard on the drive, and Henrietta's heart plummeted to her feet as Angel turned back toward her slightly. "Brandish is arrived, Henry," she stated flatly. "I wish you would accompany us. I am afraid Mr. Brandish is exceedingly bored in my company. Though he never says so, he merely stares between his horse's ears whenever the carriage is moving—which is not frequently now that I think on it. The drive could be accomplished in half the time were we not besieged by gentlemen demanding to know how his matched grays fared since the accident! Everyone is so extremely solicitous!"

Henrietta stared at her sister, astonished as she always was that Angel did not realize the attention was all for her and not for Brandish's horses.

Returning her gaze to her needle and the two pinpricks she had already left upon her fingers as she fumbled with the business at hand, she responded quietly, "It is far better that I remain here."

Angel crossed the drawing room to stand in front of Henrietta. "What are you hiding from?" she queried.

Henrietta looked up at her swiftly, jabbing the needle yet again into her skin. She gave a cry and sucked her finger quickly before the blood that had welled upon her skin could stain her whitework. Angel's question startled her not only because it represented those rare moments of her sister's when she was peculiarly perceptive, but because it was disastrously true. She knew a strong desire to prevaricate or to deny her feelings entirely. Instead, she spoke slowly. "You know that my marriage to Freddy had unfortunate consequences and I do not like to put myself forward where others might sneer or scorn my family because of the scandal that followed his death."

Angel fluffed the blue bow beneath her chin and retorted, "I think that's all humbug, Henry, I do! Since we arrived in London, I have only heard Lady Ramsdean complain about your marriage, and even then, Sally Jersey snubbed her at Almack's for speaking such nonsense! And Brandish says you are foolish beyond permission to believe the *ton* so unforgiving!"

"He said as much to you?"

Angel nodded, then asked, "Why do you not like Mr. Brandish? He is very kind and agreeable, but you scarcely speak to him anymore. I have noted as much whenever you are in company with him. And he seems uncommonly white-lipped when he is near you."

"I believe he is very angry with me of the moment," Henrietta replied quietly.

"Why?"

"I don't know."

The door opened, and the butler announced King's arrival. Angel, who stood between Henrietta and King,

204

stepped aside to remove herself from her sister's line of vision. When Brandish came into view, Henrietta felt yet again that peculiar tugging sensation that always assailed her when she but looked upon King Brandish. Some part of her cried out to him, and she felt herself lean forward slightly in her chair as she met his gaze. He was dressed in buckskin breeches, Hessians, a dark blue coat and a neckcloth arranged carefully in a mode known as *trone d' amour*. His appearance was neat and elegant, and as he entered his father's drawing room, he bowed stiffly to her then toward Angel. It was true that they scarcely spoke beyond the necessary pleasantries, but Henrietta still did not know the source of King's anger. He had been white-lipped indeed.

Angel turned toward Henrietta and opened her eyes wide as though an intriguing notion had just struck her. "Betsy told me you were—" she broke off suddenly, then pressed her hand to her cheek. Whirling back to Brandish, she cried, "Oh, I do beg your pardon, but I have just realized I forgot my gloves!"

King looked at Angel's hand still held to her smooth cheek and, with a surprised expression in his blue eyes, exclaimed, "You are wearing your gloves, are you not, my dear?" He had become well acquainted with Angel over the past sennight since he had taken it upon himself to escort her daily to Hyde Park and had come to see her as a dear younger sister over whom he had spread his mantle of protection. Henrietta had even heard him warning her against a number of gentlemen who were wont to cling to her hand at Hyde and who had dared to suggest waltzing with her at Almack's when she had not been approved by one of the patronesses to do so.

Angel held her hand out before her and blinked rapidly as she gazed upon her elegant lavender gloves. She began shaking her head firmly as she cried, "Not these gloves! These won't do at all! Forgive me, Mr. Brandish, but I must find my—my gloves of York tan!" With that she breezed quickly from the room, like a sudden whirlwind that catches up autumn leaves in its wake.

Brandish bowed to Angel as she closed the door behind her, his expression stunned as he turned back to regard Henrietta.

King Brandish had never experienced such a tearing of emotions as he did now, left quite alone with Henrietta. He had been deliberately ignoring her, speaking to her only when it was absolutely necessary and in all other respects, shutting his heart off from her. In response, she was coolly polite, though on more than one occasion he had known she was watching him. In the past, when he had chosen to ignore a female, he had always found it an easy matter. But walking by Henrietta without speaking to her always felt like he was swimming against a strong current. Several times he had been tempted to address her; but then he would remember the library, and he would set aside these strange promptings and continue on his way.

But here he was now, looking at her, trying to hold his heart in check.

"King," she called to him across the chamber. "Whatever is the matter! How have I offended you? Why are you so angry with me? Even Angel knows something is amiss."

He shook his head, feeling bewildered. "I am not angry," he said quietly. "That is, I am aggravated that Angel must suffer because of your—"

"Suffer?" Henrietta cried. "Whatever do you mean?"

King raised a brow. "Are you so blind to her, Henry, that you cannot see she is miserable? Her politeness to the gentlemen who flock about her at Hyde emanates solely from duty, not from any interest or desire in doing the pretty. Once, she yawned behind her glove when poor Golden Hare was teasing her about her being as pretty as a snowdrop. I have never seen him so discomposed—" he laughed suddenly—"though I must admit it was worth witnessing his consternation. Of course you will be pleased to know that he has since doubled his efforts to try and fix his interest with her. He is a considerable patron of the arts and would no doubt enjoy adding her beauty to his vast collection."

Henrietta knew the worst sinking sensation in her heart as she glanced down at the whitework sitting upon her lap.

"Indeed," Henrietta responded. "I am not unaware that he has begun to pursue her mightily. Flowers arrive thrice daily now with his calling card."

Brandish seemed to relax as he approached Henrietta, who sat on a settee near the fireplace. He drew a chair forward to sit beside her, his expression thoughtful. "I caught her shedding tears at the opera."

"No!" Henrietta cried as she lifted her gaze to meet Brandish's. "You must be mistaken. She—she was undoubtedly moved by the music, or—or Catalani's exquisite voice. Angel is a remarkable musician, you know! You have heard her perform."

He levelled his gaze at her. "London frightens her, Henry! She is little more than a child emotionally or mentally—a child with an amazing talent, as you say, but wholly unsuited for this mode of existence. I daresay she longs desperately to be back at Fair Oaks."

"But she cannot return to the manor," Henrietta murmured. Oh, why was life so complicated, and why did Brandish have to speak so sensibly, his words drawing back a protective veil from her mind. Angel was not happy; King had spoken the truth. "I know," she said, sighing deeply. "I had hoped that somehow Angel would adjust to life here, that she would become content, or that some young gentleman might perhaps capture her heart! Instead, as the days have progressed, I have watched her draw inward, and I fear for her. It was foolishness to have thought she would find a husband. Perhaps, given time, she could have been introduced slowly to the *beau monde*—" Her gaze was fixed away from King, upon the empty hearth.

King watched Henrietta, her large blue eyes filled with

concern. He knew a desire to hold her, to comfort her. His father had forced him to see the extent of the difficulties Henrietta faced, and ever since then, he could not look upon her without thinking how much he admired her strength. She had spoken several times about her intention of becoming a housekeeper once she saw her family settled. A housekeeper! It was unthinkable. This elegant creature, this beautiful woman with fire that flowed through every vein, into every reach of her person, who would have succumbed so easily to his embraces through no calculation of her own.

He took her hand, clasping it firmly within his own, and she glanced at him, startled. He eased himself out of his chair to sit beside her, still holding her hand. "Let Angel go, Henry," he said, falling into the depths of her eyes as he regarded her evenly. He felt a familiar desire take hold of his heart, constricting his chest, dragging him into a current of longing he did not comprehend.

Squeezing her hand hard, he whispered, "Why is it I cannot even converse with you for but a few seconds, and I find myself wanting desperately to take you in my arms and into my heart, and to hold you there forever. I am perplexed by my feelings for you. I admire you, Henry; I have hated this past sennight devoid of your company and smiles. At the same time—" he broke off, regarding her strangely.

Henrietta caught her breath, his words and the expression on his face searing her heart. "Only tell me why you left me so suddenly in the library," she asked. "You hurt me terribly."

"I did not mean to. I was certain if I stayed, I would hurt you more than if I left. And—and there was something more, something I am reluctant to define—" he broke off as footsteps were heard in the hall.

Without begging her permission, he kissed her full upon the mouth for a long, intense moment, his lips wondrously soft and beckoning. Henrietta felt awash with warmth and contentment as his mouth devoured

208

hers. She had missed him so wretchedly during the past sennight, more than she had realized until this moment. As he pulled away from her, she found herself full of hope for the future. Perhaps, as Betsy had once told her, she had fallen madly in love with Brandish, only she was unwilling to admit the truth. And perhaps, he loved her, too. But what then?

Just as the footsteps paused outside the door, King resumed his seat. He was still facing her as he asked in a whisper, "Will you not release Angel from this heinous path?"

"Tomorrow is her ball," Henrietta responded. "If Angel is still so unhappy, which I am also persuaded she is, I will release her, but on one condition only—" when he lifted a brow, she continued—"that you release me from Paris."

He smiled, nodding in acquiescence. "Of course, it was a foolish wager, and I should never have suggested it."

Angel reentered the room, saying that she could not find her York gloves and that her lavender ones would simply have to do.

Brandish then rose quickly to his feet, greeting Angel again as he took her arm and guided her from the room.

Henrietta rose to cross the formal chamber to the windows where the afternoon light now streamed fully upon her as she looked down into the street below. She watched Brandish help Angel gently into the carriage. He was tender with her, she realized, as though he understood that of all the Leighton ladies, Angel required a delicate touch. With the same comprehension, he knew that Betsy enjoyed a more rollicking manner. King frequently teased her and on one occasion had tickled her until she was laughing hysterically. With Charlotte, he conversed easily on subjects she enjoyed the most: the arts and literature, especially the poetry of an unknown by the name of John Keats.

Long after the curricle was gone, Henrietta remained by the window, feeling the warm sun upon her face, tears smarting her eyes, as she grew to an awareness that Betsy had indeed been right. Without having wished or intended to, Henrietta had tumbled irrevocably in love with King Brandish. Only what would their end be? Would King marry her? The question dimmed the sun's brilliance on her face, and she turned away from the window. Did King even love her, or did she appear to him to be a woman of easy virtue, who would give herself willingly to him without the sanctity of marriage to protect their relationship forever? She felt frightened and humbled by the thought. She had all but thrown herself into his arms once they were locked in the library together—she had all but told him that with the very mildest of persuasions, in short, the most passionate of kisses, he could command her. Yet he had promised her nothing; he had not even said he loved her.

Somehow, with each day that passed, their circumstances had grown steadily worse instead of better. Her own heart had been given to a rogue, and unless a miracle were to occur, tomorrow night, in all good conscience, she must put an end to her schemes regarding her dear sister Angel. In addition, only this morning, Mrs. Leighton had received a tradesman's bill from Madame Louise amounting to nearly four thousand pounds.

The Leighton ladies now had no reliable prospects and had fallen deeply into debt.

Chapter Twenty-Six

King stood at the edge of the ballroom floor, his gaze fixed upon Henrietta as she went down a country dance. He knew a profound jealousy of the man who touched her hand as the steps of the dance brought them together. He wanted no one to touch her, save himself, even in the innocence of a country dance.

He watched her hungrily, the grace of her movements delighting him, the glitter of candlelight on her dark brown hair making promises to him, and the faint smile on her lips when he caught her eye the second time driving an Olympian arrow straight into his heart. He wanted only one thing, for the dance to end, that he might claim Henrietta's hand for a waltz. He wanted to hold her in his arms, and he wanted to blend into the music with her; he wanted to flirt with her and look deeply into her eyes. He wanted to see a blush cover her porcelain cheeks when he reminded her of the many times he had kissed her. Then he wanted to tease her by begging for another kiss as soon as the last guest had quit the Ennersley town house. He felt his heart grow tight at the mere thought of being with her again. He may not feel prepared to offer her his hand in marriage, but he wished more than anything to give her every security within his power, to release her from the burden of her impoverished state.

The music ended, and he did not hesitate to enter the crush of dancers leaving the floor, nor to take possession of Henrietta's arm, much to her partner's dismay and high-pitched protests. King ignored him as he gazed down into Henrietta's eyes. He felt impassioned by the mere sight of her as he possessed himself of her hand. It was all he could do to keep from lifting her fingers to his lips and kissing each of them in turn. He asked her to dance the waltz with him instead, though he promised her he meant to hold her as close as he could without causing a desperate scandal.

Henrietta inclined her head. "I should like it above all things, Mr. Brandish." She smiled as she spoke, teasing him with the use of his formal name, her eyes shimmering in the candlelight. "And you may cause as much of a scandal this evening as you like. I feel very brazen and foolish of a sudden."

"My hapless influence, no doubt."

Henrietta shook her head. "No," she cried with a smile. "It is my own hopeless flaw. I blame no one but myself for my propensity to enjoy dancing with rogues."

"We are a matched pair."

He held her tightly, one hand pressed upon the small of her back, the other cradling her hand gently. The moment he drew her into the whirling pattern of the dance, he knew an ease between them that he had not known with any female before. They moved as one, gliding effortlessly about the floor.

"I love you," he said after a time. The dancers about them blurred into a pattern of glittering color as he watched Henrietta intently. "I have loved you since I kissed you in the dell. My darling, why do you cry?"

"Stupid," Henrietta whispered. "My heart is too full of the moment, and you shouldn't be saying such things to me now when I can do no more to express my sentiments than become a watering pot. Oh, King, I had hoped. I had dared to hope, but I didn't think—"

He smiled, his heart aching as he gazed down into her brimming eyes. A tear trickled down her cheek, and he repressed a desire to kiss it away. "I want to possess you," he whispered. "If we were alone, I would. I would not hesitate. I have thought of little else since I spoke with you yesterday, indeed, since I first met you. But you stole my heart as well, Henry, besides having driven me to the point of madness every time I so much as looked at you. Your *flaw* be hanged. I bless you for it!"

Mrs. Leighton sat upon a blue satin-damask chair across from both Lady Ramsdean and Mrs. Kempshott and every now and again nodded politely as though she were listening to everything the ladies had to say to one another. She hoped her expression was pleasant enough, for the truth be known, she felt unreliable suddenly, as though if someone spoke to her in the wrong manner, she might let out a terrific yell. The very thought of it frightened her, but she had been feeling this way since the late afternoon when she had last spoken with Ennersley.

It was a curious thing about men, she thought, how quickly they grew to both depend upon a good woman and to take serious advantage of her at the same time. The moment she had arrived in Grosvenor Square, she had fallen quite easily into a pleasant camaraderie with Lord Ennersley, a fellowship she had never known with her poor, late husband. Henry Leighton had been a cold man emotionally, not one to discuss any matters of import with her, and she had been left, upon his death, not only penniless but rather indifferent to her marriage. She had shed tears only once after he was buried in the churchyard, and they were not tears of grief but of fear that she had lost her ability to feel anything for a man ever again.

But when Ennersley so abruptly charged into her life and overset her vulnerable heart with his dashing good looks and breathtaking blue eyes, she knew her condition had been a result of an impoverished relationship, not a defective soul. However, she had not meant to fall in love with Ennersley, not by half! But that was precisely what she had done. It just seemed to happen all by itself, and by the time they had argued over, planned, organized and otherwise delighted in shaping Angel's come-out ball, she knew her heart was given to the viscount. In addition, she had taken to providing him with any number of services commonly relegated to the arena of wifely duty, and she had done so out of love and affection. Every night she prepared him a potion—which only she and his cook knew about—which was designed to strengthen his injured arm. In the mornings, she discussed with him various articles from *The Times* and *The Morning Post*, and more than once he had expressed his sincere pleasure in her company. In the evenings, when her daughters had all retired to bed, she would read to him from the Psalms. And yesterday afternoon she had actually made a special trip to Berry Brothers in order to procure for him his favorite mix of snuff! She had expected him to praise her for her thoughtfulness or to at least thank her, instead he nodded absently and instructed her to take it to his office.

She had stood upon the threshold of the morning room, where he was enjoying a cup of tea, and stared at him for a full minute. When he asked if anything was wrong and did she know where the office was located, she had merely nodded dumbly and quit the room, not to see him again until the family met in the drawing room for dinner.

She had dressed with great care, in hopes of impressing him with her femininity; she had even worn her hair in the manner he seemed to favor the most, but all to little avail. His treatment of her was friendly, and even a trifle autocratic when he directed her to trim the candle at his shoulder. Otherwise his behavior lacked anything bordering on *interest*. How quickly he had come to see her as his servant rather than as a woman!

Her disquiet had increased throughout the evening when she waited with each passing hour for Ennersley to ask her to dance. But it was not until he had led Sally

Jersey out for the waltz, did she actually believe that he had no intention of doing so. It was at this time that she decided to retire to the drawing room, where she settled herself beside Lady Ramsdean and pretended to be interested in her ever-flowing discourse on the proper modes of conduct necessary for the perfect functioning of society.

At least Angel's success was now assured, for nothing had been more astonishing than the flood of guests who inundated Grosvenor Square for her daughter's ball. Mrs. Leighton smiled softly to herself. Golden Hare Phillips had been one of the first arrivals, and had even begged Angel for one of her first dances. She sighed dreamily. If he were to offer for her dearest, most beautiful daughter, all would be settled, not only for Angel, but for the rest of her girls as well.

"You look different tonight, Miss Charlotte!" Golden Hare cried. "Though I confess I do not know how to account for it. You are always impeccably gowned and coiffed, yet there is something more about your expression, perhaps! Have you perchance tumbled in love with one of our fine, eligible young gentlemen?" He swept an arm in an elegant arc encompassing the entire ballroom, his smile affectionately polite.

Charlotte blushed slightly as she regarded her sister's most promising beau. She shook her head, indicating he was far off the mark, then resisted an impulse to touch spectacles that did not exist. She had left her round-rimmed glasses purposely in her bedchamber, but she was still unaccustomed to their absence. More than once she had pressed the bridge of her nose, expecting to find her spectacles, and startled when she felt her own skin beneath her finger. "Dare I confess what I have done?" she asked quietly, leaning slightly toward Mr. Phillips.

He seemed a little surprised as he lifted his quizzing glass to his eye and scanned her thoroughly. "No. Say not a word. I shall attempt to discern what you have

215

changed about your costume, or your hair—I believe the answer is simple, and yet—" he squinted at her.

Charlotte smiled, liking his warm, friendly countenance. "You will laugh when you discover it, Mr. Phillips," she teased him. "Very likely you will kick yourself for not having noticed it before!" She fanned herself lightly with a painted fan covered in soft swanskin. She was grateful that he was observing her, for it provided her the unexpected opportunity of gazing at him closely without attracting his notice. From the moment he had entered Lord Ennersley's opera box, a full sennight past, she had been intrigued by Mr. Golden Hare Phillips. There was something purposeful about him that struck a chord within her own heart. And how very much she despised his nickname. It was a coarse reference to his immense wealth and held the most demeaning sound to it. *Golden Hare,* indeed! Over the past few days, Charlotte had had many opportunities to converse with Mr. Phillips and had learned that despite his air of indifference to his nickname, he frequently cringed when someone called out, "Golden Hare." She knew also that he had initially desired to dispense with his cane altogether, once the nickname fell to general use, but upon serious reflection, he concluded he could not. His father had bestowed the elegant walking stick upon him in celebration of having attained his majority, and he did not wish to dispense with an article that held a great deal of significance to him merely because the *haut ton* chose to make sport of him and his fortune. Charlotte honored him for his sentiments and did not hesitate to tell him so. He had seemed inordinately pleased with her opinion and henceforth had made it a point, whilst he was busily courting Angel, to seek Charlotte out, politely inquire after her health, and demand to know her opinion of the weather. Very soon, particularly if Angel was beset with suitors, they would fall deeply into conversation, discussing every manner of intriguing subject from metaphysics to Leigh Hunt's most recent essay in the *Examiner,* to the value of the acquisition of the Elgin

Marbles. Beauty was a frequent theme in their discussions, one that led inexorably back to Angel's face, figure and musical ability.

By the time Angel's ball had arrived, Charlotte understood implicitly Mr. Phillips' love for her sister. He loved Angel because he was devoted to beauty. Not in the manner of the smitten young gentlemen who collected at Angel's feet and read poetry to her, but as an ethereal pursuit which had for years been the predominant force in his life. He collected paintings, statuary, fine porcelain works, elegantly crafted snuffboxes, ancient jars, glass jewelry and bronzed swords. His great country house in Oxfordshire had become a temple in which he housed the beauty he pursued and purchased. Though he never stated his intention flatly, Charlotte knew by the zeal in his eyes when his gaze rested upon Angel that he believed he had found the very female he wanted to preside over the brilliance of his home and his collections.

Only once had Charlotte tried to awaken him to one small flaw in his otherwise harmless desires. At Almack's she had asked him gently whether or not he had ever truly conversed with Angel. He had seemed slightly startled, his brow puckering in confusion as he stammered a response: Of course he had, well, not a lengthy one naturally because she was so besieged by every puppy in London, that is, he knew she was as elegant of speech as she was of person, and he was satisfied with that!

Charlotte had hid her smiles, and now as he regarded her through his quizzing glass, his eyes still narrowed, she watched an expression of enlightenment suffuse his face as he cried, "By Jove, you've left off wearing your spectacles. Well done, Miss Charlotte! You look much prettier, just as I said you would, and how kind of you to honor my suggestion by taking it!"

"There is only one difficulty in following your advice, however."

"And what is that?" he asked briskly, as was his fashion.

"My legs are bruised from bumping into furniture I

217

cannot see!"

He laughed heartily, slapping his knees and begging her to dance the waltz with him. "For I can at least protect you for a short while if you are held in my arms."

These words so innocently spoken caused Charlotte to blush faintly as she thought with a rush of pleasure how delightful such an occurrence would be. As for Mr. Phillips, he regarded her with an odd tilt to his head, his lips parted as though he, too, were considering the possibility for the first time and perhaps found the image equally agreeable. He cleared his throat after a moment and said, "That is, if I were to guide you carefully through the steps of the waltz."

Charlotte, who saw that the numbers were very quickly being made up, rose to her feet with alacrity and cried, "I should like nothing better than to dance with you, but we had better hurry before we are forced to wait out another set. Angel's ball has become a delightfully *sad crush!*"

He gained his feet promptly, took her arm upon his and led her to the floor where he found, much to Charlotte's chagrin, a place directly opposite Angel and her partner, a red-faced youth with large, adoring brown eyes. His attention was soon lost in a rapt perusal of Angel's face whenever the turns of the dance permitted it. Charlotte loved her sister very much, but for the first time in her life, as she glanced up at Mr. Phillips' worshipful expression, she wished Angel hadn't been blessed with quite so much beauty.

Angel's cheeks hurt. She had been smiling for so long, and so hard, that she promised herself once she quit London, she would never smile again. The ball had been in progress for scarcely more than three hours, with several more to follow, and she did not know how she was to bear it. As her partner trod upon her feet yet again, Angel wished she could simply sprout a pair of wings, such as her name suggested, and fly away. She glanced at

218

the young gentleman who was of the moment crushing her hand within his, but this was a wretched mistake, for his face turned redder still as he stammered out first his apology for his clumsiness and then his opinion that she must be a goddess from ancient Greece. She was sick to death of allusions to her beauty, mostly because she did not comprehend half of what was said to her. But she nodded to the young man, just the same, smiling yet again, though she thought it the height of absurdity that he would give all the appearance of being in love with her merely because she was polite!

Glancing away from him, she looked at some of the other dancers and noticed that Mr. Hare, or was it Mr. Goldy, was making a whirling progress about the room with Charlotte in his arms. She was surprised to see her sister laughing, for she could not imagine anyone being amused in Mr. Hare's company. He was so big and spoke at such lengths about his magnificent home that she was frequently overwhelmed by his conversation. She had danced twice with him already, and every time she saw him looking her direction, she feared he meant to ask her for a third set which she was certain would cause her to faint. She did not think she could bear even speaking with him one more time this evening, nonetheless dancing with him.

Still, she smiled.

The waltz seemed interminable, and Angel looked anywhere but upon her partner's face. After a fourth turn about the length of the ballroom floor, she noticed a gentleman whom she had never seen before. He stood scowling upon her, his arms folded across his chest. He seemed angry, and yet since Angel had never even noticed him before, she could not imagine how she had offended him. He was an interesting young man, though, for his hair was quite long and wild in appearance, and his brow was creased with intelligence and mood. He reminded her of one of Bach's more violent fugues which required great strength and agility to play. She looked at him every chance she had and discovered that he, in

219

turn, never took his gaze from her. For the first time in her entire existence, Angel actually found herself intrigued by a man, and she felt the oddest stir in her heart.

When she demanded of her partner to tell her who the gentleman was, he responded with a sneer, "Oh! That fellow claims to be a poet, though I have read a little of his published works, and I find it to be little more than drivel! His name is Wellow—Cornelius Wellow—and his name suits him admirably."

Angel looked at her partner directly, and for the first time that evening she failed to smile. Indeed, she had nothing more to say to a clumsy oaf who would malign a struggling young poet, particularly one so handsome of face!

From that moment she was determined to be made known to Mr. Wellow and accomplished the feat when she begged Miss Brandish to present him to her.

"He is not so much a favorite among our hostesses as you would think," Miss Brandish said, her voice lowered carefully. "Many of the young ladies of gentle birth find him rather harsh, as it happens. His opinions are well known and not greatly admired. It would seem he finds much to dislike in *tonnish* society."

Far from being disappointed by Miss Brandish's warning, her words served to increase her desire to meet the poet. He accepted the introduction with a curt nod of his head, congratulated Angel upon her success, and would have walked away had not Angel stayed him with a request that he escort her to supper. He seemed surprised, but not displeased, as he smiled faintly and said, "How original that *you* should ask *me!* It is not the accepted mode, you know!"

Angel replied, "Are you not hungry? My stomach has been rumbling in protest for the past half hour and more!"

Mr. Wellow lifted a brow, his smile now reaching up to his large, soulful brown eyes. "Truthfully spoken, Miss Angel, in which case, I should be enchanted to escort you to supper. Let it not be said that Cornelius Wellow should suffer a young lady to starve for a lack of formality."

"Is that a foreign dish of some sort? I don't recognize it. *Formality*. It is French, I think."

Mr. Wellow, who had taken Angel's arm and was guiding her toward the entrance hall, looked down at her and cried, "What? Oh—" He laughed aloud, uproariously, but when he saw that Angel's expression was confused, he said, "You spoke a witticism. Do not you see? Formality."

Angel lifted her brows in surprise and cried, "I did! How very amusing. Thank you for saying something to me. If you must know, I don't always—" she broke off, frowning slightly—"that is, I don't have a good sense of the world or the order of things as everyone else does. Words twist around in my head and upon the pages of books, and I see patterns others generally don't. I become lost in big houses. You do not have a big house, do you?"

A look of profound regret overcame his features as he patted her arm gently. "No, I am afraid not."

"How wonderful," she cried, much to his astonishment. "I like you more and more."

"And I you," he exclaimed. "But if I laugh again at something you've said, you are to pay no heed to me. I very frequently find amusement in the oddest things."

"I do too," she responded with a smile that did not hurt. "Frost on the windowpanes in November, for instance, appears like cricket players. I giggle and giggle, and spend hours watching them, but no one seems to understand what I see. Have you never noticed the frost, Mr. Wellow?" She glanced up at him and was stunned by the fierce expression in his brown eyes as he looked down upon her.

"You are my *Frost Queen*," he responded cryptically. "A favorite poem of mine, don't you know. I knew the moment I stepped foot on the flags that the Fates had ushered me forth into the streets. I once saw frost on an early spring turf that looked like netted lace over a fair lady's brow, and I called that lady, the 'frost queen.' Are

221

you my queen?"

They were standing under the archway that led to the ballroom. Various personages passed by them in the dimness of the hall, but Angel saw none of them. She saw only the poet who had shared her enjoyment of something as simple as frost, who had not stared at her blankly when she had spoken of cricket and frost together, whose eyes blazed with a warmth that swept over her. "My dear Mr. Wellow," she breathed, leaning into him slightly as several ladies pushed past them. "I am your queen, indeed, I am sure of it!"

Time was an extreme irritation to Angel. The evening heretofore had felt unending, as though eternity had caught up with her and decided to rest for a long moment. But now, the hour seemed to rush by her as supper hastened to a conclusion and she was separated, for propriety's sake, from her *dear Cornelius*. Already, she was his *beloved Angel*, and he—he was the man she meant to marry. His passion was his poetry, his life devoted to the muse, and he had promised to read her his first two volumes of verse if she wished for it. If she wished for it! She longed for it and begged him to call upon her tomorrow as early as was considered correct. He promised, but hastily quit the ball, unwilling to watch her dance with the score of gentlemen who had already laid claim to her hand.

She was dancing now, within the circle of Mr. Hare's arms, and she did not even mind that it was their third set and that a buzzing of gossip went up about the room at so intriguing a development. As she stared up into his face, she saw not the large nose and somewhat bulbous brown eyes of Golden Hare Phillips, but rather the image of her dear Cornelius.

She sighed deeply. Oh, how she loved London!

Chapter Twenty-Seven

Henrietta watched Angel dance the waltz with Mr. Phillips, and she felt a swell of delight overtake her heart. Angel was smiling at Golden Hare with all the appearance of a young lady who had just fallen desperately in love. She could not credit her eyes! Was this her mopish sister who only that afternoon had been sitting alone in the library staring down into the street, a sad frown marring her exquisite features? Impossible! And to think Angel had actually developed a *tendre* for the wealthiest gentleman in all of England. It was too wonderful, too incredible to be true, and yet she could not deny that Angel wore a beatific expression Henrietta had never seen before. And to think that a few hours alone would find the future altered so easily and so happily.

Yesterday, despondency had ruled Henrietta's spirits. King was not speaking to her, Mrs. Leighton had fallen sadly into debt and Angel was suffering from a terrible fit of the megrims. All of Henrietta's schemes had appeared destined to failure on several fronts, but now, as she watched Mr. Phillips sweep Angel into a delicate whirl about the long, candlelit chamber, she saw an end to all of their trials. She had made peace with Brandish, and if Angel were to bring Mr. Phillips up to scratch, even her mother's debts would pale to insignificance.

Her thoughts turned to King, and she knew an immediate need to inform him of this astonishing twist of Fate. Taking one last glance at Angel, who was still regarding Mr. Phillips with a rapturous expression, she moved swiftly from the ballroom, her blue silk skirts rustling to her brisk steps. For the first time in ages, it seemed, she felt happy and was able to smile and bow to several of her new acquaintances, her heart light as she wended her way throughout the chambers on the ground floor. In none of these rooms, was King to be found, and she quickly crossed the entrance hall to begin mounting the stairs. Her mind filled suddenly with images of the extraordinary dance she had shared with Brandish. How smoothly their steps had flowed together, how safe she had felt in his arms, and how greatly his love had eased every torment from her soul. He loved her, and she was now free to return his ardency. She had hoped to keep him by her side for a little while, that she might hear more of his sentiments; but the claims of society were too great, and Lady Ramsdean had quickly whisked him off to do the pretty with a plain young miss who was in desperate need of a partner for the quadrille. But before he joined his aunt, he had pressed her hand and whispered words that sent a spark neatly through Henrietta's heart. His words came to her now, as she ascended the stairs, *I have something of great significance I must ask you tonight. Do not forget! I must speak with you before you retire for the evening!* As though anything short of cataclysmic occurrence would send her early to her bed! She knew, in the deepest part of her spirit, he meant to offer for her hand in marriage. This, too, was a marvelous thing, that she had actually captured King Brandish's heart. But more to the point, she could now love him openly, admitting even to herself how greatly her affections had long since been given to the rogue. She loved him, desperately! And very soon, they would begin contemplating a life together as husband and wife!

She was teased several times for her absentmindedness as she threaded her way through the guests traversing the stairs, but she did not care. Her only desire was to find King and inform him of the intriguing shift in Angel's heart. She knew he would be greatly pleased by the news that far from disliking Golden Hare Phillips, Angel had tumbled in love with him.

The air of the library was redolent with a mixture of snuff, perfume and fine candles, the latter of which glowed from silver branches and sconces arranged carefully to keep from torching the curls, ribbons and feathers that adorned the ladies' elegant coiffures. The chamber resonated with subdued chatter, emanating from a number of ladies and gentlemen couched within the book-lined chamber. Anyone desirous of conversing quietly, away from the noise and mischief of the ballroom, stole to the library which hummed with elegant conversation punctuated by the occasional burst of laughter that frequently accompanied the anecdote told with great wit and ability.

King sat at a small inlaid table, tucked away in the corner, playing at piquet with Fanny Marshfield. He had not meant to join her in play, but somehow had found himself in the middle of a game before he realized he had even agreed to it! In addition, he discovered that the setting was quietly intimate, even though they were surrounded by other guests, and somewhere in his mind he knew a nagging desire not to have Henrietta find him situated thusly.

However, as he gazed into Fanny's large, brown eyes, which reflected a glittering of candlelight, he knew a slight stir of interest. The expression on her face was decidedly mischievous, her manners perfect, her voice melodious. She was in many ways the sort of female he had envisioned one day marrying. Would he one day offer for Fanny? he wondered.

She was teasing him about his extraordinary good fortune at cards, he responded with an acknowledging

225

nod of his head, then she promptly slayed him with a cry of *repique!* What a playful spirit she had!

Since this cost him the game, she smiled coyly upon him and asked him innocently whether or not he was courageous enough to challenge her again. He could not resist picking up such a gauntlet and immediately took the cards from her.

"And pray tell me how the Leighton ladies are faring in London," she said. "I have longed to know if they will all be married before the season has ended. Mama tells me it is their only hope for surviving the wretched will Mr. Leighton afforded them upon his death."

Her flippant tone jarred him slightly. Shifting in his seat, he responded, "As to their success, Angel's beauty and Charlotte's excellent manners have won them both the admiration of numerous personages of consequence. Henry, that is, Mrs. Harte, too, seems to be enjoying a marked degree of attention which certainly pleases my father, for she is a particular favorite of his. I cannot, however, possibly hazard a guess as to whether or not any of them shall acquire husbands by the end of May. Angel, I believe, longs only to return to Fair Oaks."

"I feel for them acutely," Fanny said, sighing deeply as King dealt the cards. "I cannot imagine the difficulties before them if the season proves fruitless. I, myself, have never cared for the phrase, *marriage mart,* to refer to our annual gatherings in the spring, but in their case—" She let the sentence hang for a long moment. Her voice dropped to a whisper as she changed the subject abruptly. "Brandish," she said, her voice soft. "There is something I have wished to say to you since our last private moment together at Broadhorn. I hope I did not leave you with a false impression or raise expectations I could not possibly fulfill." She tilted her head slightly as she leaned toward him and added, "I could never become your mistress."

He was completely taken aback as Fanny smiled sweetly upon him. He was stunned by her boldness in even addressing the matter, and a warning went off in his head.

She settled back in her chair and asked, "Do I shock you overly much?"

"Yes—no!" he cried. "That is, I am surprised you would mention it at all."

"My conduct was quite shameless at Broadhorn, though I confess I was carried away by the moment. You have a certain persuasiveness about you as you very well know, and as I considered the incident later, I feared you would hold an unhappy opinion of me were I not to say something to you. I trust I have not offended you." Her eyes were dark and sultry in the candlelight, and King had a faintly uneasy sensation as he met her languid gaze. She picked up her cards, scanning them, her appearance and demeanor all that was soft and elegant. He could sense that he was being hunted, but by a foe so silent and clever that only his instincts warned him of danger; his mind made nothing at all of her speeches save that she was a gracious, intriguing female.

She again altered the course of their conversation sharply. "I had never seen anything so lovely as the ethereal vision of Angel descending the stairs this evening. She radiates a beauty unlike any other that has graced our London seasons. Her spirits, though, were quite depressed, I thought. Even her lovely features could not disguise the fact that she has been blue-devilled since she arrived in London. I am not at all surprised that you say she has longed to return to Fair Oaks."

"It is very sad," he responded, ordering his cards, all the while trying to sort through the strange shifts in her discourse. "Upon more than one occasion, I have wished to take her back to Hampshire myself. She does not enjoy the Metropolis one whit!"

"Have you not laid eyes upon her in the past hour or so?" she queried, again giving their conversation a severe jolt. When he shook his head, she continued. "Then, you will be greatly surprised, for the most amazing transfor-

227

mation has occurred. When I mentioned her lowness of spirits, I was speaking only of her mood earlier this evening. But not an hour past, I noticed that her entire person had become alive; she seemed absolutely enthralled with her surroundings. Her shoulders no longer drooped, her smile seemed perfectly natural, and her eyes glowed with excitement. It was truly extraordinary to watch, though I suspicioned that the company she was keeping must have had something to do with her change of demeanor. As it happened, she was lost in conversation with one Cornelius Wellow."

"Who?" King queried. He felt vaguely concerned by Fanny's observations.

"A rather obscure poet whom Mr. Hunt seems to fancy, but other critics find untried and inelegant. Personally, I find him an obnoxious young man with unkempt hair and an acerbic tongue."

"You do not like him, I apprehend," King stated with a faint smile.

"I do not. However, the qualities I enjoy in a gentleman do not necessarily mean that all women should follow my suit." Here she called out her point, then continued, "But I had the distinct impression Miss Angel Leighton had tumbled quite violently in love with Mr. Wellow."

"Violently in love with a poet? Are you sure?"

"Quite. I only wonder, however, whether Mrs. Harte will approve of such an alliance. I am certain you have noticed that she rules her family with a singularly firm hand."

She lifted her gaze from her cards, watching him carefully, and King was again struck with a strong sensation that she had extended some invisible net and was attempting to gather him in. Her reference to Henrietta seemed, to his practiced hand, to carry a hint of challenge. He decided to answer her in kind, and in a subtle manner, he caressed her arm with his hand and then drew back as he said, "How kind of you to heighten

228

my awareness to Mrs. Harte's flaws. A wife would do as much. She would warn her husband away from potential danger—subtly, of course!" He stared hard at her and watched her blush faintly.

"I meant nothing by it, Mr. Brandish."

"Of course you didn't. And though you won't become my mistress, I hope I do not disappoint you when I again remind you that I have no desire to wed you or anyone else."

She laid her cards down carefully before her, arranging them in a neat stack. After a long moment, she rose quietly to her feet. "I beg you will excuse me, Mr. Brandish. But I have for so long been separated from Mama that I'm sure she's become anxious as to my whereabouts." She curtsied slightly, and King watched her go, admiring the straightness of her spine, the elegance of her acceptance of his rebuke. Fanny, at least, knew how to execute a charming retreat. He watched her leave the library, not in the least offended. Indeed, he wondered if Fanny were not, after all, a match for him.

He stared at the door for some time as he absently gathered up the cards and began shuffling them. He did not know precisely when he became aware that someone was watching him, but after a moment, he seemed to sense that he was being observed. He shifted his gaze slightly to the left and saw, standing in the shadows by the door, Henrietta.

Good God! What had he done? Her expression was accusingly blank. She did not approach him, but in a dazed manner, left the chamber in Fanny's wake.

He was on his feet instantly, his knee bumping the small table and scattering the cards over the floor. His chest felt strangely constricted with a feeling akin to panic, as though he were about to lose something very precious to him.

Chapter Twenty-Eight

Henrietta walked rapidly away from the library doors, a fierce pain taking hold of her heart. She felt bereft of air as her chest crushed her lungs. She could not breathe. Her mind remained frozen with a single picture, of Brandish touching Fanny's arm in an intimate manner. She felt foolish to have believed he could love only her; at the same time she was angry that he could not be faithful to her for even an hour without succumbing to the wiles of another female. Such then was the depth and quality of his love for her. But what did she expect from a confirmed rake?

Yes, she felt foolish beyond permission.

Quickly descending the stairs, Henrietta returned to the ballroom, where the noise and crush of guests surrounding the dancers provided a private place in which she could lose her thoughts and perhaps then gain some composure.

She had arrived in the library, her heart still full of excitement about the future, only to find Brandish flirting mightily with Fanny Marshfield. She had settled back into the shadows of the chamber just as Fanny had risen from her seat. Brandish had said something to her, and at first Fanny had appeared offended. But by the time the young widow had reached the door, she was wearing a secretive smile that cut deeply into Henrietta's confidence.

How could King have told her in one moment that he loved her and, in the next, engage in a *tête-à-tête* in the library with an acknowledged Beauty like Fanny Marshfield? She fanned herself madly and backed deeply into the throng of spectators who were watching two dozen couples go down a simple country dance. She eased herself against the wall, feeling obscure in the dim light of the ballroom, and breathed a sigh almost of relief. If Brandish had followed her, he would have a difficult time locating her in such a crowd.

When she could breathe easily, and some of the shock of what she had seen fell away from her, she was surprised to find herself addressed by one of Brandish's acquaintances, a man by the name of Hugh Farley. He was a large man, cut from the same cloth as Mr. Phillips, for though he was not handsome, he had good humor in his face, a strong jawline, intelligent eyes and massive hands. *Fit,* Henrietta thought, *for the sport found at Jackson's.* He was of the moment, however, quite in his cups, and his expression as his gaze drifted over her gown of royal-blue silk was exceedingly wicked.

"Mrs. Harte!" he exclaimed, bowing slightly, his eyes half-lidded. "Damme, but you're the prettiest female I've seen in months! Why, it's no wonder Brandish took to parading your sister about at Hyde Park! Means to slip into your good graces, what?" He laughed heartily, and Henrietta stared up at him, uncertain whether or not his words held an unseemly import.

When she did not respond to his remarks save to look at him in a bewildered fashion, he leaned close to her and asked, "You are Freddy Harte's widow, aren't you? Fine lad Freddy was! Sorry he stuck his spoon in the wall at such a tender age, though the sharps had him snabbled up but good by the time he—well, mum for that!" His speech was slurred, and his breath smelled heavily of wine.

Henrietta was deeply offended and tried to move away from him, but he caught her by the elbow and in her ear whispered, "I always thought he'd won a treasure in you! I remember thinking years ago that I wished I'd been in his shoes on his wedding night—or you might say, 'in his bed!' You're a widow now, and I thought perhaps—"

Without giving the matter a great deal of thought, Henrietta trod with all her might on his foot, called him a buffleheaded clunch, and was satisfied with the cry of surprised pain that erupted from his lips. Since he stumbled against the wall as he tried to rub his slippered foot, he bumped into another lady, causing so much chaos that Henrietta was able to slip from the ballroom unnoticed.

She intended to return to her bedchamber, for this had been a wretched blow, the very one she had been dreading since she first arrived in London: She had been connected with her deceased husband in a most unsavory light. How desperately she wished she had remained in Hampshire. Her throat closed up entirely as she choked back her tears. At least once she was safely within her chamber, she could give vent to the awful pain that engulfed her.

Just as she reached the landing that led to her room, however, she saw King standing in the hallway, directly in her path. He was frowning as he stared down at the carpet and at first did not see her. She knew a strong desire to whirl around and run back down the stairs, but before she could even decide whether or not she ought to leave, he caught sight of her. There was nothing for it but to speak with him.

As he walked toward her, she realized it was best they settle this business between them now.

"I have been looking for you, Henry," he cried. "I thought perhaps you had retired to your chamber, only tell me why you are so upset? Was it Fanny? You must not concern yourself with her! She is very little to me, I assure you."

Henrietta took a deep breath, biting back her tears as she pressed her hands tightly together. She remembered suddenly that King had told her he had something significant to ask her, and a beam of hope burst upon her mind. At the same time, however, she knew a horrible prescience that her hope was ill-founded. She looked at him steadfastly and responded, "Earlier this evening, you mentioned that there was a certain matter you wanted either to tell me or to request of me. I wish to hear it now, for then I will know what to think of Mrs Marshfield." She searched his eyes, wanting to find in them some reason to trust him. She again felt as she always did when she was with him, that in some inexplicable manner, she already belonged to him.

"Very well," King responded, a furrow between his brows.

He led her to his father's bedchamber and closed the door against the eager ears of anyone roaming about the hallways. "I know that you are overset by what you saw in the library," he began, his tone sincere. "But I beg you will not be. You have stolen a special place in my heart; you have captured a portion of my affections that I am convinced Fanny could never possess."

Henrietta moved to stand beside the tall bedstead, her heart sinking at his words. She placed a hand against the cool mahogany wood and realized that there were blank spaces between his words, a discrepancy as it were, between what he said and what he was truly feeling. Was she imagining her doubts? Or were they real. "Tell me, Brandish, does Fanny please you? I mean, she is an intelligent female, and quite lovely. How could she not, to some degree, to a man of sense—" she broke off, suddenly afraid of both asking the question and hearing the response. "How could she not command your interest, your admiration, your affection?"

She was turned away from him and heard his approach, rather than saw it. She was not surprised when she felt his hands upon her arms. "You have already guessed, then, that I am not entirely indifferent to her."

"Do you love her?" Henrietta asked, trembling. Where had she found the courage to even pose such a hateful question?

"Good God, no!" he cried promptly. "I would never describe my sentiments toward her in such terms. I am

233

mildly intrigued by her, and to some degree she suits my notion of the sort of female who ought to be the next viscountess Ennersley."

Henrietta leaned her head upon the wood post and, with a disbelieving laugh, cried, "What?"

He turned her around with a gentle pressure on her arms. Holding her gaze steadily, he said, "I do not love her. That is all I am trying to tell you. She is nothing to me, save a woman whose manners and comportment I admire. She does not fill my heart with a desperate fever as you do." He caressed her arms and back as he drew her tightly against his chest.

"You are utterly hopeless, King, and I have been foolish beyond belief to have fallen in love with you. And the worst of it is, were I to tell you that you have wounded my sensibilities with your words, I daresay you would be astonished. Am I not right?"

He smiled at her, his gaze shifting to her lips as he held her more closely still. "If I believed for a moment I had hurt you, my dearest Henry, I should thrust a small-sword through my heart, I should shower coals upon my head, I should—"

"Enough!" Henrietta cried with an anguished laugh. "A rogue to the last, full of silly speeches and an underlook even Byron would covet!" She understood clearly now that he had no intention of wedding her; still she loved him and took great joy in his flirtations. But neither the adoration she felt for him nor the pleasure she took in his company could diminish the terrible ache that had begun weighing upon her heart. "I love you, King Brandish. You are a rascal and a rogue and everything meant only to hurt me. Pray, keep me in suspense no longer and tell me what you desire of me."

He pressed his lips upon the tender slope of her cheekbone and drifted feathery soft kisses in a slow, languid trail across her cheek, until he reached her mouth. He smelled delightfully to her of a fine soap as he paused in his gentle movements, his breath light upon her lips. "I do love you, Henry," he whispered. "More

234

than I can tell you with these meager words and protestations." His lips sought hers as he kissed her roughly, and Henrietta felt her own longing for him increase a hundredfold as she returned his embrace. She held him tightly, slipping an arm about his neck, and believed in her heart she would never be so close to him again. The very thought of so great a loss caused her to cling desperately to him. He responded in kind, bruising her mouth and pressing her hard against the bedstead as he eased his body fully against her own.

After a moment, he drew back from her slightly and, in a low voice, asked, "Do you remember the first day I met you? It was a Monday I think. I desired nothing more when I first saw you than to find some means of holding you in my arms. I shall always be grateful to Vincent for providing me the most paltry excuse of my career for assaulting a female, when I returned him to you! Oh, my dear Henry, I was lost to you even then upon discovering you alone in the wooded dell near Fair Oaks. But do you also remember a time later that evening when I arrived at the manor to say good-bye to Betsy?"

She nodded, looking into his eyes and feeling each of his words pulling her more deeply still into a terrible pit of aloneness.

He smiled softly upon her as he continued, "I'll never forget that moment, how you refused to leave, how you told me that were I to stay at Broadhorn you would become my mistress. Tell me you recall giving voice to such a desire?" Again she nodded, her throat tight. His expression was full of love as he stated, "I want you to become my mistress, Henry. I will shower you with every delight within my power. You shall have an establishment of your own, jewels, servants, anything you have the least yearning for. I have thought of little else since yesterday, of possessing you, of offering you my protection, a *carte blanche* if you will. Pray tell me that you are of a similar mind, that my hope is well founded upon your professed passion for me, upon our shared love."

Henrietta was grateful that he had finally told her

precisely what he wanted of her; at the same time, she knew a despair that sunk her spirits entirely. She had been prepared to take a position as housekeeper, to give up forever either knowing love or being loved. And it seemed so harshly unfair to her that Fate should have thrown this wretched man in her path, to so disrupt the careful schemes of her life and show her all that she would be giving up forever once she stepped into a position as a household servant. She would never know love, or have children of her own, or a house over which she would reign as mistress, and King had for the briefest moment given her hope that she would have these very things after all. Instead, he wished only for her to become his paramour, and she could not.

She placed her fingers gently upon his lips, her eyes filling with hot, painful tears as she cried, "Kiss me again, Brandish, before my heart breaks."

"Oh, my love!" he cried ecstatically, believing she had acquiesced to his hurtful suggestion.

As he kissed her hard, holding her fiercely in his arms, Henrietta pretended he had not spoken such heinous words to her. Instead, she saw in her mind the images of King that she loved the best, of a man who spoke softly and kindly to Angel, who took the time to converse with Charlotte and who readily teased Betsy whenever she but bounded into the room. This was the man she loved, not the one who had so cruelly ground her pride and self-respect into the earth by asking her to become his mistress. Perhaps she might have done so, had they remained in Hampshire where they would have met in secretive copses where their shared pleasure would have been hidden within the purity of the earth and sky. But in London, the reality of such unmaidenly behavior was too clear to be ignored. She could not bear the thought of being pointed out by the interested *beau monde* as King Brandish's latest mistress, a woman who one day would be cast aside, like so many others before her. She knew also that one day, Brandish would marry—a woman like Fanny perhaps.

She received his mouth upon her own with painful pleasure, for she was saying good-bye to him. After a moment, as his lips began seeking a tender spot beneath her ear, she said, "More than anything, King, I wish to express my appreciation to you for all your kindnesses and attentions to my family, to my sisters. I know that Betsy holds you in particular esteem; she values your friendship nearly as high as Vincent." She felt his ardor diminish as he ceased kissing her ear. He seemed to comprehend that her demeanor toward him had shifted slightly. She continued, "In addition, you have given Angel, especially, a great gift, for she has at long last fallen in love. And with what wondrously happy results! Neither my beloved mama, nor Charlotte nor Betsy, will ever know poverty again. For this, my dearest King, I shall always be grateful since I have little doubt that it was due entirely to your position in society that Angel has enjoyed such remarkable success."

He leaned back in order to better see her. He searched her eyes, all the while holding her close. "What are you saying, Henry? You speak as though you are bidding me *adieu!* Why are there tears in your eyes? Why do you cry?" He frowned deeply, angrily. "Do not say you are refusing to become my mistress! Henry, you cannot have thought I meant to offer for you merely because I said I loved you!"

"It was silly of me, wasn't it?"

"But I told you in Hampshire I have no desire to wed anyone of the moment. You knew as much. Tell me you are only teasing me, that you knew very well I meant only to offer you my protection."

Henrietta felt a warm tear spill from her eye and trickle down her cheek. "I am as foolish as every other female of my acquaintance," she said with a watery smile. "When you said you loved me, I supposed it meant you intended to make me your wife. I trust you will forgive my lapse of common sense."

He appeared boyishly confused. "Your tone is edged with bitterness. I never meant to hurt you. I thought you

237

understood my sentiments."

"Mr. Farley also asked if I cared to partake of his bed. It would seem that *Mrs. Harte,* by her prior association, commands a certain disagreeable mode of address. I didn't realize until this moment, however, just how odious the idea is to me, but where you are concerned, I realize I am as much to blame as you. I misled you, and I am sorry for it."

She had not meant for her words to do anything more than to reveal to him how much she despised the notion of becoming any man's mistress. Instead, King's face grew quite red as he exclaimed, "That hellborn babe dared to speak to you in such a fashion! By God I'll have his head! He was always one to cross the line!"

Henrietta pulled away from him, traversing the elegant Aubusson carpet of red and blue, moving to stand beside Lord Ennersley's dressing table. She could not keep from chuckling at Brandish's odd sense of outrage. On the polished wood surface of the table, a large snuffbox bearing a mother-of-pearl lid sat quite alone. There were no other accoutrements present. With her finger, Henrietta traced the pastel lines swirling on the smooth lid, and she cried, "You cannot mean what you are saying, King. Do but listen to yourself; you are like the pot calling the kettle black. Perhaps Mr. Farley spoke through his wine-laden sensibilities, and perhaps his suggestion was coarse. It was certainly done without anything approaching your extraordinary address, but he was proposing nothing very different from yourself. My end would be the same. I would be left alone." She paused and turned to face him, holding his gaze steadily. "Or did you imagine that such a relationship as ours would be destined to last forever? I think not. It is the unfortunate nature of the agreement—it is love without honor. Surely respect would die in such an unhappy entanglement."

"You are wrong!" he cried, appearing astonished and angered by her words.

She continued relentlessly, "You will take a wife

someday, King, for your progeny's sake, whether you like it or not. And I've little doubt that the bride of your choosing would rather see you dead, than permit you to keep a mistress. I'm certain Fanny would be of such a mind. Even you must admit that."

He appeared as though he had been blown about by a strong wind. Henrietta could not read his thoughts, but he appeared quite enraged. He was silent for a long moment as he removed his snuffbox from his pocket and took a pinch between his thumb and his forefinger. He stared at the fine, brown mixture, letting the powdery grains sift back into the box. He clamped it shut and finally said, "What will you do then? I at least offered you an end to your penurious circumstances."

"Have you not known me, King? I have no need of wealth. I have had only one desire, to see my family settled comfortably. Once Angel is married to Mr. Phillips, as I have reason to believe she very soon will be, I intend to pursue my original course. I shall become a housekeeper, hopefully, in a very fine establishment."

She was surprised by the look of quick anger that overspread King's features as he cried, "What do you mean, when Angel marries Mr. Phillips? She cannot be in love with him, though I daresay he hopes to make her his bride that he might display her along with his other possessions."

Henrietta clasped her hands before her, sensing that a familiar quarrel was about to rise between them. She said quietly, "I am referring to what I observed not an hour past. My sister was dancing with Mr. Phillips and gazing into his face with an expression of rapt adoration! I saw her clearly! And I tell you, she is in love with him."

"You must be mistaken. Golden Hare frightens the poor child out of her wits! He has but to come within a few feet of her and she trembles. You know this much is true."

Henrietta responded, "Then she has recently overcome her aversion to him. Undoubtedly she grew to comprehend his kindly and generous disposition and now

239

sees him for the unexceptionable gentleman he is."

"Fanny mentioned to me that Angel had been quite taken by a young poet this evening, a fellow by the name of Cornelius Wellow. I doubt, however, that you have heard of him, for his origins appear to be somewhat obscure along with his verse."

Henrietta knew the strongest distaste as he mentioned Fanny. "As for Mr. Wellow, you are correct—I know naught of him. But as for Mrs. Marshfield, I do not comprehend how you can believe she knows Angel's sentiments better than myself."

"You are blinded," King cried, "by your ambitions for your sister. You speak nobly of wanting merely to see your family well settled, but you do not consider their feelings one whit! And I tell you again, regardless of Fanny's opinion, or what you believe you saw in Angel's expression as she looked at Golden Hare, your sister is not in love with him. I would wager five thousand pounds on it!"

"An idle boast," Henrietta cried harshly.

"Hah! I'll wager you again our original sojourn in Paris against five thousand pounds that Angel does not love Golden Hare Phillips, nor will she marry him!"

Henrietta lifted a brow, stunned by the large sum he was willing to bet in support of his opinions. For the smallest moment she knew a doubt that perhaps she had been mistaken. But as she considered again the love that radiated from Angel's face, her confidence returned. "You cannot be serious. Why, I would be robbing you, cheating you of a small fortune. I know what I saw!"

"You misunderstood what you observed," King insisted, an irritating smile playing upon his lips. "Well? Do we have a wager? Will you care to risk yet again your virtue, this time as a reflection that you have full confidence in your opinions?"

Henrietta, convinced she was right, took great delight in agreeing to his stakes and suggested he visit his bank very soon to ascertain whether or not he could cover his part of the wager.

He bowed with much irony to her and strolled to the door, where he turned back suddenly and said, "I will say only this—you will believe Angel has fallen in love with Phillips, because you wish it. This is your flaw, Henry— you choose to believe only what you want to."

Henrietta stared at him, and with a slight catch in her throat, she responded quietly, "You may very well be right. After all, I not only believed you loved me but that you wanted to marry me as well! I am flawed, indeed! And how very kind of you to have made me aware of this dreadful rift in my character."

He opened his mouth as if to speak, his expression for a moment one of regret. But he reconsidered the words that sat upon the tip of his tongue, and he remained silent, inclining his head to her as he opened the door and passed through.

He shut the door behind him, and Henrietta was left standing near Ennersley's dressing table, her throat painfully tight. Tears started yet again to her eyes, and she would have shed them had not the door to the viscount's wardrobe—a sizeable room adjoining his bedchamber—begun to open with a jarring creak.

Henrietta knew the worst fright and could not imagine who had been privy to their entire conversation unless it was Lord Ennersley himself. Oh, but he could not have been listening to all that was said between herself and King! He could not! She pressed her hand to her cheek, opening her eyes wide as she watched the door part to a distance of about a foot.

Lord Ennersley peeked his head through and whispered, "Is my son gone?"

Chapter Twenty-Nine

Henrietta stared at Lord Ennersley in shocked disbelief. Her hand was still pressed to her cheek as she exclaimed, "Merciful heavens! Do not tell me you were privy to our—our conversation. I am mortified beyond words! She felt the deepest blush burning upon her cheeks as she whirled away from him, pressing her other hand to her face as though by doing so she could somehow keep her embarrassment at bay.

"Please, Henrietta!" he cried. "I beg you not to fall into a fit of strong hysterics. I know that I should have made my presence known to you both at once, but—oh, the devil take it—my curiosity bested me. I had to know what King meant to say to you, though I will confess I suspected his intentions were of a dishonorable nature—and how very right I was! How could he have been such a codshead to have supposed you would become his mistress! Lord, what a cawker I have raised for a son."

Henrietta bowed her head and in a low voice said, "I gave him the distinct impression I would not be indifferent to such a proposal. I am equally to blame."

"Nonsense!" Lord Ennersley cried.

Henrietta whirled around to face him. She did not want the viscount to be under a misapprehension, to think that his son was entirely at fault. "But I told him as much!" she exclaimed. "When I first met him in Hampshire, my words precisely were that should he stay,

I would become his mistress! So you see, you cannot blame King completely. He had cause to believe I would agree readily to his request."

Ennersley approached her, shaking his head. He patted her shoulder in a fatherly manner and said, "I hold my son responsible for this, and I suggest you do not refine too much on what foolish words you may have spoken to Brandish at Fair Oaks. You are grown wiser now; your innate common sense has held sway. At the same time I cannot help but feel part of King's interest in you is because you are a forthright young lady, willing to admit your errors, besides possessing a—a disposition to equal his own." He cleared his throat and slipped a finger around the edge of his neckcloth as though it had grown too tight. He stepped away from her, moving toward his dressing table where he lifted the lid of the mother-of-pearl snuffbox and took a pinch.

"You refer, I suppose, to my enjoyment of his kisses!"

He inhaled the snuff loudly and cried, "I would not have said anything so ungentlemanly, but since you are being so very bold, yes—you are well suited for King. My suggestion, however, is that we provide you immediately with a suitor with whom my son must compete for your affections. You must trust me when I say that frequently a challenge to a man's domain will turn the trick!"

Henrietta considered his scheme for a moment, remembering how quickly King had fired up at the mere mention of Hugh Farley's reprehensible conduct. "But who?" she queried, after a moment. "I have met several delightful gentlemen, but none who seemed especially enamored of me. In time, perhaps—"

"There is one whom King would take quite seriously," the viscount responded readily. Henrietta frowned, wondering to whom Ennersley could possibly be referring. Finally, he smiled, his expression reminding her of his son, as he exclaimed, "Why, myself, of course. He knows I have a special fondness for you, and I daresay it would not take too great a mental effort on his part to recall he suggested the very same thing to me but a few weeks ago. And why not choose a young bride!"

Henrietta blinked several times at Lord Ennersley and said, "You cannot be serious. You would become my suitor? You would send me flowers and love-billets, for I should require nothing less, I assure you!"

He laughed at her lively response and said, "As it happens, I think we ought rather to dispense with a formal courtship and instead become engaged. We haven't much time as you well know. In little more than a month, the Season will draw to a close, after which I feel certain that all our paths will separate, our destinies radiating from London like the spokes of a wheel."

Henrietta stood very still, her hands now resting at her sides. The scheme was an excellent one, save that it presumed Brandish loved her enough to overcome his aversion to marriage. She expressed grave doubts on this score, and Lord Ennersley responded promptly that he was certain Brandish was in love with her and that all the boy needed was a push!

Though the viscount tried to persuade Henrietta to agree to his stratagem, in the end she refused to feign an engagement with him. The very nature of such a scheme was fraught with difficulty, the greatest of which was the awkwardness of ending such an engagement should King prove entirely unmoved by the spectacle of it. No, she had rather not become embroiled in yet another clever design to try to shape the future to her own will. It was enough that her schemes where Angel was concerned were progressing happily. She thanked him profusely for his kindness to her as well as his interest in seeing her happily settled with his son, but she insisted upon declining his offer.

Henrietta decided that she was calm enough to return to the ball. As she stepped into the hallway, she turned to thank him yet again and on an impulse leaned quickly toward him and kissed his cheek.

*   *   *

Mrs. Leighton watched horrified as her eldest daughter emerged from Ennersley's bedchamber. She had just that moment crossed the threshold of her own chamber, into the hall, but at the first glimpse of Henrietta, she had melted back into the shadows of the doorway. She could not, however, close the door completely. She was transfixed by the sight of her eldest daughter actually chatting so freely with Lord Ennersley. Was this possible? But when Henrietta kissed the viscount upon the cheek, she felt her heart dip deeply into the pit of her stomach and remain there until Henrietta had disappeared entirely from view. Only then did she shut the door, and that slowly, for she felt as though she was walking through the midst of a ghoulish nightmare where each step she took was weighted and sluggard.

Was it possible that Lord Ennersley had fallen in love with Henrietta? He certainly enjoyed her company and had even commanded her to sit beside him at nearly every meal! They were always laughing together, but he was so much older than Henry! Surely he could not be contemplating marriage! Surely not!

And yet, as she sank into a chaise longue before the fire, she realized now it must be true. From the first, Ennersley had wanted them *all* at his house in Grosvenor Square. Furthermore, he had insisted Henrietta join in every social occasion. Indeed, he had been firm upon this point in particular.

Now, Mrs. Leighton finally understood why. The viscount was in love with Henrietta and meant to make her his wife.

So this was to be the end of Angel's ball, she thought drearily. She was to see the man she loved give his heart to her eldest daughter. And she couldn't reside with them after the wedding! Her heart would break! No, she would undoubtedly have to beg to reside with Arabella and that wretched Huntspill! Was this truly to be her fate? She covered her face and her guinea curls with her peach shawl of fine cashmere, leaned her head on her arm, and wept.

Two days later, on Monday afternoon, Angel sat upon a chair covered in gold damask awaiting the arrival of those visitors paying their "morning calls." She was seated in the drawing room, near the windows, where a gentle afternoon sun shone upon an embroidered reticule she clasped lovingly upon her lap. She was certain Cornelius would be numbered among the callers as she touched her reticule for perhaps the hundredth time. Secreted within were three love-infused missives from her beloved poet. She sighed deeply, her gaze drifting toward the window as she listened intently for the sound of either carriage or horse upon the street below. Alas, every wheel that grated upon the stone-flagged street rolled unconscionably past the Ennersley town house. Oh, when would Cornelius come!

She had been reluctant to discuss her fledgling love with either her mother or her sisters. Betsy would surely have laughed at her, and she strongly suspected that neither Henry nor Charlotte would approve of Mr. Wellow. She knew in her heart a terrible fear that were anyone to discover that Cornelius Wellow had gained her affections, she would be sent back to Fair Oaks. She had heard Henrietta ask Miss Brandish about Cornelius and learned to her horror that the poet was sadly impoverished. To Miss Brandish's knowledge, he had not a feather to fly with.

Angel did not give a fig whether or not Cornelius had a groat to his name, but she was well versed in Henry's sentiments. Her sister's instructions to her had been quite clear at the outset of the Season: Angel was to lure a wealthy gentleman to her side, coax him to fall in love with her and then marry him. She shuddered, knowing that both Henrietta and her mother believed Mr. Goldy, that is, Mr. Phillips, would very soon do just that, and she could scarcely bear the thought of listening to his proposals, if he were indeed prepared to offer for her. He had called upon them yesterday, and Angel had found it worked quite well to endure his visits by pretending she was conversing with her dear Cornelius. Mr. Phillips had broken the spell, however, by pressing her hand and informing her that he rather thought in a few days he had something of tremendous import to ask her. At first, Angel had thought he meant to inquire about her recent musical compositions, but in the middle of the night, she had awoken from a violent dream in which Mr. Phillips rode toward her on a giant rabbit covered with gold-plated armor, a lance poised at her bosom. As she pulled her bedclothes up to her chin, she realized London's wealthiest man had actually meant he intended to ask her to marry him. Whatever was she to do?

Angel gave her head a shake, clearing the wretched visions from her mind. She glanced about the long, blue chamber, which she had only this morning finally grown accustomed to, and discovered that she and Henrietta were the only ones present.

Henrietta smiled at her, and Angel knew a rush of affection for her oldest sister, who had always shown such patience with her intellectual deficiencies but who, at the same time, had encouraged her to pursue her interests in the harp and pianoforte. On an impulse, Angel rose from her chair and joined Henrietta, sitting beside her on a settee near the fireplace.

"I have been meaning to tell you something, Henry, only I have not known precisely how to begin." Angel sat well forward, her heart beating rapidly as she watched her sister ply a delicate piece of whitework with a silver needle.

Henrietta responded, "I was hoping you might confide in me. Ever since your ball two days ago, I have longed to ask you about your beau. You were very happy on Saturday, were you not?"

"Oh, yes," Angel breathed as she smiled seraphically upon her sister. "I have never known such delight as possessed me when he but looked into my eyes. And he thinks as I do! It is all so wonderful! I wanted to tell you sooner, but I was afraid you would not approve of him."

"*I*, not approve of *him!* But how absurd. He is all that is congenial and kind. I *approve* of him tremendously. He is by far one of my favorite gentlemen."

"Oh, Henry," Angel cried, greatly relieved as a tear formed in her eye and plopped upon her bronze-green round gown. "And to think I feared you would not like him at all. But when did you meet him?"

"Why, just as you did—at the opera, of course."

Angel glanced sharply at her sister, the happiness that had overtaken her heart dimming quite suddenly. "But he was not—" she broke off, unwilling to say more. "That is, of course, the opera! I had almost forgot. But then there were so many persons who trampled in and out of Lord Ennersley's box. It was a very confusing evening." She swallowed hard, searching in her mind quickly, trying to remember, hoping desperately to recall if Cornelius had made an appearance in Ennersley's box, but she knew he had not. Henry clearly thought she was referring to someone else.

Angel forced her mind to work rapidly, though a habitual fog intruded upon the functioning of her brain. She chewed on her lower lip and stared at the blue carpeting beneath her slippers of Denmark satin.

She felt a pressure on her arm, and when she looked up, she saw Henrietta watching her with a concerned expression in her eyes. "Angel, dearest, is something the matter?"

Angel stiffened slightly and shook her head. Henrietta smiled gently upon her and said, "You know, I was prepared on Saturday to release you from our original agreement—that you would do all in your power to secure a husband. I knew you had been very unhappy, so you cannot imagine what relief I felt when I saw you, as you danced with Mr. Phillips, smile so adoringly into his face. And it seems the most wondrous of occurrences that you should actually fall in love with quite the wealthiest gentleman in all of England. Oh, my dear Angel, you shall want for nothing, and your future will be full of everything good and wonderful. And to think I meant to return you to Fair Oaks if you did not fall in love with a gentleman of means by Saturday!"

Angel could see that her sister was smiling and that her words were meant to be playful, but she could not comprehend in the least why Henry would joke over such a serious matter. What she heard in her sister's voice and cloaked within her speech was the simple threat that if she did not marry Mr. Phillips, Henrietta meant to send her post-haste back to Fair Oaks. She rose quickly from the settee and, pinning a smile on her face, said, "I do not wish to return to the manor at all. Please do not make me go. I promise I shall not disappoint you. I shall of course become engaged to Mr. Phillips if he wishes it—" She was trembling, and her knees felt weak beneath her, but she would say anything of the moment to keep from being forced to part from her beloved Cornelius. "I shall do anything—only do not send me away!"

Henrietta cried, "My dear! What have I said to distress you? Of course I will not return you to Fair Oaks. I wouldn't think of it, not when you are so recently tumbled in love, not when your future appears so brilliant and full of hope."

"Oh, thank you, Henry! I'll be very good, I promise!" she exclaimed, her mouth feeling dry and cottony.

In all their conversation, they had not heard the arrival of several carriages. Just as Angel spoke these words, the doors opened, and the butler began announcing a veritable river of visitors, the first two being Golden Hare Phillips and Cornelius Wellow.

Angel looked from one to the other and promptly crumpled into a dead faint at Henrietta's feet.

Chapter Thirty

It was generally concluded that Angel's fainting fit
had resulted from the exigencies of a first season. Mr.
Phillips, gravely concerned for the state of dear Miss
Angel's health, recommended strongly that a physician
be sent for to attend her. But Angel refused to be
cossetted, explaining to Henrietta in private that the
mere sight of the gentleman for whom she had formed a
lasting passion, had caused her to swoon. She was certain
it was merely the shock of having him appear so suddenly
before her that caused her legs to betray her, but she was
convinced it would not happen again!

She soon rejoined the morning visitors, greeting
everyone affably, yet indicating with careful smiles
directed toward Mr. Phillips her partiality for him.
Henrietta approved of the delicacy of her conduct, and
when the drawing room was again bereft of callers, she
did not hesitate to tell her how very proud she was of her
success. She was also amused to learn that the wild-
looking young man who had marched beside Mr. Phillips
into the drawing room was none other than Cornelius
Wellow. Henrietta could not imagine how Fanny, for all
her abilities, could suppose Angel would be in the least
intrigued by a gentleman who not only sported a loosely
tied belcher kerchief about his neck in place of a proper
white neckcloth, but who stood dramatically apart from

his company, scowling upon Angel the entire duration of his visit. Angel, she knew quite well, could not be attracted to so arrogant a creature, and Henrietta took pleasure in the knowledge that very soon she would be able to inform Brandish that he had lost his wager with her. Angel would marry Mr. Phillips. It was all but settled between them! Even a ninnyhammer could see that Golden Hare worshipped Angel and that she in turn received his attentions with quiet gratitude.

As for Mr. Wellow, he had taken his leave not ten minutes after his arrival. His gaze had scarcely wavered once from Angel's face, but this was hardly unusual since that could be said of half the gentlemen present. Angel, for her part, showed little interest in Mr. Wellow's society, though she seemed quite distressed when he bid her *adieu* by possessing himself of her hand and placing a passionate kiss upon her fingers. Henrietta would have protested his behavior had he not quit the drawing room immediately afterward.

By Wednesday, Mr. Phillips' attentions had become so particular that it was generally known he meant to beg for Angel Leighton's hand in marriage. So it was that when the ladies entered the Almack Assembly rooms that evening, a veritable hush fell over the crowded room as scores of young ladies and admiring gentlemen turned to regard the Beauty. The most courageous of the men descended in a violent rush upon Angel in hopes of claiming her exquisite hand for a country dance, or the quadrille, or—if the heavens were smiling—a waltz!

Henrietta watched Angel accept these honors with gracious indifference as she was led almost immediately out to the ballroom floor where an unexceptionable country dance was forming. Mr. Phillips had not yet arrived, and Henrietta glanced quickly about the long chamber searching for—no, but it was silly. Why should she be concerned whether or not Mr. Wellow was in attendance? Only, there he was, chatting politely with Emily Cowper, who seemed intrigued by his conversation. Miss Brandish had told her the young gentleman was something of an oddity, and not greatly admired amongst her own acquaintance, but Henrietta thought his companion seemed agreeably pleased with his company.

She fanned herself mildly as she let her gaze drift about the assembled guests, the music a balm to her ragged sensibilities. For several days now, since Saturday, she had felt a creeping loneliness overtake her heart, and with every venturing-forth from Grosvenor Square, she had succeeded in buoying her spirits only with the greatest of efforts. Several times, she had been of a mind to pack her trunk and bandboxes and scurry back to Fair Oaks for a sennight or more until she could secure a position of employment elsewhere. London had become a torture to her and not more so in this moment when she found, as her gaze lit upon the broad shoulders and elegant dress of King Brandish, that he was flirting with Fanny. She was not surprised when the country dance ended that he led the fawn-eyed beauty out for the quadrille.

She glanced down at her hands which had begun trembling as they lay in a politely cupped shape upon her rose silk ball dress. Her heart knew a sadness that struck so deeply she wasn't sure if she would ever be happy again. What if Brandish decided to marry Fanny? The thought caused her heart to beat in a wildly fearful cadence. Perhaps she ought to make a push to secure his hand! But how, when he would scarcely speak to her? She thought again of Lord Ennersley's proposal, to become engaged to him. How many times over the past several days had she considered so bold and reckless a gambit. Yet each time, her conclusion was the same; there were simply too many flaws in such a scheme to warrant the risks.

Later, when Mr. Phillips arrived, Angel bestowed the next dance—a waltz—upon him. Holding her hand lightly in his, he lifted her to her feet and smiled adoringly upon her. Angel responded with a sweet smile of her own, but before they had taken more than five steps toward the perimeter of the ballroom floor, Angel held him back with a gentle pressure on his arm and whispered something in his ear. Henrietta exchanged a smile with her mother, who sat beside her. Was there anything prettier than the sight of Angel whispering secrets to the man she hoped to marry? The ladies fanned themselves in unison, taking great delight in the tender scene before them. Henrietta watched Mr. Phillips glance back at Charlotte, who sat quietly on the other side of Mrs. Leighton. Henrietta noticed that Charlotte blushed hotly as he smiled at her; then she quickly lowered her gaze. A funny suspicion entered her mind as she realized Charlotte had begun busying herself with smoothing out her gloves so that she might not have to look at Mr. Phillips.

As Henrietta scrutinized her sister for a moment, she noted that Charlotte appeared uncommonly pale beneath the blush that still held her features captive. In all her concerns for Angel and her success among the *haut ton*, Henrietta had paid little heed to Charlotte. She did not know, for instance, whether or not her sister was enjoying her London Season. Why, Charlotte was not even wearing her spectacles! And for how long had she dispensed with them? Henrietta wondered. She was about to address Charlotte, when Mr. Phillips suddenly returned Angel to her seat, and begged Charlotte to dance in her stead.

Charlotte was thrown into a flurry of confusion, refusing at first to dance with him, until Angel pressed her arm very hard and begged her to please her in this one small matter.

What a great heart Angel possessed! She at least knew a compassion for Charlotte while the rest of them were idly fixed within their own interests. She was about to express her gratitude to Angel for her exemplary display of sisterly affection toward Charlotte, when Cornelius

Wellow swooped down upon her. Before Henrietta had finished her speech, he had swept Angel away.

Cornelius Wellow! What an impertinent young man! She only hoped Angel's feet would not be sadly crushed by this impetuous gentleman's abrupt movements.

"What a strange fellow!" Mrs. Leighton cried. "Why, he did not so much as incline his head to me. Who is he? I wonder. I do not recall having made his acquaintance." When Henrietta informed her of the young man's name, vocation and otherwise penurious state, she shrugged her shoulders indifferently. "How very grateful I am that Angel at least shall have a contented future. I could not want for a more gracious son-in-law than Mr. Phillips!"

Once Angel was firmly fixed within the circle of Cornelius's arms, she whispered frantically, "I have been sick with worry that you might have misunderstood my conduct toward you. I have searched my mind a thousand times attempting to discover a means by which I could speak privately with you. But alas, I am guarded carefully by my family. I could not even send you a billet in response to the several you have written to me! And how much I cherish each one, only, tell me you realized the difficulties of my position. Tell me you did not believe me to be inconstant of heart!"

Cornelius regarded her with impassioned eyes as he clasped her hand painfully. "You could not be inconstant! You are my frost queen! Remember, dearest? I have implicit faith in you."

Angel breathed a great sigh of relief. "Yes, oh, yes," she cried. She then quickly informed him of Henrietta's threat to send her instantly back to Hampshire if she did not agree to wed Mr. Phillips.

"Are you engaged to him?" Cornelius cried. "You cannot be!"

"No! No!" Angel exclaimed, then quickly lowered her voice lest they attract too much notice. "But I fear he will offer for me given the least encouragement. Indeed, I am sure of it! Oh, what am I to do? If I do not agree to marry him, Henrietta will force me to return to Fair Oaks! And I know she would not permit me to become your wife! Oh, how unhappy I am become!''

Cornelius was silent for a long moment, his steps even and sure as he led Angel about the ballroom to the lilting rhythm of the waltz. His expression was grave as he spoke with a sad note to his voice, ''Were I a man of fortune, your sister would no doubt look favorably upon my suit.''

Angel agreed and again queried, ''Whatever shall we do?''

''For the moment,'' Cornelius responded, ''I think we ought to try if we can to—to meet clandestinely, if possible. Could you, for instance, be at Hookham's at two o'clock tomorrow afternoon, alone?''

''An assignation,'' Angel cried gleefully. ''How wonderful! Only, I don't think I would be permitted to roam about London unchaperoned unless one of my sisters were to accompany me. Charlotte would do so, and she at least is sympathetic to my plight, for if you must know she has developed the most amazing *tendre* for Mr. Phillips—only he does not love her! It is such a sad coil! Whatever are we to do, Cornelius?''

Mr. Wellow squeezed her hand as they whirled about the floor and said, ''We shall come about, never you fear, even if we have to elope!''

''Elope?'' Angel cried. ''But how romantic! I should like it above all things.''

''But would your family ever forgive us?''

Angel's heart sank yet again. ''I don't know, and I cannot live without my dear Henry, and my dear Betsy and Charlotte and Mama, though I can't say I would feel too wretched were Arabella to disown me. She was forever pinching at me, you know. She thought I didn't *apply* myself to my letters and such, but I did, *I did!*''

Cornelius nodded his head wisely as he responded. ''It is because you have great genius that you get the simplest things confused. Now, tell me more of your composition, and I shall quote one of my poems to you, a recent work, entitled, *Fairest of Angels*."

"Oh, Cornelius," Angel sighed at the sound of her name gracing the title of her beloved's poem. She leaned into him, looking up at him in adoration; but he promptly rebuked her, saying that if she continued to regard him in that delightful manner, he would be forced to kiss her, and then they would be in the basket!

"You cannot mean to tell me, Henrietta," King cried, as he gestured toward the dancers, "that you do not perceive a fledgling, mooncalf love upon Angel's pretty features!"

Henrietta turned her gaze from Angel and lifted a brow regarding King directly. "I see a polite young woman conversing with painstaking propriety," she responded with some asperity. "She has, over the past several days, scarcely acknowledged Mr. Wellow's presence, nonetheless tumbled in love with him. You are expressing opinions based upon Fanny's imagination."

"And you are still blind, m'dear! Still wishing for what cannot be!"

"And you are merely afraid for once you might be wrong!"

"Have it as you will, then. I argue with you out of vanity and pride, rather than a belief in my own perceptions. But I shall win our second wager, and you shall accompany me to Paris!" He bowed to her after that and stalked away.

Henrietta watched him go, furious that he could be so stubborn. At the same time, she knew the strongest desire to follow after him, to gentle his temper and to prevail upon him to dance with her. She missed him dreadfully.

As though comprehending her thoughts, he stopped suddenly and turned around slightly to look at her over his shoulder. His expression was fraught with concern and perhaps even longing. She wanted to reach a hand out to him, to call him back to her side, but whatever the source of his hesitation, he soon overcame his impulse and continued on his way.

Lord Ennersley brought a cup of iced lemonade to Mrs. Leighton and settled himself beside her. "Well, then!" he cried. "How do you answer me? I have given you enough time, I am certain, to consider your responses—that deuced servant overfilled the cup three times, and I was not about to bring you a sticky handle to hold on to. So, what say you? Why do you not read with me in the evenings? Have you been ill? I have missed your company sorely, and with only my sister to converse with, I only wonder that I have not gone mad!"

Mrs. Leighton felt a sweet wave of hope float over her as she looked up into Ennersley's face. At last, he had finally noticed her—better still, he admitted to enjoying her society. She felt her cheeks grow pink with pleasure as she sipped her lemonade and responded quietly, "Why, Charles, I find myself flattered. I, too, have come to miss our evening discourse and readings. Of late, however, I questioned whether you took pleasure in it at all."

He looked at her intently, nodding as though he had heard every word she had spoken, but he didn't offer any comment. She frowned at him slightly, prepared to ask him what he was thinking, when the object of his true attention became known to her. With a sinking of her heart, she watched his gaze slip suddenly from her face as he turned bodily toward Henrietta.

"I just realized, Lavinia," he said, his tone one of concern, "that Henry looks positively blue-deviled. What transpired while I was procuring your refreshment to have brought such an expression of unhappiness into her eyes?"

Mrs. Leighton bit her lip. How was it Ennersley could not converse with her but two minutes before he shifted his interest to Henrietta? There could be only one answer, she thought, her spirits plummeting. He must be in love with her. "Henry quarrelled with your son, I think—something about Angel and Mr. Phillips. King walked away after but a few minutes. He did not even dance with her."

Ennersley nodded absently. Picking up his quizzing glass as it dangled on a long silk riband, he peered through it to examine his black slippers. He fell into a brown study and finally glanced back at Mrs. Leighton. "I am sorry," he cried. "I do beg your pardon, but I did not hear your answer. Let me ask you again, why is it you do not read with me in the evenings anymore?"

Mrs. Leighton felt her hopes rise again, her heart emitting the faintest note of a song, only to have the melody shattered before it had begun. Just as she was about to speak, he patted her arm and said, "We must talk later. Of the moment, I feel the most pressing urge to speak with Henry. You'll understand, I'm sure, only I insist you read to me after the children have all gone to bed—from now on that is, in the evenings. Do not disappoint me!" He seemed quite distracted as he rose to his feet, crossed to where Henrietta stood watching the dancers whirl about the chamber, and begged her for the next set.

"Well, of all the absurdities," Mrs. Leighton muttered to herself, tossing her head. *"Do not disappoint me!* Do not disappoint me, indeed! I intend to *disappoint* you very much, my lord Ennersley!"

Chapter Thirty-One

Two days later, Henrietta paced the landing outside the drawing room. She was waiting, in a state of extreme excitement, for Charlotte and Angel to return from Hookham's where they had gone nearly two hours earlier. She could not imagine what had detained them, though ordinarily she would not have been concerned overly much, save that Mr. Phillips had been sitting in the drawing room with Mrs. Leighton for nearly an hour. He had arrived, his stolid, well-bred features full of every good tiding as he finally made his intentions known to Mrs. Leighton. He wished to offer for Angel's hand in marriage.

"That is," he had queried, his brow knit, "if you find such an arrangement agreeable?"

Mrs. Leighton had laughed, delighted at his modesty. "You are a very good man, Mr. Phillips," she responded, patting his arm affectionately. "And I should be pleased to have you wed any of my daughters, though I have long since known you had a decided preference for my dearest Angel."

He appeared satisfied, a warm smile suffusing his face. "I am not unaware of your difficult circumstances," he responded haltingly. "And I hasten to assure you that I mean to provide amply for your needs as well as Angel's. I have come to cherish your entire family nearly as much

259

as your daughter's beauty—that is, I mean of course, almost as much as Angel's beauty of person and character." He had appeared slightly embarrassed by his speech, but Mrs. Leighton set him at ease, assuring him that she had known from the first he was a generous, kind gentleman, then informed him she would be happy to let him address Angel the moment she returned from the lending library.

Henrietta had been privy to this entire exchange and in addition had saluted her future brother-in-law fondly upon her cheek. But her impatience to have the matter settled, her thrill at having had her schemes work to such perfection, had filled her with such an agitated exhilaration that she was forced to quit the receiving room where she could pace the landing quite at her leisure. She enjoyed immensely the sense of triumph the moment brought her—Angel to marry Mr. Phillips! She sighed with deep satisfaction, and when she heard a carriage on the flags, she immediately glided down the stairs, her morning dress of soft sea-green cambric held lightly in both hands, to greet her sisters.

She was greatly startled, therefore, to find King regarding her from across the portal when the butler opened the door, and she found a blush burning on her cheeks. She knew she appeared as though she had been eagerly awaiting his arrival.

His eyes lit up with surprise and pleasure as he caught sight of her. His notorious gaze drifted appreciatively over her entire person, and Henrietta felt the blush deepen upon her cheeks. He handed his hat, cane and gloves to the butler, then approached her saying, "Mrs. Harte! How charming you look today. Were you hoping I should call?"

"Mr. Brandish," Henrietta responded, inclining her head to him. She ignored his question completely, refusing to answer him as she turned back toward the stairs to retrace her steps.

He quickly joined her, holding her elbow lightly as he

led her up the stairs. He leaned close to her and whispered, "You must tell me which you prefer—to travel in easy stages from Calais to Paris, or to cut a dash through the countryside?"

She glanced at him, at his smug expression, and she retorted with great pleasure, "My preference cannot signify to you in the least. Indeed, your only concern ought to be whether or not you can afford to part with five thousand pounds! Mr. Phillips is abovestairs, if you must know, awaiting Angel's return. He intends to offer for her."

She expected her words to disturb Brandish, but he merely smiled in response, appearing more confident than ever. "I wouldn't care if the Archbishop of Canterbury were standing beside him prepared to perform the ceremony. There will be no wedding!"

As they achieved the landing, Henrietta faced him boldly and said, "Were you not listening to me? Mr. Phillips is in love with Angel and has expressed his desire to marry her. She, in turn, has encouraged his advances. What more remains to be said! Come! Admit you have erred!"

"Oh, but I haven't," he responded coolly. "And in but a few seconds, you will know why."

Henrietta was about to demand he explain this cryptic speech when another carriage was heard upon the street. She stared at the finely carved wood door, wondering what Brandish could possibly mean. She heard the faint sounds of her sisters' voices and knew at once they were engaged in a heated argument. She glanced at King, who returned her gaze with a firm nod, and suddenly she felt the worse qualms assail her. Something had happened, and Brandish knew of it already. But what?

The door flew open, and Charlotte, bearing a parcel of books, exclaimed, "But you must tell Mama! Indeed you must! Mr. Brandish saw you! He will surely expect you to explain what you have done!"

Angel burst into tears. "I cannot!" she cried. "I will be

261

sent to live with Arabella, and I don't want to."

At this point, Henrietta called softly to her sisters, only to have Angel utter a distressed shriek. She tried to escape into Lord Ennersley's office, but Charlotte caught her arm, held her firmly and whispered something in her ear.

Angel grew very quiet at her words, though her chest heaved with ill-concealed sobs. She nodded several times, then began ascending the stairs with Charlotte, her lower lip quivering.

Henrietta watched Angel wipe several tears from her cheeks with the back of her gloves of lavender kid. Whatever was the matter, she wondered, a sense of foreboding taking hold of her heart. She glanced at Brandish, who merely lifted a brow as if to say he had given her sufficient warning.

Henrietta descended several steps, meeting Angel before she had reached the landing. She slipped an arm about her sister's shoulders and begged to know what was amiss. But all that Henrietta could determine between her sister's hysterical sniffs was that for some reason Angel was convinced she was about to be cast from London society and exiled to Fair Oaks forever, where she was certain Arabella meant to beat her because she could not read very well!

Glancing at Charlotte, Henrietta asked her softly what had happened to cause Angel to grow so irrational. Charlotte's expression grew worried as she gazed down at Angel and pressed her sister's arm. Addressing Angel, she said, "I wish you would confide your difficulties in Henry. She is not the ogre you seem to believe her to be. Pray, tell her what is in your heart! Tell her about— about your *assignation* at Hookham's."

They reached the landing on a slow, labored tread. King drew away from the sisters and busied himself by taking a pinch of snuff.

"An assignation?" Henrietta queried, feeling as though she had just breathed in a vast quantity of frosty air. Her entire being felt stunned and cold. "With whom?"

Angel could not speak as she glanced wildly from one sister to the other. Pressing her hand to her mouth, she gave a startled cry and ran toward the drawing room.

"Angel!" Henrietta cried. She had meant to stop her from entering the chamber where Mr. Phillips awaited her, but Angel opened the doors abruptly and passed through. Henrietta and Charlotte were not far behind.

When Angel realized that Mr. Phillips and her mother had been closeted together in the long, blue chamber, she stopped abruptly, a hand pressed to her cheek.

Henrietta was beside her at once, holding her gently about the waist. She hoped to avert a disastrous scene as she said, "Mr. Phillips has come to call upon you, but he could not know that you are fatigued from your excursion to Hookham's. Perhaps we could persuade him to speak with you later, to return—"

But before she could finish her speech and lead Angel from the room, Mrs. Leighton, full of joy at her daughter's good fortune, rose from her seat by the fireplace and crossed the chamber to engulf Angel in her arms. "Oh, my dearest child! How glorious your future shall be! Look! Here is good Mr. Phillips come to call upon you, and he has something of a particular nature to ask you as well. Come!"

Mrs. Leighton tried to sweep her daughter toward Mr. Phillips, but Angel dug her heels into the carpet. "Mama!" she cried. "I cannot! Oh, dear. I feel dreadfully, dreadfully—" She got no farther but again crumpled to the carpet just as she had done a few days earlier.

Henrietta could not keep from looking back toward the doorway where Brandish stood frowning his grievous disapproval. He held her gaze rigidly as he closed his snuffbox shut with a snap. Henrietta had never seen him quite so angry. She glanced toward Angel, whom Mrs. Leighton and Charlotte were attending to, and she felt sick at heart. She did not yet fully comprehend all that was going forward, but she finally realized that her poor sister had been laboring under some misapprehension that unless she did as Henrietta bid her she would be sent back to Fair Oaks. Henrietta recalled her last conversation with Angel. She remembered how anxious her sister had grown when she had but suggested she could return to Hampshire if she wished to. She now understood that for some reason Angel had believed Henrietta was issuing her a threat—in short, that if she did not wed Mr. Phillips, she would be forced to retire to Fair Oaks.

Henrietta moved forward, and as Angel began coming around, she held her hand gently and felt tears of humiliation burn her eyes. She never meant to place so great a burden upon her sweet sister. Never.

At that moment, a commotion was heard on the landing, and in the next instant, Cornelius Wellow burst into the room. He bowed stiffly to Brandish, who, in return, inclined his head with considerable aplomb. "Mr. Wellow," he said. "I compliment you on your having chosen to address the matter at hand. You are, I perceive, a man of honor!"

Mr. Wellow's cheeks were quite red as he strode past Brandish, ignoring the taunting savor of his words, and entered the drawing room. He begged pardon for having disturbed the ladies, but the moment he caught sight of Angel, reclining upon Mrs. Leighton's lap, he cried, "What have you done to her?" He was immediately beside her, displacing Henrietta, who gave way to him as though she understood he was meant to be with her.

Angel's eyes fluttered open. When she saw that Cornelius was with her, she cried, "My dearest love!"

Charlotte and Henrietta fell back as one, while Cornelius quickly took Angel from Mrs. Leighton's lap and gathered her up in his arms. Mrs. Leighton joined her daughters, and they remained at a discreet distance as though Angel's words of professed love had acted like a carefully placed whip that landed neatly at their feet in warning.

"Whatever does she mean, 'my dearest love'?" Mrs. Leighton cried in an anguished whisper, a hand pressed to her bosom. "She cannot be in love with Mr. Wellow! How is it possible? How could I have not known her sentiments?"

Henrietta felt dumbfounded by the revelation before her. She had been deeply prejudiced against Mr. Wellow, partly because he was not in the usual mode, but primarily because he was not plump in the pocket. She had not for one second believed Fanny could have observed correctly when she said Angel had tumbled in love with Mr. Wellow. She had not *wanted* to believe Angel loved anyone else but Mr. Phillips. Brandish had been correct in this.

Glancing at Mr. Phillips, she saw that the good gentleman had risen from his own chair and was staring in shocked disbelief at the tender scene before him. He leaned forward on his cane, his brown eyes unblinking.

Charlotte, who was standing next to Henrietta, whispered, "I should have said something to you, Henry, but I learned only yesterday—when Angel kept her first assignation with Mr. Wellow!—that she had fallen in love with him. And yet I couldn't believe it was true! It seemed so sudden and quite at odds with Angel's usual mode of conduct where gentlemen are concerned. I suppose I merely wished to be certain of what was going forward before I spoke to you—or Mama—about my concerns. As it was, when I asked Angel yesterday whether or not she had formed a *tendre* for Mr. Wellow, she told me emphatically that she had not—that she was merely being polite. She had seemed deeply distressed, and of course I did not press her.

"When she asked me, however, to attend her again— to Hookham's, where Mr. Wellow made a *convenient* appearance—I waited until they had enjoyed a lengthy *tête-à-tête* before confronting her. I was in the process of doing so when Mr. Brandish appeared and suggested to

265

Mr. Wellow that he speak with Mama immediately or he would be forced to call him out! I was so very frightened! Fortunately, Mr. Wellow did not demur, but rather seemed grateful for the opportunity and insisted we repair to Grosvenor Square at once.

"Angel, however, grew quite distraught, and I had no small degree of difficulty in ushering her into the town coach. I did not comprehend her distress at all, particularly when I knew Mr. Wellow was welcome in Miss Brandish's drawing room. But it seems Angel has been laboring under the impression that unless she wed where you wished her to, Henry, she was certain you would banish her to Fair Oaks, and then she would not be able to see Mr. Wellow again. I could not persuade her otherwise." She glanced at Mrs. Leighton, who appeared as though she had been struck hard across the face. "I am sorry, Mama, that I did not inform you yesterday of Angel's strange conduct. I believe in this I erred greatly."

Henrietta remained firmly fixed in one spot, as did Charlotte and Mrs. Leighton. The three ladies watched Cornelius minister gently to Angel, and there was little doubt that the prettiest of the Leighton ladies had fallen desperately in love with the impoverished Mr. Wellow.

Painfully aware that for the second time in the space of a month she had become indebted to Brandish to the tune of a sennight in Paris, Henrietta turned back to look at him, to admit her misperceptions with an inclination of her head, but he was gone. For the moment, since her shock was still so great, she was glad to be rid of the necessity of not only speaking with him, but enduring his gloatings as well. Time enough, she thought, to face his censure.

Chapter Thirty-Two

A fortnight later, the Leighton Ladies stood grouped about Angel and Cornelius as they spoke their vows to one another. The wedding ceremony took place in Lord Ennersley's library which the sisters had decorated with streamers of white satin, garlands of ivy, and huge bouquets of pink rosebuds.

Angel's large blue eyes sparkled with devotion as she pledged her love to Cornelius. He, in turn, won the hearts of all the ladies present, Miss Brandish included, when he drew the ceremony to a close by quoting his *Frost Queen* poem to his new bride before ever he kissed her. Mrs. Leighton sobbed into her lace kerchief, Charlotte and Henrietta also dabbed at their eyes and cheeks, and even Betsy proclaimed Cornelius's poem to be well rhymed!

The celebration was both small and private, with only the family, Lord Ennersley, Miss Brandish and King in attendance upon Angel and Cornelius.

Brandish stunned everyone after the ceremony by presenting the impoverished couple with a small annuity as a wedding gift, an arrangement his father had agreed to with hearty approval of his son's generosity. Angel had kissed him tenderly upon the cheek, shedding tears of her own. "Now we shall have sufficient paper upon which to compose our music and poetry," she exclaimed, hugging Brandish. "I have come to regard you as an elder brother,

King. You have been most kind to me throughout my first season. I could only wish you as much happiness with a wife as I intend to have with my dear Cornelius." She turned back to her husband and said, "And he has promised me we shall live in a very small cottage—oh, how happy I am!"

King wished her much joy in her marriage, and Henrietta was startled when he turned to gaze at her suddenly, a burning question in his eyes, as though he was wondering. . . .

Henrietta turned quickly away from him, unwilling to give hope a chance to blossom in her breast. King had accepted her humble apologies for having disbelieved his perceptions where Angel was concerned. At first, his demeanor toward her had been haughty and cold. But as each day unfolded and he realized Henrietta was delighted that Angel had found a love so sweet as the one she bore for Cornelius, King's posture toward her softened.

"I was blind, Brandish, not hardhearted or uncaring," Henrietta had said to him after three days of his curtness toward her. "Will you not forgive me? Do you not think that I have felt like a beast to have caused my dear sister so much anguish?"

He had unbent a little after that. But today, his wondering eyes slayed Henrietta. Until this moment, he had given her not the least indication that his own heart had changed, that he might desire more from her than just a sennight in Paris. Dare she hope?

When Angel and her new husband clambered aboard Lord Ennersley's town chariot, embarking on their honeymoon, Henrietta returned to the blue drawing room, her heart heavy and anxious. Whatever sentiments Angel's wedding may have forced King to acknowledge, they were not sufficiently strong to prompt him to do more than bid her good-bye politely in the same manner in which he addressed both her mother and Charlotte.

Whatever was she to do, she wondered. It was already the middle of May. June loomed closer with each advent of the morning sun, and the Season would end in little more than four weeks. Already Lord Ennersley spoke of adjourning to Brighton once London grew thin of company.

Henrietta stood by the windows, holding back the blue, satin damask drapes with her fingertips as she gazed down into the street. A breeze swept across the square, whipping the skirts of three ladies strolling leisurely, arm in arm, along the flags. A Stanhope gig rolled by, followed at a trot by two gentlemen astride neatish bay horses. A hidden child called from among the shrubbery in the center of the square. All seemed peaceful and so completely at odds with her spirits. Angel's departure brought the full import of her sister's marriage—unattended by the fortune she had hoped such an alliance would afford her family—bursting upon her. What were they going to do? What of Betsy and her mother? And as she turned to regard Charlotte, who looked quite fetching in a round dress of wine-colored satin and lace, she knew an intense desire to see her sister settled, *not* in a position as governess, but in a home of her own with a hearty brood of children clustered about her knees. Charlotte deserved as much.

Mrs. Leighton, gowned elegantly in a robe of gold silk, approached Henrietta, her face creased with worry. "Oh, Henry, as much as I am thankful Angel is so very happy in the choice of her husband, our hopes were pinned on her. And—" her voice sounded choked with tears as she turned to face the window "—and I am fallen so deeply in debt! My chest burns with fear! I cannot tell you how miserable I am become."

Henrietta took her mother's arm and squeezed it tightly. "You mustn't distress yourself, dearest!" she whispered. "We shall come about—you'll see! If nothing else, Lord Ennersley made a certain proposal to me—" She sighed deeply, biting her lip, wondering if perhaps

269

she ought to consider his scheme after all.

"What?" Mrs. Leighton cried in an astonished voice as she turned to regard her daughter.

Henrietta averted her gaze. "It is nothing, a whim of his perhaps; I'm not certain. But, if it would mean that my family would be secure, I would do it. Oh, Mama, I don't know what to do. What should I do?"

Mrs. Leighton lowered her head, her features wrinkled with concern. "Only tell me this," she cried intently. "Do you love him?"

Henrietta felt sudden tears rush to her eyes. "Oh, yes, Mama! I love him ever so much. Sometimes it hurts when I but look at him."

Mrs. Leighton gave a small cry. "Oh, my dear! I had no idea you felt as you did. I knew that he held you in high regard; anyone could see that! But I didn't know that you returned his sentiments! Why, then, by all means you must follow your heart's desire! Do not let anything stop you! This is my advice to you, my dearest Henry!" And with that, she burst into tears, covered her face with her damp, lace kerchief and walked quickly away from her, nearly colliding with Ennersley as she quit the chamber.

Henrietta watched her go, startled that her mother had fairly run from the room. Her encouragement, however, had struck the proper chord in Henrietta's heart, and when the viscount crossed the room to join her by the window, she said, "I have given the matter a great deal of thought, sir, and I wish to become your—your betrothed, if you are still of a mind!"

Chapter Thirty-Three

Brandish sat comfortably ensconced in a striped, sabre-legged chair sipping his coffee. He wore a dressing gown of burgundy satin and scanned the various columns of *The Morning Post*. He read the sundry notices of engagements, some with surprise and others with an expression of distaste. But when he ventured upon one involving his father and Mrs. Henrietta Harte—lately of Fair Oaks in Hampshire—he spewed a mouthful of coffee all over the newspaper as well as his neatly pressed dressing gown. Profanities of a varying nature erupted from his lips and rent the air. So violent was his outburst that his butler scurried into the morning room, obsequiously demanding to know if the coffee had not, after all, been to his taste.

"The coffee?" Brandish asked, bewildered. "Good God, man! What are you blathering about? Do you not know what has happened? That—that woman has somehow seduced my father! And to think I had begun to believe her an exceptional female, regardless of her stratagems. This is beyond bearing!" He rose hastily from his seat, knocking the chair backward onto the floor as he hurried from the room. If Henrietta thought he would permit her to marry his father, when he knew she was not in love with him, then she did not comprehend his character in the least!

271

Within the hour, Brandish found himself standing before Lord Ennersley, his temper further exacerbated by the fact that his papa recommended he keep his discourse brief since he had a great deal of business to attend to. "Sir!" he cried. "I have something of enormous consequence to discuss with you! I beg you will attend most seriously to what I am about to say."

Lord Ennersley lifted his gaze from a letter he was writing to his solicitor. He regarded his son with a faint lift of his brow. "And pray tell, King," he asked, dipping his pen into the brass inkwell before him, "what has put you in such a passion?"

Brandish stared at his father, his outrage taking strong hold of him as he slapped his copy of *The Morning Post* down upon the desk in front of the viscount. "This!" he spat indignantly.

Lord Ennersley glanced at the stained newspaper and said, "I should be very unhappy, too, were my butler to deliver my newspapers in such a wretched condition. I suggest you dismiss the fellow; he is clearly an incompetent servant!" He then continued scratching out quick words upon the page before him, ignoring his son.

Brandish at first did not comprehend what his father meant. "What does my butler have to do with this!" he cried, gesturing to the announcement of his father's engagement to Henrietta.

Lord Ennersley glanced up at him and said, "If you are not in the boughs over your soiled paper, then I cannot imagine what else could have put you in such a temper."

King realized his father had been taunting him, but he was not of a mind to engage in verbal swordplay. He grabbed the paper from off the desk and cried, "You know very well I did not come here to complain about the condition of my newspaper. What I wish to know is how you came about to ask for Henry—that is—Mrs. Harte's hand in marriage? Surely you know she does not love you." He rolled the newspaper up and began striking his thigh in a hard staccato.

At these words, Lord Ennersley set his pen down and leaned back in his chair, his expression cool. "I know nothing of the sort," he responded quietly. "As it happens, Henrietta has expressed a great deal of fondness for me. I consider that a proper form of love. I do not pretend, of course, to arouse an immense passion within her breast, but I am certain in time, I shall be able to coax her into warmer sentiments toward me. I would like to think I am not unversed in how to love or please a woman." He held King's gaze steadily, his blue eyes sharp and cutting. "I intend to be the very best of husbands to her, and I expect you to wish me joy!"

King began pacing the small panelled chamber, still beating his leg with the rolled-up newspaper. He had not known precisely how his father would respond to his censure of the engagement, but he was surprised at how steadfast he appeared, how determined he was to marry Henrietta! "Father," King began, as he turned abruptly back to the desk, throwing his hands wide, "is not your decision uncommonly sudden? You are speaking of taking a wife, not hiring a companion, or a servant! Did you give due consideration to your proposals before they passed your lips?"

"Just because you may think ill of the married state does not mean that I must! I have long since contemplated marrying again, and in Henrietta I have found a woman of extraordinary charm, grace and beauty. Why should I not marry her when she took up my hints so readily? She even permitted me to kiss her!" Here he cleared his throat and added softly, "And she is beautiful, is she not?"

King frowned at him, nodding his head faintly, feeling battered by all that his father was telling him. "I suppose I simply cannot conceive of your marrying anyone, nonetheless a——a lady whose age is but half yours!"

"I might even manage to produce another son by her," he added absently, gazing toward the window where a beam of morning sunlight struck the carpet through a space between the olive-green draperies. "I had not thought of that before. What a charming notion."

These words, however, spoken so calmly, had the very strange effect of causing King's stomach to ball up into a fierce knot. "Another son?" he queried, feeling as though his father had planted him a flush blow to his chest.

"Why not!" Lord Ennersley exclaimed. "The more I think on it, I daresay I could fill up that nursery myself, just as you suggested I should do. Then I might rest easy." He shook his head. "And to think all these years I have been pressing you to marry when I should have simply taken a wife myself. I feel like the worst nodcock for not having considered it before!" He rose to his feet, rounded the desk and slipped an affectionate arm about King's shoulders giving his son a hug. "I must say, King," he continued, drawing Brandish toward the door, "I am very grateful you spoke to me as you did, for now I am fully persuaded I have made the proper decision. Oh! I almost forgot! Your aunt is giving a small engagement party in honor of the event tomorrow night. I will of course expect you to be here."

King quit his father's town house in a daze. His father to marry Henrietta! Impossible.

The *beau monde* soon proclaimed the *small party* a wretched *squeeze*, which guaranteed it a place as one of the most fashionable fetes of the season.

Henrietta stood beside Lord Ennersley, holding a red rose he had given her in honor of their forthcoming nuptials. As she greeted all her well-wishers, she smiled graciously, but her conscience weighed heavily upon her. From the first, when she had informed her mother and Charlotte of her intentions, she had been beset with nervous palpitations by the mere thought of the monumental sham she and Ennersley were about to foist

274

upon the *ton.* Her mother had appeared stunned by the news and immediately pointed out that she was not at all persuaded a man of King's stamp could be herded into marriage by such a scheme. Henrietta would have argued with her except that Charlotte had joined ranks immediately. "He seems to abhor machinations of any kind!" Charlotte had exclaimed. "Are you certain this course is a wise one? Oh, Henry, I fear you've made a grave error."

Betsy, upon general agreement, had been kept ignorant of the true state of the engagement, as was Angel, who was enjoying her honeymoon and who would not have comprehended half of Henrietta's explanations anyway. A letter to Arabella informing her of the ruse, resulted in a hastily penned letter in response, a three-page diatribe upon the evils of deceit and an exhortation that Henrietta mend her ways for the sake of the *entire* family. Miss Brandish, who knew from the outset something was rotten in Denmark, had merely nodded and announced somewhat unsympathetically that if nothing else it would supply an endless variety of *on dits* throughout the habitually lean summer months.

With these varied, yet unencouraging responses still spinning about in her brain, Henrietta lifted the red rose to her nose and inhaled deeply. The die was cast, and she had but now to graciously wait out the game. She wondered if Ennersley was experiencing similar qualms, but as she glanced up at him, she could see he was in high gig. He smiled broadly upon everyone and did not seem in the least disconcerted that he was fobbing off a lie to all of his friends and acquaintances.

She soon discovered, however, that he had reason for feeling hopeful and at ease. During a lull in the arrival of guests, he leaned toward her and whispered that King was behaving precisely as he hoped he would: "Like a jealous suitor—enraged, morose, inclined to fall into a fit of the megrims! We have only to stand fast, and he will come about—you'll see!"

Henrietta was not convinced, especially when later that evening King drew her apart and demanded angrily to know just what tricks she had played off in order to entrap his father into so ridiculous an engagement.

Henrietta unfurled her fan with an indignant snap. "If you must know," she cried, "I had no notion Charles meant to offer for me, and I certainly was not pursuing him. Did he perchance tell you, though, that he had begged for my hand in marriage some four weeks ago?" King appeared stunned as he shook his head. Henrietta continued, "At the time, I refused him. My hopes had been placed elsewhere, as you may well imagine!"

"Upon Angel," he retorted crossly.

"Not precisely, King," she responded, regarding him unwaveringly. "As you once told me, my flaw is to believe what I wish. Well, now I have come to learn that opportunity is a fleeting thing. And whether you choose to accept it or not, I do love your father. He is the most generous, large-hearted gentleman I have ever known. What other man of your acquaintance would have taken on a passel of strangers as your father did when he brought us to London. I admire him prodigiously, and I intend to become an excellent wife to him." Henrietta started to turn away, but stepped back toward him and in an undervoice said, "I trust you will release me from our sennight in Paris. Even you must admit that my approaching nuptials must cancel that particular debt." Henrietta did not flinch as she made this speech; at the same time her knees fairly knocked together as she awaited his response.

"Paris is nothing," he replied with a wave of his hand, his expression one of puzzlement. "But you do not love him; you cannot love him," he whispered, reaching his arm toward her, then letting it fall back to his side. "You once said you loved me. How can you so easily accept my father's addresses when your heart cannot be given to him, or do you give your love so carelessly?"

Henrietta felt overcome by the look of hurt in his eyes,

and she lowered her gaze to stare at a diamond pin tucked between the folds of his neckcloth. "I do love you, King; I believe in my heart I always shall. But you forget that I am not free as you are to choose my course so randomly, to pursue my desires wherever they might lead me. Perhaps if Angel had wed Mr. Phillips—who had expressed a sincere desire to provide for my mother and Betsy—I should not have felt obliged to accept your father's proposals." She paused, thinking that this much at least was true. "But whenever you and I argue on this subject, I am frequently struck by how little you seem to comprehend my situation. Do you not realize, for instance, that if I do not marry your father, the season will draw to a close within a few weeks and my family will have nowhere to go! You are fully versed in Huntspill's sentiments. He would not receive us back at Fair Oaks." She smiled faintly. "And besides, I will not be the first young lady to accept a promising alliance because my family was in need of it. I expected Angel to do as much. Now I am merely partaking of my own supper, as it were." Since it appeared her words had silenced Brandish, she curtsied slightly and walked away.

King felt a gentle touch upon his elbow as he watched Henrietta greet several of his father's friends. He looked down to find Fanny gazing up into his eyes, a wicked smile upon her lips, as she queried, "You must tell me what you think of your papa's betrothed! I for one had not believed her to be quite so mercenary, though even I will admit she shall grace your father's arm to perfection. Lord Ennersley's acquaintance also seem to find a great deal in her to admire. Do but look how they fawn over her hand. Do you suppose they each wish they could take so young a bride?"

King listened to the hint of sarcasm in Fanny's voice and found himself irritated. As he gazed into her confident doe-eyes, he noticed the scornful though faint curve of her lips and realized she represented all that he despised in *tonnish* society. She was witty, but her charm carried a sharp edge; she was beautiful, but the self-interest that characterized her every word and move hardened her exquisite features to a marbleized coldness; she was elegant, but in every trained gesture he found deceit. He had even learned earlier that the wager in which she had once professed to have engaged with her friend, Miss Taverner, was a sham. "Fanny?" he asked. "Do you possess Miss Taverner's fan? It was pearl-studded, I think, but I have never seen you with it. Did you not tell her you had succeeded in winning a kiss from me thereby winning your wager with her?"

A dull blush began to creep over Fanny's cheeks, spreading downward quickly across her neck. She carried a fan, but it was painted with soft clematis flowers and bore no pearls or other finery. It was pretty, soft and elegant, but it was not Miss Taverner's. "Why, King!" she cried. "You cannot suppose I would actually reveal to such a hopeless scandalmonger that I had actually permitted you to kiss me! I have forgotten all about the wager as I'm certain she has as well!"

He turned toward her, and possessing himself of her hand, pressed it very hard. "My dear Mrs. Marshfield," he said, shaking his head. "You are a hopeless fibster. Miss Taverner was quite affronted, for all her jollity of person, when I suggested you had engaged in a wager with her, a bet she found repugnant in the extreme. The fan in question belonged to her grandmama; she would never have set it as a stake. Somehow, I believed her."

"And you do not believe me!"

"No, as it happens, I do not. Farewell, Fanny, and good hunting! You are a female of exceptional abilities, but I find only recently I have come to value something else a great deal more than cunning and artifice."

"And what is that, pray tell?" Fanny asked with considerable pique.

"Courage, my dear Mrs. Marshfield," he said, his gaze drifting toward Henrietta. When Fanny stalked away, he took a pinch of nut brown snuff and knew that he had been a decided sapskull not to have recognized the truth of his feelings for Henrietta. He had told her he was in love with her, but until this moment, he had not comprehended the depth of his respect and esteem for her. He smiled, as he closed his snuffbox quietly. She was grievously flawed. She did not hesitate to implement ploys and stratagems he despised; at the same time her concerns were always outward-reaching and not the actions of a woman, like Fanny, who was entirely self-consumed. She might also sacrifice her ideals to the need of the moment; still he had come to treasure her forthrightness as well as the fact she never hesitated to blast his own conduct when the occasion required it.

How odd, he thought, to have fallen desperately in love with a harsh female, who spoke her mind forcefully and who had just become engaged to his own father. How Nemesis had pursued him in the form of this most wearying of females! And how much he wished, had the hours been turned back, he had seized the moment and made her his wife instead of humiliating her by asking her to become his mistress. He felt extremely foolish of a sudden, and decidedly chastened.

With a heart that grew heavier as each minute passed, he realized there was nothing more to be done or said than to endure with equanimity the joining of the woman whom he adored and his father, in wedlock.

Chapter Thirty-Four

"Charles!" Henrietta cried, a slight blush warming her cheeks, for she disliked immensely calling him by his Christian name. "Are you certain we have made progress? Our supposed wedding is to take place in only a sennight, and still there is no indication that King is in the least moved. He seems so—so very *accepting* of our engagement. I am frightened!"

Henrietta and Lord Ennersley were conversing alone in the library. Over the past fortnight, since the engagement party, she had grown increasingly anxious, disbelieving that their scheme would bring about a happy conclusion. She stood now near the fireplace and upon impulse glanced up at the portrait of Lord Ennersley and King. The eyes were the same, shared between father and son, and the chins were both decidedly mulish. Was it stubbornness, then, that prevented the son from begging the father to release Henrietta from the betrothal? Or was it simply that both she and the viscount had completely mistaken the depth of King's regard for her? Oh, why had she been persuaded that this was a reasonable course! Gifts had begun flowing from every quarter, and each one brought a wave of guilt and shame beating upon her conscience. St. James had been secured for the supposed sanctification of their union, and every day well-wishers poured through the town house, expressing their hopes that the marriage would be a happy one. Ennersley had even brought the Reverend Baughurst down from his country seat in Oxfordshire to lend credence to the betrothal.

Henrietta did not know how much longer she could bear being part of so onerous a sham.

"Courage, my dear!" Lord Ennersley said, as he joined her by the fireplace and took both of her hands in his. "You must believe me when I say that I know my son. And though I, too, have had my doubts as to the wisdom of our course, every now and again I see King staring at you with such an expression that my spirits again regain their confidence. If nothing else, while he is standing beside me at the church, even with several hundred personages of rank and privilege present, I shall ask him if he should desire to take my place!"

"Oh, no!" Henrietta cried, withdrawing her hands from his and pressing them against her cheeks. "What a perfectly horrifying notion! You know very well he would refuse! You know his greatest flaw is his obstinance."

Lord Ennersley turned away from her, crossing the book-lined chamber to stand before a small, round, inlaid table by the window. "Indeed," he sighed. "We are too much alike, he and I. And you are quite correct. Were *I* to suggest he marry you in my stead, he would likely stomp from the church!" An elegant snuffbox sat upon the gleaming wood of the table. Ennersley lifted the lid, took a pinch, then let the top fall shut with a slap that sounded oddly loud in the small room. He glanced out the window, which fronted the street, and noticed that Golden Hare Phillips was descending from a landau lined with an emerald-green velvet. "Good God!" he cried. "What wealth! Only a month ago that same landau was decorated with a royal-blue silk. It is Phillips again. I wonder why he has continued to call when only painful recollections can attend him here?"

Henrietta strode to the window, where she watched

Mr. Phillips give instructions to the small tiger mounted behind his carriage. "He is a very good man and seems to find comfort in our small family circle," she responded.

"I can certainly understand that," Lord Ennersley commented. "I do not look forward to this summer, no matter how all our stratagems fall. I shall miss Betsy's playfulness and Charlotte's refined conversation. And why did your mother cease, yet again, reading Psalms to me in the evening?"

Henrietta looked up at him, surprised. "Does—that is did she do so?"

"Why, of course she did—that is—oh, I forgot! You girls were always long in your beds by that time." He cleared his throat as though an uncomfortable idea had begun to steal into his thoughts. "She read to both my sister and me, if you must know! It was not just for me that she performed this ministration. Augusta, too, took great delight in your mother's fine elocution." His brow drew together sharply as he added softly, almost to himself, "I shall miss her very much."

An intriguing light burst suddenly within the shadowy webs of Henrietta's brain. "My mother reads to you? What a *wifely* chore, m'lord!"

"*M'lord!*" he cried. "I thought we had settled that business. You must call me Charles! And as for *wifely*, why it is no such thing! I simply enjoy hearing her read."

Henrietta stared very hard at him and watched a faint blush cover his cheeks and spread downward upon his neck in stark contrast to his white neckcloth.

Thrusting his chin forward in a manner that reminded Henrietta decidedly of the son, he cried, "I do not like your expression! I do not like it at all! You are presuming a great deal!"

Henrietta smiled sweetly and responded, "Why, whatever do you mean, m'lord? I presume nothing. You like to hear my mother read. What else could I mean by looking at you?"

At that moment, just as Ennersley opened his mouth

to take Henrietta strongly to task, the door opened and Mrs. Leighton was suddenly with them. "Oh! Oh, dear!" she cried. "I had no idea you were in here. I do beg your pardon." She wore a gown of pale amethyst, trimmed with Brussells lace. Her gold hair was coiffed to perfection, with charming ringlets dangling in front of each ear, and Henrietta thought she looked quite pretty save for the unhappy shadows beneath her large blue eyes. Why had she never noticed her mother's dejection before?

"I will leave you, of course," Mrs. Leighton said. She turned to quit the library, and Henrietta saw to her dismay that her mother's lip was actually trembling. How could she have been so blind to her sentiments—and worse—how could she have stolen so much time and attention from Ennersley that could have been better spent upon her mama?

Because she stood near her mother, she caught her arm and prevented her from leaving. "You do not intrude, I assure you. I was just about to return to my bedchamber to dress for dinner. As it happens, Lord Ennersley wished to ask you something. Did you not, m'lord?" She smiled devilishly upon the viscount.

"Why, yes," Ennersley said, clearing his throat. "That is, it is nothing of great import, but I beg you will stay for a moment, Lavinia. Please."

Mrs. Leighton turned back toward the viscount, an expression of surprise on her features as she clasped her hands tightly before her. "As you wish," she answered quietly.

Henrietta excused herself, intent upon leaving Ennersley alone with her mother. Until this moment, until she saw the wistfulness in the viscount's eye when he realized perhaps for the first time that he would not see Mrs. Leighton again once the season drew to a close, Henrietta had not even considered the possibility that he might have fallen in love with her. She now believed there was a strong possibility he had. But, if the father were as much like the son, the likelihood of Mrs. Leighton bringing Ennersley up to scratch would prove as easy as it had been for Henrietta to do likewise with King. What a horrid coil, but at least she could give her dearest mama this opportunity of engaging his affections.

Mrs. Leighton regarded the viscount steadily, her heart laden with pain. She had never known such longing for a man in her life, yet she did not know how to proceed. Even though she comprehended fully that Ennersley's engagement to her daughter was part of a great deception to bring King Brandish to an awareness of his love for Henrietta, Mrs. Leighton had never quite recovered from the jolt the original announcement of the engagement had brought to her. With the reading of the banns, she had herself come to a degree of self-knowledge that had since cut up her peace entirely. She loved Charles Brandish, fifth Viscount Ennersley, to the point of madness. But the very strength of her passion had caused her to withdraw from him, lest he discover her love and despise her for it. She was convinced in her heart, in the secret place where her feminine instincts held sway, that if he did not conceive of the notion first—that they ought to belong to one another forever—she would lose him before she had even begun. It was a wretched place to be caught. How mysterious the course of love and marriage was. And what was it he required of her now? And how ought she to answer him?

"This is quite ridiculous," Lord Ennersley began, a nervous laughter playing uneasily upon his lips. "Henrietta should not have insisted you stay to hear my request. It is an old one. I merely expressed a regret that you had, yet again,"—he seemed annoyed as he said these words—"ceased reading to me, that is, to Augusta and myself in the evenings." He glanced at her warily.

Mrs. Leighton felt as though she were standing upon the edge of a precipice. She knew that her words were

284

critical, that in this very moment, her fate would be decided. Several notions about how to proceed blew through her mind, as though carried upon a strong wind. She captured one, and discarded it. She grasped for another, but tossed it aside. For what seemed an eternity, she paused, her mouth partially open as she waited for some inspiration to strike her, or at least to guide her through this most dreaded confrontation.

Finally, when no Olympian wisdom shed light into her mind, she responded quietly, "Charles. I have lived in your home, in Augusta's home, most contentedly for several weeks now. And in but a fortnight I must move on and find another course for myself and my beloved daughters. I, too, have enjoyed reading to you, as well as to your sister, but I have of late discovered that I am far too comfortable within your small family bosom. If I do not take great care, I shall find my heart broken by having to leave Grosvenor Square. Do not take offense, I pray. Only understand that I must now see to my own future." Here, a feeble light glowed dimly in her mind, and she added, "In fact, more than one kind gentleman has expressed an interest in me. And though I had not considered marrying again, I believe now it would be the prudent course. You see, I don't rely overly much on your son's coming about, though I too believe he loves Henrietta. But for all these many weeks now I have most selfishly placed the burden of securing my future upon my daughters, and I shan't continue to do so."

At this juncture, the butler arrived to inform Mrs. Leighton that Mr. Phillips had come to call upon the ladies and that of the moment, Miss Charlotte sat alone with him—an improper arrangement given Charlotte's maidenly status.

Mrs. Leighton thanked the butler for informing her of this lapse in propriety, and she promptly excused herself from Lord Ennersley's presence.

The viscount remained in the library for quite some time. He did not at all like the unsettled emotions that had begun romping about in his chest. He did not like his life to be quite so disordered. At his age, he considered it unhealthful to be in a state of extreme apprehension. And whatever did Lavinia mean that several gentlemen had expressed an interest in her? What fellows were these? He felt violated in some manner, as though another buck had come to challenge his territory. At the same time, his common sense forced him to realize that of course Mrs. Leighton was free to marry where she wished. It just seemed unnatural somehow, though he was damned if he knew why!

Chapter Thirty-Five

Henrietta waited discreetly in the hall for her mother but pounced on her the moment she was certain Lord Ennersley could not hear them converse. She demanded to know if what she suspected was true. "Do you love him, Mama?"

Mrs. Leighton's eyes filled with tears. "More than I wish to!" she responded angrily as she wiped her cheeks with a lace kerchief. "Oh, my dear Henry! How is it possible that you and I fell in love with such *hopeless* men! Stubborn, intractable and so very determined to remain in their bachelorhoods. I could scream with vexation, for I know that should I speak the wrong word or display an unexpected sentiment toward him, he will be lost to me forever! I do not know how to proceed, and every step I take fills me with such dread. You've no idea!"

Henrietta slipped her arm about her mother's waist. Mrs. Leighton did the same as she leaned her head against Henrietta's dusky curls.

"What do you intend to do?" Henrietta asked as they progressed toward the drawing room.

"I do not know precisely. I can only guess from day to day what course to set my feet on. This I do know, however; I shall not hesitate to get up a flirtation with one or two willing gentlemen of my acquaintance if for no other purpose than to keep my spirits from sinking into oblivion. Everytime I but look at Charles, I feel as though I have fallen into the greatest pit. Do you have any notion how much I have suffered over the past several weeks?"

Henrietta laughed. "I am afraid I comprehend your distress perfectly."

Mrs. Leighton squeezed her daughter's waist. "Yes," she responded with a heavy sigh. "I suppose you do at that!"

They arrived at the drawing room, and Henrietta opened the door, gesturing for her mother to precede her. She was a little surprised when her mother stopped abruptly, placed a hand to her lips and, with an expression of shock suffusing her features, whispered, "Good God! Who would have thought! My second-born! My *dearest* child!"

Henrietta followed the direction of her mother's gaze and gasped, for there, standing before the fireplace, was Mr. Phillips with his arms locked about Charlotte in a crushing embrace.

If the *beau monde* flocked to Grosvenor Square when Henrietta's engagement was announced in *The Times* and *The Morning Post,* the fascinated *ton* swarmed into Miss Brandish's drawing room from morning till night when it became generally known that Miss Charlotte Leighton, a female of retiring manners and indifferent beauty, had actually succeeded in capturing the greatest Matrimonial Prize of them all—Golden Hare Phillips. How was it possible that so ordinary a young lady could have garnered Mr. Phillips' affections? It was generally agreed that some form of witchery must have occurred.

Henrietta watched her sister's success with nothing short of immense pride and pleasure. Charlotte's coup far outshone her own supposed betrothal, and it was a great irony to her that for all their fine scheming, it was Charlotte—the least advantaged with beauty of either

288

face or figure—who had won the very gentleman who could easily have saved them all a great deal of anguish and absurd stratagems. After the same fashion, Henrietta realized that of all the ladies, Charlotte deserved to be blessed in so glorious a manner. She had never put herself forward during the course of the Season, nor had demanded the attention lavished solely upon Angel, nor had she caused the least fuss when it seemed an engagement between Angel and Mr. Phillips would soon transpire. Having so recently learned of Charlotte's love for her betrothed, she now understood that Charlotte's loss would have been horrendous had such an engagement come to fruition.

"I am happy beyond words, Henry," Charlotte told her five days before Henrietta's wedding was due to take place. "And we have such plans and hopes for the future. We intend first to travel the Continent in search of the finest works of art for our home in Oxfordshire. How I have always longed to see Rome! We mean to take Betsy with us as well, for you know how much she wishes to escape from England."

Henrietta nodded, clasping her sister's hand and pressing it hard. "You cannot know how glad I am that you are not to be locked away in some dreary country manor, playing the governess to another woman's brood of nursery-brats! You will have your own children in time, and what a great mother you shall be." Tears spilled from her eyes and trailed down her cheeks to plop finally upon her morning gown of twilled emerald sarsenet.

Charlotte queried, "But how do your own schemes progress? We have scarcely seen Mr. Brandish this past sennight and more. You must miss him dreadfully. Why, I've never known anyone to tumble so violently in love as you!"

Henrietta gasped, "Is it so very obvious?"

Charlotte smiled and fingered the bridge of her spectacles as she responded facetiously, "I know it seems unlikely to you that anyone should have guessed the truth when you were forever regarding him with such an adoring expression! But there it is! I suppose I am simply more perceptive than most." She trilled a refrain of happy laughter and cried, "Mooncalf, m'dear! Decidedly, wretchedly, mooncalf!"

"Oh," Henrietta groaned playfully. "And I had thought myself amazingly clever."

"And so you probably were with most of society, but not with me, nor with Richard." She blushed faintly, and Henrietta could not keep from teasing her about how easily Mr. Phillips' Christian name rolled from her tongue. Charlotte responded by blushing more darkly still, but refused to be put off from her original train of thought. "Whatever do you mean to do, when several hundred guests will be sitting in St. James's expecting to see you trip down the aisle."

"I haven't the faintest idea," she said, shaking her head and staring at nothing in particular. "I begged Lord Ennersley to cease this horrid farce not two days ago, but he is intent upon it. He believes King will realize his great love for me and steal me away from the church doors, I suppose. But enough of my difficulties, tell me about your wedding plans!"

Their wedding was set for a fortnight following Henrietta's and promised to be the season's grandest occasion of them all. Even the Prince Regent, who was a particular friend of Mr. Phillips', expressed his hope of attending the happy festivities. No greater approval than this could be graced upon Charlotte, and suddenly the *ton* found the impoverished Miss Charlotte Leighton to have acquired more *beauty* than at first was supposed, to have developed in the course of but a sennight an exceptional countenance, and to have revealed by means of her betrothal a heretofore hidden, rapierlike wit. The latter was pronounced by many to be equal almost to that of Scrope Davies, a bosom beau of Byron's known for his penetrating observations of English manners and mores.

Charlotte, much to her credit, as well as to Henrietta's

satisfaction, merely nodded politely to the effusive compliments paid to her in deference to her forthcoming nuptials. "I am of a similar mind as King," she told Henrietta not three days later. "I despise toadeaters of all things, though I must say it provides an endless source of amusement for myself and Richard." She then looked very hard at Henrietta and asked, "He was here last night—I am referring of course to King—but he seemed so quiet and *accepting* of your imminent marriage. Does Lord Ennersley still insist—?"

Henrietta pressed a hand to her bosom. "I have been quaking with fear the entire day! I can mark the hours, with little stretch of my intellect, until I am to step across the portals of the church! Oh, Charlotte, what madness seized me to travel this path? King is polite and friendly and—and indifferent! In two days' time, how will I face those who have showered their gifts and congratulations upon me! I am sick with unease! I have considered putting an end to this dastardly business myself. Tonight, Brandish is taking Betsy to Astley's Amphitheatre, and when he brings her home, I have all but decided to confess the whole of it; only what will he think of me?"

Even through the din of two hundred horses pounding in apparent chaos around the ring of the amphitheater, King Brandish saw only one vision before him—the sight of Henrietta, gowned in satin, lace and orange blossoms, striding down the long aisle of St. James, preparing to wed his father. The vision, which had taken strong hold of him since early that morning, had grown increasingly vivid, so much so that even when the roar of a cannon threw the crowd of the theater into a tumult of excitement, he still saw only Henrietta. When Louisa Woolford danced upon the back of a white circus horse, he saw Henrietta, his chin in hand, his heart compressed with fear.

He had been so proud, so certain that all he wanted of

her was a sennight in Paris, or several months' pleasure were she to become his mistress. But as each day surmounted the next, since the announcement of her engagement to his father, he had been forced to comprehend the truth. He could not bear the thought of Henrietta becoming any man's wife, nonetheless his father's. He wanted Henrietta for his own; he wanted to take her as wife. His wife! He had finally owned to the truth. He wanted to marry her.

But she was betrothed to his father!

The numbing reality of their engagement grew steadily upon him throughout the evening, to the point that when *The Battle of Waterloo*—as the program was called—drew to a close, he wasn't even aware that Betsy was speaking to him.

"Oh, Mr. Brandish!" she cried, though her voice reached him through a thick haze. "I have never enjoyed anything half so much! Thank you—why, whatever is the matter?"

He glanced down at her, blinking several times until her freckled nose came into focus. "Nothing, my dear! Why do you ask?"

"Because you look so *absent,* and your skin has a gray tinge to it. Are you bilious? Mama has an excellent purgative if you are suffering overly much!"

He laughed at that, at her innocence and the sweetness of her concerned expression. "I am in excellent frame, I assure you. I was merely distracted for a moment with certain unhappy thoughts."

"For a moment!" she exclaimed. "Throughout the entire performance, more like! Why, you did not even jump when the cannons exploded. It smells awfully thick and dusty in here, now that I think on it. Could we not leave?"

He rose immediately and guided her out of the theater. When they returned to his town chariot, he settled a thick lap robe across her knees, adjuring her to tuck her hands deeply within her muff against the chill evening

292

air. Once the horses were set in motion, he again fell into a brown study, until Betsy's voice intruded.

"Well!" she cried. "I have a secret I am longing to tell you, only I greatly fear that if I do, Henry will murder me in my bed when I am asleep!"

He turned toward her slightly, restraining a yawn. Ordinarily, he enjoyed her buoyant spirits and playfulness. But tonight he wished to hear nothing of her pranks and mischief. Rather, he longed to return home, to a warm fire and a snifter of old brandy. He sighed and asked perfunctorily, "And what secret is that? Only I am in a sad temper, and I warn you not to try my patience too far this evening with your prattlings!"

"Why, only that Henrietta is not really getting married—she is only pretending to. Now, what do you think of that!"

"What?" Brandish asked, uncertain he had heard correctly. "What do you mean, little hoyden, that your sister is pretending to get married?"

Betsy, wearing an impish smile on her lips, leaned toward him slightly, her head lowered as she whispered, "I heard her speaking with Charlotte. And though I usually don't propagate tittle-tattle—for I have an abhorrence for such creatures that do—I thought you, in particular, could benefit from knowing the truth! Besides, you saved Vincent's life, and I felt I owed you a favor."

"Are you certain you have the right of it, Betsy? It is of the utmost importance that what you are telling me is absolutely true!"

Betsy nodded slowly, a furrow forming between her brows. "There is only one thing, and I know you will be angry when I tell you; but I believe it was entirely your father's idea. He thought if you faced losing Henry forever, you might come to know your heart. I, for one, think his ploy has succeeded."

Brandish, who was struggling to comprehend the full import of Betsy's confidences, responded curtly, "Do you, indeed!"

"Yes," she retorted, lifting her chin and leaning back against the squabs. "How else can you account for your complete disinterest in Mr. Ducrow's performance this evening? He nearly fell from the two horses he was straddling as they raced wildly about the ring, and you sat staring at the chandelier, your eyes open and blank, as though you were seeing a specter. I think you love Henrietta more than you will admit. The problem is, you are hopelessly flawed."

Brandish found himself extremely irritated and responded haughtily, "And pray tell, my precocious little bluestocking, just what is my flaw?"

"You are mulish beyond permission. Even Angel said as much just before she left on her honeymoon. And you know how rare it is she draws the sum of a character! Stubbornness, that is your true vice! But at least you are not high-in-the-instep or something equally as horrid, like Mr. Huntspill! I detest Huntspill, even though he is my brother now! You may be obstinate, Mr. Brandish, but I could never detest you."

"And I suppose you gleaned this opinion of my character primarily from Henrietta!" he responded crossly, a growing sense of ill-usage and outrage burning within him.

"Oh, no!" she responded happily. "I saw from the first how it was! You want everything precisely the way you want it! You even kissed Henry—I saw you outside the barn that first night at Fair Oaks—and you kissed her solely because you wished for it, not because it was proper." She was silent apace, then continued, "Though I must admit that the real reason I can judge you in this harsh manner, is because we—we share the same flaw. Charlotte tells me I'm spoiled; but I do like things to be just so, and it irks me to no end when I cannot have and do the things I wish to. That is why I am especially grateful that Charlotte is marrying Golden Hare, for I shall be able to travel with them which is what I want

294

above all things. That, and Vincent and the colt. Did you know that Mr. Phillips intends to purchase the colt from Huntspill?"

Brandish merely grunted in response, sinking low into the leather seat, his arms folded across his chest. Forgotten almost entirely was the fact that but a few moments earlier he was beset with anguish that Henrietta was wedding his father. The knowledge that the engagement was a sham served only to infuriate him since its purpose was but further evidence that Mrs. Harte was as wicked as his aunt Margaret, full of every odious wile. That his father was involved only increased his ire.

Light from the gaslamps along the street pulsed across his face as the carriage swayed upon its sturdy springs heading toward Mayfair. King knew an intense desire to exact revenge upon both his parent and Henrietta. He again fell into a brown study as Betsy chattered contentedly beside him, apparently oblivious to his dark mood. Throughout the duration of the journey back to Grosvenor Square, he conceived and summarily dismissed at least a dozen vengeful schemes of his own. One, however, finally brought a sweet peacefulness to his inflamed sensibilities, and when he found Henrietta anxious to speak with him upon his return to his father's town house, he was able to address her in perfect union with his own carefully concocted designs.

Chapter Thirty-Six

Henrietta coaxed King into the library, her heart wrenched by the sight of the melancholy aspect of his expression. She heard him sigh heavily when she closed the door behind her, shutting them both into the book-lined chamber in a most forbidden *tête-à-tête*. To her surprise, he came to her at once, taking both her hands in his and exclaimed, "Do not speak, my dearest one! Pray do not torture me by giving utterance to a single regret you might have for your present course. You do not know how I have suffered these several weeks, watching you and my beloved parent greet the *beau monde* as one! How my soul strives within me at the mere sight of you!"

Henrietta, her stomach bubbling unhappily and her heart nearly ready to burst from her chest, tried to interrupt him, to proclaim her iniquity, but he would not have it as he released one of her hands and pressed his fingers to her lips. "I will not permit you to speak!" he cried, his blue eyes burning a pathway into her own as he held her gaze. "I could not bear to hear one word of longing cross your perfect lips!" At the same moment, he slipped an arm about her waist and drew her painfully close.

Henrietta lost her breath completely as well as her

ability to charm her carefully prepared speech from her throat. "Oh," she responded, a familiar weakness invading her legs, causing her knees to tremble. "King, my darling!"

"This is the very last time I will ever be free to express my love for you." He looked deeply into her eyes, and some of the forced theatrics of the moment faded into the recesses of his mind. He saw her now as the woman who had somehow worked magical fingers into the marrow of his spirit, gripped him firmly, and refused to either let go or to be forced out by his own will. "My darling Henry," he continued, his voice dropping to a whisper. "I do love you, so very much! Do you know how your eyes sparkle in the candlelight? I could devour you, in an effort to take within my being the brightness of your own. I have complained loudly of your flaws, but have I ever told you how much I admire your selflessness? Your thoughts have all been for your family, whereas mine have been for my pleasure alone."

Henrietta listened to him, her heart drinking in the sincerity of his words. She leaned into him, lifting a hand to stroke his cheek. The faint smell of gunpowder from the spectacle at Astley's clung to his clothing and black hair. "You reek of battle, my love," she said, chuckling softly.

He laughed at her words. "You are so very right, but of the moment I have only one desire, not to quarrel with you, but to kiss you, my dearest, most beloved Henry." His words had grown soft as he leaned down to her, his lips brushing her mouth gently.

As he pressed his lips to hers, Henrietta felt as though for a long time she had been marching over a hilly countryside, through muddy lanes for hours on end, and just now, in this moment, she had finally come home. She felt wondrously safe and comfortable within the circle of his arms. He was rife with imperfections; this much she knew to be infinitely true. But she loved him so much as he kissed her with increasing fervor. She returned his embraces, tasting of his lips as if it would be the last time, even though she knew their life together was just beginning.

As he pulled away from her, Henrietta felt warm and desired nothing more than to beg his forgiveness for her stupidity in embarking on such a ridiculous course. She was about to speak, when he said, "Henry, I cannot let this happen. I must speak with my father and beg him not to marry you. Will you not await me here while I approach him on our behalf, though I know it shall break his heart to learn that it is me you love and not him. I wish to make you my wife if you will have me."

Henrietta felt such relief flood her mind and heart that a dizziness assailed her. She was about to confess the whole of her schemes to him, but since King meant to address his father, she decided to remain silent for the present. "I would like it above all things, my love. Do—do go to your father! I am persuaded he will not hesitate to release me from this engagement."

For the barest second, Henrietta saw a funny light enter King's eye as he bowed slightly to her, then begged her to remain where she was until he could conclude the matter for both of them.

When the door closed behind him, Henrietta sank into the settee and shed tears of relief. The deception was over at last, all had ended well, and King wished to marry her—Ennersley had been right after all.

After a few minutes, she heard a carriage pull away from the town house, and with a vague feeling of unease, she rose to her feet and crossed the small chamber to see who had left. She was startled to find that King's town chariot was disappearing quickly into the misty evening air at the end of the street.

A panic assailed her as she quickly ran from the room and flew down the stairs. The butler confirmed her fears, whereupon she ran equally fast up the stairs only to find

Lord Ennersley sitting quietly by the fire reading a copy of *The Times*. He did not appear in the least flustered.

"Did King speak with you?" she asked, her breath coming in painful gasps from her exertions on the stairs.

Lord Ennersley appeared quite bewildered as he shook his head. A confusion raced about in Henrietta's mind. *Why did King choose not to confront his father? What could he mean by leaving without having accomplished his task?* Even though the viscount pressed her to tell him what was amiss, Henrietta kept her counsel, waiting to receive word from Brandish himself. None was forthcoming that night, nor even the next day, and she began to question what had actually transpired in the library. Had King not been sincere? Was he afraid to speak with his father? Did he perchance believe that Ennersley was in love with her after all, that the viscount wished to marry her?

When she realized how her horrid scheme could have been interpreted by Brandish, she hastily penned a letter and dispatched it to him. She informed him of everything she had meant to tell him on the evening before. The letter was returned forthwith, however, and much to her shock, unopened.

In response, he sent a note of his own which read,

My dearest Henry, I know you will understand when I tell you I cannot disappoint my father so grievously by stealing his bride from him. He loves you. I have seen how he looks at you, his eyes are always full of adoration and I cannot bring myself to hurt him. I know you will respect my sentiments for I have learned such a familial loyalty at your hand. I will of course attend my father at the wedding; until then, do not torment me further by trying to correspond again. Yours, etc., King.

Henrietta took the missive to Lord Ennersley, who remained staring at it for a long moment as though he had been carved from a block of marble. "Good God," he cried at last. "I sired a sapskull, a—a gudgeon, a dullard of the meanest order! However could he suppose I had fallen in love with you?"

"We are engaged to be married, you know," Henrietta reminded him with a twinkle in her eye. "And though I am not half as beautiful as Angel, I have been told by more than one gentleman that I am not a complete antidote!"

"Bah!" he retorted. "You know very well what I mean. But what does this letter signify? Do you know, Henry, I believe he is calling our bluff. There is something about this missive that does not ring true!" He struck the thick paper with his hand and said, "He'll be at the church tomorrow, and then we shall see just how far he will permit the ceremony to go!"

On the following afternoon, both Charlotte and Betsy helped Henrietta don her wedding gown of white satin trimmed with seed pearls and lace. She wore her dark brown locks drawn into a knot at the top of her head and dressed in feathery ringlets. A white, net veil draped to her waist from a garland of orange blossoms encircling the crown of her head. As she regarded herself in the looking glass, she saw a bride reflected back to her, and she wondered yet again how she had let this scheme come to such a pass.

Henrietta drew on her white lace gloves and glanced from one sister to the next. "Has there been no word from Brandish?" she queried.

Charlotte, long-faced, shook her head, and Betsy stated, "I think you should be wedding King, not his father!"

Henrietta realized in that moment that Betsy still did not know the wedding was a sham and informed her of the truth, adding that it seemed unlikely anything good would come of her wicked schemes.

Betsy, whose face grew quite red during the recital, cried, "King will not forsake you now, Henry! He loves you! If only you had seen him at the amphitheater. He did not even hear the cannons roar so consumed was he in his thoughts of you!"

Henrietta smiled upon Betsy, thinking she was so very sweet, but so very innocent. After a moment, she queried, "But what is the hour? I suppose we must leave very soon."

Charlotte replied softly, "It wants only ten minutes until we are to depart. Lord Ennersley's carriage awaits us." Both younger ladies were gowned in matching lilac round gowns of fine silk trimmed with several rows of elegant ruching about the hems.

Henrietta clasped Betsy's hand and pressed it hard. She rose to her feet suddenly and with a smile said, "I must finish what I have begun, though my knees quake at the very thought of walking down the aisle of St. James. I shall trust that Lord Ennersley will know how to proceed! Though I begin to wonder."

The ladies formed a solemn party as they descended the stairs to the well-wishes of the servants lining the hall. The female servants curtsied, smiled and giggled at Henrietta, who grew increasingly uncomfortable with each step she took knowing that they believed she would soon become their mistress. She could hardly bear to look at the assorted maids and footmen who greeted her, and she quickened her steps, inclining her head slightly as she passed by.

Once on the flags, two liveried servants—one of whom kept a hand pinned to his powdered wig in an effort to keep the wind from blowing it off—awaited the ladies, prepared to help them board Lord Ennersley's gleaming town chariot. Henrietta's heart failed her as she lifted a foot to mount the two steps into the carriage. She could not go through with it. She could not!

301

At that moment, another coach and four drew up sharply beside the viscount's equipage. Henrietta glanced with mild curiosity first at the pawing, snorting horses and then with considerable surprise at a gentleman who burst from the coach's door. Her heart leapt within her at the sight of Brandish as he fairly ran toward the ladies.

Bowing to Henrietta, he said, "I have come to escort you to the church, Henry. Please come with me!" He held an arm out to her and gestured toward his coach.

Henrietta looked about her, feeling slightly confused, wondering what she ought to do. Charlotte decided the matter for her instantly when she gave Betsy a push toward Ennersley's coach and called over her shoulder, "Do go with Mr. Brandish, Henry. I'm certain your *betrothed* would not have the least objection, and Betsy and I do not mind travelling alone, do we Betsy?"

"Not at all!" Betsy cried as she scrambled into the coach with Charlotte fast behind her.

Before Henrietta could protest, or consider whether or not she should go with Brandish, the viscount's coach bowled away from the flags with Betsy leaning out the window and waving at her.

King wasted no time in guiding Henrietta toward his town chariot, his hand gripping her elbow firmly.

Once inside, Henrietta was astonished when Brandish drew the shades down, took her roughly in his arms, and kissed her hard upon the mouth. She was inordinately shocked and pushed him away, wondering what had taken possession of him to accost her in this unexpected manner. For all she knew, he still intended for her to wed his father.

"I don't understand, King!" she cried. "Whatever are you doing? First you tell me, not two days ago, that we are to be wed, then you choose quite abruptly not to confront your father after all. And now you kiss me?"

The coach pulled slowly away from the town house,

turning about entirely to head in the opposite direction. Henrietta glanced around the darkened interior, trying to gain her bearings. "We are not travelling in the proper direction!" she cried, with a start. "Brandish, do you not mean to take me to the church? And if not, what are you about?"

He still held her gripped tightly about her shoulders and waist, the length of his leg pressed scandalously against her own. He smiled in a perfectly odious manner as he responded, "Why, I intend to take that which is due me—a sennight in Paris, my little scheming wench, your stake in our wager, if you remember!"

Chapter Thirty-Seven

At half past two, with the *haut ton* whispering excitedly in their seats, Betsy and Charlotte left the confines of their antechamber—where they had been awaiting Henrietta's arrival—to go in search of Lord Ennersley. Henrietta was nearly forty-five minutes overdue, and though Charlotte considered the possibility that Brandish's town chariot had suffered an accident, it seemed more likely that Mr. Brandish had simply spirited Henrietta away. Charlotte had never been entirely comfortable in King's presence. She admired his brute energy a great deal, but she did not trust him to always follow suit. It would be just like him, she thought, to have eloped with Henrietta, if nothing more than to punish his father with whom he was frequently at odds.

Charlotte found Ennersley pacing a room adjacent to the nave, with the Reverend Baughurst looking on. The latter wore a pinched expression as he watched his patron march to and fro in quick, nervous steps. Charlotte explained her fears to the viscount, having been unwilling until this moment to reveal to him that Henrietta was with his son.

Ennersley listened intently, and when she had done, he slapped his hand against his thigh. "That miserable whelp!" he cried. "I should have known he was up to some devilment! But if Henrietta did not reveal our scheme to him, however did he discover it?"

"I told him," Betsy squeaked, taking a step behind Charlotte and peeking around her to stare wide-eyed at Ennersley. "A full two days ago!"

"Astley's, eh? Why didn't you tell me? Now everything is made clear! His speech to Henrietta was all a hum! Damn and blast—oh, I do beg your pardon, Mr. Baughurst!—do but let me think! Whatever is to be done now! And where do you suppose he has taken her. Mark my words, he has done this out of pique! *Betsy*, I could wring your neck, you little hoyden."

Betsy, who remained crouched behind Charlotte, merely smiled wickedly to this threat and retorted, "King is my very good friend, and he deserved to know the wedding was a sham!"

Ennersley scowled and clucked at her, but in the end he merely cleared his throat, admitting it was probably for the best, though he still confessed he did not know how next to proceed.

Mrs. Leighton, and her newly acquired suitor, Edward Rowledge, stood outside the door of the chamber in which her daughters, Ennersley and Baughurst were closeted. They had followed Charlotte and Betsy, unbeknownst to the young ladies, when Miss Brandish had recommended to Mrs. Leighton that she discover for herself what delay had occurred—in effect, where Henrietta and Brandish were. Both Miss Brandish and Mrs. Leighton had been seated in a forward pew some thirty minutes earlier, at Lord Ennersley's request, in an effort to allay the restlessness of the assembled guests. To little effect, however. The cause of so much ferment they had learned from the willing lips of Mr. Rowledge, who had been seated behind Mrs. Leighton, and who had happily informed both ladies that a rumor was circulating which declared that Henrietta had eloped with Ennersley's son. "A most delicious scandal," he had whispered, "if it is indeed true!"

Mrs. Leighton had looked into Edward's haughty blue eyes and knew a strong desire to give him a sharp setdown. He was a fine-looking man, of an age with her, who wore his brown hair clipped conservatively short and brushed *a la Brutus*. She admired him in many ways, but she soon realized he persevered in the odious belief that he was far above any of the company he kept, including Lord Ennersley. Instead of telling him he was an overbearing sapskull, she held her peace. It was then that Miss Brandish suggested she find out whether or not Henrietta had arrived safely.

Mrs. Leighton had gripped her gloved hands tightly together and surreptitiously glanced back at Mr. Rowledge. A most daring and frightening stratagem occurred to her. Over the past several days, she had been able to collect a not unformidable court about her much to Ennersley's extreme annoyance, and occasional bewilderment. Time had been so very compressed, as each day melted into the next, that she was not convinced that a dance with this gentleman here and a flirtation with that one there had truly been sufficient to arouse within Ennersley's breast a sense that he was about to lose something of irreplaceable value to him were she to wed another.

She glanced about the nave, where feathers bobbed with titillating conjectures as to the accuracy of the *on dits* travelling among the pews. Here was an unequalled opportunity, she realized—a wedding seemingly short of a bride. But would the groom take another?

Her heart beat rapidly within her breast. She again glanced back at Mr. Rowledge, and in a sweet voice, with a hand laid upon his arm as he leaned well forward to hear her whispers, she begged him to help her find Lord Ennersley. "For you must know it is a matter of the utmost importance. I am gravely concerned as to my daughter's whereabouts, but I do not know my way about this labyrinthine church." How much she disliked telling whiskers!

As she waited now outside the chamber, she took several deep breaths, and when all conversation ceased within the room, she graciously took Rowledge's arm, at the same time rapping lightly upon the door.

Ennersley, much to her surprise, opened it. He glanced from her face to Rowledge's, scowled at the latter and bid them enter.

Mrs. Leighton took great care to lift the demi-train of her amber silk gown. She moved slowly and elegantly, giving the viscount every opportunity to see her and to notice how attentive and solicitous Mr. Rowledge had become. As Ennersley stood aside, permitting them to cross the threshold of the antechamber, she glided softly into the room.

"Charles?" she queried. "Where is my daughter, Henrietta? And what of your son? Should he not be here by now? The guests are nearly frenzied with anticipation. It seems there is a rumor going about to the effect that Henrietta would not be wedding you today."

Ennersley approached her, and stepping between Mrs. Leighton and Mr. Rowledge—fairly pushing her beau aside—he possessed himself of her hands. "My dear, I am sorry, but I think I've bungled it! I greatly fear King has abducted Henry, and I've little doubt he means to take her to Paris. Henrietta told me she had entered a quite reprehensible wager with my son involving a scandalous sennight in Paris staked against King's help in bringing Angel into fashion. We—none of us—had ever been informed of the true stakes to that ridiculous wager! But it seems Betsy, here, told Brandish of our stratagems when he took her to that absurd equestrian spectacle at Astley's some two days ago. It would seem King has been playing off his tricks again, leading us all to believe he first wanted to marry Henrietta, then disappeared for a day and a half! And now he's disappeared with my bride, just to make me mad as bedamned, though I've little doubt he will take an equal pleasure in setting the *ton* by the ears!"

"Then, you must send your guests home," Mrs. Leighton said quietly. "The farce has run its course. You must address them; you must tell them something!"

"Indeed, you must!" Mr. Rowledge agreed readily, regarding the viscount through his quizzing glass. "This whole affair has gone quite beyond the line, if I do say so myself!"

Lord Ennersley, his face turning a ruddy color, glowered at Mr. Rowledge and retorted with no small degree of asperity, "I don't recall anyone asking for your opinion! And what the devil do you mean by intruding in my family's affairs!"

Mrs. Leighton pulled her hands away from Ennersley and turned back to Rowledge with a reassuring smile. "Pay no heed to Lord Ennersley's temper, I beg you, Edward!" She took up his arm again and addressed the viscount. "If you must know, Charles, I asked Mr. Rowledge to support me in this trying hour."

Much to Mrs. Leighton's pleasure, she watched Lord Ennersley bristle at the sight of her arm upon Mr. Rowledge's.

With apparent effort, Lord Ennersley said, "If you don't mind, Rowledge, we need a bit of privacy here of the moment. I only beg you will say nothing of what you have heard, at least not until we have decided what to do."

Rowledge took the hint in a gentlemanly manner, though before he quit the small chamber, he took the opportunity of kissing Mrs. Leighton's fingers.

"What a paltry fellow," Ennersley remarked, irritated.

"He is nothing of the sort," Mrs. Leighton retorted quickly, though to a large degree she was in accordance with his sentiment. "The fact is, Charles, he has asked me to marry him. His fortune is quite comfortable, and of the moment, I am of a mind to accept his kind offer."

Lord Ennersley stared at her as though she had just

308

struck his cheek with a crackling whip. "Marry Rowledge," he cried, disgusted. "You? Why the man's a born bleater! And as for his fortune, why he's the most clutch-fisted, nip-farthing I have ever known! You'd do far better to reside with Golden Hare and Charlotte than to become leg-shackled to the likes of Edward Rowledge! I recommend you do so."

Mrs. Leighton stiffened her shoulders as she met his gaze squarely. "I don't give a fig what you recommend I should do. I have not lived in London these past two months without realizing how much I have missed society and the company of a good, worthy gentleman. Mr. Rowledge appreciates the little attentions I show him, unlike a certain man I could mention."

"You refer to me, I suppose! And in what way have I not appreciated you, Lavinia! I have all but begged you to read to me in the evenings because I adore to hear your voice—Augusta, too!"

"There, you see! You cannot even say that *you*, and you alone, have enjoyed my society. You must forever combine your praise with the laud of another. And as for *begging* me to read to you, all I ever desired was that you might *ask* me to read. Instead, you commanded I attend to your every wish! Only a wife has the onerous task of submitting to such scurrilous treatment and then only under the profoundest protest. You are one of the most inconsiderate men I have ever known!"

"You are very harsh with me today, Lavinia!" he cried, taken aback. In his clear blue eyes, Mrs. Leighton noticed a boyish hurt that struck deeply into her own heart.

In a more subdued voice, he continued, "I never meant to be so tyrannical as you suggest I have been. And if this has been the case, I do most humbly beg your pardon. As for your voice, *I* adore it. I, and I alone, have enjoyed the sweet musicality of your expression when you read." He took a step closer to her and again possessed himself of her hands. "Only, tell me you do not really intend to wed Mr. Rowledge. I don't think I could bear it!" For the first time since she had known Ennersley, she saw in his face, in the look of real concern that constricted each most beloved feature, a reason to hope.

Mrs. Leighton regarded the viscount steadily as she blinked back her tears. "I must consider my future, Charles. I cannot depend on your good graces and generosity forever. You have been so very kind in helping to establish my daughters this season, and for that I will always be grateful. But you must realize that I, too, need a home that I can call my very own."

Even the air in the small antechamber seemed suspended in time for the longest moment. Lord Ennersley gazed into Mrs. Leighton's large, blue eyes, and in a whisper he finally said, "I can give you a home, my dearest Lavinia. Will you not marry me, instead? Will you not become my beloved wife that I might hear your voice at the close of each day and when I arise each morning?"

Charlotte and Betsy, who were both leaning toward their mother and Lord Ennersley, gasped aloud in unison.

"Oh, Charles!" Mrs. Leighton cried, her eyes misting over completely. "Do you really wish for it?" When he nodded and smiled and drew her very close to him, she continued, "I had dared to hope, but in my heart it seemed so impossible."

"I love you," he responded sweetly as he placed a gentle kiss upon her lips. "Why did I not see it before? Now that I think on it, I believe I loved you almost from the first. Will you forgive my blindness, and if I have been unkind, my pet, you must take great care to instruct me in a better way. I know I can be a brute, but I promise you I shall endeavor to make you the best of husbands, if you'll have me!"

"Oh, yes, yes!" she cried.

He enfolded her in his arms, and much to the embarrassment of the young ladies, he kissed her passionately, until even Mr. Baughurst began coughing his disapproval. Afterward, there remained only one thing to be done.

To both the astonishment and the general delight of the wedding guests, Lord Ennersley took as his bride that afternoon, not the daughter—who had mysteriously disappeared—but the mother. After the ceremony, the wedding party and guests returned to the Ennersley town house for an elegant reception where Henrietta's absence was commented upon at least a thousand times. Where had she gone? And where was King Brandish! It was all too mysterious, too exciting, too delectable! The choicest morsel of gossip, one destined to reign supreme throughout the duration of this London Season, appeared in the making! The most innocent to the most scandalous of conjectures flew about the town house until Mrs. Leighton could bear it no more.

After an hour had passed, upon their return to Grosvenor Square, Mrs. Leighton turned to her new husband and expressed her dismay that if King had indeed eloped with Henrietta then there was the strongest of likelihoods that he had no intention of wedding her poor daughter. "And she loves him so very much," Mrs. Leighton whispered, "that I have the worst fear she will go willingly to Paris with him. And then what would become of her?"

Ennersley took her hand firmly in his and cried, "I have been considering the matter ever since we quit the church. You must believe that I shall do everything in my power to force him to marry her! If he thinks he can behave in this abominable fashion, and not pay the piper, then he knows nothing of the pressure I can bring to bear, though it would be a far sight better if the deed could be done before they leave England."

"But do you really think he means to take her to Paris?"

At that moment, Mr. Baughurst passed by, a cup of iced champagne in his hand.

311

Lord Ennersley frowned at his retreating back, then broke into a broad smile. "Why, it is the very thing!" he exclaimed. "Baughurst! Come here, at once! We have need of you, immediately. Do you think, if we set our minds to it, we could procure a Special License?"

"But you are already wed, sir!" Baughurst responded, shocked.

"Not for me, you idiot! For my son!"

Chapter Thirty-Eight

Henrietta sat contentedly upon a settle, her gaze mesmerized by a thick mound of coals burning red and white. The warmth of the fire made her slightly drowsy, for she was at peace with herself. They had arrived in Dover after a sluggish journey across Kent through sodden lanes and chill, damp air. Once arrived, King quickly ensconced them in a private parlor of The Ship Inn.

The ancient sea-town was saturated with a salty sea mist that smelled wondrously of adventure to Henrietta. She had occasioned considerable comment upon her arrival since she was still gowned in a manner fitted for a stroll down the aisle of a church instead of for a crossing of the English Channel. But she merely smiled at the curious stares and audible comments upon her unusual costume. She had long since removed her veil, but no one could doubt that here was a woman ready to be married. Only the groom, it seemed, appeared reluctant, for even the innkeeper's wife, a woman not particularly noted for her perception, agreed that Henrietta radiated a bride's joy and happiness while the gentleman looked like he was being led to the slaughter.

Henrietta heard this last comment and felt a twinge of sadness. She was not to be a bride—not today, not tomorrow, not forever. This, she had at long last concluded. She looked up at King, who was standing, deep in thought, before the mantel. His head was in his hand as he, too, stared down into the coals. They had exchanged but a few words since their departure from Grosvenor Square. She had admitted to him at last that she no longer cared whether theirs was a union sanctified by God; she wanted only to be with him, and to be done with her ridiculous machinations. She had begged him to forgive her for making such a cake of herself with a scheme as stupid as it was manipulative. He had been furious with her, taking great delight in giving voice to the advantage he meant to take of her while they were in Paris. But he could not rail at her for very long, because she no longer struggled against either the depth of her love for him or his indifference to marriage. Somehow, it just didn't matter to her anymore.

Perhaps part of the reason was simple. Her family was well situated now, and she could at long last be at ease where they were concerned. She said as much to King, and after that he had fallen silent. For hours they had travelled with scarcely a word uttered between them.

Henrietta watched him now, wondering what thoughts were rummaging through his brain. He pushed away from the mantel slightly, shaking his head as he looked down at her. A rueful expression overcame his features, almost of pain. "I have been humbled," he said, surprising tears springing to his eyes.

"King!" she cried, wondering at this remarkable change in his countenance. "Why, whatever is the matter? I have never seen you like this. And what do you mean, you have been humbled?"

"I was so certain of my course when I brought you into my carriage this afternoon. I meant only to use you ill, as I felt I had been used—to hurt you in every manner I could, to force you to accompany me to Paris, to take a vengeance upon you by wresting your innocence from you."

Henrietta replied quietly, "But I was married at one

314

time. I am not innocent, neither in heart nor body."

"When a man takes what is not given to him freely, he is robbing a woman of her *innocence* regardless of her former experiences. I meant to do as much, out of anger toward you. But these past few hours, when you seemed so reconciled to your fate—"

"Not my fate, King. Do you not think that I do not have enough intelligence to know that all I must do, in order to extricate myself from your clutches as it were, is to raise a cry and hue to the rooftops of this esteemed establishment? I promise you, I could do so, if I had the heart for it. But I do not!" He seemed struck by her words as she continued, "I have surrendered only to my love for you. This is not what I wish, to charge off to Paris; that much I will admit to you. But I have realized over these past several weeks that all I desire in life is to be with you. If the terms are as your mistress, then so be it and know that I have chosen to surrender willingly! You once said that my greatest flaw was believing what I wished to believe, but I think in truth, the larger flaw is the passion of my heart which must forever rule my head."

"Why do you torture me!" he cried. "Cannot you understand what I am trying to say to you? You speak of flaws and of becoming my mistress, when I—" he broke off and dropped to his knees before her, taking her hands in his. He cried, "I want you to be my wife! Will you marry me, Henry? Will you forgive me for being stubborn and foolish and for being so completely careless of your affections and of your good nature? I promise from this moment forth that I shall care for your heart, if you will but entrust it to me. I shall do everything in my power to ensure your happiness, only will you marry me?"

Henrietta could not believe he was actually speaking the words she had only dreamt of one day hearing. It seemed so impossible! Especially when she had finally reconciled herself to living out her life as his paramour.

"My heart was long since placed in your care, King. Of course I will become your wife, but are you certain you wish for it?"

"Damn it, Henry!" he cried, as he rose abruptly and pulled her to her feet. "Have you not heard what I have been saying to you?"

"My love!" she whispered, tears now burning her own eyes as she realized he was fully persuaded upon his course. He took her roughly in his arms, kissing her harshly as Henrietta leaned into him. A sob had caught in her throat, of mingled relief and joy, as she submitted to the wildness of his embrace as he kissed her lips, her cheeks, her forehead, her neck. Was she truly to become his wife?

A knock sounded upon the door, and as King pulled away from her, the landlord entered the chamber informing him that the packet to Calais was due to sail within the half hour.

"We will not be leaving England just yet," he responded.

"Very good, sir. Would you care for a little supper, then?"

The late afternoon drifted into evening as King and Henrietta sat before the warm fire and lingered over a fine repast of poached turbot and oyster sauce, a sirloin of beef, peas, an orange pudding, salad and a fine plum cake. An abundance of plans were laid for the sharing and building of a bright future. Candles guttered, and the hours passed too quickly until Henrietta suggested that if they were to return to London before dawn they ought to begin their journey forthwith.

Just as they rose from the table, a din sounded in the street. The rumbling of dozens of coaches, as well as the accompaniment of the cries and shouts of postillions as they jockeyed for position outside the inn, could be heard even to the parlor.

"What could it be?" Henrietta cried. "I have never heard such a commotion in my life!"

316

King responded, "Perhaps there was a mill nearby earlier today and the gentlemen decided to adjourn to Dover for a tidy supper!"

Within but a few seconds, Henrietta knew that Brandish had been quite mistaken, for his father's booming voice could be heard calling for King the moment the viscount crossed the portals of the inn. "Oh, dear," she whispered with a faint smile. "We are undone, though I must confess I feel more like a child who has been caught stealing brambleberry tarts from the kitchen than anything else!"

When the pounding of dozens of pairs of boots, shoes and sandals shook the planked floor of the inn, King drew Henrietta back to the fireplace. "It would seem my father has brought a prodigious contingent with him to contend with me! Had I not begged for your hand already, I could very naturally suppose the meaning of this assault." He looked down at Henrietta, who met his softly smiling gaze with an answering smile of her own. King slipped an arm about her waist and whispered, "Courage, m'dear!" just as Ennersley shoved the door open and stormed into the parlor. He was followed by Mrs. Leighton, Charlotte, Betsy, Mr. Phillips, the Reverend Baughurst, Miss Brandish and at least three dozen assorted personages, all dressed in wedding finery.

Henrietta stared at the ogling assemblage of friends and acquaintances. She could not believe that so many people had actually followed King and herself to Dover.

"Henry, my dear," Mrs. Leighton called to her, crossing the room quickly to embrace her. "How glad I am that you have not left England before we could arrive to tell you our excellent tidings!" She cleared her throat nervously as she whispered, "Are you all right?"

"Of course," Henrietta whispered in return. She was not certain what next to say, and felt an embarrassing flush begin creeping up her cheeks and down her neck. She knew she must present an odd and scandalous figure, dining alone with King, dressed in the wedding gown she

317

was supposed to have worn for her marriage to Lord Ennersley. Mrs. Leighton supported her on one side while King increased the pressure of his arm about her waist.

The chamber fell silent, even as several late arrivals pressed in at the crowded doorway, trying to gain admittance.

Brandish started to speak, but Lord Ennersley cut him off with an abrupt gesture of his arm. "How could you, King! How could you abduct this poor, unfortunate young woman and, with the vilest of intents, have eloped with her to Dover—though I've little doubt your destination was Paris!"

"Yes, sir, it was!" King answered with considerable aplomb.

The crowd gasped and moaned in delighted shock at this wicked confession.

"You admit it, then!" Ennersley continued. "That you meant to elope with Henrietta, against her will, against every fine and decent principle upon which our society is governed?" His brows were drawn together in outrage over his son's heedless conduct.

"Oh, not against my will!" Henrietta exclaimed, her cheeks burning hotly. She refused to permit King to bear the entire guilt for their elopement.

"Pay no heed to her, father!" King interjected quickly. "She—that is Henry became violently carriage-sick on our journey here. Even now she speaks from a state of delirium!" He directed an admonishing glance at Henrietta.

A sniggering rippled through the crowd, and even Henrietta could not resist chuckling.

"What a rapper!" Betsy called out. "Henry is never ill when she travels." The sniggering and chortling increased as Charlotte told her to "stubble-it!"

Lord Ennersley continued, "Whatever the case, I have brought Mr. Baughurst with me, and I must insist, before these many witnesses, that you marry poor Henrietta!

318

None of your nonsense now, King! And I won't argue with you—I won't hear a single protest either! I expect you, as a man of honor, to marry this girl!" When King did not respond, but merely looked down at Henrietta and again smiled, Ennersley lost a little more of his patience, as he cried, "Good God, boy, why are you silent! Why are you not hurling your habitual threats at me!"

King glanced back at him and responded quietly, "Because I am in complete agreement with you. I desire nothing more than to marry Mrs. Harte."

"Well, I don't care what you say!" the viscount stormed, apparently not having understood his son. "You will marry her, or before God and this company I vow I shall disinherit—eh? What's that?"

The crowd gasped, murmured, shouted and laughed their amazement. "You'll wed her?" Lord Ennersley asked, astonished.

King nodded. "Yes. It was all settled several hours ago. But you are quite right to chastise me."

Mrs. Leighton quickly hugged her daughter, crying upon her neck and wishing her every happiness in the world. She then revealed the extraordinary fact that she, in place of Henrietta, had become Ennersley's wife.

"Why, you are a viscountess!" Henrietta exclaimed, holding her away slightly and smiling through her tears into her mama's face. "And a very pretty one, too! My only regret is that I was not in attendance upon you!" Henrietta hugged her mother very hard, yet again, then immediately crossed the chamber to embrace her new papa.

"My dear Henry," he whispered. "I suppose all's well that ends well. But I would never have forgiven myself had we not found you here!"

Henrietta pulled away from him and whispered in return, "What nonsense! You had nothing to do with this! Now salute my cheek and tell me you are happy that I am to wed your son."

"Oh, yes, my dear! More than you'll ever know." He then kissed her cheek lightly and afterward accepted his son's congratulations upon his nuptials, smiling self-consciously at King. Brandish slapped him on the back and, after meeting his gaze for a long moment, said, "I love you, Papa, and I am indebted to you forever for giving Henry to me."

Ennersley swallowed very hard, and afterward did not hesitate to grab his son and hold him in a rugged embrace, though he could not keep from muttering, "Damme, you always were the most hopeless scapegrace!"

The gentlemen in the crowd cheered at this exceptional display of sentiment while the ladies grasped wildly in their reticules for their handkerchiefs.

Amidst considerable sniffling, and dabbing of eyes with perfectly useless lace confections, Lord Ennersley then brought Mr. Baughurst forward, explaining as he did so that with no small degree of effort, they had been able to procure a Special License. "That is, of course," the viscount added, "if you wish to be joined in matrimony at this time."

Both Henrietta and King agreed readily to be married that very instant. Again the onlookers blessed themselves with a cry of wonder at having been fortunate enough to witness so many social solecisms in the course of one brief day, not least of which was an unexpected wedding between the infamous Mrs. Harte and the most elusive Matrimonial Prize of them all—King Brandish.

Before the fireplace, therefore, in her creased wedding gown, a veil that somehow in the midst of her elopement with King had suffered a tear, with orange blossoms that had curled up and grown brown within the garland, and white slippers now dirty from wear, Henrietta married King before an awestruck assemblage who would remark on the scandalous event for the rest of their lives.